IN THE SHADOW OF THE LAW

IN THE SHADOW
OF THE LAW

KERMIT ROOSEVELT

FARRAR, STRAUS AND GIROUX

NEW YORK

Farrar, Straus and Giroux
19 Union Square West, New York 10003

Distributed in Canada by Douglas & McIntyre Ltd.
Printed in the United States of America
ISBN 0-7394-6206-7

Designed by Jonathan D. Lippincott

To my family, which I like to think includes Larry Hardesty

IN THE SHADOW OF THE LAW

PROLOGUE

September 23, 1999
Alanton, Virginia, 6:30 a.m.

Detective Ray Robideaux pulled his cruiser to the curb in front of a small clapboard house. Morning shadows hung long down the empty street. People in this neighborhood tended to sleep in, perhaps because few of them had much to get up early for. Through the quiet air Robideaux could hear the rumble of traffic from a highway overpass. Approaching the house, he flipped open the snap of his holster and glanced at his partner. Bill Campbell's gun was already out, held low at his side. Robideaux tried the doorknob, which turned in his hand, and he knocked. The wood was soft under his knuckles and resounded hollowly. "Police," he called. "We have a warrant to enter this building." By his side Campbell counted seconds off in a whisper. At eight he nodded and Robideaux threw the door open.

The uncertain dawn spilled inside the house, revealing shabby furniture and the faint glow of a television. From the couch a man turned dull eyes on the officers. He wore a sleeveless T-shirt that looked like it had been slept in, and from a quick whiff, Robideaux guessed he'd made a start on the day's drinking. Or, at this hour, that the night wasn't quite over.

"Earl Harper?" he asked. The man grunted an affirmative. "Where's your boy?"

"He ain't here," Harper answered. "What right you got to come bustin' through my door?"

"We have a warrant for the arrest of your son," Robideaux told him. "For the murder of Leslie Anne Clarke. It'll go easier if you cooperate with us, now." He looked up as a woman in a housecoat entered the room. "Mrs. Beth Harper?"

The woman ignored him. "Don't you lie to the police, Earl," she said. "You know what they're here for." Harper shook his head. He lifted a bottle from the floor and took a deliberate pull.

"Ma'am," said Robideaux. "We need to ask your son some questions."

Harper gave a guttural laugh that exploded into a phlegmy cough. "You can ask him all you want. I don't think you'll be getting many answers." His wife's face tightened. She drew the coat closer around her and, as Robideaux watched, jerked her head almost imperceptibly to the side. He followed her gesture down an unlit hall. The door yielded to his touch, and he entered, one hand on the butt of his pistol, squinting into the darkness.

The room was small and cluttered. As Robideaux's eyes adjusted to the gloom, he could see clothes on the floor and clumps of dust that looked long undisturbed. Squalor and solitude, the parents of violence. Unidentified shapes slowly resolved themselves into tattered dolls and children's toys, used and broken beyond repair. For a moment Robideaux wondered if he'd stumbled into the wrong room, but the figure in the bed bulked man-sized. The detective fumbled for a light, found the switch, and flicked it on. The figure sat up, blinking.

"Wayne Harper?" A slow puzzled nod. Robideaux pulled the cuffs from his belt and wrestled the man facedown, pulling his wrists behind his back.

"You hurtin' me," Wayne complained thickly.

"You are under arrest for the murder of Leslie Anne Clark," Robideaux said. "You have the right to remain silent. If you give up that right, anything you say may be used against you. You have the right to an attorney. If you cannot afford one, an attorney will be appointed to defend you at the state's expense. Do you understand these rights as I have read them to you?"

"You hurtin' me," Wayne repeated. "What'd I do to you?"

Robideaux pulled him to a sitting position, let him sag against the wall. Wayne Harper was a big soft man, his cheeks sprouting the tawny stubble of early morning, his close-cropped hair thinning on top. His face was empty of expression, his eyes a pale, vacant blue. Robideaux felt a familiar disappointment. Eighteen years he'd been on the force, working his way up, making his share of arrests. Tracking down the predators. Just once he'd have liked to have them spit at him in defiance, cry out that they would never be taken alive. Or at least resist. Many times, at the end of an investigation, steeped in the crime, he'd hoped for a little resistance at the collar. But no. The drunks on the street resisted, unable to calculate consequences. But the ones he came for with a warrant had time to think it through, to act innocent and surprised. Too many cop shows.

"Do you understand these rights as I have read them to you?" Robideaux repeated.

Campbell stepped into the room, holstering his pistol. "That him, Ray?"

"Seems so."

"Ugly son of a bitch, ain't he? He ask for a lawyer?"

Ray shook his head. On the bed, Wayne Harper frowned, his lips moving. He looked toward the two officers. "A what?" he said.

Mayfield, Texas, 5:30 a.m.

Janette Guzman was getting blisters. The work boots she was wearing had been on sale, but they weren't quite the right size, and they were men's, and they pinched her feet in some places and let them slide in others as she patrolled the perimeter of the Hubble factory. She hadn't wanted to be a fencewalker in the first place. It was lonely work, with bad hours and occasional danger, but there weren't a lot of opportunities for a girl with a GED and no job training. There were tech dollars in Austin, there was oil cash in Midland, but none of that was coming her way. At least not yet. Things might be different with a junior college degree or vocational schooling. But that took money, and money in Mayfield was mostly locked into the operations of Hubble Chemical. Which was why she was pacing the grounds of the main factory with a burning sensation growing on the outside of her right heel.

The factory was a gray concrete block, featureless but for infrequent windows. It was the tallest structure in Mayfield, save the water tower, but wide enough to look squat. In the daylight it seemed to have dropped from the sky, flattening on impact. Now it was just a dark bulk looming in Janette's peripheral vision. Her flashlight's beam played across the fence, up to the razor wire, down to the hard-baked dust. Some feet beyond, an incurious armadillo trundled by. She took a deep breath of the cold night air, looking up to the vastness of the spangled sky, then raised the radio to her lips. "West four," she said. "All clear." Then she bent down to pull on her sock, and that was how she missed the first shy flames showing through the factory windows. She saw what followed, though.

With a deep roar, a blast swelled up through the building. The windows burst in a glistening rain of glass, and thick black smoke followed. For a few moments Janette watched, stunned, as backlit figures struggled from the plant, turned strange pirouettes, dropped to the ground. "Marty," she said into the radio. "Something's happened. There's been an explosion. There's a fire."

The reply crackled back. "What? Say again."

"You'd better send someone. There's a big fire. There are people running out of the plant." She paused, watching the figures against the glow. Another explosion shook the building. "They're dancing. I don't know. They're falling down. They're sort of twitching." She stumbled and realized that she had backed up into the fence, its chain links pressing against her body. The firelight dimmed, obscured by smoke, then reasserted itself. She turned and through the fence saw jackrabbits bounding away, the armadillo lumbering awkwardly, its scales a fading gleam. A thought flashed irrelevantly through her mind, a rhyme learned from a library book: *Something wicked this way comes.* "Marty, the gate's locked."

"What?"

Janette tugged the handle. "This gate's locked. I can't get out." The radio made no reply, and she let it fall to the ground, taking hold of the fence, pulling herself up. Her boots scraped uselessly against the metal, too large to find a foothold, and she gave a high cry of frustration as she dropped like a supplicant to her knees, fingers meshed with the unyielding wire. She caught her breath and looked back at the factory, watching the roiling smoke, black against the fire, blacker than the black sky. A chemical scent laced the air now, stinging her eyes, burning her throat. She fumbled for the radio. "Marty, this smoke is poisonous. I can't . . . Tell . . . Oh, God, I don't know . . . Tell . . ."

In a room across town Martin Jessup laid the silent radio on his desk and looked at it. Out the window he could see a garish glow, a lewd carnival light growing in the sky. He dialed a number on his phone, and two hundred miles away Roger Allen woke from dreamless sleep.

"Jessup here. There's a problem at the plant," Martin said.

"What kind of problem? Worth waking me up for?"

"It sounds that way, sir." Martin felt oddly calm. Janette was dead, he was pretty sure of that, and a lot of other people, most likely. But he was responding appropriately. He was doing what he was supposed to, and if everyone simply performed their designated tasks, what was there that the system couldn't handle? "There's a fire, and some sort of toxic smoke."

There was a moment of silence on the line. "I see," said Roger Allen.

"What should I do?" Martin asked. "Should I call Disaster Response? The state people?"

"No, no," said Roger. "Call Morgan Siler." Martin said nothing. If he waited just one more moment, he thought, he might understand. "And the local counsel," Roger continued. "Weiland Hart. They're our guys on the ground. And the in-house people."

Martin could contain himself no longer. "Who?" he asked. "I'm sorry, but aren't those—"

"Yes," Roger said. "They're our lawyers. And that's who you call. Get on it now. That's the first thing you do. You call all the lawyers."

Martin Jessup hung up the phone. He had his orders now, but they still didn't make any sense. As he picked up the receiver and began to dial again, he could feel the first sting of tears.

1 TIME AND MOTION STUDIES

September 18, 2000
Washington, 7:00 a.m.

Every weekday morning at seven o'clock a powerful black car made its way through the Georgetown traffic to a redbrick house. For fifteen minutes it waited outside the door for the occupant of the house to emerge. Peter Morgan kept it waiting because he could, and he wanted the driver to know that. He did it for precisely fifteen minutes every day because, in addition, he wanted the driver to know that he knew.

Peter Morgan's mornings did not dare to vary from his routine. The soft glow of a progressively luminous alarm clock cajoled him from slumber; the aroma of coffee brewed by an automatic espresso machine drew him from between the smooth white sheets of his bed. With a fond glance at his sleeping wife's soft swell, he alit and padded to the scalding benison of a high-pressure shower. Beneath its steaming pulse he shaved with a wet/dry electric razor before stepping forth into a plush cotton robe. A fog-free mirror held his image while he applied costly unguents to his body, his face, his head. He dressed inside a closet. Fifteen suits were arrayed on the cedar rails, a crisp army of shirts, a bright artillery of ties, and below, a battalion of shoes like dragons' teeth. Breakfast, a sop to the doctors, was half a grapefruit and two crusts of penitent's toast, the espresso like a song in his blood.

This morning, diverging from the pattern, he was out the door precisely at seven. Today he felt too eager to take any pleasure in making others wait for him. Today there was a meeting of the steering committee of the firm. Of course, he could make even them wait if he chose, wait a virtually indefinite time, since they were powerless to act without him. They were powerful men in their own right, and had Peter Morgan been less accustomed to command, he might have been tempted to that sort of extravagant display. But there was no need. He could make them wait if he chose; he knew it; they knew it; and he knew they knew he knew. Peter Morgan realized that things were seldom this simple in life, truths seldom so unitary, but he was the managing partner, son of the firm's founder, Archibald Morgan, and for him, they were.

Morgan Siler occupied thirteen floors of a large building on K Street. Other businesses shared the space—a consulting firm, some lobbyists— but Morgan was the dominant presence. Peter walked through the lobby, heels clicking on the marble floor, and absorbed with half-conscious majesty the greetings of the security guards. An elevator bore him upward. The steering committee would be meeting on the top floor, which held the firm's conference rooms, but Peter stopped first on the twelfth. He needed to pass by his office to gather some papers, but he wanted also to make his morning rounds, check on the inhabitants of his fiefdom.

Most of the office doors on his floor were closed, which was to be expected. A few were canted slightly inward, their occupants' attempt to suggest that they had already arrived at work and were simply being industrious at some other location: the library, the records center. This displeased Peter, who liked certainty. He did not see the need for associates' offices to have doors; indeed, he did not see why associates needed offices at all. He would have preferred them to work at computer stations on an open floor, or in transparent cubicles, their every act circumscribed by the rigid intelligence of time and motion studies. But the law had yet to find its Frederick Taylor, and the recruiting committee had advised him that moving associates into cubicles would hurt hiring efforts.

Failing a wholesale reorganization, Peter had more than once considered instructing the night cleaning shift to lock each office, instead of leaving the doors as they were found. But this posed the risk of shutting out those who were actually working late and had made a run to the library or the all-night deli in the lobby. It was better to let ten guilty go free than to punish one innocent, lawyers were told. Peter Morgan had invoked this maxim frequently, though he remained agnostic as to its truth. He did believe, however, that it was a wrong of the first order to interfere with the productivity of associates burning the midnight oil, and he knew that the chicanery of those who simulated early mornings would lead to nothing. Leaving the door open didn't bill any hours, and at the year's end, part Santa Claus, part Minos, Peter Morgan would judge his flock on the basis of how many hours their time sheets had recorded.

A few doors, Peter saw, were flung wide, the inhabitants of their offices basking in the cool early-morning glow of the computer screen. A soft tide of contentment loosened his belly at the sight of these dutiful souls; his patrician features softened. They were making money for him, true; each hour an associate billed returned a fixed sum to the firm, generating profits to be shared among the partners. But Peter felt a more fraternal warmth. He too had been an associate once, punching the same clock, running the same treadmill, and he remembered the satisfaction of noting down the hours, tabulating his worth. His diligence had made him a partner, and for some of the young lawyers working away this Monday morning, it would do the same. Coming up on the last open door before his corner office, he paused and flashed an avuncular grin. "Good morning," said Peter Morgan. Without waiting for a response, he continued on his way.

Mark Clayton was at the customary point in his day when panic gave way to resignation. His office was small, smaller even than the norm for first-year associates, but a compensatory window offered a partially obstructed view of downtown Washington. Once this had seemed cause for optimism, as his sensible gray suits and framed diplomas had seemed confirmation of his place in the professional world. Both now struck him differently, the suits a poor camouflage, the diplomas almost a silent rebuke.

Mark was twenty-six. He had placid brown eyes and dark hair that rose in alarmed clusters if not carefully tended. He had a degree in political science from Rutgers and one in law from Penn. And he had a growing sense that at some time in the recent past he had made a crucial mistake whose effects were now, irrevocably, emerging.

His current assignment substantiated the impression. Like most of his work, it was a case he'd been switched on to after the associate initially assigned had left. For a while he had wondered what happened to those people, who had left only initials studding billing records and memos in the file to prove they had ever existed. Now he did not wonder; he simply envied them. Whatever they were doing, they no longer had to worry about whether the odor of rotten eggs could count as a product defect sufficient to void a contract.

Mark did. One of the firm's clients had ordered natural gas from a Canadian supplier only to find that, as required by Canadian law, the gas was infused with sulfides for safety reasons. A neighborhood near the client's plant now smelled like a Halloween prank, and outraged homeowners were threatening suit.

The assignment was to write a memo detailing the ways in which the client could refuse to accept the remaining supply. An evening of research had yielded nothing, and the fresh start the morning had promised was turning up more of the same. Worse, he was nearing the end of the ten hours he'd been told to dedicate to the project. Partners gave instructions like that, he was beginning to believe, simply out of spite. Unable to finish the project in the allotted time, an associate had three choices. He could confess his failure and appear stupid, or underreport the hours he'd actually worked during the day, which would knock down his billable total and make him appear shiftless. Or he could spend early mornings and late nights at work, in order to shave down the hours for that particular project and still meet his billable target for the day.

Mark tended to choose the third option. In his heart he knew this was a self-defeating ruse, since it had earned him a reputation for efficiency that required ever-later nights to maintain. And now sleep deprivation was robbing him of whatever focus he'd been able to bring to the work; more seriously, it was stealing the acuity required for day-to-day life. His mornings were perilous: an intemperate blast from the unpredictable shower, brutal hand-to-hand combat with the razor, precious minutes repairing the most visible damage. He couldn't understand how people found the time for hygiene. Doubtless some were cutting corners; he himself had begun to wash only on alternate days, or when time permitted. He could feel his body softening from lack of exercise, and in its spreading flesh and unaccustomed smells he saw the transformation worked by the operation of law. He was becoming something else.

Now, with his freshly dry-cleaned shirt already soggy against his sides and his face burning from the razor's metallic kiss, he was confronting the fact that despite his machinations, he was most likely going to end up with a full ten hours on the time sheet and nothing good to tell the partner in charge. The prospect had once been terrifying, but now the fear was fading and he was beginning to feel the onset of despair.

The transition point was not a bad moment, but it had been coming earlier and earlier, sometimes before he even made it into the office, and that was starting to disturb him. He'd grown used to a particular pattern of emotions arriving as the workday progressed, but now they were packing themselves closer and closer together, as though his emotional life were accelerating while the rest of it maintained the same plodding place. Initially, he'd woken with a sense of excitement, the new job beckoning like the big football games of high school. Those had tended toward anticlimax, involving chiefly a period of waiting until the outcome was sufficiently removed from doubt for his name to be called. Now, likewise, he sat at his desk for long hours while the day's excitement dulled; then, usually midafternoon, he'd realize how little he'd accomplished, how much there was to do, how outrageous it was that some poor slob was paying out one hundred and fifty dollars an hour for his fecklessness. Then the panic would start. Finally, toward evening, after an afternoon spent in futile attempts to justify his salary, he'd resign himself to the fact that today was not the day he came up with a case-breaking insight, found some overlooked and pivotal authority, turned around a losing cause. Instead it was a day he spent six hours poring over numbingly boring FCC reports only to find he'd been researching the wrong section of the Telecommunications Act, a day he realized he'd been charging his time to the wrong client number and spent four hours trying to pull the records from the depths of the computer system.

Still, it had been a routine, something he thought he could get used to. Or at least the sort of thing one was supposed to get used to. But then the excitement was crowded out, as panic began to hit him in the mornings, or sometimes in his dreams. Despair was the noontime respite, a signal that it was time to grab lunch. That schedule had held for four months, but now the panic was fleeting and his days consisted largely of boredom and low-grade melancholy. Sometimes, staring blankly at an assignment as the unrecoverable hours trickled by, he felt that he wanted to cry; more frequently he felt he wanted something worth crying for. He wasn't making as many stupid mistakes as he used to, but given the character of his work, he was astonished that he'd made as many as he had.

Back when there'd been periods of satisfaction in the days, when he'd conquered the panic and gone on to actually produce something—bang out a memo, rearrange a file drawer, it didn't matter what—he'd thought that each day was a microcosm of what the future had to offer: a period of adjustment, then long solid years of productive work. Now that they were simply tedium, he was growing increasingly confident that he'd been right. This was what time held in store, patient and unrelenting. The prospect earned Mark a stab of dread. He smiled at the variety, then began one more pass through the oil and gas case reporters on the chance that he'd missed something.

It was at that moment that Peter Morgan's leonine profile passed down the hallway, that his head made a brief turn to address Mark's office, that the morning greeting fell from his lips.

Mark jerked upright in his chair, banging his knee on the underside of his desk and simultaneously giving a solid kick to the PC hard drive nestled beneath it. Recovering his balance, he knocked a mugful of coffee onto the papers in his lap. "Oh, fuck," he said. He lifted the papers, letting the coffee they'd not yet absorbed slide onto his pants, and cursed again.

"Good morning," another voice said.

Mark raised imploring eyes. Katja Phillips slowed her progress past his door long enough to give him a look of amused concern and walked on, wringing water from her black hair. Katja lived across the river in Arlington, and as often as she could she ran to work, passing the commuters stuck on Key Bridge. Through car windows the drivers watched her, but Katja didn't notice. She had trained herself in obliviousness from an early age, and law school had taught her the costs of distraction. She watched only the sidewalk in front of her as she ran, moving forward, turning up M Street and into Georgetown, her feet pounding past the bars and restaurants and clothing stores until the world of retail and leisure gave way to the coffee shops and corporate enclaves of downtown Washington.

The building had a single shower, adjacent to what the firm called the nap room and the lawyers called the Morgan Hotel, a windowless office equipped with three cots and an alarm clock. In the event of an all-nighter, it allowed lawyers a few hours' respite without the inefficiency of returning home or the indignity of sleeping under their desks. Also, more rarely, it was a place for nervous breakdowns, where employees could rock and moan in relative privacy. Katja occasionally encountered people making one or the other use of the place as she showered and changed into her business attire, but this morning it was vacant, and she passed through its dimness with bright-eyed good humor, ready to start her day.

She always felt better after running, more alert, more confident, more capable of meeting whatever challenges the world might throw in her path. The routine limited her fashion options—she kept three suits at the office and usually skipped the run in favor of a bus at least once a week, giving her four—but Katja was a bottom-liner. A morning run made for a more productive day, and Katja had always believed that productivity was the ultimate metric.

Her two years at Morgan Siler had not changed that belief, but she sometimes found herself wondering what exactly it was that she was producing. Countless memos, various contracts and agreements created largely by exhuming their predecessors and changing appropriate names, dates, and dollar amounts, and, during her brief stint in the litigation department, some fragments of briefs arguing one or another point of law too esoteric or tangential to attract the interest of anyone more senior. That was one way of looking at it. Some quarter of a million dollars for the coffers of Morgan Siler—that was another. And from the last perspective, which she tended to adopt only late at night, in times of extreme fatigue or unrest, she had produced . . . what?

Hours, that was the answer. She had produced hours. Katja had gone to law school, in the crisp and distant air of Ann Arbor, because she thought it would give her a challenging career, because medicine and banking and consulting hadn't interested her. There are three different kinds of jobs in the world, a law school professor had told her civil procedure class their first day. There are people who make things, people who buy and sell those things, and people who provide the intellect and the analysis that make everything else possible. You will be that last group. You will be the lawyers.

That had sounded good to Katja. She had no interest in buying and selling. There was a certain nobility and satisfaction to making things, tangible creations, laying the stamp of order upon the stuff of chaos, but in the end, asked what she made, she would rather answer: I make it all possible. She had said this to herself a few times, toward the beginning of the job, once to shut up an investment banker talking salaries on a forgettable blind date, and not since then. For the fact was that it simply wasn't true. It might have been in the halcyon days about which her professors reminisced, though none of them had spent more than a year in the world of practice; it might still be for the partners. But for the young associates, law was industrialized. They were assembly-line workers, and what they made was time. Torts, contracts, antitrust cases came through the doors of the firm, and associates took these raw materials and turned them into hours.

Katja didn't mind. She was good at her job. She had the brains and, more important, the stamina. Partners appreciated her diligence and reliability; with increasing frequency they would stop by her office with assignments, and always the same request: Can you make some time for me? Katja pushed back her hair and got to work. She wasn't a sprinter, and she knew it, but she could clock ten hours a day without breaking a sweat. In at eight, an hour for lunch, out the door by seven, with a little luck. Any later and she could order dinner on the client and take a firm car back to Arlington, but Katja was making an effort to spend enough waking hours outside the office that she didn't begin thinking of it as home. Today that would be a challenge; she'd been given the task of revising a master loan agreement to take account of the addition of several new lenders. Katja pulled the documents together on the desk and turned on her computer. She surveyed the contents of her office with a nod that was almost a greeting: a plant on the table and on the walls two diplomas and a Chagall print. She took an elastic band from her pocket, tied back her damp hair, and took a deep breath. The clock was ticking.

2 THE MAIN ORDER OF BUSINESS

Upstairs the meeting was under way. Peter Morgan sat at the head of a teak conference table bearing breakfast pastries, coffeepots, and pitchers of orange juice. On his right was Harold Fineman, head of the litigation department; on his left, Anthony Streeter, in charge of corporate business. Across from them, looking somewhat uncomfortable, sat Wallace Finn, the partner who ran the pro bono program. Wallace was pale by nature, with close-cropped gray hair and sky-blue eyes; in a cloud-colored suit windowpaned with soft blue checks he seemed barely visible. He had participated in steering committee meetings years ago, when Streeter was just his protégé and Wallace himself had ruled over the complex web of deals that constituted the firm's corporate practice. Wallace had been a legend in his day, able to maintain an intimate familiarity with the details of each of the most important transactions, appearing like a gray ghost to place his seal of approval as they closed or, more often, to restructure with a few bold strokes what it had taken others weeks to conceive.

The godlike omniscience came at a cost; he had worked so hard that his wife left him, and then he had worked harder in response. That had earned him a heart attack at fifty-three, and though the firm would never part with such a luminary, it became clear on his return that his run was over. The firm continued to use his name to promote its corporate work, but he hadn't done any in eight years. Instead they parked him in the pro bono department, where he organized the firm's representation of people who couldn't otherwise get a lawyer. He was still ghostly in appearance, and much more seldom seen. Pro bono didn't usually qualify for steering meetings, and he was here today only because a problem had come up.

Peter Morgan didn't like pro bono, and he didn't like problems. He passed a cold gaze around the room and turned his eyes back down to the papers in front of him. "What do you have for us, Wallace?"

"The Harper case," Wallace said. Receiving no reaction, he continued. "As part of the summer program, we agreed to represent a prisoner on Virginia's death row." Peter gave a nod of grudging acknowledgment. Every summer a fresh crop of law students, just out of their second year, descended upon the firms, part of the mutual feeling-out process intended to lead them to their permanent homes. These summer associates were a necessary evil, to Peter's mind. The summer program was the only way to assure a continual supply of new blood for the firm, but on the other hand there wasn't much to do with the summer associates, and no way to turn a profit. Paid a prorated first-year's salary, the law students were usually entirely lacking in basic legal skills, and often in basic knowledge as well. You couldn't give them any significant work to do because there was no way to know what glaring errors they would make, and you couldn't charge clients for more than a small fraction of the hours they billed because no client would stomach their inefficiency. They could reasonably have been put to work as document clerks, though even then the small number of hours they billed would have made them a losing proposition, but no summer associate would return for a permanent position to a firm that had treated him that way. Most of them ended up with interesting research projects that either had no relevance to any real case or would be entirely redone by someone who knew what he was doing. Typically, they did little enough work on even these fictitious assignments and spent most of their time dining out on the firm's credit cards and going on various outings arranged for their benefit.

Pro bono was the perfect solution: cases on which summer associates could take positions of significant responsibility without any worry that their incompetence would cause problems for the firm. Furthermore, it gave them an unrealistic idea both of the sort of work they'd be doing and of the firm's commitment to pro bono practice, something law students seemed to value. And finally, it boosted the number of hours Morgan Siler could report that its attorneys had spent on pro bono work, which again helped in the recruiting process. Death penalty cases were ideal for these purposes, something the kids could get really excited about. Each summer had one, like a class project or a hamster brought in to delight kindergartners. Like kindergarten projects, the cases typically amounted to little, and like hamsters, the prisoners usually ended up dead.

"What did he do?" Peter asked. "Oh, never mind. What's the problem?"

"Well," Wallace said, "we thought that once his case had gone all the way through the Virginia state courts, we could try to get relief from the federal courts. You know, file a habeas petition, make some constitutional arguments."

"Of course," said Peter. Law students loved constitutional arguments.

"He was sentenced to death in December, and we thought the appeals process would go pretty quickly. There's automatic review of every death sentence by the Virginia Supreme Court, but it's usually minimal. The family paid for a lawyer, but the guy wasn't all that aggressive. So that was over by February. Then there was the state post-conviction review process, which again is perfunctory. The same lawyer filed a petition in April arguing that the imposition of the death penalty was disproportionate to the crime. That argument never works, so we figured the case would be ready for us to take it into the federal system by May. But the lawyer got sick and the Virginia Capital Defenders Office took over. They got some more time to prepare their motions and they made a real run at it—ten different issues, affidavits, expert testimony, the works. The Virginia Supreme Court refused to hear any of it, but the preparation took so long that the decision didn't come down until mid-July. Then the Capital Defenders, who'd gotten pretty invested in the case, wanted to handle the federal petition too, so we had to convince them that we were going to do a good job on it, and by the time we got substituted in as counsel it was August."

"And then?"

Wallace remained silent. "And then," he said finally, "there were only four weeks left in the summer program and I didn't think that the kids could do a reasonable job in four weeks. There's a lot of material to go over from the trial, and none of them had actually written a real brief before."

"Your loyalty to the client," Peter said carefully, "is . . . commendable. So we erred in taking the case. Why don't you give it back?"

"I don't think the Capital Defenders Office has the staff for it now. I mean, they've got lots of these things, and just a handful of people working, and I think they're fully committed."

"I see," said Peter. "But we can still withdraw as counsel, can't we?"

"We'd have to get court approval," Wallace said. "Which I'm sure we could do with the Virginia courts; they don't care. But it would be unusual." Peter regarded him impassively. "It would look bad," Wallace continued. "I think the Capital Defenders people would make a stink. There could be some bad press."

"That's a point, Peter," Harold joined in. "That's not going to make us look good."

Peter Morgan put one hand over his eyes. "Okay," he said. "Okay, give it to some first-year." A flick of the wrist dismissed the matter. "I don't want to hear any more about this." His eyes fell back to the papers. "Main order of business," he said. "Hubble. I've got some reports here, and it sounds like this is going to be a substantial undertaking for us. Harold, tell me more."

Harold cleared his throat. "The good news," he said, "is that this is a fucking mess." A slight frown creased Peter Morgan's tanned brow. Harold was loud, profane, and an astonishingly effective litigator. In Peter's private calculus, this made him an asset. The tumult of red hair, the cheap suits, the air of perpetual surprise all combined to work an insidious magic in court. Peter applauded the results. He had watched as Harold developed this identity; more, he had assisted. Still, Peter wished that Harold could drop the role for other occasions. "They need us," Harold continued, "and they need us bad. The bad news is that this is a fucking mess. Our boys were storing some unpleasant chemicals—ammonium nitrate, methyl bromide, paraquat, endosulfan, carbofuran—and none too carefully."

"What are those?" Peter asked.

"Ammonium nitrate is our friend from Oklahoma City. Fertilizer, but you can blow it up. Also emits very toxic fumes when cooked. The others are pesticides, herbicides. Chemicals to kill things. The cloud that came out was mostly ammonium, but the other stuff got in there too. Methyl bromide's a neurological agent, and from the reports we have it looks like there were neurotoxins at work. A very bad air day, in short. Not anything you'd want to get too close to."

"What's the situation?"

"Well, they called us as soon as it happened, which was smart. Then they dicked around for a while with their in-house counsel, trying to settle it, which was a mistake. If we'd gotten there fast enough, we might have been able to go right to the victims and buy them off on the cheap, before they knew what was going on. But now the vultures have gathered. There are some pretty serious plaintiffs' lawyers in town, and we can't even talk to their clients. They're looking to get it certified as a class action, take care of the liability issues in one trial, and start counting the money."

"They're not talking settlement?" Peter asked.

"They're feeling pretty cocky right now. With good reason. You should see the place. I mean, it looks like Dresden. Like Bhopal. I don't think we could offer them anything less than all of Hubble's assets."

"That seems more like surrender than settlement. How could we do any worse in a trial?"

Harold blew out his breath in a sigh. "Well, here's the thing. Hubble Chemical is a decent-sized corporation. It's worth a couple hundred million as a going concern. The liquidation value is substantially less, but still, break it up and sell it and you've got over a hundred million. Problem is, give this case to a jury, and if they get all excited about sending a message, they could award punitive damages well above that. So the jury doesn't just kill Hubble; it kills them a lot. Ordinarily, that makes no difference, very dead being the same as dead. But Hubble is a subsidiary of Parkwell International, and Parkwell is a *very* big corporation. If there's a jury award that's far beyond what Hubble itself can pay, then it starts to look like Parkwell sent its subsidiary out there without enough money to cover the damages it was likely to cause. That's going to make the judge more willing to hold Parkwell itself liable. And then we're talking serious deep pockets."

"Are they going after Parkwell?"

"We won't know until we see the complaint. But I expect so. It's a lottery ticket, but it doesn't cost them anything. The problem it gives us is that the only way they can get to Parkwell is by making Hubble look underfunded, and the only way they can do that is by getting a monster judgment against Hubble. So they're not inclined to settle."

Peter looked almost pleased. "Well," he said. "That certainly makes things interesting. What do you think, Anthony?"

Anthony Streeter was deep in thought, hands steepled before his face as if in prayer. A glistening skullcap of dark hair covered his head; a black bespoke suit embraced his body. An expensive monochrome tie lay like a silken chameleon in the folds of a similar-colored shirt. He raised his eyes to Harold and spoke without expression. "How much time do we have before anyone gets an enforceable judgment?"

Harold was taken aback. "Up to three years, probably. The trial will take some time, and there are always appeals. It's a steady paycheck for us, but it's not going to do Hubble a damn bit of good unless we come up with a pretty clever move."

Something glittered in the depths of Streeter's dark eyes. "You just hold them off awhile, Harold." He turned to Peter. "We've been making arrangements. We can do it. This is a perfect opportunity."

Peter Morgan smiled. "All right, then. That wraps it up for today. Let's go make some money." He looked at Wallace. "Or do whatever we do." The lawyers rose and left the room.

3 WHAT'S IT LIKE?

Peter's elevator brought him back down to the twelfth floor. Another elevator was coming up, and as he passed his electronic key card through the reader controlling the door to the offices, it disgorged a young lawyer. Peter noted the man's overcoat, the tousled blond hair, the headphones covering his ears. As Peter opened the door he glanced at his watch. Ten-thirty. Peter Morgan's face assumed a stern expression. One of his eyebrows raised itself upon his forehead and bent into an arch of skeptical inquiry. Humming audibly to himself, Walker Eliot gave a slight wave as he approached. With Peter's gaze, now even sterner, fixed upon his back, he stepped through the doors and passed musically away.

Still humming, Walker fished keys from his pocket and unlocked the door to his office. He shrugged off his coat and laid his bag on the floor. Walker's office was larger than Katja's or Mark's, but it had none of the usual associate's decorations, no diplomas, no certificates of admission to practice in particular jurisdictions. For a while the wall had held a poster of the female star of a popular television series, but the show's writing had faltered and with it Walker's desire to proclaim that particular allegiance. Now there was a single signed photograph, framed in basic black. The man in the photograph was Justice Marshall Arlen, for whom Walker had clerked the year before.

What's it like, other lawyers often asked him, clerking for the Supreme Court? Walker had one stock answer, and one that he didn't use. A fascinating experience, was what he usually said. An extraordinary opportunity to glimpse an important institution from the inside, a chance to work with some great legal minds.

Some of this was true. The law clerks worked intimately with the Justices, researched the cases, discussed each difficult wrinkle, drafted opinions. Among themselves they batted ideas around, lobbied for their positions, engaged in sometimes heated debate. But as Walker thought about it more and compared his life now to the way it had been that year, he was coming up with a different description. What it was like, he was thinking, was dating a girl in college and thinking that all relationships were probably like that, and realizing only after it was over that you would never have it so good again. He'd known, for a year, the purest sort of passion, spending his hours in a transport of research, touching the most secret and delicate places of the law, its hidden contradictions, its mysterious heart.

That much he could have done anywhere, as a student or professor- ial voyeur. But Walker was also working with a Court that always had the last word, that had the power to make the law what it said. *Fiat lex*, the missing day of Creation. No contradiction he discovered was too knotty to dispel, no blemish so great that the Court could not banish it with a word. The Court sought out these problems; from the myriad of cases lobbed hopefully its way, it took those that presented the most serious flaws in the law, the gravest rents and divisions among the lower courts. Its resolutions of these splits issued like blessings and reassurances, and always to Walker's ears came an undertone of affection for the law: How much more beautiful you are become, said the Court, how much more pure.

The Court was not perfect, of course. Sometimes it erred; sometimes it strayed on purpose. Part of Walker's time was spent trying to shield the law from these outbursts of violence, or registering a futile protest, leav- ing optimistic blueprints for future Courts' repair. There were whole ar- eas of law so ravaged by the shifting tides of battle that he could barely bring himself to think about them. But most of the time, it worked; and its working strengthened the Court. The Court made the law, and the law made the Court, a perfect symbiosis. Ten years a widower, the Justice he'd served was married now to the law. Walker had had a fling.

He looked once more at the photograph and sighed. Justice Arlen's face wore a slight, mysterious smile. Before, Walker had been tempted to attribute this to the television starlet's proximity, but the Justice bore her absence with the same quiet good humor. Walker envied the stoicism. Clerking at the Supreme Court, he had come to decide, was like being in love. What he was doing now . . . that was just taking advantage.

4 THE BEAUTIFUL MOVE

By midafternoon, a different atmosphere pervaded Morgan Siler. What in the morning had been a relatively homogeneous group of lawyers was now divided into two classes: those who were going home that evening, and those who weren't. Katja was in the former group. At four o'clock she had billed seven solid hours, and she was far enough into the drafting assignment that she knew she wouldn't need the night to finish it in time. Just one issue troubled her. The bankers they were working with would know the answer, presumably. But Katja was discovering that she didn't really get along with bankers. She hesitated a moment, then picked up the telephone and dialed.

The voice at the other end sounded displeased. "Are you saying you can't do it? That's what we pay you for, to do it."

"No," said Katja. "I can do it. But I don't really understand what we're accomplishing here."

"Why does that matter?"

Katja sighed. A spiky-haired young associate walked past the door, glancing inside her office with a smile. "It helps me in drafting the language if I understand what the purpose of the transaction is," she said. "And it looks to me like there's a problem."

"What's that?"

"Well," Katja said, "in the original deal, we had the loan collateral held by bankruptcy-remote subsidiaries, so we walled off the risk that the borrowers would default."

"Yeah."

"But now you're adding these lenders and you've got a chain of guarantees going back to the subsidiaries. So you've shifted the risk of default back onto yourself."

There was a pause. "That's big-think, counselor. I do big-think. You're a lawyer; you concentrate on the small stuff."

I do big-think, Katja repeated to herself silently. She shook her head. You monosyllabic Wall Street monkey. This is some twenty-four-year-old in suspenders. The A students end up working for the B students. Who had told her that? And why hadn't she listened? She swallowed and answered, "Right," while making obscene gestures to the empty air. One of these caught the eye of the associate who'd passed by before, now headed in the opposite direction. He smiled again.

Katja hung up the phone. "Sorry," she said quickly.

Ryan Grady waved a dismissive hand. "I get that a lot. I'm used to it. Is it the outfit?"

Katja looked at him more closely. Ryan's suit was unexceptional, though its stripes were a bit wider than the norm. The shirt too . . . well, some of the older partners favored blue shirts with white collars. But the tie . . . the tie, she could now see, bore the printed likeness of a woman in a bikini. "No," she said, pulling her eyes away. "The client was being difficult."

Ryan's hand ran briefly over his clothing, a proprietary caress. His face curled in a practiced smile. "Don't let it get to you," he said. "The client can't take a piss without three lawyers holding his dick for him."

Despite herself, Katja laughed. "I saw you go by earlier," she said. "Are you lost?"

"No," Ryan said. "This is a good floor to be on. Lots of important people."

"Are you looking for someone?"

"Just walking around." Ryan lowered his voice to a conspiratorial hush. "You could walk around with me if you want."

Katja reevaluated the situation. "I don't think so," she said.

Ryan shrugged and walked away. Katja turned back to the documents. The drafting wouldn't be too hard. Possibly she could even fix the structure by writing in additional covenants. Bearing down hard for the stretch run, she didn't notice Wallace's shadowy figure at her door, or even respond to his first gentle knock on the wall. He cleared his throat and she looked up. "Can I help you?"

"Do you have any time?" Wallace asked. "I've got a pro bono project that needs staffing."

Katja considered. She would have some free hours coming up, and she liked the idea of pro bono work. But law had a way of defeating her expectations, of turning out quite unlike the ideas that had seemed so appealing. As a first-year student, before the chain of events that culminated in the catastrophe of third year had begun, she'd signed up for a pro bono program. The students staffed a small office in the Washtenaw County Courthouse, advising people who came to apply for thirty-day restraining orders. It was an appealingly simple idea. Temporary restraining orders had certain standard legal prerequisites—a close relationship with the person to be restrained, a threat of abuse—that law students knew but the applicants did not. The point of the TRO project was to dispel for these people the mystery of the courtroom, to distribute more broadly the concentrated power of a legal education.

That was what the third-year directors said. Katja, trained already to distill substance from rhetoric, understood that she was to coach applicants into reciting the correct formula. Facilitating the process: that worked for her. Three days a week she walked from Hutchins Hall to the corner of Huron and Main and read her torts casebook on the second floor of the courthouse, sitting in a molded plastic chair behind a card table covered with domestic violence flyers. Business was slow; it picked up after weekends and holidays. There were more men than she would have expected, but usually women, young and old, married and single, offering variations on a few themes: drunkenness, infidelities real or imagined, refusal to accept the end of a relationship.

She told them what to say; if they asked, she went with them to court. The judges varied; the courtroom employees, who did not, grew to recognize her and offered greetings. And the restraining orders issued like clockwork. Katja felt useful, productive, a gear turning in the machinery of justice.

"How can I help you?" she asked a man one Wednesday afternoon.

"You think you can tell me not to go near my wife?"

Katja stiffened. The directors had mentioned the possibility of these visits. "I can't," she said, "but the law can."

"You think so," the man said. He bent down and planted his hands on the table, his voice dropping almost to a whisper. "Tell me something, little girl. Where's the law *right now*?"

Katja could smell his breath—it was, surprisingly, minty—and feel it on her face. She didn't lean back. "You're in the middle of a courthouse," she said. "There are marshals walking up and down the halls."

The man straightened. "Yeah," he said. "That's right. This is where the law is."

When he'd left, Katja took two deep and calming breaths and put the incident aside. But his parting remark recurred in her mind.

"Did you ever see the police about your injuries?" she asked during an interview.

"Yes."

"And what did they say?"

"They said I better not make my husband so mad at me."

I'm not even scratching the surface here, Katja thought. A wheel attached to nothing. She started doing research on the effectiveness of restraining orders, the frequency and speed with which police responded to violations. She watched the local paper for reports of murders. Sooner or later, she thought, I'll read about one and recognize the name. Three months in, with the Christmas and New Year's application surge looming, she quit.

"I don't know," she told Wallace now. "Will it accomplish anything?"

He looked around the office. On the desk an ailing plant shed long tapered leaves. "Not if you want to win," he said. "It's a death penalty case."

Katja looked alarmed. "I don't think I'm qualified for it."

"Don't worry about that," Wallace said. "You'd be a world of improvement from the other lawyer he had."

"Still. I'm not a litigator anymore. And I'm not sure I'd want to get involved with death penalty litigation even if I were. Have you had a lot of these?"

Wallace sighed. "A few. And it is upsetting. You think you're prepared for it, but you never are. I didn't care one way or the other about the death penalty before I got into this. And when I started, I thought we'd just be helping the system work." He stopped.

"But now?"

"I shouldn't be taking up your time with what I think," Wallace said. "Well, let me know if you change your mind."

He walked quietly away, and Katja went back to work.

Mark was struggling with conflicting emotions. He'd told the assigning partner of his failure to come up with anything useful, and the man hadn't seemed disappointed or even surprised. Instead, he'd shrugged his shoulders and given Mark another research project. This one too seemed hopeless, and Mark was again facing the dilemma of whether to sink unreported hours into it in order to be sure he wasn't missing anything. Possibly, he thought, he was trying too hard to make something from nothing. But why would they keep giving him impossible tasks? At this rate he might as well be overstating his hours. "I don't know," he told Wallace. "It sounds interesting, but I've got a fair amount on my plate already. I'll have to see if I get any big projects in the next week." Wallace nodded and moved on, passing Walker's office without a pause.

At four-fifteen, Walker was about to start work. This was not to say that he hadn't been busy the rest of the day. He had recently bought an MP3 player, and he'd been enjoying using the firm's speedy Internet connection to download music. Typically he spent only an hour or so a day on this project, billing the time to clients with the rationalization that brief diversions made him more productive. But recently he'd been sparked to greater industry. His favorite site was facing legal problems, and once Walker had used the Net to find and read the briefs, he could see that the great buffet would soon be closing. So today he'd given it six hours of concentrated work. Charging even that much to a client didn't cause him concern. The brief Harold had assigned him was supposed to be complicated, but though he hadn't looked at it yet, he knew he could do it quickly. He turned to the papers, primed for serious work. He had four hours till the deadline. In that time he had to produce something that could credibly be the product of twenty hours' effort. All right, he thought. Let's get going.

Half an hour later, Walker was near despair. It wasn't that the question had turned out to be difficult. On the contrary, it was simple. The desired answer was so easy to reach that there was no way he could claim to have spent twenty hours on it without branding himself a moron. Walker got up from the computer and began to pace his office. The issue had to be made more complicated, which meant that he would have to destroy the position he'd been told to establish. But then, unless he was going to report a failure—which he would never do—he'd have to build it back up again. He'd have to prove the opposite of an obvious truth, and then the opposite of *that*. Walker began to hum softly to himself. For the first time, he felt the job was fully engaging him.

One hour later he had a draft. The firm's client manufactured automotive parts and, after repeated disputes with distributors over product placement, had decided that the solution was to acquire a chain of service stations through which to sell its products. Not wishing to alert potential rivals to its plans by making the purchase itself, it had hired an arbitrage firm to locate and obtain a suitable partner. The arbitrageurs had done this but, in the spirit of arbitrage, then decided that they would do better to auction their acquisition off among the client and its rivals. That was a breach of contract, the manufacturer claimed, and the lower court agreed. The manufacturer had made an offer and the arbitrageurs had accepted. Offer and acceptance create a binding contract. This much every first-year law school student knew. It was an open-and-shut case, as simple as these things could be. Which meant, of course, that it was far too simple for Walker's purposes.

Why *isn't* this binding? he asked himself. His mind roved over the terrain of contract law. Was there a binding contract once the arbs agreed to find and buy the service stations? Maybe not. If they hadn't found a suitable acquisition, they wouldn't have been liable for breaching their obligations. No, Walker thought, nodding his head in satisfaction, they didn't have any obligation at all. If I tell you I'll pay twenty thousand dollars for a '57 Chevy, I've made an offer. But the only way you accept that is by giving me the car. You're not bound to do that. Legally, it was called a unilateral contract, and though the doctrine was esoteric, it was still good law.

"Unilateral what?" Harold protested, five pages into the draft. "I don't understand what you're saying. You're supposed to argue that there *is* a contract."

"Wait," said Walker. "There's more." What the arbs had been asked to do, his brief went on to explain, was find and acquire the chain of service stations. True, they could have backed out before making the purchase. Having identified a suitable target, they could have stopped and tried to renegotiate the deal. But they hadn't stopped, and that was the fatal error. Once the acquisition was consummated, they had done everything the client had asked. With the requested performance complete, the brief concluded triumphantly, a contract came into being, binding the client to pay for the chain and the arbs to turn it over.

Harold looked at Walker as though he'd just realized he was in the room with a dangerous lunatic. "You know that no one raised this issue at the trial level," he said. "The court didn't consider it. The parties didn't mention it."

"Yes." Walker smiled. "It just occurred to me while I was thinking about the economics of the deal."

"Do you think there's a danger that they'll argue it?" Harold asked.

"Well," Walker said, "I thought that as officers of the court we had a duty to point it out."

"Yeah," said Harold. "One of the things they might not have taught you at the Supreme Court was that you don't go out of your way to make things hard for your client." He paused. "People often compare litigation to chess, and there's some truth in that. But what we're trying to do here is win. We're not looking for the beautiful move. I think we'll wait and see if the other side comes up with this and save your excellent rejoinder for the reply brief."

"Okay," Walker answered, rising and heading for the door. "Just trying to be thorough." Inwardly, he was a little shaken. It had been a close call, and though he'd pulled out a solution, it had come at the price of making him appear demented. That's the last time I trust anyone who tells me a case is complicated, he thought.

"Got something else for you, if you're interested," Harold said.

Walker paused. "What is it?"

"Big case," Harold told him. "Toxic tort. It's not an appeal, but there'll be some interesting legal questions to work on, motions to dismiss and things like that."

"Sure," said Walker, halfway into the hall. "Just send me the stuff." On the way back to his office he looked in on Katja. She had changed back into the morning's running clothes. "Hey, there," Walker said, but Katja didn't hear him. She was lacing up her shoes, imagining herself already out the door, pushing away through the darkness. Walker shook his head.

Katja pulled on a sweatshirt still bearing the tang of the morning's run. It smelled to her like life, like liberty. She rode the elevator down to the ground floor and waved to the security guards. Then she was out the door, striding into the night. Her suit and its world behind her now, she was stepping lighter, moving faster, breaking free.

5 PUMPING WATER INTO THE SEA

Mark Clayton was heading back to work with a sandwich when memory tugged him abruptly into the past. He had missed the five p.m. deadline to order dinner from the firm's dining service, not through any misplaced optimism about his ability to get the work done and go home early—those days were long past—but simply because he'd lost track of time. It happened with surprising frequency, alarming, really, given that hours were what he was supposed to keep the closest eye on. If he had plenty of time, he'd go and get takeout from the Chinese place on Nineteenth Street; if he was in a frantic rush, he'd stop in the lobby. But the deli inside the building served a captive audience and knew it. They skimped on the chips and even essentials like mayo and hot peppers. So when he could, Mark walked half a block to a pizza place run by gruff Greek brothers, who also did the best cheesesteak he'd had since Philadelphia. Later at night, especially on weekends, it would be crowded with college students, but weekday evenings he could order what they unaccountably called a "steak and cheese with everything" and be in and out in under ten minutes.

He made his way back along the sidewalk, feeling heat rise through the tinfoil and the paper bag, inhaling the aroma of the crusty bread and the sharp, slightly sour odor of the hot peppers. As he neared the firm he let the bag fall to his side and another scent came to him, something sweet and floral drifting through the dusk. The bushes by the door, he assumed, gardenias or sweet olive or something like that. And he was seized by memory, thinking of other fragrances in another night.

Nantucket got very dark. That was perhaps the most surprising thing. You wouldn't know it walking around, most of the time; the streetlights and the houses spread their glow over most of the places you were likely to go. But if you got off by yourself away from them, the night was around you like a cloak, a darkness you kept expecting would lift as your eyes adjusted. It didn't; it remained inky and impenetrable, broken only by the occasional flash of a firefly or sweep of a lighthouse beam. There was none of the general ambient light of a city, the inescapable illumination of hundreds or thousands of close-packed buildings. Growing up in New Rochelle, Mark had seen the sky glow orange at night, the clouds absorbing and diffusing the light the city cast off. In Nantucket, if there were clouds, you couldn't see anything. If there weren't, you could see the stars, more and brighter than Mark had ever known, the Milky Way actually a visible smudge, the constellations clear and distinct, if you knew what they were, which of course he didn't.

Mark had taken a year off between college and law school, though given his uncertainties about the future, it hadn't seemed necessarily a year between. It might have been the beginning of something, but he'd worked mostly odd jobs with one eye on the LSAT. And then in February he'd started with Ambrose Marine, and in June, when he'd already been accepted at Penn, they sent him to Nantucket to fix the beach by digging holes for pipes and pumping stations.

The trouble with the beach was that it was moving, heading inland at a pace of five to ten feet a year. Sometimes more, so fast that it outran the sand and became a jagged margin of dirt bleeding mud and shrubs into the ocean. The beach moved, but the houses didn't, or at least they weren't supposed to. That was the real problem. Back on the mainland the project supervisor had showed them a Boston newscast taped in the fall of 1991, a cottage floating out and breaking up in the waves. That was the perfect storm, which took the *Andrea Gail*. On the island they didn't need a video. There was a path along the bluff that had gone up to the lighthouse on the point and now stopped short, plunging into space. There was the lighthouse itself, separated from the advancing cliff by a few yards of grass and the trembling raised hand of a chain-link fence. Down in Codfish Park, by the public beach, there was a house on stilts, like an old woman who'd hiked up her skirts at the water's approach, showing tubes and cables not meant to be seen.

Dewatering had been discovered by accident, in Denmark, they were told. The idea was that running perforated pipes underground and collecting water and pumping it back out to sea would stop the process of erosion, fix the beach in place, or even reverse its course, send it away from the houses. Eight thousand gallons a minute sounded like a lot of water. On the other hand, there was a lot of water in the ocean already. Mark didn't care about the history, or even the theory. He liked walking the sleepy streets of Siasconset, looking at the houses with shingles faded gray by the salt air and names on small boards by the door. Willow Harp, Sans Souci, Fortune Cookie, Nepahwin. They meant something, presumably, to the owners, just like the license plates on the lines of Jeeps parked along the street out front, usually some variant on ACK, the airport code for Nantucket.

The Jeeps had oversand permits for driving on the beaches, fishing pole racks, and crusts of sand on their bumpers. The houses had weathered lobster claws and painted clamshells in the windows, Adirondack chairs on the lawn. Mark and the rest of the crew were staying in one of the larger houses. It was named Decked Out; it slept eight in comfort; and it would have rented for seven thousand dollars a week had the owner not offered it gratis. Much of the dewatering project was privately financed by those whose houses were threatened, and one of the things Mark had most eagerly anticipated when he'd learned of it was the prospect of meeting these people who hoped to hold back the sea.

He met a couple, though no one he hadn't seen already in Boston. The construction workers kept mostly to themselves. They hung out with the housepainters, the Irish kids who'd come over for kitchen work, the caddies at the local golf club, who were younger but reliably hosted beach parties. When the weather was bad they went to bars in Nantucket Town, the Rose and Crown and the Atlantic Café. On the rare free afternoon they borrowed the house clubs and chipped golf balls inexpertly around the lawn, or went to the beach and displayed the T-shirt tan lines that distinguished them from the children of leisure. Occasionally, walking down to their beach, where the earthmoving equipment ferried expensively from Hyannis awaited, Mark passed by the tennis club. The courts were ringed by fences and thick privet hedges. Through the leaves Mark could see flashes of tanned arms and legs; he could hear the repetitive thwack of a ball against strings, men muttering curses or compliments, and female voices raised in cries of mock despair.

Once a fuzzy yellow sphere soared out into the street, trailing a high-pitched lament: "Keep your eye on the ball!" Mark caught it on the fly, surprising himself, and tossed it back. The same girl's voice called out thanks.

"Oh, now you're in," said Ty, the foreman. "She wants you. Gonna have dinner at the country club." Mark peered through the hedge, catching a glimpse of dark hair in a long ponytail, then felt himself being pulled away. "Joking, buddy boy," said Ty, who was fond of dispensing advice. "There's a league. That they are in and you are not. The only way you'll meet girls like that is if you're working for their dads. Come on. Tide's a-wasting."

Not even, thought Mark. He *was* working for their fathers, indirectly at least, and still he never met them. He saw them sometimes, slim and bronzed and elegant. The regulars, the house owners, were called the summer people, and even the name had a flavor of the otherworldly, the untouchable. He saw them in the little market, on the beach or the narrow streets, and he exchanged waves or smiles but never spoke.

That night the construction workers went shopping at a seafood place near the airport. In the house they raced lobsters on the kitchen floor, through a track of quahogs and surf clams, an exercise that left Mark unable to participate in the cooking or eating. Instead he stepped outside and looked at the stars, the sweep of the beam from the lighthouse, the black ocean and the white foam of the waves. That was when he noticed the characteristic scent of the air, the slight salt tang of the sea and the sweetness of wild rose and honeysuckle on the breeze. Anything could be out there, behind the darkness, in the future; anything could happen.

Walking through the glass corridors of Logan on his way back, changing terminals from Cape Air to Continental for the flight to La Guardia, Mark felt the satisfaction of tangible deeds. The experience had been unreal in some ways, but he had done something, made a difference. It was that feeling, he thought, that made those weeks return so often to his mind. In law school, as he'd struggled with the vagaries of doctrine and rule, and even more since he'd joined Morgan Siler. If he'd told anyone, it would have sounded ridiculous, he knew, even pathetic. But he missed the sense of accomplishment he got from pumping water back into the sea. Compared to what he was doing now, it seemed the establishment of an empire.

Above the main reception desk on the second floor of the Morgan Siler offices, there hung a large oil portrait of Archibald Morgan. Many firms had similar paintings, the stern and confident gaze of their founders assuring prospective clients that here was an assembly of lawyers like no other. Archie's portrait was different. He wore an expression of gentle perplexity, as though the answer to a difficult question hovered just beyond his reach. The clients waiting on the leather couches could only wonder, as they returned *The Wall Street Journal* to the oak coffee table and glanced up once more, whether the man had ever grasped the understanding toward which he strained. The portrait would be puzzled forever.

The firm's lawyers, some of them, could have given an answer. Archie had never lost his air of bemusement; that was how they remembered him, if they remembered him at all. But Archie had not always looked that way. There was a time, in fact, when he felt he understood the world very well.

Archibald Morgan arrived in Washington in the summer of 1937, ready to begin his clerkship with Justice McReynolds and feeling like a latecomer to the bloody fields of Gettysburg. He owed the sentiment in large part to Harvard professor Felix Frankfurter, who saw law diplomas as conscription papers and sent a yearly wave of recruits south to the Capitol to do battle. But even without Frankfurter's influence, Archie hardly could have avoided being entranced by the struggle between the President and the Supreme Court. No law student, no American, could. The branches of government, after a century and a half of reasonably peaceful coexistence, had finally been pushed, and pushed each other, past a succession of breaking points.

That was how Archie thought of it, watching from afar. In reaction to the sudden swoon of 1929, the unyielding grip of the Depression, the President and Congress pushed one way. The Court pushed back, striking down federal attempts to regulate the economy, always by the same 5–4 majority, sometimes through the voice of the archconservative McReynolds.

With the legislature stymied, the matter was thrown to the people. That was what it had turned on, Archie decided. They'd voted for Roosevelt, giving him that historic margin in 1936, and Roosevelt decided he'd had enough of the Supreme Court. If the Justices didn't see things his way, he'd appoint some extra ones who would. But suddenly there was no need. In March of Archie's third year, the battle unexpectedly ended; the Court backed down as Owen Roberts went over to the President's side. The Court-packing plan went down to defeat in Congress— "A Switch in Time Saves Nine!" the papers announced—but it no longer mattered. Another of the conservatives, Justice Van Devanter, resigned the same term, and it was clear that a new era had arrived. The law responded to the voice of the people, and Archie had missed his chance to serve.

From Union Station, Archie walked the few blocks to the new Supreme Court building at One First Street. Only Sutherland and Roberts had moved into their chambers within; the other Justices, including McReynolds, worked as accustomed in their own apartments. Standing at the foot of the massive staircase leading up to the great bronze doors, Archie half expected to stumble over evidence of carnage, the bodies of corporation lawyers fallen where their last charge had broken and spent itself, papers charred and bloodied on the ground. Perhaps they were to be found in farther recesses; on the outside all was glistening marble. Too pristine to admit even the rays of the sun, the building shot them back at viewers. The guards on the plaza wore colored glasses; Archie squinted through a hand in front of his face and considered donning the green eyeshade popular with his classmates. Instead he took a cab to 2400 Sixteenth Street, where McReynolds awaited.

Frankfurter had done his best to shape Archie's view of the law, but he'd done nothing to help with the clerkship. That marked Archie as a rarity among Harvard men, to have obtained a Supreme Court clerkship without Frankfurter's sponsorship, but Frankfurter of course held no influence with McReynolds. Archie had gotten the job through family connections, a means equally traditional and efficacious. His father, a partner at Stowe and Bingham in New York, dropped a word with a friend in the D.C. legal community who golfed with McReynolds at the Chevy Chase Club, and a month later Archie received a letter inviting him to Washington for the Justice's personal scrutiny.

The interview was perfunctory. Archie, too smart to be complacent, had read McReynolds's recent opinions and tried to prepare a statement about the New Deal. The latter task proved difficult. Archie had absorbed his parents' disdainful fear of Roosevelt in college, but law school posed questions to received wisdom. Archie didn't doubt that men, like his father, who succeeded in the marketplace deserved their wealth. But with wealth came responsibility, the need to assume the duties of one's station. Not all of the nation's successful men were like his father. And if they would not foster the public good of their own will, what was the alternative to compulsion of law? Sitting in McReynolds's apartment, he was still unsure what words would come out of his mouth. But few were called for. McReynolds asked if Archie could type and take dictation in shorthand and whether he used tobacco; Archie divined that the correct answers were "yes" and "no." Then McReynolds requested a handwriting sample, which he inspected while peering alternately at the nails of his left hand.

Archie took the opportunity to perform an inspection of his own. Even defeated, as he then must have known he was, McReynolds cut an impressive figure. Still slim and elegant at seventy-five, he possessed height evident even when seated and a bold shock of white hair over his craggy features. His shirt cuffs projected from his jacket, gleaming and immaculate. The Justice frowned at his fingernails; Archie sat attentive. "I shall expect you on July first, Mr. Morgan," McReynolds said.

And so on that day Archie presented himself once more, eyes still smarting from the Supreme Court's reflected glory. McReynolds greeted him as though they'd never met and set him to work on the five hundred or so petitions seeking the Court's review that had accumulated during the spring.

Archie donned his green eyeshade and buckled down. For each cert petition he was to prepare a one-page memo describing the lower court's decision and making a recommendation as to whether the Court should hear the case. McReynolds, passing in the hall, peered into his room. "What is that you're wearing?"

Archie explained that the eyeshade reduced distraction and was customary among his classmates.

"You look like a bank teller," McReynolds said. "Take it off."

In the weeks and months that followed, Archie learned there was a reason that he'd heard McReynolds called the rudest man in Washington. Archie worked each day in one office of the Justice's thirteen-room apartment, with his eyeshade off and his suit jacket on. McReynolds himself was seldom around. When not at the Court, he preferred to play golf or dine with one of his female admirers.

Left most days to the company of McReynolds's Court messenger, Harry Parker, Archie absorbed the unwritten rules of the household. As instructed, he had taken a much smaller apartment in the same building, but now he learned he was required to spend the day in McReynolds's rooms. "If he calls and you're not there, he'll fire you for sure," said Harry. Nor was Archie allowed to drink or entertain women. Lacking a kitchen, he waited until the Justice returned in the evenings and then walked to a Chinese restaurant on Eighteenth Street for dinner. And then, while the glories and mysteries of the nation's capital swung around him like constellations, filling his vision but impossibly beyond reach, he turned back to the apartment.

In their infrequent interactions, McReynolds generally confined himself to the description of assigned tasks. When the cert petitions ran out, he used Archie to handle his personal correspondence, declining requests for autographs and acknowledging the receipt of calling cards. On occasion, almost as an afterthought, he voiced his disapproval of some practice or person. Gradually Archie concluded that these negative opinions collectively constituted the entirety of his personality: McReynolds was a bunch of prejudices held together by sheer force of ill will. He frowned on wristwatches, tobacco use, red nail polish on women, and Harvard Law School, which he deemed respectively effeminate, filthy, vulgar, and overrated. He loathed the two Jewish Justices and forbade any contact with their chambers personnel, a particular blow to Archie, whose good friend was clerking that year with Brandeis. And McReynolds railed, though now with some resignation, against the New Dealers and all their handiwork.

As the clerkship drew to a close, Archie could honestly tell himself that he'd done well merely to survive. Many of McReynolds's clerks did not last the year, so it was possible to do worse. But not to do better; Archie racked his brain without success in an effort to come up with any opportunity he'd had to learn something about the law. He'd had one chance to write an opinion, when McReynolds was away for the weekend. In those two days, Archie had torn through four drafts and presented the latest, along with the parties' briefs, to McReynolds upon his return. The Justice retired to his study and an hour later called Archie in. The briefs and some case reporters lay upon his desk, as did Archie's draft. McReynolds leaned back in his chair. "And now, Mr. Morgan," he said, "we shall begin to write this opinion properly." For five or ten minutes he dictated extemporaneously, eyes on the ceiling, then, examining his nails and dictating the while, he picked up Archie's draft with his right hand and dropped it softly into the wastebasket. The assignment, Archie decided, had been given merely to keep him busy over the weekend.

Perhaps, Archie told himself, McReynolds simply had nothing to teach. In response to a direct question, the Justice had once agreed to share his accumulated thoughts on the practice of law. But wherever he thought he was reaching for the burnished wisdom of the years, his hand strayed into the kit bag of peculiar prejudices Archie had already encountered.

"A lawyer should never wear a red tie," McReynolds observed at last. "They're effeminate." Archie hung his head. To be so close to the churning heart of law's empire, and yet no part of the machinery.

From the outside, of course, things looked different. After the clerkship ended, Archie considered a return to New York. "With your Supreme Court experience," his father said, "I expect you could demand fifty dollars a week from one of the New York firms." But Archie wanted to make his own way, to make his own firm. And he felt he'd yet to take the measure of Washington. The city excited him, the buildings resembling the temples of Greece and Rome, the brilliant New Dealers coursing through their corridors, avid to shape the land afresh. World-building was in the air.

Archie looked up George Tutwiler, a few years ahead of him at Harvard Law School and now associated with the firm of Rose and Stone. Tutwiler took little persuading, and in the space of months the firm was launched. They hired two secretaries and took office space. Tutwiler and Morgan—the concession to George's age seemed only fair—opened its doors at 2300 K Street on October 17, 1938.

For an alarmingly lengthy time thereafter, nothing happened. No phones rang, no hand disturbed the heavy brass knocker of the door; the virgin sanctity of the office remained unsullied by any visitor. Tutwiler had been too junior to bring with him any clients, and would in any case have considered it a breach of trust to poach from Rose and Stone. Archie hit the cocktail circuit to no effect. He listened eagerly as aged matrons lamented the obstinacy of their estate planners, and earned a reputation as a sympathetic ear. But Washington was choking on legal talent and competition was fierce. The firm teetered on the brink of insolvency. To his parents' chagrin, Archie cut costs by marrying his secretary, Cynthia, a spirited girl two years out of Smith and destined for better things. Tutwiler's secretary—plainer, less fortunate, or both— was given three weeks' notice. More than once Archie considered abandoning private practice and heading for the looming shelter of the government, but the world he wanted to build was a private one. At last he called upon his father, with customary results.

The firm survived its early years on castoffs and leftovers, the unwanted work of the larger legal establishment. These were relatively plentiful; the Morgan connections put Archie first in line for such references. But he was disinclined to scavenge for hand-me-downs. His vision of himself, though unclear in his mind, was not that of a hyena in last year's suit. This approach also meant engaging in a large amount of litigation, something the reputable firms disdained. Pride lay in giving advice that kept one's clients out of court, not descending to the arena as a hired sword. Archie lay awake nights dreaming of the big corporation that would rely on him for counsel and offer him steady suck in return: General Electric, U.S. Steel, Standard Oil. Or better, one of the large commercial banks to which the firm might attach itself, as Milbank did to Chase Manhattan, something huge and buoyant to hold tight through the roiling years.

Then war came, and almost simultaneously Archie and Cynthia's first child, Peter. Tutwiler was caught up in the draft, never to return from the sands of Sicily. But Archie sat this one out too. A new brass plaque, names reversed, was screwed to the wall. Archie buffed it with melancholy ardor and soldiered on. He had more to work for now. Myopia kept him safe, and history smiled on his vision. For the first time in its life, and never to be repeated, Washington was experiencing a shortage of lawyers.

Morgan and Tutwiler moved up through the vacuum, not itself unchanged by the ascent. Archie quickly hired two graduates from Georgetown—Catholic, but there was no time to be choosy—and lured more Rose and Stone associates with the promise of partnership. Morgan, Tutwiler, Stevens, Raymond, and Cox began to establish itself. One of the first things established was that Tutwiler, having left the world, was not to linger on wall or letterhead. The legal community knew firms by their first two names, and while a deceased founder might have merited pride of place to emphasize continuity, Archie's firm was still protean and could use the second space to advertise Bert Stevens's growing real estate practice. Demotion smacked of disrespect, and so Tutwiler was simply erased. Archie would have laid a wreath on the grave had it been nearby; instead he wrote a modest check to the American Legion and raised a quiet glass of Scotch.

Morgan Stevens prospered moderately. Archie continued to accept references from his father's friends, but increasingly he was pleased to welcome first-time—or better still, repeat—clients who came of their own accord. And not just litigation either. Stevens was increasingly known as a wizard with a lease, a soft touch with the zoning board. A K Street cobbler joined their list of regular clients; Archie brought in the Chinese restaurant where he'd dined during his clerkship. Even a tobacconist, apparently through word of mouth. Archie celebrated the evidence of growing reputation, particularly pleased by imagining what McReynolds would have thought. The man would never know, of course; he'd died in 1946, his funeral notable for the fact that no Justice attended.

By the 1950s, Archie could look with satisfaction upon his circumstances, daring to entertain the thought that he'd succeeded in making something of himself. Peter, developed into a precociously serious young lad, attended St. Albans, where he excelled with a determination that surprised even Archie. Cynthia bore him two more children, twin girls; Archie sold his Dupont Circle apartment and bought a house in Spring Valley. He joined the Chevy Chase Club and retraced McReynolds's steps along the links. And the firm, his first baby, continued to thrive. The fledgling businesses whose leases Stevens had negotiated turned to Raymond to deal with suppliers. Archie's father's friends, in a last gesture of loyalty to the old man, offered up their wills, allowing the firm finally to break into the trusts and estates practice.

Those middle decades of the century, Archie often thought later, were the golden years. Peter went to Harvard College, left it with a magna in economics, and without a pause headed north of the Yard to the Law School. The girls rode horses at Madeira and made their debuts during their first year at Vassar. Morgan Stevens grew to forty lawyers, then to fifty, taking additional floors in its K Street lodgings. It competed for new graduates with the best of the D.C. firms, interviewing at Harvard and Yale and the New York schools. Its roster of partners swelled to twenty. Some were promoted from within. One had been passed over for partner at Covington; one came from a position as general counsel to the Securities and Exchange Commission, vaulting the firm almost overnight to the front ranks of Washington's securities regulation bar. And none of these additions required a revision of the letterhead. That, Archie realized with satisfaction, was the final indicator that he'd created something enduring. That new partners did not feel entitled to add their names, were in no position to make such demands—that was a good sign, of course. But for Archie it held a more metaphysical significance. The partners changed but the firm continued; its name referred no longer to the lawyers who'd sired it but to something else, something independent of them all. Morgan Stevens had been emancipated from mortality.

Archie presided over the firm's growth with a father's pride and a degree of control no parent could hope for. As it expanded, he'd divided it into departments according to practice area, each with its own head. Those heads formed the steering committee, and the steering committee reported to him. Archie's authority was absolute, not because the partnership agreement entitled him to it—indeed, it was a point of some pride that Morgan Stevens had never had a formal partnership agreement—but because it had always been so, and every new lawyer who joined the firm understood. Archie decided who would make partner, which clients would be taken on, how many litigators would be loaned out to Legal Aid and the Public Defender's Office. The associates did not complain; monarchy and oligarchy were indistinguishable from their perspective, and Archie treated them well. Starting salaries were pegged to the going rate set by the big New York firms and rose steadily, and Archie, unlike some of his managing partner peers, made no fetish of the billable hour.

Indeed, the associates loved Archie. He was reaching the peak of his powers as a lawyer, a respected fixture of the Washington bar with a stable roster of clients. He sat on the boards of Sibley Hospital and the National Cultural Center; he was one of the District of Columbia's representatives in the American Bar Association's House of Delegates. All these things were good for the firm. But they were not what caused the young associates unconsciously to mimic his slightly duck-footed amble down the corridors, his habit of doodling geometric marginalia during meetings. They were not what made the young lawyers treasure and repeat the cryptic apothegms he let fall at the meetings' conclusions. You could tell a Morgan Stevens lawyer, Archie liked to think, by the way he carried himself, by the quality of advice he offered clients, by his wisdom and judgment and general rectitude. All the firms liked to think this about themselves, and of course all were more or less self-deluding. But for a space of five years or so there was a certain type of Morgan Stevens associate who was indeed recognizable, a young man who wore a hat and a gray flannel suit long after they were out of fashion, who walked like a middle-aged man and said things like, "The window's faster than the door, but you only go out it once." These were Archie's loyal sons, and they loved him for his fatherly attention to their lives, for knowing their names and the names of their wives and children, for sending the lobby shoeshine man to their offices if he noticed a scuffed toe.

And the partners? They too respected Archie's legal acumen; they too appreciated his solicitude. As for the question of management, well, the partners did not complain, because they agreed with his vision of what the firm should be. Archie never entertained any serious doubts on this score. The firm was what it was: his firm. Of course the partners agreed with his vision. Why otherwise would they have signed on to the venture?

Even later, reproaching himself in private conference for having missed the warning signs, Archie maintained that this assessment had been correct. He'd created a firm according to his vision, and that vision had been shared. But he'd relied also on a stable backdrop—the world in which the firm was created—not taking account of the possibility that it might look different to others if the backdrop changed. In the final analysis, Archie blamed the world. Morgan Stevens had been betrayed not by any flaws within itself but by an unexpected contextual shift, a sea change in the nature of legal practice.

7 THIS IS WHO YOU ARE

Two words, thought Walker Eliot, bounding briskly from his apartment. Cashmere socks. Peter Morgan had imparted this valedictory wisdom at the close of one of their first meetings, and Walker was finding the advice sounder than ever as the days grew colder. Cashmere did not wick away moisture in the manner of wool, and in the uncertain heat of the fading summer, he had more than once felt damp doubt in his shoes. But as the air turned crisp, his doubts evaporated and his feet reveled in their luxury. In the socks' warm embrace he felt the world's appreciation, an almost erotic thrill of recognition. Others did too, partners, probably, and Walker felt a silent kinship with them. He had entered into the fraternity of the wealthy, been vouchsafed its secret stimulation, the succor of objects. He was loved.

Cashmere socks never would have occurred to Walker a year ago, or even six months. When he'd anticipated the young-associate phase of his life, he'd imagined himself monastic and intense, reaping the harvest of earlier achievements, laying away a bounty for winters to come. Now, when he had more money than he'd ever thought he'd need, he was finding needs he'd never thought he'd have. He was learning that there was a whole industry devoted to creating needs for people like him. And it was powerful. It was hard to resist. *You can have me*, the voices said. They emanated from shopwindows, from fine topcoats and shirts of varied hue. *We're meant for each other*, the cell phones implored. The digital cameras, the GPS watches, the baubles and gadgets. *You deserve me. This is who you are.*

You can have me. Ryan Grady heard the chorus too. Not from objects; his basic nature was too stolid to be molded by the blandishments of commerce. Ryan heard the voices of people. In a way this made it more natural, but only in a way, for the people were not speaking. Still Ryan heard them, a synesthetic murmur from bared shoulders and angled eyes. Walking down the street, standing in the subway's jostled crowd, he heard them and wondered: How much? How much would it take? One hundred, two hundred, three hundred thousand? Not onetime figures but annual income: How much would I have to make to get that woman to go out with me?

Everyone was available in principle, Ryan realized; it was just a matter of haggling over price, of demonstrating sufficient buying power. And power was what it came down to. You didn't, if you played your cards right, even have to do the actual spending. The proven ability to do so was enough, the promise that one day you might. Not right now, not immediately; there's no need to rush these things. But eventually, when the time was right, when things had grown clearer. In that sense, Ryan thought, money and love were much alike.

Ryan was accumulating money, but he was willing to wait on love. More, he was avoiding it. Love led to marriage, and when marriage entered Ryan's mind it came with the same fear and reverence that accompanied his visions of the grave. For what was the point of all his strivings, if not to make himself appealing to women? To give that up, to forsake life's purpose, was surely a kind of death. Certainly, to do so prematurely could only be understood as suicide, or at best grave misfortune. That so many men married before reaching the peak of their attractiveness— something Ryan estimated would happen to him in his mid-thirties if he kept his hair—was astonishing. They weren't idiots, not all of them; they were, Ryan decided, simply unlucky. Waylaid by love, struck down as by a sudden injury, taken out of the game.

Ryan steeled himself against the possibility. He performed mental exercises designed to prevent the formation of crippling attachment. Chiefly these consisted of imagining every attractive woman he saw naked, an attempt to preserve emotional flexibility in the same way that daily calisthenics ward off the snapped tendon. It was like stretching, but somewhat more enjoyable, and Ryan likely would have done it even if not convinced of its utility as an anti-love exercise. But not with the same fervor, not with the same dedication. It was an enduring project he had set himself, a life's work, and it demanded all his effort.

He walked out of the Farragut North metro stop, silently calculating. Two-fifty, he thought, nodding appreciatively. Three hundred. Out of his range right now, but years passed swiftly; annual raises incremented each other. He'd seen the partners' wives. Five hundred for that one; she's probably a model. He followed a woman in expensive clothes around the corner, straining for a glimpse of her face. Five hundred there too, but for the wrong reasons; she's probably a partner herself. An elegantly dressed man passed in the other direction; his eyes swiveled.

He's totally checking her out, Ryan thought, amazed. That's sick. She's got to be like thirty-five.

Harold Fineman heard one voice in his head, insistent and repeating. It was his own voice, and it was directed not at him but at the surrounding crowds. *Not all of us are going to make it. Who's it going to be?* He shot a sidelong glance at the man to his left on the sidewalk, his substantial bulk draped in a double-breasted suit. You're not healthy, Harold's interior voice pronounced. You don't work out four times a week, an hour of squash, an hour on the StairMaster. Who's going to get colon cancer? Harold thought. Who's going to drop dead of a heart attack? Between the two of us, is there really any doubt? It's you, tubby. You'll die instead of me; you'll die so I may live.

Life was a competition, and in any competition there were bound to be losers. In law school, his professors had told him so: "Look to your left, look to your right. One of you won't be here for graduation." Those were the old days. Times had changed; the dictum meant nothing to law school students now, inspiring more hilarity than fear. Instead its significance had followed Harold into middle age. Look to your left, look to your right. One of us won't make it to sixty. Harold was at an age where he heard the whispers of mortality, the actuarial scythe passing close. The classmates whose wedding announcements had graced the pages of the *Times* were now cropping up in the obituaries.

Harold's own family history, truth be told, was less than spotless. There was the grandfather who'd dropped in his tracks at forty-eight; there was his father, who'd shuffled and wheezed out of the world before

Harold's college graduation. The Fineman men were not known for longevity. But had any of them graduated from Columbia Law School, been Kent scholars, joined prestigious firms? Were any of them called partner by men with names like Morgan? How many had even gone to college? Rising above his origins was something Harold had always done.

Hard work and ferocity had brought him this far, and he saw no reason to change a winning strategy. Things had gotten more difficult, admittedly, more competitive. But that was how life worked, as the weak were winnowed away. High school, college, law school, partnership: always a stronger field, always the same need to be at the top. Okay, Harold said to himself, answering his own voice. As he neared the firm he raised his chin and squared his shoulders. Okay, he said again. Bring it on.

Katja Phillips heard only the even flow of her breath, felt only the percussive shocks of her feet on the cement of Key Bridge. Running was the only thing that calmed her nowadays, the steady pounding of her stride eating up the miles, the rhythm of her exhalations. Keep your head up, she thought. Keep moving. One foot in front of the other. If you're fast enough, nothing will stop you, nothing will mark you. If you're fast enough, nothing can hurt you.

Others competed; others desired. Katja just performed. There was isolation in that creed, but also safety. It was true, she thought, what her coaches had told her. In the end, other people were incidental. In the end, you were running only against yourself.

IN THE CIRCUIT COURT FOR
THE WESTERN DISTRICT OF TEXAS

FELIX GUZMAN, as administrator of the estate of JANETTE GUZMAN, deceased, for himself and a class of others similarly situated,

Plaintiff

vs.

PARKWELL INTERNATIONAL, a Delaware Corporation, and
HUBBLE CHEMICAL CORPORATION, a Delaware Corporation

COMPLAINT AT LAW

1. Plaintiff's decedent JANETTE GUZMAN and other members of the plaintiff class are residents of the State of Texas.
2. Defendants PARKWELL INTERNATIONAL ("PARKWELL") and HUBBLE CHEMICAL CORPORATION ("HUBBLE") are corporations organized under the laws of the State of Delaware and registered to transact business in the State of Texas. At all times relevant hereto, Defendant HUBBLE regularly and continuously did business in the State of Texas by operating a chemical plant at 1300 Oakview Avenue, Mayfield, Texas. Defendant PARKWELL regularly and con-

tinuously did business in the State of Texas by controlling and directing the operations of Defendant HUBBLE.

3. On or about September 23, 1999, the chemical plant at 1300 Oakview Avenue was destroyed in a fire. As a result of the fire, numerous toxic chemicals were released, exposure to which caused the death or grievous injury of Plaintiff's decedent JANETTE GUZMAN and other members of the plaintiff class.

COUNT I
WRONGFUL DEATH

4. Plaintiffs incorporate by reference herein paragraphs 1 through 3 of this Complaint.
5. Defendants HUBBLE and PARKWELL did wrongfully fail to exercise due care in the manufacture and storage of chemicals at 1300 Oakview Avenue and thereby did proximately cause the death of JANETTE GUZMAN and other members of the plaintiff class.
6. Defendants are liable pursuant to the Texas wrongful death statute, Revised Code Section 13.26.

WHEREFORE Plaintiffs demand judgment against the Defendants in an amount in excess of $100,000.

COUNT II
NEGLIGENCE

7. Plaintiffs incorporate by reference herein paragraphs 1 through 6 of this Complaint.
8. Defendants are under a duty to manufacture, market, and store their products with reasonable care to avoid inflicting physical injury or death on members of the public, which includes Plaintiffs.
9. Defendants breached their duty to Plaintiffs in that:
   a. Defendants knew or should have known that the chemicals manufactured, marketed, and stored at 1300 Oakview Avenue were highly combustible and dangerous to human health.
   b. Defendants failed to use reasonable care to warn the public of the presence of highly dangerous chemicals and the potential for catastrophic injuries.

c. Defendants failed to use reasonable care in the manufacture and storage of their chemicals so as to prevent the fire which consumed 1300 Oakview Avenue and caused death and injuries to Plaintiffs.

So it continued for another eighteen pages. Mark rubbed his eyes and put the papers down. Like twenty or so other lawyers at Morgan Siler, he was getting his first look at the Hubble complaint. Filed that morning in Texas, it had been quickly faxed to Washington, then photocopied and distributed. He hadn't received a personal visit from a partner offering the assignment, just a curt e-mail from Harold to a large group of litigators telling them to clear the decks and get ready. Then a paralegal, walking door-to-door, handing out copies. To a certain extent, Mark was happy about this. He was finally involved in something important, and though he had no doubt that his role in it would eventually prove minimal and tedious, he appreciated the feeling of being engaged in a weighty and perilous venture. On the other hand, he was starting to see the facts behind the legalisms of the complaint, like figures hidden in a complicated picture or animals straining against cage bars, and they were disturbing. He pulled some news stories from the Internet, and they were worse. Mark drained his coffee mug and headed toward the bathroom.

Ryan Grady was walking the halls again, a project to which he devoted a couple of hours every day. Getting ahead at the firm, he had decided early, was not a matter of sitting cloistered in your office churning out memos. Billing hours was important, of course, but he had that under control. The other component was recognition, not by name but by face. When the time for selecting partners came around, people had to know who you were. For that purpose, it was essential to be seen both frequently and in the right places.

Ryan's office was on the fourth floor, an assignment he had protested vigorously, but to no avail. Most of the floors were allocated to particular practice groups, and as a litigator he belonged somewhere between nine and twelve. Twelve, in particular, was attractive, for it contained not only litigators but also the most senior partners and their favored associates. Four, by contrast, was sandwiched between the tax and corporate groups and had no distinctive character of its own. Or at least not one associated with a practice group. More than once Ryan had heard it called the "dead man walking" floor, and though the reference was usually explained in terms of the presence of Wallace Finn and the pro bono program, Ryan was beginning to doubt that story. Four, he was coming to believe, was the place for old partners being pushed toward retirement and associates who weren't fitting in. Refusing to accept this as his lot, Ryan spent as much time as possible elsewhere. Twelve was his favorite; there was pleasant artwork on the walls, and he'd several times encountered Peter Morgan himself. Though Peter gave no evidence of remembering who he was, or even that they'd seen each other before, Ryan believed he was making progress.

Rounding a corner, he almost collided with Mark Clayton. "Good to see you again," said Ryan Grady affably.

Mark frowned. "Have we met?"

Ryan nodded knowingly. "I look familiar, don't I?"

"Yes," Mark admitted.

"You've probably seen me in the halls," Ryan said. "I'm a high-profile kind of guy. Or the elevators. Sometimes I just go up and down in the elevators."

"Oh," said Mark. "Doesn't that make it a little hard to get work done?"

"You're not supposed to get work done. You're supposed to bill hours. And I do. How many hours have you billed today?"

Mark considered. "Probably two."

Ryan Grady smiled. "I've got six."

"Six?" Mark said. "But it's only ten-thirty."

Ryan's face assumed an expression of dull cunning. Don't really want the secret to get out, he thought. Especially not with the other associates, who would be his rivals for partnership in a few years. But doubtless few could match his dedicated application of the system, and with six hours clocked already, he found it hard to contain himself. He felt like a warlord, sacks of loot swinging from his belt, like a giant with enormous moneybags clutched in hammy hands. More, he felt the value he'd created swelling inside him, expanding him to godlike proportions, glowing from within like Lucifer's light. He was the buck bearer, incarnation of cash.

"It's simple," he said. "We bill in fifteen-minute increments, right?"

"Right."

"So what you do is, you just work for like five. Or less. Then you bill for fifteen and switch over to something else."

"Oh," said Mark. "Is that ethical?"

"Ethical?" Ryan looked distressed. "They told us fifteen-minute increments. I don't make the rules." A ringing telephone interrupted him. Ryan fished it from his pocket and consulted the display. "Sorry," he said. "Got to take this."

"Sure," said Mark, and continued, bemused, to the bathroom.

Peter Morgan stood at one of the two urinals. Mark anxiously took his place at the other. A weakly musical noise arose at his side, trickling up and down the scale like an idiot child practicing piano. That man has prostate problems, Mark thought.

"What are you thinking about?" Peter Morgan asked.

Mark's face flushed. "Work," he said quickly.

Peter zipped his fly emphatically. "I could tell," he said. "Make sure to bill it."

"What?"

"Bill it. Bill this time. You can't let the moments slip away from you. You'll never get them back."

"Uh," Mark said. My God, he thought, I can't pee with the managing partner talking to me like this.

"There's an Emerson quote that I often think of," Peter Morgan went on. He ran water in the sink and doused his hands. "'The lubricity and evanescence of things that makes them slip away then when we grasp them hardest, this is the most unhandsome part of our condition.'"

I'll come back later, Mark thought, giving up. Halfheartedly he feigned a shake and moved to the sink.

Peter Morgan treated his reflection to a searching stare, consumed with the importance of what he was saying. The irretrievability of time tortured him; he saw the unbilled thoughts of associates as a mist of dollars drifting away from the firm, confetti on the breeze. He dreamed of wiring their brains to mark each fitful electric squall, like hairnets catching each fleeting moment of attention. He wanted an infinitely fine mesh to subdue the fretful instant, to trap their quicksilver lives. "What's the case?" he asked.

"Oh," Mark said, "I was just thinking about different assignments.

Wallace Finn was talking about a death penalty case in Virginia that I was going to take, but there's also this Hubble litigation coming along."

"Harper, right?" Peter Morgan asked, calculating. He didn't recognize this associate, and though there were plenty of senior associates Peter wouldn't know on sight, this one seemed young enough to be a first-year. And based on this conversation, he seemed neither bright nor ambitious—all in all, exactly the person Wallace should have turned up for Harper. But Peter was feeling expansive. He had opened his heart, however briefly, to the young man, and doubtless there were other slack dullards Wallace could find. "Harper's a pro bono case," Peter went on, as Mark, seeing nothing else to do, dutifully took a place beside him at the sink. "Do you know what that means?"

They regarded each other's reflections. "We're taking it for no fee?"

"No. I mean, yes, but . . . do you know what pro bono means?"

"For the good?" Mark ventured.

"No," said Peter, relieved to be back on the definitional track. "That's the trick. 'For the good' sounds nice. That's why they call it pro bono. But that's not the real name. It's really *pro bono publico*. For the public good. The good of the public. Now, do you know who the public is?"

Mark opened his mouth to answer.

"I'll tell you who they're not," Peter continued. "They're not you. They're not me. They're not our clients. The public is the mob in the street looking for lawyers to hit each other over the heads with. Lawyers are weapons, and this firm is the heavy artillery. We're meant for serious stuff. The market understands that. But pro bono takes away the discipline of the market. It gets you involved in cases that—well, literally, they're not worth your time."

Mark dropped his eyes. "I see," he said. From one of the bathroom stalls there came the trumpet of a mighty fart. Mark flinched. He dared a look at the mirror and saw, as he'd feared, that he was blushing again.

Impervious, Peter Morgan offered what he thought of as a friendly smile. "What I'm saying is, there's no reason for you to get mixed up with that sort of stuff." He laid an affectionate damp hand on Mark's shoulder. "And you need to think about yourself. How you want your career to develop. Don't fool yourself into thinking that you have unlimited time because you're young. Whatever case you take, you'll never again have the hours you spend on it." He paused. "Think about what you'll regret," he said.

When Peter Morgan looked back on his life, he found he regretted most what he called failures of nerve, and others might have called pity. Opportunities to be uncompromising, to extract a few hundred thousand more in settlement, to destroy a rival's reputation, to pile up fees for an inattentive client; these were what haunted him. It was no consolation that such moments clustered toward the beginning of his career and occurred now only with great infrequency. Their increasing distance simply magnified the gap between his present situation and what might have been. Every day found him fallen further from the perfect trajectory he imagined; each day, in comparison, made him poorer. For compunction bears no interest, but forgone dollars do, ghostly sums piling up in the unchosen otherworld, ectoplasmic reproach to all remembered ruth.

Peter looked intensely into his mirrored eyes. He nodded slowly and let a small sigh escape, then with a valedictory pat he was gone, leaving Mark to survey the wet fingerprints on his shoulder and dab at them ineffectually with a paper towel.

A toilet flushed, and a man emerged from one of the stalls. Gerald Roth was bearded and heavyset, entering middle age in a navy blue suit. He shot Mark a companionable glance. "Getting the party line?"

"I guess it makes sense," Mark said warily. Gerald's face was sympathetic, almost inviting confidences, but he was an unknown quantity. What will I regret in twenty years? Mark thought. All of this, probably. Right now I do.

Gerald touched his beard as though uncertain it was there. "Listen," he said. "You don't have to say that to me. I'm not a partner. I'm a third-year associate. I know, I look older, and I am. I did some other things before I realized law was my calling. But you don't need to tell me that makes sense. It might if you're Peter Morgan and you're going to make partner if you keep your head down and bill your hours. But if you're actually concerned about your professional development, pro bono's a great opportunity. When else are you going to get the chance to actually argue a case? Not for five years."

"Yeah," Mark said. "I suppose that's true."

"And the other thing," Gerald said. "The discipline of the market. 'We're meant for serious stuff.' What he means is, we're meant to work for big corporations and oppose other big firms. One corporation has a team of forty lawyers, so the other one wants fifty. You get a lot of bright people sitting around trying to outsmart the other bright people who were sitting next to them in class four years ago. If you ever wonder what lawyers make, they make other lawyers necessary. It's an arms race, all right, but it adds up to nothing. Take a pro bono case and you might actually change something. We wouldn't have gotten this one if there wasn't something to it."

"What, you think he's innocent?"

"No," said Gerald. His blue eyes studied Mark intently from behind black-rimmed glasses. "Probably not. And you don't want him innocent. The defense lawyer's greatest fear is having an innocent client. You want him guilty, and you fight the good fight because it's your duty, and you lose and go home and think noble thoughts about helping the downtrodden. And your client gets what he deserves. Most of the time the appointed lawyer is giving last rites. It's a ritual. But there's a value to ritual.

"And who knows what he deserves, anyway? Sure, he's probably guilty. But does he deserve to die? There's loads of murderers who will be out in twenty years. Not a reassuring thought, but that's how the system works. How it works for people like you, anyway. For people like Wayne Harper, you are the system. If it's going to work for him, it's up to you. Basically, what you know about someone who got the death penalty is that he's pretty damn unlucky. Probably didn't have a good lawyer, maybe got some state's attorney looking to make a name. If he'd had just one break, it might have been different. And you could be that break." He raised his hand, looked at Mark's shoulder, and let it fall. "We're all better than the worst thing we do. Think about it."

Mark stood alone before the mirror, waiting in case any other lavatory oracles emerged. What did he regret? There had been no cataclysms in his life, no great failures or disappointments. No great successes either. Looking back, very little stood out. There had been a girlfriend in law school whom he'd helped move into a new apartment. They bought furniture together; he assembled it for her; and then she broke up with him. He'd felt embarrassment then, and even anger, imagining what someone else was doing with her in the bed he'd built. But in the end he'd been happy to have done her one last favor. Maybe a pro bono project was that kind of gesture.

Mark looked more seriously at his reflection, seeing the wrinkles in his jacket, the coffee stain on his pants. He thought of Peter Morgan's impeccable suit, the shirt crisp and white as a glacier. That man had never been dumped after putting together a bookshelf. Conversations died at his approach; silence trailed behind him like a heavy imperial cloak as he swept through the halls. Maybe, Mark thought, he should be regretting much more than he did. The furniture-building was at least something he should try not to repeat. Why seek out disappointment? He considered the options again. Managing partner says no; mysterious old associate says yes. I don't think so, he decided. Wayne Harper's going to have to find his break somewhere else.

"So I hear you're shopping a pro bono project," Walker said.

At the other end of the phone Wallace was puzzled. "Yes," he answered. "But I was looking for someone a little more junior. You're a third-year, aren't you?" Walker had been at the firm only since March; after leaving the Supreme Court in August he'd taken a long vacation. But they gave him credit for his time clerking with Justice Arlen, and for the Court of Appeals clerkship before that, and so in the firm's internal accounting books he was a third-year, which made his time too precious to be squandered on the public good.

"Three years in six months," Walker said cheerfully. "At this rate I'll be a partner by Easter. But I thought this would be a good opportunity to get my feet wet. And I don't want to look back one day and say I never did any pro bono work."

Wallace gave a sad, dry laugh. "I doubt you'll ever find yourself regretting work you didn't do," said. "More likely the reverse."

"Yeah," said Walker distractedly, inspecting his shoes. These are getting a little shabby, he thought. I should get a new pair. It was easy for his mind to stray, since Walker Eliot regretted nothing at all. He was dazzled by how good his life was. Work was easy for him, moderately interesting, remunerative beyond reason. The firm's lawyers treated him with kid gloves, hesitated to offer him anything but the most important tasks, stopped by his office for anticipatory reminiscence about the delirious future sure to unfold should he grace them with his presence a few years more. Don't be intimidated by the quality of lawyers at our firm, they told law students in interviews. Not everyone's a Walker Eliot.

By the silence on the phone he judged it was still his turn to speak. "All the same," he said.

"Of course I'd love to have you," Wallace said. "But don't sink too much time into it. Get someone else to help you with the legwork."

Walker scowled. "I'll only spend as much time as I have to," he promised, putting down the phone. Leaving Harold's office, he had been racking his brain for a task to which he could claim to be devoting the hours he put into other pursuits. Real assignments, as he'd learned, were dangerous; there was always the risk that they'd turn out to be trivial. But pro bono had seemed perfect: there was no client to complain if he billed absurd amounts of time, no one supervising who'd know the complexity of the work and question disproportionate hours, and, best of all, no pressure to win. The firm wouldn't be happy, he'd realized, but they wouldn't dare tell him no either. Walker was a rare commodity, and if one firm didn't treat him as he wanted, there was a sweaty press of others waiting. Well, he thought, this can still work. I'll delegate most of it and save just a couple of things in case the real work lets me down again. Now, who's going to be my errand boy?

9 SECURITIZING THEIR RECEIVABLES

"The question before the court," said Harold, "is this. Does the law allow recovery in this situation? Now, my friend and colleague over there is going to tell you a lot about the facts of the case. Some of what he'll say might even be true. Much of it won't be. But we've brought a motion to dismiss the complaint, so at this stage we must take the allegations at face value. For the purposes of this argument, then, we can assume that the design of the car in which the plaintiffs were riding was such that it exposed the gas tank. And we can assume that this design made it possible for a relatively low-speed impact to cause an explosion. We can even assume that the alternative design my friend mentioned would reduce the risk of explosion, and that it would have cost two thousand dollars more to implement that design. The legal question is not whether what happened to the plaintiffs was a terrible tragedy. And it is not whether we would spend two thousand dollars to prevent it. It is whether the law allows the conclusion that the design my client adopted was unreasonably dangerous."

He paused and smiled at Katja. She met his eyes briefly, then looked away, surveying the conference room. It was set up to resemble a court, with a podium from which Harold was delivering his argument, and a bench behind which the mock judges sat for these rehearsals. Usually there were three or more, partners aggressive with their questions. But Harold had suggested they try it by themselves, which left Katja alone to impersonate the judiciary. Silence lingered in the room. Katja looked back at Harold and, with an effort, turned up the corners of her mouth in what she hoped was an encouraging expression. He shrugged and continued.

"This court may take judicial notice of the facts stated in our motion to dismiss, that there were approximately thirty thousand cars manufactured with this design. To outfit those thirty thousand cars with the design the plaintiffs suggest would have cost sixty million dollars. Now, according to the U.S. Department of Transportation, there have been only ten accidents of the kind at issue here. The cost that's relevant to this case, Your Honor, is not two thousand dollars a car but six million dollars an accident. I would further call the court's attention to a Department of Transportation study analyzing traffic fatalities associated with different makes and models of cars, which indicates that the American consumer is willing to pay for increased safety at a rate of fifty thousand dollars for each accidental death prevented. Plaintiffs seek to hold my client to a safety standard one hundred and twenty times more demanding than the one consumer behavior indicates is desired. One hundred and twenty times. Now, we admit that compliance with a market measure of cost-effectiveness is not always a defense to a products liability suit. The standard applied to a private manufacturer is not always the same as the standard that consumer buying behavior reflects. But we maintain, and we ask this court to hold, that it cannot be one hundred and twenty times more demanding."

Harold consulted his watch. "That's only about five minutes, and they've got us scheduled for twelve. Of course, there's no chance I'll get through that. She's going to be jumping in with questions before I say ten words. Which is what you were supposed to do."

"Right," said Katja, trying to collect her thoughts. She looked out the window, down toward Constitution Avenue where the real D.C. District Court sat, then back at Harold. He rose slightly on his toes, anticipating interrogation. "I'm sorry," she said. "I have absolutely no idea what to say to that."

Harold chuckled. "I don't think the good Judge Keene is going to be quite so accommodating. Why don't you think about it and write up some questions for me?"

"Right," said Katja again. It was this case, in no small part, that had made her ask for a transfer into the corporate department, and it seemed particularly unfair that she'd been forced to continue working on it. Harold had explained that no one else had the degree of familiarity with it that she did, and that it wouldn't be fair to make the client pay for the time another attorney would have to spend getting up to speed. Which was true enough, Katja admitted, but fairness to the client wasn't uppermost on her mind. Four people had burned to death inside the car after it was rear-ended at a stop sign, not the sort of impact that was supposed to cause the gas tank to rupture. The family barbecue, the lawyers had called it, which was about the point Katja decided that maybe litigation wasn't for her. After some hotly contested discovery motions, it had turned out that the manufacturers were aware of the potential for explosions after low-speed collisions, that they'd estimated the cost of fixing the problem and simply decided not to do it. What was unforgivable, from the lawyer's perspective, was that they'd actually recorded their decision-making process. There was a memo detailing how many people were expected to die, how much the lawsuits would cost, how much more expensive it would be to recall the cars and make repairs.

"They're really innocents," Harold had said. "In a not-guilty-by-reason-of-insanity kind of way. They actually thought they were doing the right thing. But they don't seem to have factored in the punitive damages."

Innocents, thought Katja. Punitive damages. Four people burned alive. And, rumor had it, a dog as well. This fact was not in the complaint, and Katja hesitated to credit it. Rumor had packed the subcompact with such a menagerie that it was starting to sound like Noah's Ark. "I hear you got crispy critters," an associate had said, jealous of the good fortune. Black humor would not be her life's work.

Katja inclined her head to one side and then the other. "Questions," she said. "I'll get on that."

Harold watched her leave, feeling something sinking inside his chest. He liked working with the young associates; he gained more from their perspectives. By the time they reached the fifth or sixth year, if they made it that far, the associates were lawyers. They had internalized the norms of the profession; they had entered into the world of the law. This made them useful in some ways. They were competent draftsmen; they could argue unimportant motions and take depositions without suffering catastrophes. But they had lost the sense of how things appeared to those in the world outside. The young associates had not, and this was their value.

They were Harold's periscope, his parallax view. They let him see matters through the eyes of jurors, or the young judicial clerks, fresh out of school. And in return he showed them how things looked to the law.

They were frequently puzzled, of course; sometimes they were shocked. Harold explained things, joked and instructed. He eased their passage between the worlds. But things were different with Katja.

Harold couldn't quite figure out how to describe what was happening. It wasn't that she complained or raised objections; it wasn't that she rebuked him for losing touch with his humanity. Those things were familiar to Harold, who understood rebuke, from above or from below. If judges were shocked and troubled, he did damage control; if associates were, he laughed them through it. But this was coming from neither above nor below. It wasn't explicit; Katja didn't have to say anything at all. He'd see her face, reacting to something he'd said, and somehow *feel* it, a tightness in his chest, a squirming in his guts. It was coming from everywhere and nowhere, Harold thought, almost, in some strange way, as if it were inside him.

That was something Harold could not understand, and he dealt with it as he did all imponderables, through a quick mental triage. Is it an immediate problem? No, he decided; it is not. Then put it aside, he told himself; there are briefs to be written, fires to be put out. Harold thrust the thoughts back into the dark cabinets of his mind and girded himself for the day's next struggle. There was work to be done.

Katja walked back from the conference room toward her office, reflecting. Her heels sank into the carpet; her hand traced idly along the wall. Law school had been easy enough to understand. There were rules of law; she had learned them. There were exams to be taken, and places on journals to be won, and clerkships to be obtained. She had done all those things. There were mistakes to be made; she had made a big one and suffered for it, and that too had been a lesson. And beyond it all there had been the promise that after graduation she would go out into the world as a lawyer and make it run more smoothly.

Practice did not fit the promise. Not litigation, anyway, in which she was now seeing that half the work—more, for defense-oriented firms like Morgan Siler—consisted of trying to prevent people from enforcing the legal rights they claimed. Victory in such cases, the best possible result, meant that the complaint would be dismissed. No rights would be enforced; the parties would return to the status quo ante, and the only tangible consequence was that both sides had spent a lot of money on lawyers. This was the correct result in some cases, perhaps most; Katja knew that well enough. But it struck her as less a satisfying achievement than a terrible waste, the sort of thing that never should have happened, and she disliked the idea of building a career on the repeated squandering of resources. And then, of course, there were cases like the family barbecue, which she disliked in its every aspect, from the jokes of the other associates to Harold's constant questions about how to get a jury to see it from the carmaker's point of view. She had not gone to law school to change other people's perspectives.

Hence corporate practice, the deal-making, where the aim was not to argue for a viewpoint but to make sure that minds met, that every contingency was identified and planned for. And it was better, she had to admit, despite the strain of working with the boorish bankers, the grandiose and ignorant clients, the obstreperous lawyers on the other side. It was better because it was fundamentally a cooperative venture where at the end everyone could assemble on a conference call and congratulate one another for getting the documents all drafted and executed by the closing date.

At least, it was cooperative as far as the parties to the deal were concerned. But there were others to worry about, and here the shifting multiplicity of perspectives returned with a vengeance. Different perspectives existed at the beginning of litigation; each side presented one and tried to convince the court of its truth. But they were the object and end of the corporate work, where the deal had to look one way to the parties and another to the government, one way in its form and another in its economic substance, one way for accounting purposes and another for the tax code. This led, in Katja's view, to a waste that rivaled that of litigation, to tremendously complicated structures built up at great cost and effort for no reason other than to respond to particular provisions of tax or bankruptcy law, which would themselves be changed in response, necessitating the construction of new devices of avoidance.

Admittedly, it made a kind of sense for any individual deal. Given a particular set of legal requirements, they found the best way to structure a transaction; they made things as cheap and easy as possible for their clients. They helped people. But this wasn't triumphing over the harsh and ineluctable laws of physics; it wasn't perpetual motion or cold fusion. It was outsmarting some congressional staffer who, like a disappointed plaintiff, would likely as not dust himself off and come right back at you with something new. And that, again, seemed a slender foundation for a career. It certainly did not explain the conviction and enthusiasm of people like Anthony Streeter, the fervor with which he'd explained to her the benefits of securitization.

Securitization was, apparently, a new financing technique. It was, more obviously, the thing on which she spent most of her time. Working on small pieces of deals, as she had been, it was easy enough to find reason in them. The problem was that, when assembled, the pieces formed a figure she could not comprehend. A corporation might, for example, sell its assets to a subsidiary it owned and had created for that purpose, a special-purpose vehicle. That was understandable. But then the SPV would lease the assets back, and the corporation would continue to use them as though it owned them. And what was the point of that?

"We're securitizing their receivables," Streeter had said when she was first staffed on the deal, and she had nodded. "We're securitizing their receivables," he'd said again when she'd asked him what the deal was supposed to achieve. "Don't you know what that means?"

"That we're making them safer?" Katja asked. That was what had come to mind the first time she heard the phrase, and she was ashamed to admit that it was part of what had made the project sound appealing. Bankruptcy remoteness, the elimination of risk. Those were good things, surely. Actually, she had no idea what it meant, securitizing their receivables. When she thought about it now, it sounded like the kind of vaguely pornographic jargon that unattractive men used for unfunny jokes. "I'd like to securitize *her* receivables." But there had to be an original meaning, didn't there? Things couldn't come into being as parodies. No one was born a middle-aged lech; there had to be a process of falling off, a prior state from which to fall. Then the recognition that self-parody was all that was left, the pretense that something purer remained to stand outside and mock what the self had become. Appearing repellent on purpose so as not to take the risk of doing so accidentally. Securitize their receivables—once it was sleek and hopeful and full of promise; once it had a mother that loved it. "What does it mean?" she asked.

"Say you're a corporation," Streeter said.

"I'm a corporation," Katja said.

Streeter looked at her suspiciously. "You want to borrow money to run your business. And you should be able to; you've got a lot of assets; you've got an income stream from products you sell. You're a good credit risk. But there's always a risk: demand could dry up, you could have bad management, some competitor could come along and make you obsolete. If something goes wrong, you could go into bankruptcy, and the people who loaned you money will be fighting it out with other creditors. So they charge you a higher interest rate to compensate themselves for the risk of bankruptcy.

"Securitization lets you borrow against your assets without paying a premium for the risk of bankruptcy. What you do is, you sell your assets to another corporation that you create specially for that purpose. And then you lease them back, so you can use them. Now the other corporation can borrow, using those assets as collateral. The money that it borrows is what it uses to finance the purchase of the assets from you in the first place. And it services the debt to the lenders with the payments that you make on the lease. In substance, it's just like you're borrowing, but all the payments go through this intermediary. And in case you go into bankruptcy, your creditors can't reach the assets that the intermediary holds. So the lenders don't have to worry about it, and you get the lower interest rate. Makes sense?"

"I guess so," Katja said. "But selling your assets to an SPV you create and own? It seems kind of fake."

Streeter shook his head. "You're a lawyer. You should know better than that. You have these ideas about what's real and what's fake, but they're just intuitions. They don't mean anything. Your intuitions wouldn't tell you that a pebble falls as fast as a cannonball, or that moving clocks slow down. Law says what's real, and if you want to learn the truth, you have to ask a lawyer. That's what the clients hire us for. And legally, this is a true sale. We give a true sale opinion letter saying so, and they rely on it. Like a scientist saying the rocket will go up. We'd never have gotten to the moon if we trusted our intuition. Morgan Siler is a leading firm in securitization work, you know. Wallace Finn was one of its discovers. You wouldn't guess it to look at him now, but he was a pioneer."

Katja looked at Streeter's gleaming eyes, imagining him in a lab coat and glasses. Discoverers, she thought; pioneers. He was a believer. She could almost understand how it seemed to him, the deal provisions whirling through his mind like subatomic particles in an accelerator,

ever faster, ever more complicated. They met and annihilated one another; no economic substance was left. But in the residue of the explosion
there persisted ghostly traces, undetectable by any but the keenest in-
struments: legal consequences. That was what allowed people to find this
work satisfying, she decided, the belief that law constituted the ultimate
reality, that it imposed itself on the universe, held the world within its
sweep and bent it to its will. Very possibly, she thought, this man is insane.

"So it doesn't have anything to do with making them safer?"

"It makes the investments safer," Streeter said, a consoling tone in his
voice. "Less risky." He considered. "Actually, it does make the corporation
safer, in a sense. It makes them liability-proof. They have no assets to pay
a judgment. But that's not what it was developed for. It's good for the corporation because they get debt financing on more favorable terms. And as-
set-backed securities are good, reliable investments. Everyone's better off."

That piqued Katja's interest. It really did sound like perpetual motion. You can't eliminate risk, her torts professor had said. You can only
make someone else bear it. "Everyone?" she asked.

Something shifted in Streeter's face. "Well, all the parties to the
deal," he said. "Creditors of the parent company don't have as many assets to look to, but they know that going in. Basically you're contracting
out of bankruptcy, and bankruptcy's very inefficient. The only people
who might complain are involuntary creditors of the parent. Say, tort
plaintiffs. But you know what, we're getting kind of far afield here."

The hallway outside Mark's office was obstructed by a large number of
cardboard boxes, and by Mark himself, cross-legged on the carpet. He
turned wearied eyes up as Katja stepped delicately past. "Looks like my
apartment," she said.

"What?" Mark asked.

"After I first got here," Katja explained. "I didn't finish unpacking before I started work. Then it took about a month to find the time. It was a
week and a half before I got sheets on my bed."

"Oh," Mark said. "This isn't your apartment. It's more like the
maximum-security wing at Sussex." He gestured toward the side of the
box he'd opened. It, like all the rest, bore a black-inked legend:
Commonwealth v. Wayne Harper.

"You took that pro bono case?" Katja asked, mildly surprised.

"Not on purpose," Mark said. "Walker took it and then asked me to help him. Or told me to. It's hard to tell the difference with Walker."

Katja's surprise edged up a notch. "Walker took it?"

"Yeah," Mark said. "Which is noble, or something like that, but so far it seems like I'm doing the grunt work."

Katja smiled at him. "Good luck," she said.

Luck, thought Mark, consumed with sudden visions of a happier world. There were such things, he had read; according to the physicists there were infinite numbers of universes in which every possibility was actualized. And thus there was a Mark Clayton out there who, like him, had met this girl at an orientation cocktail party and noticed her pale composed face and sleek black hair, her green and luminous eyes. Who had noticed her and found her thereafter recurring to his mind, but who, unlike the Mark presently sitting on the carpet amid his documents, had then done something about it. A Mark Clayton who'd asked her out, taken her to dinner, found himself no longer alone in the night.

But that was a different world. In this one, Mark had never worked up the nerve. Instead, for practice, he'd invited a less intimidatingly attractive associate to have coffee. *Terribly swamped right now*, she e-mailed back; *maybe next week?* Mark read this as a lack of interest and sought to give her a way out. *Just let me know when you're free*, he wrote. She never did, and he took this as something like success, a communication achieved, implications grasped. He smiled fondly at her in the halls now. They understood each other; he hadn't embarrassed himself, or forced her to embarrass him, and it felt like a kind of intimacy. Or what passed for intimacy in his world.

From his position on the floor he regarded Katja's knees, then turned his eyes back up. There was also, he supposed, a Mark Clayton who'd tried to ask her out and choked to death on his tongue in the process, one who'd been stabbed through the heart with a letter opener in response, one who'd gotten a date and in his happiness wandered into the path of a laundry truck. He wasn't doing so badly when you considered all the possible alternatives. "What are you working on?" he asked, hoping to keep her there a few moments longer.

Katja's smile faded. She shrugged. "Defending murderers." And what, she wondered, would Anthony Streeter say about that? That if we can get the suit dismissed, the client did nothing wrong? What would Harold say? If law was the ultimate reality, then the firm was the real world, and what went on outside mere illusion. The thought would doubtless be consoling to some lawyers, those who had embraced the job and lost themselves in the work. But not to Katja. She had compartmentalized her life, segmented herself. There was a person who went to work, and a person who stayed outside; there was a brisk and competent lawyer, and there was a girl who read Rilke at night. Sunday mornings she cooked German potato pancakes from a grandmother's recipe and did the *Times* crossword in blue ink.

That was how to stay sane, her professors had counseled. Katja listened, a dutiful student. It had been hard at first, the feeling that each morning she pulled on one identity, discarding it as she headed home. She faced herself in the mirror, willing the transformation, trying to catch its traces. She'd been able to, those early days. At work she'd spot her reflection in a window, suited and serious, and feel no recognition. But not anymore, and the shift was becoming easier, almost imperceptible now.

This was not encouraging. Mothers told children that an ugly expression would freeze their features. Or they were supposed to; Katja's mother never had, perhaps because she had no habit of grimacing, perhaps for the adequate reason that it was demonstrably false. Increasingly Katja found herself wishing that she had received the warning, something to fix itself in a childish mind and transmute over the years. It might have been more useful than her professors' advice. They told her what worked for them, for the summer or six months they spent to pick up the clerkship bonus before jumping to academia. But no one had said anything about what happened over the longer haul, as year succeeded year. No one told her that we grow into our masks, that we become who we impersonate. A novel a week won't hold it off. And that, thought Katja as she picked her way through the boxes, was starting to seem a crucial piece of information.

10 ALL CLEAR FOR THE CLERKS

Still sitting on the floor, Mark watched Katja's shoes recede, then went back to the boxes. He pulled out a document at random and looked at it. *Report of Peter D. Samuels, Ph.D.* What's this? I have no idea what I'm doing, what I'm looking for, he thought. Time to ask for advice. He went back inside his office and picked up the phone.

"Look, Walker," he said. "I don't know what to do here."

Walker's yawn was almost silent. "Read the stuff they gave you," he said. "Figure out what we're trying to achieve. Then write me a memo about it. A short one."

"Well, I know what we're trying to achieve," Mark said. "We're trying to save this guy's life."

"We're what?" Walker asked.

"But I don't know where to start on it. I don't know the first thing about the death penalty."

The howl of dismay was entirely silent, but veins stood on Walker Eliot's neck. He clenched the phone in shock. Oh, shit, he thought. This is a death penalty case? I took a death penalty case?

Walker took a deep breath, trying to regain composure. He contorted his face into a grimace of distress, on the theory that a physical manifestation of his sentiments would remove them from his mind. It was partially effective. "Where are we now?" he asked.

"Filing a federal habeas petition, I guess."

"Okay," said Walker. "So he's gone through the state system. What we need to do is look for errors in the trial. Or the penalty phase."

"What's that?"

Walker twisted in his chair, which did not twist with him. With one hand he massaged his temples. He had explained the workings of the death penalty before, most often to groups of schoolchildren visiting the Supreme Court. He had developed a speech he could deliver by rote. Then in the course of one long night he had experienced what he described, and now he found he didn't want to talk about it anymore.

"Here's what you need to know," he said finally. "There's a trial, there's a conviction. That's the guilt phase. Then there's a penalty phase, to determine whether a death sentence is appropriate. We're going to identify errors in those phases. Ideally, they'd be constitutional errors, because that's what federal habeas is for. But they don't have to be. The Constitution guarantees you a lawyer. And not just any lawyer, a reasonably competent one. That doesn't mean much, but it does mean that if your lawyer missed a winning argument, you can say that he was constitutionally ineffective. So a big enough mistake can give you a constitutional argument. That's what you're looking for."

"What if I can't find any?"

"Then the habeas petition will be dismissed. And then we can appeal to the Fourth Circuit, and if they affirm the dismissal, we could file a cert petition with the Supreme Court. Or you could—the Court doesn't allow clerks to work on Supreme Court cases for two years after they leave."

"And what does the Supreme Court do?"

"Usually they deny it," Walker said uncomfortably. It was starting to seem easier just to give the talk. "They don't have to hear any case they don't want to, and most death cases don't present the sort of legal issues they spend their time on. That's pretty easy with an ordinary habeas case. It's the last-minute stuff that causes the problems. When the death warrant actually issues, prisoners almost always try to get last-minute stays from federal courts, and if they can't, they appeal the denials up to the Supreme Court. That's what makes the clerks stay up so late. The Justices go home, and the clerks wait for the filings, call the Justices to get their votes, and keep doing it until the all-clear signal comes around."

"All clear?" asked Mark.

"It means nothing more will be filed," Walker said. "So it's all clear for the clerks. For the guy on the gurney it means something very different. But you don't need to worry about that yet. Here's what you should do. Start with the Virginia Supreme Court opinion. Just give it an issue-spotting read—look for legal problems, or factual descriptions that seem odd. They should be candid about the issues, but sometimes they like to hide the ball. If something strikes you as unfair, note that. It's probably just Virginia law, but it might be unconstitutional."

"Right," said Mark, hanging up the phone. He took the opinion from a box and began to read.

11 NEITHER EXCESSIVE NOR DISPROPORTIONATE

Supreme Court of Virginia

Wayne Lee HARPER
v.

COMMONWEALTH of Virginia

F. Anson Henry (Law Offices of F. Anson Henry), for appellant.

Alexander Reiner, Asst. Pros. Atty. (Caleb M. Kite, Senior Pros. Atty., on brief) for appellee.

Present: FAY, C.J., ELLMAN, FESSENDEN, MILLER, JAMESON, ANDERSON, BUCK, J.J.

BUCK, Justice.

In this appeal, we review the capital murder conviction and sentence of death imposed on Wayne Lee Harper.

I.
PROCEEDINGS

An Alanton grand jury indicted Harper for the capital murder of Leslie Anne Clark and Michael Clark as part of the same act or transaction.

vestigative search of the house. They discovered that the lock on the back door had been broken.

At the Norfolk Crime Lab, Dr. Arthur Dole, assistant chief medical examiner, performed autopsies and forensic examinations on the bodies of Leslie and Michael Clark. The autopsies revealed that both victims had been struck with the same object. In addition, the autopsy of Leslie Clark revealed that she had been sexually assaulted.

Examination of a red handkerchief found near Leslie Clark's body revealed the presence of spermatozoa. Jonathan R. Dunn, a forensic scientist, performed DNA tests that revealed that the spermatozoa found on the handkerchief were consistent with Wayne Harper's DNA profile. The HLA DQa type found in the crime scene sample appears in approximately 7.8% of the Caucasian population.

III.
THE CONFESSION

On September 21, 1999, the Alanton police department received a phone call from an anonymous informant implicating Wayne Harper in the murders. Based on this information, Detectives Robideaux and Campbell went to the house where Harper lived with his parents. After obtaining entry, they arrested Harper and took him to the police headquarters. Arriving at the police headquarters at about 7:00 a.m., the detectives took Harper to an interview room. The interview began about 7:15 a.m. and was recorded on the police station's videotape. At 7:30 a.m., the detectives falsely informed Harper that his fingerprints had been found in the victims' residence. At 7:32 a.m., the detectives created another ruse by telling Harper that a witness had seen him entering the victims' house. At 7:45 a.m., Harper admitted that he had been inside the house on the night of the murders. At 8:00 a.m., Harper admitted that he had killed the victims. Following arraignment and consultation with his lawyer, he entered a plea of guilty to all the charges.

Code §§ 18.2-31 and 18.2-10. The grand jury also returned an indictment for first degree sexual assault of Leslie Clark and statutory burglary. He pled guilty to all charges.

Before accepting the guilty pleas, the trial court questioned Harper and determined that his pleas were made voluntarily, intelligently, and knowingly. In response to questioning from the trial court, Harper stated that he was satisfied with the performance of his lawyer.

Before determining punishment, the trial court held a separate hearing and received evidence in aggravation and mitigation on the capital murder counts. The prosecution introduced evidence showing that Harper had committed the crimes in a wanton and depraved manner and would pose a danger to others in the future. Upon consideration of the evidence, the trial court sentenced Harper to death for the capital murders, based upon findings of "vileness" and "future dangerousness" as prescribed in Code § 19.2-264.2. The trial court imposed two additional sentences of life imprisonment for the crimes of statutory burglary and sexual assault.

II.
THE CRIMES

On September 18, 1999, Annabelle Meadows had made plans to m
her daughter, Leslie Anne Clark, for lunch at an Olive Garden resta
in Alanton. After her daughter did not arrive at the restaurant, Me
telephoned her house at around 2 p.m. No one answered the ph
around 4 p.m., Meadows went to the house in an effort to
Leslie's whereabouts.

Arriving at her daughter's home, Meadows found the
locked. She went around to the back of the home and was
through the back door, which was unlocked.

Meadows proceeded through the house in an effo
Clark and her husband, Michael Clark. Leslie Clark's
body, covered in blood, was lying on the bed. She h
ous injuries to her head, and her clothing was soake
Clark's body was on the floor of the bedroom. He,
in the head.

Meadows called the police. A team of local
Detectives Raymond Robideaux and William C

IV.
PENALTY PHASE

During the penalty phase of the trial, the prosecution offered expert testimony as to Harper's mental state. Peter D. Samuels, a clinical psychologist, examined Harper and opined that Harper suffered from an antisocial personality disorder, had poor impulse control, and was unlikely to be deterred from criminal or violent acts by the threat of punishment. He concluded that Harper would likely pose a threat to others in the future. In opposition, Harper relied on Samuels' analysis in order to present evidence indicating that he had a subnormal IQ and had completed no schooling beyond the fourth grade. He also offered the testimony of his parents and Katherine Woods, a neighbor, that he had no history of violence. Katherine Woods stated that she had allowed Harper to watch her children while she was away in the past and that she would still do so. Harper also offered his lack of a prior criminal record as a mitigating factor weighing against imposition of the death penalty.

The trial court concluded that the death penalty was appropriate because the crimes were committed in a "vile" manner, and because Harper posed a threat of future dangerousness. Code § 19.2-264.2. Harper argues on appeal that the trial court erred in giving weight to Samuels' testimony because Samuels admitted on cross-examination that he had not read four of the six documents relating to Harper that were mentioned in his report. But Harper himself relied on Samuels' report to present mitigating evidence of his mental capacity, and he cannot simultaneously attack that report. Moreover, even if Samuels' concession did reduce the weight properly given to his expert opinion, Harper's failure to offer any contrary expert evidence prevents this Court from finding error in the trial court's finding of future dangerousness. And even if we did conclude that the trial court erred, the imposition of the death penalty would still be supported by the "vileness" finding, which the trial court could have found to outweigh Harper's mitigating evidence.

The trial court, in fact, found the mitigating evidence insufficient. Harper argues that this was error because the court failed to consider fully the testimony of his parents and of Katherine Woods. Our review of the record leads us to disagree.

During the hearing at which the sentence was imposed, the trial court stated, "It is the court's duty to take into consideration all the evidence produced in mitigation of the offenses. I have considered all the mitigating evidence produced. It includes the fact that the defendant pled guilty to these offenses, that he had no prior criminal record, and the testimony of his family and neighbors. I find that the defendant has failed to establish a mitigating factor to outweigh the statutory aggravating factors and I impose a sentence of death."

While the evidence that Harper presented did tend to mitigate, it did not require as a matter of law that the death penalty not be imposed. The trial court was not required to give it controlling weight.

V.
SENTENCE REVIEW

Code § 17-110.1(C)(2) requires this Court to review the death sentence imposed to determine whether it was imposed under the influence of passion, prejudice, or any other arbitrary factor, and whether it is excessive or disproportionate to the penalty imposed in similar cases. Upon review of other similar cases, we hold that the sentence of death is neither excessive nor disproportionate. Further, we find nothing suggesting that the sentence was imposed under the influence of passion, prejudice, or any other arbitrary factor.

VI.
CONCLUSION

We find no reversible error in the issues presented here. Consequently, we affirm the judgment.

Affirmed.

Jesus, thought Mark. Now what? Harper hadn't put on any mitigating testimony by psychiatric experts. Maybe that was something. But on the whole, Mark had no idea what the weak spots in the opinion were, or even if any existed. And he didn't want to tell Walker that. He sighed and started reading again. HLA DQa type, he thought. Struck in the head. Soaked with blood. Poor impulse control. Watch her children. Neither excessive nor disproportionate. My God, this is depressing.

12 ALMOST A SYLLOGISM

In her office, Katja gave a cup of water to the plant on her desk. It wasn't doing well, and lack of water, she suspected, wasn't the problem. An excess of water, if anything. She had found the plant sitting forlornly by the trash chute in her apartment building and brought it in to work hoping to nurse it back to health. But maybe she had been too aggressive; maybe those early ministrations had induced some kind of root rot that was responsible for the wilting and discolored leaves, the gradual defoliation. She didn't even know what kind of plant it was, which probably would have been a useful datum. She could hear Streeter's voice: Your intuitions will tell you that water's good for a plant, but if you want to know the truth, ask a lawyer. Despite herself, Katja laughed, and when the phone rang, she answered with a smile on her face.

"You sound happy," said a familiar voice.

Katja lost her smile. "I don't understand why you keep calling me, Jason. What have I not been clear about?"

"You haven't been clear about how you're going to manage to live without me."

Katja sighed. "Not as happily as if I'd never met you, but I'll cope."

"You know you miss me," he said. "Put your hand down your pants," he said. Katja hung up.

I made a mistake, she thought. I paid for it. Why can't it just be over?

Jason had been a first-year at Michigan during Katja's third year. He was from California, tall and good-looking in a rangy sort of way, with the tan and the legs and the springy, graceful walk that suggested he'd spent a lot of time playing beach volleyball. He was, in short, not at all her type, which ran rather more to the bookish.

But they hadn't met socially, and her guard was down. They met through the student peer tutoring program, to which she had turned as a less distressing venture than the TRO project, and he on the strong and unanimous advice of his first-semester professors. Jason wasn't stupid. He was, she thought, probably a little bit too smart for his own good, the kind of person who'd been able to get by in college with a short burst of effort at the end of the term, who'd scored well enough on his LSAT to make up for the few times the technique had failed him. Some people were smart enough to do that in law school. Possibly Katja, if she'd taken the risk, which she would never do. But not Jason. "You're not going to be able to get away with that here," she told him, and he gave her a lazy, insouciant smile.

"Then I guess you'd better help me," he said.

She helped him. He had no trouble learning the law, when he put in the effort. And he did, for her, sometimes. His confidence outstripped his diligence, infuriatingly so; he seemed to believe that joining an outline group or buying a commercial nutshell guide and cramming for a night would be enough. But Katja still found that she was coming to enjoy their sessions, to anticipate them. Jason admired her intellect and ability and dedication, and this was nice for Katja, who was more used to being admired for her legs. And at the end of a bunch of wisecracks about the students, the professors, the school, the legal profession in general, he'd tell her so, in a sweet and plaintive way that made her think a lot of his disdain was just the preemptive rejection of a world he feared would give him trouble.

When he turned back from the door one day as though he'd forgotten something and kissed her, when they started going out, she was surprised at how natural it felt, how easy. Jason wasn't challenging in the way some of her college boyfriends had been. He didn't demand that she justify her position on affirmative action; he didn't ask her to rethink things from a Rawlsian perspective or tell her that Kant had proved her wrong. And this, Katja found, was quite a relief. Jason was easy, relaxed, comfortable like an old sweatshirt. They'd go running together, rent movies, play with his dog down by the athletic fields. She didn't think about the question of whether they'd stay together after she graduated — she'd be clerking for the federal appeals court in Cincinnati — and that was a relief too, a change from the boys who seemed to have their lives perfectly planned, the space a wife would occupy already rigidly defined.

And then there was the sex. Jason had a very uncomplicated relationship with his body. It did what he wanted, because that was what it wanted. Sometimes she doubted that there was any distinction between the desires, between the body and the self; she'd see him stretched on her bed, long and languid under the sheets, and marvel at his seamless unity. Things were different for Katja, who commanded her body's obedience but not its love, and was painfully aware of it as a thing apart from her self, sometimes recalcitrant, sometimes embarrassing, and frequently the object of attention she'd rather have been without.

But with Jason she could at least begin to glimpse the possibility of unity. "Dualism is always wrong," a college boyfriend had told her once, and begun to discuss Wittgenstein. Jason had more effective arguments. Ten minutes and she'd be gripping the sheets with white knuckles, eyes screwed shut, issuing sounds she'd never suspected were inside her. Twenty and she'd be beyond thought, lost inside herself, moving without willing it or even noticing, until a sudden peak of awareness rose through the sea and she said, "Come with me," as though inviting him out for a walk, and he did.

Or not. Sometimes he didn't; sometimes he continued on his own path, leaving her to gasp and recover and build again until some stunning curvature of space, some glorious improbable non-Euclidean twist brought them around to each other again, reunited them spent and drenched and panting. Katja had never come just from sex, just from a man inside her; not once, let alone twice, and as she felt herself clench and release around him, she couldn't believe this was the same disciplined body that rose each day at six a.m. and ran five miles, the same voice that recited facts and holdings with calm professionalism in class. Now she heard it saying different things, words like "more," and "harder," and "again." She would sit in class, shifting in her seat, mentally replaying her workouts and wondering why she was sore. And then a different memory would come back and she would think, That's why, and blush up to her ears. Her body looked different to her, infused with purpose, awake in all its parts.

All this was a revelation for Katja, a world of difference from the respectable, unimaginative Connecticut preppies she'd grown up with, the kids whose fathers took the train to New York in the mornings and gave their affection to martinis when they returned. "Most men are a disappointment in bed," a sophisticated friend had told her once, and she'd nodded, affecting weary agreement, while inside her head the word flashed like neon, buzzing with possibility: Most? And now for the first time she could say, "So that's what all the fuss is about," and mean it as a statement and not a question.

She had a happy life with Jason, a small and private and comfortable world. The larger world, the one outside, was different. It gave him trouble when exams came around, as she had suspected and he perhaps had feared. He'd built a reputation as a slacker, and the study groups wouldn't have him. Katja gave him her old outlines, graded his practice exams. She blamed herself, in part, for his lack of preparation; there was a time, at the beginning of their relationship, when he'd started to take her admonitions seriously, when he'd shown a real willingness to work. But that was just the time that she had started to appreciate their lazy evenings together, their long mornings in bed, and she'd stopped pushing.

She'd been distracted too; her own studies had slipped. She came to class unprepared; some days she skipped entirely. It was a far cry from the days of first year, when she'd dragged herself to every session despite anxiety that had her vomiting in the bathroom before class all the first week. School didn't matter for her anymore; she was a third-year with a clerkship in hand and a job in D.C. after that. It was Jason who should worry. Katja put aside the anxieties about her exams and tried to help. She brought her books over to his apartment to study, though often enough they'd end up in bed, working at problems they knew they could solve. She took his phone calls when they weren't together. And she was helpful. She knew the law; she answered his questions easily, off the top of her head, barely looking up from her books. Right up to the day of his exam. "Promissory estoppel isn't an argument about a contract," she said. "It's an argument you make in the absence of a contract." Only later, checking the time, did she wonder about that phone call. He didn't, she told herself; he wouldn't.

But he would; he had. Stupidly, with the belief that he could get away with anything, he'd called her on a cell phone from the bathroom. The law school trusted its students; the proctors assumed a certain degree of honesty. But they weren't fools; they weren't blind. And when they stood on the other side of that thin door, they weren't deaf.

Would he at least have tried to protect her by refusing to disclose her identity; would she have stepped forward? The questions were academic; her number was in his call log. Katja admitted the substance of the conversation but protested innocence. Jason supported her on that, which might have been to his credit if it had cost him anything. Or if he'd understood that there was no possibility of forgiveness, which to Katja was immediately clear. The disciplinary committee accepted her story; no formal sanction was imposed. "But you understand we have to inform the judge," her recommenders told her.

Katja understood; she understood too when the judge withdrew the clerkship offer. Academic dishonesty was a serious matter, and even unknowing participation showed a lack of judgment. Human error, thought Katja, analyzing the wreckage. Distraction. Sympathy leads to affection, affection leads to distraction, distraction to errors of judgment. Sympathy is an error of judgment. It was almost a syllogism, the perfection of structure to which legal reasoning aspired.

She learned the lesson: eliminate distractions. The smiling boys in the hallway, the instant messages sent in class over the school's wireless network. Ridding herself of these things was in some ways a relief. The men on the street. Since high school she had practiced the art of not seeing, not hearing, of moving smoothly through the grasping world. With Jason she had felt herself open, but it was a simple matter to close again. She cut her hair short, and lesbians hit on her. She counted this a modest success. The haircuts were cheaper, if more frequent; she went to a barbershop instead of the salon. The barber hit on her, and she grew it out again.

Jason tried in various ways to get her back. There were jokes at first. What's the big deal? Then a tearful confession: I did it for you. Because I wanted you to be proud. And finally, a flash of anger: I'm the one who's getting an F.

She answered these easily too, off the top of her head, no research required. Actually, it is a big deal. Why would I be proud of you for cheating? And last: You should be getting an F. In fact, it had been slightly different: You should be getting an F, you asshole, her voice strident and rising at the end. Jason was still bad for her self-control.

And he wouldn't give up. Not for the remaining weeks of law school, and not, astonishingly, after she'd moved to D.C., the firm indifferent to her blemished reputation. There had been a time when she felt sorry for him, when it had been difficult to hang up the phone. Now it was just an annoyance, but a potent one. She'd paid for her mistake. She'd paid for it and moved on, and for the past to keep reaching out to her was wrong. It wasn't fair. As she returned the receiver to its cradle, her eyes flashed such fury that Ryan Grady, passing in the hall on his daily rounds, stopped dead in his tracks.

That's PMS, thought Ryan, or I know nothing about women.

13   ALWAYS IN THE RIGHT

Did he, in fact, know anything about women? Back in his office, Ryan considered the question. The yardstick he'd always used was success in dating, and by that standard he'd deemed himself quite an expert. High school had been good. He'd owned a car, played varsity lacrosse, had parents with a large house and a penchant for leaving town. College was a triumph. There was still the lacrosse, and in addition the fraternity, and a welcoming and supportive environment, an institution that provided him with proximity to several thousand girls and asked very little in return. It was a world that seemed to have been set up for no purpose other than to facilitate dating. But law school had been an undeniable step down, and the firm was worse, far worse. Ryan wasn't sure what the firm's purpose was, but it plainly wasn't to make it easy for him to hook up. Since he'd joined Morgan Siler, his scores were dropping; his average was down. By those indications, his extra years of education and on-the-job training were sapping his knowledge. By those indications, he was getting dumber.

Of course, it wasn't entirely his fault. Much of the variance had to do not with his native talents and acquired wisdom but with environmental factors. College had been supportive and law school largely indifferent to his efforts, but the firm was actively obstructionist. It tolerated office romances, but the relationships had to be horizontal. The term had not troubled Ryan when he first encountered it in the course of reading the firm's sexual harassment guidelines. It sounded like a typical bureaucratic euphemism, and of course a horizontal relationship was precisely what he was looking for. But further investigation and one closed-door meeting with the head of personnel had impressed upon him a more precise meaning: hands off the paralegals. The rule avoided imbalances of power, Ryan had been instructed. Another euphemism, but one he was able to clarify for himself. It took away from him precisely those women most likely to be impressed by his job.

There were compensations. On the whole, Ryan very much liked being a lawyer. The lifestyle was not quite what he'd expected, not quite what television and movies had promised. There were fewer beautiful clients, mysteriously troubled, to collapse weeping into his arms, and more documents to be sorted and stamped and placed in various files. There was less pacing around the courtroom, wheeling to fire unexpected questions at cowering witnesses, and more solitary research and tedious memo-writing. But there was one thing that television and movies hadn't even hinted at: there was certainty.

As a lawyer, Ryan was realizing, as a litigator, you had a license to say anything. You're not responsible. In a way it was like being crazy, being given a free pass for whatever nonsense came out of your mouth, but it was better, because people didn't try to pretend you weren't in the room or lock you away in an attic. Instead they praised you for zealous advocacy, for doing your duty to the client. Duty to the client made things wonderfully clear. Is a promise enforceable if made in gratitude for a benefit already conferred? That was the sort of question professors had tortured him with in law school, and the answer was always that it depended on a maddeningly complex set of factors. But once you were out of law school, it depended only on one thing: what outcome favored the client. That was the answer you were duty-bound to give, and no one could reproach you for it.

This gave him a confidence and clarity he wished he could bring to other areas of his life. Duty to the client propelled him ever forward. Argue as forcefully as you can, it told him; never doubt. And if you're judged wrong in the end, your arguments broken and thrown back in your face, you just say: we caught a bad break with that judge. We're considering an appeal. You never have to admit that you're wrong, and if other people think you are, they also have to concede that you're supposed to be wrong—supposed to be a zealous advocate, supposed to be occasionally on the far side of the accurate. Law is the license to be always in the right, Ryan thought; law means never having to say you're sorry. Things were much simpler when you didn't have to worry about the truth.

Truth, thought Mark Clayton happily. Truth will set you free. At the least, it would free him from the Harper case. Truth had been the furthest thing from his mind when he started reading the Virginia Supreme Court opinion, looking for legal issues to raise. But after stumbling through the opinion like a darkened closet for a couple of hours, he had bumped up against something that seemed obvious now that the lights were on: the DNA test. He would have noticed it immediately if he hadn't been thinking about the law.

Reading the memos left by the summer associates—something else he now realized he should have done at the outset—confirmed his suspicion. One of the summers, apparently someone with a science background, had expounded at great length on the deficiencies of the HLA DQa analysis. Human Leukocyte Antigen testing was quick and easy, but far from state-of-the-art. The crime lab should have done a Restriction Fragment Length Polymorphism-Variable Number Tandem Repeats test, or used a Polymerase Chain Reaction to increase the sample size and allow Short Tandem Repeats. The jargon meant nothing to Mark, but it showed that better tests could be done. Then it would be over, one way or another. Mark smiled to himself. The way he looked at it, he had a 7.8 percent chance of getting an innocent man off death row. A 92.2 percent chance of finding out his client was actually guilty, of course, but that was still resolution. Either way, it beat researching rotten eggs. He picked up the phone.

Half an hour later, he was still holding the phone, and his enthusiasm was wavering. He'd been able to find the number of the Norfolk Crime Lab, but not to reach anyone there who had any idea what he was talking about. In the Prosecutors' Office, only an assistant named John Miller was authorized to take his calls, and Miller would be unreachable for days. How could such a simple task become so complicated? A sign the legal system was working, perhaps. What he needed, Mark decided, was an ally, someone who was on his side in this case, someone who knew something about the process of challenging convictions. Someone like the Capital Defenders.

Again he had the sensation of stumbling belatedly over what should have been the first step. Of course the Capital Defenders would know about DNA testing. Possibly they had pursued the matter already; possibly somewhere in the case files was a document that would hold the answer. Mark looked at the stack of cardboard boxes. Despite his lack of success thus far, the phone still seemed a better choice.

Short minutes later he was in conversation with Anne Brownlee, whose name he'd picked more or less at random from among the attorneys listed as counsel on the state postconviction proceedings. "The Harper case," she said. "Sure, I remember Wayne. What can I do for you?"

"What I was thinking," Mark said, "is that we could probably clear this up pretty quickly if we just got a better DNA test. Do you know who I should talk to at the crime lab?" There was no answer. "We'll pay for it," he ventured. "That's no problem for the firm."

"I'm sure it's not," Anne said. The pleasant tone was gone. "But there are a couple of things you should know. First, we didn't give you this case so that you could come in and clear it up. We gave it to you so you could defend Wayne Harper against the death penalty. He's your client, in case you'd forgotten. And second, of course you can't get a better DNA test. We would have done that if it were possible."

"Why isn't it possible?"

"Because the state destroyed the crime scene sample after the conviction and direct appeal."

"They what?"

"Why would they keep it around? That's standard procedure." Anne paused, and when she spoke again there was pity in her voice. "You don't have any idea what you're up against, do you?"

Walker Eliot hunched in concentration, his mind speeding gracefully through a field of appealing possibilities. He flipped a page in the catalog, surveying the candidates, imagining his body against them. How would they feel? Better than the one he had now, that was certain. With one hand he massaged his lower back, working against a knot that had started forming, a twinge of pain. The firm had a wide variety of chairs available for associates, as the catalog confirmed. There was the Ratchet Back Molded Foam Task Chair, the Multi Function Ergonomic Leather, the Executive Fabric Task Office Chair with optional Loop Arms. And the pinnacle, the ne plus ultra, the Ultimate Ergonomic Mesh Office Chair. That's the one for me, Walker thought, reading the description. It was a marvel of human ingenuity, more a loyal and affectionate companion than a piece of furniture. Its polymerized plastic frame breathed; its active lumbar support changed shape to match the curve of your back. It had synchro tilt control, pneumatic lift, and three-inch dual wheel casters. Walker did not know what these last things were, but he knew that he wanted them. Even the name was enticing. Aeron! It spoke of grace and majesty; in Walker's mind it conjured images of dragonlike creatures that dwelt on mountaintops and slept coiled in clouds, their spines untroubled by any lack of lumbar support.

"Aeron," he said out loud, nodding. His current chair was the Executive 2800, one of the lower-end models. Unsynchronized, unpneumatic, uncomfortable. Unacceptable. But also unchangeable, at least according to the people in office services, at least for a while. Walker had inherited the office of a departed fourth-year associate, which he appreciated. But the departed associate had recently upgraded his chair, which Walker had also inherited, and chair upgrades were done by office and couldn't be done more than once a year. "What did he upgrade from?" Walker asked incredulously. "A tree stump?"

"Some people like the cushions," the office manager explained.

They like the cushions, Walker thought. No wonder this guy left the firm; he probably upgraded to an Alaskan salmon cannery. "Look," he said. "I don't like the cushions. I want a different chair."

"You want a different chair," the manager said. "Have I given you false hope? Have I not been clear about this with you? Your office isn't due for an upgrade for ten months."

"There's one with a mesh back," Walker said. "It breathes."

The manager was silent for a moment. "I'm sorry," she said. "Your upgrade has been done. We can't replace your chair unless it's broken."

Walker's mind raced. "If you imagine that this is the chair I want," he said, "it's broken. The pneumatic lift doesn't work. The lumbar support isn't active."

The office manager hung up on him. When he called back, she didn't bother with salutations. "Not unless it's broken."

"If my chair were broken," Walker said, "hypothetically speaking, how soon could you get me a new one?"

"Same day," she said. "They're in stock. But you're not getting a new one."

"Right."

He called again a short time later, panting slightly. "My chair is broken."

"What happened?"

"I think it lost the will to live."

She was at his door in five minutes, a thirtyish blonde with a hair-band. Her blue eyes surveyed the scene dispassionately. The Executive 2800 was broken, emphatically so. Its cushions were ripped, its spine bent. One armrest had snapped free of its moorings and dangled to the side. "Looks to me like it put up a fight."

Walker shrugged, wiping sweat from his forehead. "There may have been some persuasion involved." The office manager closed her eyes as if in pain, then opened them and scowled at him. Walker was getting used to that look, the mixture of bafflement and outrage, the what-kind-of-crazy-person-is-this expression. It bothered him less as time went by. "So," he said. "Do I get a new chair now?"

The surprising thing about the world, Walker was coming to realize, was how plastic it was, how malleable to will and intellect. At times it seemed almost pitiably vulnerable, at times almost defenseless. Around him for years he'd seen others barrel through obstacles, overcome with force and labor what he'd learned could simply be thought out of existence. The possibility of doing that—his own ability to do it—was thrilling, but it was also frightening.

Walker had gone to Yale Law, not seeing much of a choice. Harvard, where he took his undergraduate degree, was ideal for college, the philosophy department nestled in the red brick of Emerson Hall, the residential houses lining the river. He still felt warmth for Cambridge, still liked to linger by the chess players and street musicians in Harvard Square. But the law school was different, colder and a bit strung out from competition. "Harvard Law School is like the Chinese army," an advisor told him. "It just keeps churning them out."

So New Haven for three years, darkened Gothic buildings with leaded glass windows, the Metro North trains into New York for diversion. Yale had its share of neurotics, the psycho types who slept in the library, kept changes of clothes in their carrels. Exams were bad if you let yourself get caught up in the fog of stress that descended, the rumors about the different outline groups. Some people showed up at the copy centers with fake IDs, impersonating members of a storied group in order to steal an outline. "It's a shame," one professor said, "that the people who used to go to Harvard for the reputation are starting to come here."

Walker avoided the groups. And, exams apart, there *was* something different about Yale. At other law schools, faculty struggled with the question of whether they should allow unprepared students to pass when called on. At Yale, prepared or not, you couldn't shut them up. Part of it was bootlicking, competition for the attention of the professors, the clerkship recommendations, but part of it was just raw enthusiasm. Walker sat silently in the back of the room, taking notes and musing. He'd gone to law school for no particular reason, mostly from a lack of anything better to do, but it was proving tolerable. Not especially difficult; not as time-consuming as he'd been led to believe. He'd heard the stories about the incredible intellects of Yale, and he'd been prepared to feel outclassed.

But he didn't, and after a month of searching vainly for geniuses, he had another thought. It's me. I'm the one they're going to tell stories about. Walker kept up with his philosophy; he read further in Joyce, perched on the dorm room couch with *Finnegans Wake* and the McHugh annotations. He learned to play squash; he wrote acrostic sonnets spelling the names of fellow students and involving them in various situations designed to illustrate the operation of rules of law.

And somewhere along the way, he fell in love.

It wasn't philosophy of law that won him over, stole his heart before he fully realized what was happening. It wasn't the theory so prized at Yale, the critical deconstruction of claims to objectivity. It was the law itself, in its pureness and intricacy. Walker had hated philosophy of law, and he had little use for theory. Thinking about the law wasn't interesting; what was interesting was doing it, finding the answers. From this perspective, the school was slightly frustrating. They weren't being taught the law, not really; not at Yale. They were taught methods of argumentation, ways of looking at problems. No one wanted to hear the right answer on exams; they wanted arguments on both sides. That was what it meant to think like a lawyer. Yale was still gripped by the legacy of realism, and the idea that there might be a right answer was seen as a symptom of naïveté, unworldliness. When you get out of here, his civil procedure professor said, you will be capable of inflicting immense harm on people. You will be sharp and uncompromising; your minds will have been forged into lethal weapons. You will be lawyers. Use that power wisely.

Nonsense, thought Walker. He didn't feel like a weapon; he felt like an explorer pushing the borders of the map, like a suitor eager to learn every detail about his beloved. This was discovery, not invention; of course there were right answers. After graduation he went on to a clerkship on the federal court of appeals for the District of Columbia Circuit, and there he found vindication. The questions the cases presented were every bit as complicated as the exams his professors had dreamed up, but his judge didn't ask for arguments on both sides. The idea that law is just what judges say is fine for lawyers, Walker thought. It's fine for law professors. They can say that, in talking about how a case should be decided, they're only forecasting what the courts will do. But that attitude doesn't get you far as a judge. And not as a law clerk either. Judge Andrews didn't hire me to predict his behavior.

Walker worked out the issues from the ground up. He ignored the parties' briefs; he traced the applicable doctrines back through hundreds of years of decisions, untangling the skein of opinions until the authorities had been reconciled, until the answers lay clear and irrefutable. From his Capitol Hill apartment he walked to the courthouse on Fourth and Constitution, feeling the empire of the law spread around him, passing through his body like gamma rays, ordering the world like a magnetic field. All of it unseen but visible to the mind. Walker closed his eyes and there it was, the streaming code of statutes, amendments, and repeals; judicial decisions spawning other lines of authority, interpreting, distinguishing, overruling; the law's endless conversation with itself. Judge Andrews looked into Walker's small office with an expression of polite curiosity, surveying the sea of papers around the desk, the stacks of nineteenth-century treatises. He listened to Walker's breathless recitations, nodding, and explained that he'd reached the same conclusion, though typically by a somewhat shorter route.

That was the clincher. They agreed on everything, and not because of ideology. Andrews was an efficiency-minded libertarian; Walker was basically uninterested in politics. But they agreed on the law, just as they'd have agreed on a question of mathematics. Twice the other judges on the panel hadn't; twice Walker had been set to work drafting a dissent. And twice the others had read what the Andrews chambers circulated and changed their minds, signing on to his opinion. It was the exercise of judgment, not will; it was the rule of law. The D.C. Circuit was heaven, Walker thought at times, the perfection of reason.

In his sober moments, he knew it wasn't. Heaven was where the gods lived. It was six blocks away, at One First Street, Northeast, a plaza with clear-running fountains, a building with marble pillars and great bronze doors. The Supreme Court.

Walker had applied for a Supreme Court clerkship without really thinking. It seemed as if everyone who'd been at Yale did, at least those who got federal appellate clerkships on the first go-around. It was when the invitations to interview began to come his way that he first considered the prospect seriously, and then he was troubled. He knew that the Court posed problems for his vision of the world. Walker had done what most thought impossible, gone to Yale and emerged a formalist, convinced of the law's abstract purity. His appellate clerkship had only strengthened his belief. The appellate courts ironed out wrinkles in the law, and

Walker had warmed to the task, explaining Supreme Court decisions, instructing the trial courts, glossing the authoritative texts. But the Supreme Court was bound by nothing, not even its earlier decisions, which it could overrule if it chose. It was engaged in a fundamentally different venture, with no fixed points by which to navigate. It made the law.

This was not something Walker was sure he wanted to be a part of. Being able to discern the right answer, to deduce it from certain unquestionable givens—that was a power of sorts. Being able to make an answer right was a greater power, something altogether different, and that was the power of the Court. It smacked of the godlike, and Walker did not want to be a god. There were principles out there, Walker believed. Beyond the malleable words, the cases to be dissected and distinguished, there was something else. There was the law. But that was not a perspective the Court could take, at least not always. It came down to this, Walker thought: gods have nothing to believe in. How do you decide, he wondered, when whatever you say will be right?

In the interviews he hid his misgivings. He talked of his admiration for Oliver Wendell Holmes and the great judge Learned Hand; he discussed the finer points of the Court's recent opinions. And he was hired, in the end, by Marshall Arlen, the Court's oldest Justice, a holdover from the earlier days, a man plucked from the Mississippi governor's office to serve with Blackmun and Brennan and Douglas.

The clerkship began in July. The city was hot; when it rained, steam rose from the pavements and the streets smelled like a swimming pool. On his first day of work, Walker showed up in a suit, sweat clinging to his ribs and his heart jumping inside him. He had to admit he was a little scared. Scared by what the job might do to him, what it might call upon him to do. Knowledge cost innocence, and learning what law was made of, its basic force and nature, might bear a heavy price.

But the first weeks were a relaxing introduction. Most of the Justices had left D.C. to escape the heat, and the clerks dressed casually and played basketball in the upstairs gym. The summer months were downtime before the arguments started up again in October, and with no cases to be decided, the workload was relatively light. Walker processed the cert petitions, requests for the Court to hear a case, writing summary memos to spare the Justices the work of reading each petition, and learned quickly how to pick the few credible ones from the vast heap of those that never should have been filed. Over lunches, in the clerk dining room separated from the public cafeteria by soundproofed glass doors, he got to know the other clerks and picked up what institutional wisdom he could from the holdovers who'd be there until August.

Walker had read the clerkship memoirs; he'd heard about cabals and conspiracies, clerk shouting matches late at night in the red-carpeted hallways and vicious fouls on the basketball court. The summer offered none of this. There were strong personalities among the clerks, certainly, and eccentrics. One had tried to walk through the bronze doors on his first day of work, unaware of the clerks' side entrance. The doors were locked, of course; he'd lost his balance on the marble steps and eventually made his way to the orientation session scuffed and bruised, his scraped palm spotting the forms they filled out. The intake supervisor was amused. "No need to sign it in blood," she said. "We're not a law firm here." And there were some clerks identifiable by ideology, crew-cut conservatives from Chicago, liberal throwbacks from the appellate courts in California. Their grounds of disagreement were already staked out, their arguments readied for deployment when the opportunity arose. For the moment, though, it felt friendly, even familial.

The executions were harder. These still went on in the summer, heedless of the Court's calendar. The states scheduled them; at the Court a permanent employee known as the death clerk made up a list and circulated it to the various chambers each week. There the law clerks read it and prepared. Each Justice was responsible for certain states, and that Justice's chambers took the leading role in overseeing executions in those states. Running the execution, the clerks called it, though it didn't mean they were involved in anything more than coordinating the Court's review.

Walker didn't like executions. No one did, he suspected; the facts were invariably depressing and the process macabre. The late-night vigils, the hours waiting in the deserted building for some lower court to act so that the lawyers could make the final appeal, raising arguments the clerks had hashed out days before and almost always rejected. Some of the clerks took it harder than others. Some felt compromised simply by participating, by the fact that they'd been the ones to report the vote, to give the go-ahead. For days afterward they would be pale and withdrawn. Walker lacked that visceral reaction; if the people wanted the death penalty, they could have it. But he disliked the Court's involvement in what was usually a fact-driven question, and worse, an emotional one, divisive for reasons of policy more than law. It should have been left to the lower federal courts, he thought; it was a needless strain. But the clerks generally worked through the issues cooperatively, and the occasional arguments about the fairness of state procedures did not disturb Walker.

It was the merits work, the cases the Court actually decided, that scared him. The reason there were right answers at the appellate level, he'd realized, was largely that the lower courts were bound to follow the decisions of the Supreme Court. Those decisions mediated between the intangible law and the thousands of courts around the country. They were the clanking armor that housed the hidden spirit, unquestionable and authoritative as a plate of steel. For practical purposes, for the lower courts, they were the law itself.

But not for the Supreme Court, which knew the law directly and could shape it as it wished. That was the problem; that was the seed of doubt. A lower court that tried to twist the law could be slapped down, its judgment reversed. The Supreme Court guarded the law from all others. But from the high court there was no appeal; for its wrongs there was no remedy. Nothing could protect the law from the Court, and Walker looked for vandals in its marble halls.

Justice Arlen returned in September, seeming an unlikely ravager. Small and cheerful, he arrived punctually in the mornings and took a midafternoon coffee break to regale his clerks with tales of the older days, his Southern accent swelling as the memories poured forth. The work ahead would be difficult at times, he told them, but he had confidence in their abilities and confidence in the Court. Walker wasn't sure, but as Arlen's four clerks looked over the argument calendar and divided the cases among themselves, he began to relax. Many of the cases, it turned out, were actually quite easy. Many of the splits among the federal circuits were the products of errors that were relatively obvious. Walker could spot them; so could the other clerks; so could the Justices. The Supreme Court was unanimous almost half the time.

In December Walker drafted his first opinion. Arlen struck paragraphs in a looping cursive hand, added new sections, inserted phrases. At the third draft he nodded approval from behind his desk. "You're learning," he said. "Most clerks write as though they aren't individuals; they try to sound like the law itself. They fear to be present in the opinion; they want to suggest that there's no person at work, no intellect, just the mechanical functioning of the law. That's why they resort to the legalisms, the jargon. But individuality and objectivity are not incompatible. And the law is not mechanical. It needs human intelligence to give it life."

Walker felt a deep satisfaction. At the D.C. Circuit, he had explained the law as it existed, but now he was at work fixing it, correcting mistakes. And more: he was bringing it into being, extending and making tangible the promise and implication of earlier decisions. The law could not create itself, but no more did he create it; it existed independent of his will, waiting for the light of reason to reveal.

Winter draped the Court's marble in snow. The morning sun was blinding; Walker squinted as he walked to work, straining to read the inscription on the lintel. EQUAL JUSTICE UNDER LAW. The clerks played football outside, before an audience of nine carefully constructed snowmen. There were dissents now, especially in the constitutional cases; the clerks carried the drafts down the red-carpeted hallways, past the marble busts of former Justices, to each chambers. The majority opinion was revised in response, footnotes added. New versions circulated and the process began again.

Walker drafted his share of dissents, and, unlike at the D.C. Circuit, they did not become majorities. He accepted this. The words of the Constitution by themselves left many cases unresolved. Reaching an answer required a theory, or at least an interpretive methodology, and on these matters the Justices differed. Arlen did not compromise to troll for swing votes; he would not shade the facts to avoid a difficult issue that might fracture his majority. Left to his own designs, Walker might have. If the facts threatened the law, he thought, so much the worse for them. The Court was not there for the facts. But Arlen did not write for the other Justices; he wrote for himself, or for history. "There's more to this job than counting to five," he said. Walker admired that. He admired his Justice; he respected the others. They were wrong at times, he thought, but not knowingly. And he liked the other clerks, who still played basketball together and gathered for weekly happy hours at the Court's interior courtyards. It might not have been heaven, but for Walker it was close to paradise.

It wasn't until March that he encountered a problem case, and then it stopped him cold. He read the briefs again, and then once more; he embarked on his usual forays into the doctrinal history. The papers welled around him, the books piled up. And after it all his mind retained the same neutral, appraising cast it had had at the start, the same curiosity about what the right answer was. Walker rapped his knuckles against his head, perplexed. Usually at this stage he brimmed with passion, determined to vindicate the correct rule of law, outraged at the chicanery of the lawyers who argued otherwise and the idiocy of the judges who believed them. But he had no reaction to this case.

He moved on to the next one, worried that something had broken within him. Mathematicians may lose their powers in an instant. But his blood boiled reassuringly: the Seventh Circuit had failed to grasp the difference between exhaustion and procedural default. Not me, then, he thought. He returned to the problem case. There were tools of legal analysis, canons of interpretation, modalities of argument. Text, structure, doctrine, history, the scalpels that law school had trained him to wield. None made an impression. For a week the briefs lay on his desk, the case crouched within his mind, squat and obdurate, impenetrable. He consulted with the clerks in other chambers. "Tough case," said one. "But it's a stupid law." And another: "You know subsection (d)(3) was actually inserted by a senator who hoped the whole thing would get voted down." Walker stopped his ears. These were extralegal considerations, irrelevant, impure. Still he could make no headway. Finally he went to see Justice Arlen and confessed his failure.

Arlen looked at him in amusement, half hidden behind the large mahogany desk. The Justice's chambers were well lit and modern in their furnishings; despite his age, Arlen had been one of the first to embrace new technology. Nonetheless, there hung around him an air of the ancient and the inscrutable. From the wall peered down a portrait of former Justice Hugo Black, a native Alabaman and one of Arlen's inspirations.

"You think that legal reasoning gives no answer," said Arlen softly. "Perhaps it does not."

Judgment, thought Walker, not will. But when judgment runs out, what then? "So it's a gap," he said. "The Court is going to have to make law here."

Arlen gave him a cryptic smile. He leaned back and laced his fingers over his small belly. "There are no gaps in the law, Walker. There are only answers we have not yet found. It may be that you cannot see an answer here. Perhaps if we waited, it would become clear; perhaps progress in another direction, in other cases, would shed some light on this one. But we do not have that luxury; we must decide it now.

"So we decide the case. That is what judges do. But it does not mean we make the law. We have the power to make the law if we choose, but our duty is to the truth, and power is not the measure of truth."

Interesting but unhelpful, thought Walker, wondering what he'd stumbled into. With his elfin smile and small goatee, the Justice resembled a sprite perched on a toadstool. "But how do you decide?" he asked.

Arlen raised his eyebrows. In earlier pictures Walker had seen thick white curls on the man's head; now years of intellectual focus had burned them away and Arlen's skull rose, a gleaming sun over receding fog. "As a judge does. Or a clerk. Judging is not a mechanical process, Walker. A computer could not do it. But you are a human, and you have resources. Value-free adjudication is an illusion, and a dangerous one. Too often it allows the judge to blind himself to his own values and deny their influence. Choose the right values, and they can be acknowledged openly."

Walker returned to his desk, still wondering. A judge's values were not supposed to enter into decisions; that was the point of the elevation of judgment over will, the ideal of the rule of law and not of men. So what value could Arlen be suggesting? Not the ones his fellow clerks had offered, surely; not the desire to help out a sympathetic litigant or frustrate the operation of a malicious statute. A judge could not favor a party or impose his vision of wise policy. A legitimate value would have to be one implicit in the nature of legal reasoning itself.

Walker turned back to the analytic tools that had failed him, considering them not in application to the case but in their collective nature, seeking a unifying quality. An idea began to dawn in his mind. There is a purpose here, he thought; there is a theme. The interpretive canons, the principles of adjudication, were in large part aesthetic. They demanded doctrinal coherence, elegance, harmony between different lines of cases.

That's adjudication, he thought. Choosing the interpretation that shows the law in its best light, that makes it most beautiful. And that's what a computer cannot do.

Walker nodded rapidly, his mind gathering speed. A computer cannot make aesthetic judgments, he thought; a computer cannot love. The permissible value is love for the law, the desire to make it beautiful. And that value identifies the correct answer. The measure of truth is beauty, and where judgment runs out we turn to love. This is the meaning of the oath we swear, that pledge of fidelity to the law.

He sighed aloud, and the clerk who shared his office looked up from her computer. Walker did not notice. He was overcome by revelation, and his heart was lost all over again, to the law not in its majesty and omniscience but in its limits and its frailty. He saw now what breathed inside the armor of the Court's opinions, the ghost in the machine. He saw the law not as an all-encompassing matrix but as a finite vulnerable creature that needed him, that grew within his mind and for its perfection required his love. "You," said Walker. "I favor only you."

Rachel glanced over without moving her head. Like most of the other clerks, she had come to the conclusion that there was something very strange about Walker. Addressing the air was only slightly beyond the range of his usual behavior. She cleared her throat cautiously. "Do you want to make another pot of coffee?" she asked. Walker did not hear. He was communing with the ineffable, as happy as he'd ever been.

Short months later it was over. A few more memos, one majority opinion, one dissent, and Walker was done. At the end of the year, the clerks put on a skit for the Court personnel, impersonating the Justices, singing comic songs about the cases decided that term. Walker played Justice Arlen, while the man himself sat in the audience and slapped his knee with delight. As he took off the borrowed robes, Walker felt a terrible pang of loss. For a year he'd been able to do just that, playact the part of a Justice. And then he was out in the world again with the sneaking suspicion that nothing else would quite measure up.

Walker pulled a lever on the side of the Ultimate Ergonomic Mesh Office Chair. With a soft sigh of air his seat descended. The pneumatic lift wouldn't bear him up again; if he wanted to raise the seat he would have to stand. This was probably a good thing, he decided. The distraction would otherwise have been too great. He had spent a good hour tinkering with the lumbar support and the tilt control, which was synchronized with some other feature he'd yet to identify. An hour during which he was supposed to be writing a brief, an hour he'd charge to the client anyway, because he couldn't very well construct an unassailable argument while tilted at the wrong angle.

The brief was for Larry Angstrom, and it was the appeal of a class certification decision. Much of the firm's work consisted of opposing class actions. "It's coercion," Larry Angstrom said, outrage in his voice. "The companies have to settle because they're threatened with bankruptcy if they lose. It's blackmail." He meant extortion, Walker thought, indifferent. He wasn't concerned with the policy issues; he was there for the law. Legally, the key question was whether the individual claims presented sufficient common issues to make a single trial feasible. Here the plaintiffs seemed to have a strong case, which was probably why they'd won at the lower court level and why Morgan Siler had been called in for the appeal. The Vendstar Corporation had marketed household products over the phone, their salespeople following a script that included a promise that the price offered was the best deal available in the community. Fraud, said the plaintiffs, and more importantly, common and uniform fraud: Vendstar set the same price nationwide and made no effort to find out local prices.

Walker leaned back in his new chair, considering. He had learned something in the practice of law that had not been apparent to him while clerking: you could always find a route to the conclusion you wanted. It might not be an obvious one; it might not be one that would occur to many lawyers. He remembered Harold's baffled expression when Walker had asserted that their case against the arbitrageurs was really about a unilateral contract. There he had been throwing up a roadblock in order to give himself something to overcome. But he could do it the other way too; he could find a way around the obstacles that most lawyers would simply charge at again and again. He could shift the way the case looked, so that there weren't any obstacles at all.

In a way it was like changing the subject. In a way it was like changing the world. For those who sought guidance through the invisible realm of law, any competent lawyer could draw a map. But Walker could draw multitudes, and that was his value. Embroiled in litigation, parties sought the particular map that would lead them to victory, and Walker could provide it. Lay a road through the forest, carve a river to the ocean, throw up a range of mountains: the legal landscape bent to his touch. He could call Atlantis from the sea, pinpoint Avalon and El Dorado, weld Pangaea from the shattered earth. Invoke the right doctrines, focus on the right facts, and geography yielded to the mind.

The falsity of the best-deal promise looked like an issue common to all the suits, but Walker was quite confident that from the appropriate perspective it wasn't. He leaned farther back, clearing his mind. For five minutes or so he remained almost motionless, then he jerked emphatically upright and began to type. Two important thoughts had occurred to him. First, if the price offered actually happened to be the best deal, then the promise wasn't false. That might not have been the case in any significant number of the transactions; indeed, the evidence suggested it wasn't. But it was an issue that had to be dealt with for each individual purchaser and each individual purchase. That should be enough to stop the class action from proceeding.

Second, the tilt of the chair back was synchronized with the movement of the seat.

It took almost two hours to hammer out a draft of the brief. There were some issues that demanded a good deal of finesse. Walker had found a path to the desired conclusion, but it was a narrow one, depending on a couple of delicate conceptual moves. Angstrom might not get it, might not be able to present it properly in the oral argument, and even if he did, there was no guarantee the court would understand. But what was the worst that could happen? They'd lose; Vendstar would be forced to settle. Walker was indifferent to that prospect. His job was to identify a rule of law under which they could prevail, and he'd done it.

He took a final look at the opposing side's brief to see if there were any other points that needed to be addressed, first skimming, then reading more slowly, and finally stopping altogether. The brief hadn't impressed him much when he'd gone through it the first time. A competent, workmanlike job, the sort of thing any major firm could produce. But as he read it now, his subtle arguments fresh in his mind, it seemed different.

They've anticipated this, Walker realized. They didn't address it directly, but they're slanting the facts, positioning themselves to argue that there was an implicit promise to check local prices. That would have been uniformly false; that would be a common issue. He flipped the pages, sensing something at work. He felt a presence; he felt an intelligence pushing back against his.

He felt a flash of recognition.

Walker turned to the cover of the brief, where the names of the lawyers were listed. There were a couple of different firms and he had to go to the inside cover before he found the one he was looking for. Jennifer Caputo, who'd clerked for Justice Lambert the same year he had been with Arlen. A good clerk, a friend. They had worked together on a couple of cases, one about the free speech rights of abortion protesters, one about state funding of parochial schools. In each they'd agreed, struggled to make sure everything came out right. And now they were on opposite sides, battling over sales practices for dishwashing detergent and carpet shampoos.

Walker frowned. Jennifer had written a good brief; he had to admit it. If you looked at the facts the way she did, she might even be right on the law. It troubled him, but only for a moment. The case would come down to competing descriptions of the facts. As long as both sides were right on the law, he didn't see what could go wrong.

15 INNOCENCE IS NOT AN ARGUMENT

Outside Mark's window, a sunset cast the city in gold. A spume of clouds spread across the sky, orange in the evening night. Even the large building that occupied half his field of view now loomed a pleasant burnished russet.

Mark, though, was staring blankly at the wall.

It wasn't just the knowledge that the crime scene DNA sample had been destroyed. His one bright idea extinguished, he was back in the dark, but that was familiar enough. It was the other thing Anne had said, the first thing—that he was bound to Wayne Harper, not as an associate to an assignment but as a lawyer to a client. Bound to a man 92.2 percent likely to be a murderer.

A soft tapping at the door roused him. "Busy?" Gerald asked.

Why is he always talking to me? Mark wondered. That was his second question. The first had been, Who is this guy? It had proved surprisingly easy to answer. Everyone, it seemed, knew who Gerald was; he was a legend at the firm. Mark's secretary, Glynda, knew about him; so did the cafeteria ladies and the people at the copy center. And the paralegals. Of course the paralegals, for Gerald had been one of them.

The Morgan Siler paralegals were not the usual crew of recent college graduates hoping to find out if law school might be right for them. Nor were they the glorified messengers and secretaries who swelled the profit margin on clerical work at other firms. They were talented, quirky people willing to work three ten-hour night shifts a week to free up their days for other interests. They were actors, writers, even a lawyer who hadn't liked the nine-to-nine routine.

Even among this group, Gerald stood out. He picked up substantive law from the work with surprising speed, and his intuitions were astonishing. More, he had the judgment so many of the whiz-kid Ivy Leaguers lacked. Partners took his advice over that of associates; associates pretended they needed files sorted in order to ask his counsel. The night school law degree they eventually told him to get was just a formality. Three years after starting as a paralegal he was an associate, proudly referred to as a graduate of the Morgan Siler school of law.

And now, for no obvious reason, he was regularly knocking on Mark's door. "Not busy," Mark said. "Just looking through some of the papers in this pro bono case."

Gerald smiled, sliding into the office and closing the door behind him. "I heard that you were on that. I'm glad you decided to give it a try."

"Yeah," said Mark. "Well, that's how it worked out, anyway."

"So how does it look?"

"I don't know. Not as simple as I was hoping. I had this idea we could just get a better DNA test and figure out if he did it or not."

"That's what the summer associates thought too. Looks fishy they only did the HLA DQa analysis, right?"

"Isn't it?"

"It's unfortunate for Wayne Harper if he's innocent," Gerald said. He pulled a chair to the opposite side of Mark's desk. "But innocence is not an argument for habeas relief. To get that back on the table, first you'd need to withdraw the guilty plea, which would be hard. You'd have to show his lawyer was unreasonable in advising him to plead guilty. And even if you could get a different test that didn't match Wayne, it wouldn't necessarily clear him. The state will just say that there were multiple perps. Someone else may have left the sample, but your guy was still there. And the other thing . . ." Gerald fingered his beard, his voice trailing off.

"What?" asked Mark. "What's the other thing?"

"I don't want to be discouraging," Gerald said. "I was hoping you'd take the case; I think it's a good thing that you did. But you're not Perry Mason here. The reason they only have an HLA DQa test is probably just that it's the first one they do, and when the defense lawyer said he'd plead guilty they stopped the lab work. Why should they go any further? I'm not saying bad things don't happen in crime labs. They're run by the state police, after all; they're not independent. Every so often it turns out someone's been cooking the results. It happened in Virginia just a couple of years ago."

Mark nodded. The Harper file had contained printouts of a number of Internet stories on disgraced lab technicians. The summer associates were masters of the Internet. The Virginia episode, featuring someone named Roman Fleischer, had made his heart leap when he saw it. But everyone convicted on Fleischer's testimony had been given a new trial already, by order of the Virginia Supreme Court.

"You could do a better test," Gerald said, "and it would probably still be a match. It's not very likely that you actually have an innocent guy. You don't necessarily want certainty about that. Doubt is what keeps people alive. And you could still save his life."

"How am I going to do that?"

"Well," said Gerald, "realistically you do have something going for you. Getting the death penalty is like getting struck by lightning. It's pretty random; there's little rhyme or reason to it. But getting a big firm to take your case pro bono is kind of the same. It's like lightning striking the prosecution. They have to prosecute a lot of cases; they can't blow their budget trying to go toe-to-toe with Morgan Siler. If we'd been there in the first place, they probably would have offered a deal. If you can make it look like you're going to cause a lot of trouble for them, they might still be willing to talk. Whoever's on this case probably has a lot of other things going on."

"Yeah," said Mark, nodding. In addition to the memos on DNA analysis, now revealed to be useless, the summer associates had filled the Harper file with a large number of cases in which habeas relief had been granted, showing little selectivity in terms of factual or legal similarity and linking them with theories that probably seemed convincing to people with one year of law school behind them. Reading through the cases, he had noticed the same few names recurring on the state's side. "Like that poor Caleb Kite guy."

"What?"

"It seems like he's on every brief. I don't understand how he has the time."

"Don't feel bad for Caleb Kite," Gerald said. "He's not writing the briefs. He probably doesn't know anything about them. He's the head of the Prosecutor's Office, that's all. He wouldn't have anything to do with this case; it's not high-profile enough."

"Oh," said Mark. He regretted his disparaging thoughts about the summer associates' theories. That there are people who know less than you doesn't mean you know much. "But so what would cause trouble for them?"

"Something the trial lawyer didn't do. Some way you can argue he was ineffective, say you need a hearing in federal court to develop the factual basis for an argument he didn't make. Have you read the Virginia Supreme Court opinion?"

"A couple of times."

"It probably seems pretty convincing," Gerald said. Behind the glasses his blue eyes were large and soft. Mark was silent. "Don't be discouraged," Gerald continued. "There's a particular way you have to look at these things. Don't let the opinion cloud your mind. Listen to what they're not saying."

"What?"

"Think about it this way. They know the lower federal courts are going to look at this. They know the Supreme Court will look at it eventually. Almost every death penalty case ends up there, often more than once. And they want to bury this guy. They're going to put everything they have in the opinion. Everything in there is calculated to make sure he gets the needle. So when you read through it, think about what would have made it more convincing. If there's something that would have been damning that isn't in the opinion, that's probably because it doesn't exist. And if it doesn't exist, that might be an opening."

"Like what?"

"Let me take a look," said Gerald. He picked up the opinion. Mark watched seconds tick past on his computer's clock. Can I bill this time? he wondered. Do I note it down as a conference with the bathroom guy?

Gerald flipped the pages, his face grown suddenly intense. "That's interesting," he said finally.

"What is?"

"Well, there's a lot of stuff here. Did Walker read it?"

"Not yet," said Mark. "He wanted me to spot issues for him."

"Okay," Gerald said. "Probably what you want to do is focus on the penalty phase. There's something funny there. Wayne didn't have a psychiatric expert testifying for him. He should have. You can find an expert to tell the court a Bengal tiger makes a good house pet. You can definitely find one to say your guy didn't understand the meaning of his actions and that he'll be a solid citizen from now on."

"Anything else?" Mark asked.

Gerald shrugged. "Well, there's some legal stuff. But you're never going to win one of these cases on the law. You need to have some facts to get a court's attention. Walker will get the legal issues. Make sure he reads the opinion."

Walker Eliot tapped the "hands-free" option on his phone. "Give me a second," he said. He clicked a button on his computer's toolbar, hiding the Internet browser window and replacing it with the firm's internal e-mail. He spun his ventilated, ergonomically sound chair a half turn so that it faced away from his desk, straightened his legs, and considered his new shoes. "What do you have for me?"

"I went through the Virginia Supreme Court opinion," Mark said.

"And?" Walker asked. They weren't shoes, even, really; they were driving moccasins, and hardly practical, but they had been so appealing in the store, smooth as bullets, soft as rain.

"Have you looked at it?"

Walker frowned. He pulled one shoe off his foot and examined it more closely. ZENO FOOTWEAR, read a legend on the bottom, and in smaller script, *When you don't need to go anywhere to know you've arrived.* Walker's face assumed an expression of mild displeasure. "I was hoping that you'd spare me the experience."

"I think it might be better if we went through it together," Mark said. *I can't believe this,* he was thinking. *Gerald was right. Walker wasn't even planning to read it.*

Why did I buy these? Walker was thinking. He had window-shopped before, passing with an ascetic's aloofness through aisles of finery. But then he was on a government salary, and now he was flush with cash, ready to yield to the merest velleity. Having money made matters very different; nothing seemed to cost as much as it had before. The firm's seventy-thousand-dollar signing bonus had passed through the gauntlets of state and federal taxation like an infantry column through enfilading fire; barely forty-four made it to the shelter of his checking account. But even those heavy losses had not dented the dollars' morale; they were eager to see action, ready to lay themselves down in exchange for tangible goods.

"Okay," said Walker. "Let me get in Westlaw. What's the citation?"

"It's 540 Southeast Second 214," Mark said. "But I've got a copy. I can bring it to you or run off another."

"Don't bother," said Walker. "I don't think the client is going to be complaining that we spent too much on electronic research." He spun back to the desk, clicked open a different window, and accessed the computerized database of judicial opinions. "Okay," he said. "What have we got here?"

It hadn't actually been the shoes so much as the salesmen. In the store, business-suited servitors took away the shoes he'd worn in, whisked them off for a free polishing. Walker padded in stocking feet, open to new experiences. Ordinarily he wouldn't try on shoes. Lift them from the shelf, perhaps, eye the leather. But with his own off he was halfway there already, and these had slipped on so easily. "Those are handmade," said a little man who'd appeared at his elbow. "It's a full leather lining. It molds to your foot, almost like having a custom-made shoe." Walker took one off, peered into the dark recess, inserted an inquisitive finger. Indeed, the leather lining extended to the toe.

"Well," said Mark. "We probably can't do anything with the DNA."

Walker's own shoes suddenly appeared in the little man's hand. They sported a fresh polish, but they bore the new coat unwillingly and with little grace, like someone's roughneck cousin dressed up for a wedding. The man hefted them dubiously. The gaze he turned on Walker was more of sorrow than anger, more pity than contempt. "How much did these cost you?"

"I don't know," said Walker. "Maybe seventy bucks."

"At first I thought we could get another test, but it turns out the crime scene sample's been destroyed," Mark said.

"You get what you pay for," the little man told Walker. "This is a three-quarter leather lining, but the toe is canvas. That doesn't get soft; it gets stiff. You see how they're wearing? Here." He pointed to a crease in the leather. "And here." A looseness to the sole. "It's cracking. Now, you could have taken better care of these, probably, but they'd still come apart. For a little more than twice that you can get shoes you'll have for the rest of your life. I mean that. If they start to go on you—which won't happen for a good five years, I promise—bring them back here and we'll repair them."

Walker was impressed. He'd never thought of repairing shoes. "Okay," he said. "I'll take them."

"But I was wondering about why Wayne didn't have a psychiatric expert testifying for him at the penalty phase."

The salesman smiled. "You won't regret this. Now, do you want new heels on the ones you wore in?"

Walker decided he had to draw the line somewhere. "No," he said firmly.

"I don't know about the legal issues," Mark concluded, "but that's what seemed odd on the facts."

"Legal issues," said Walker, his attention snapping back like a rubber band. "Let's see." He began scrolling down the computer screen, muttering to himself. "Capital murder . . . guilty plea . . . satisified with the performance of his lawyer, yeah, right . . . future dangerousness, that's a good one . . . vile crimes, whatever . . . no mitigating factors, well, there's a surprise. Okay."

"What do you think?" Mark asked.

"We probably can't do much with the guilty plea," Walker said. "So we're looking at the penalty phase. There are three legal issues there. One we win, one we lose, and one I don't understand yet."

"What are they?"

"Okay, you remember I said that you could turn an ordinary error into a constitutional one by saying that it was ineffective assistance of counsel? Of course, the state courts don't like that. So the clever guys in the Virginia judiciary decided that at every trial they'd ask the defendant if he liked his lawyer. If he says yes, then, under Virginia law, he's waived the right to argue that the lawyer was constitutionally ineffective. Which is a load of crap, because obviously when you ask if he likes his lawyer, you find out if he likes his lawyer. You don't find out if the lawyer missed a winning argument, because the defendant doesn't have any idea. They're going to try to use that doctrine to cut down the claims we can present in federal court, but no federal court will accept it. So we win that one.

"Then there's the future dangerousness finding. One of the justifications for imposing the death penalty, under Virginia law, is that the defendant will pose a threat to people in the future. Which makes sense if you're considering someone who's going to be back on the streets. But this guy had two life sentences already for burglary and sexual assault. If he hadn't gotten death for the murders, he was going to get two more. With four life sentences, he's not getting out. So who's he a danger to?"

"Can we challenge the death sentence on that ground?" Mark asked.

"No," Walker answered. "That's the one we lose. The answer is that he's a danger to his fellow inmates. He might kill someone in prison.

Maybe someone on death row. We can't have that. So future dangerousness in conjunction with a life sentence is fine. You can thank the Supreme Court for that little gift.

"The last one is the psychiatric testimony. Good catch there. If the state is going to put on psychiatric testimony at the penalty phase, they have to give you money for your own expert. That's also from the Supreme Court. We can be pretty sure that this guy got examined by a defense expert, but they didn't have him testify. So something strange happened there."

"Okay," said Mark. *Ineffective assistance of counsel*, his notepad read. *Future dangerousness* (crossed out). *Psychiatric expert?* (now underlined). "What should I do now?"

"Future dangerousness is what we need to work on," Walker answered. Mark frowned at his notepad and added the phrase again. "If we can knock that finding out, the only aggravating factor left is vileness. Vileness by itself isn't enough, because the term 'vile' is too vague to support the death penalty. It doesn't give the judge or jury enough guidance. There are cases on that. And future dangerousness is one thing Harper's psychiatric expert should have addressed. So we're going to say that there was ineffective assistance of counsel for failing to present expert psychiatric testimony in mitigation."

"Right," said Mark. "And what was it I should do now?"

"Oh," said Walker. "Well, we probably need to enter an appearance in the federal district court. And we should file a motion letting the judge know what we'll be arguing. You can handle that. Then we need to figure out what actually happened with the psychiatrist. Talk to the trial lawyer, this Anson Henry guy."

"Is he going to be upset that we're saying he was constitutionally inadequate?"

"No, he'll understand. It's the only way to get the claims heard. Everyone knows that. He'll be helpful. What you should do is go down there and do some interviews. Do it the same time you make the preliminary motion. It'll be like a vacation, get you out of the office."

"Okay," said Mark dubiously. "Is there anything more I need to know about the motion?"

Walker hesitated. "Well, I guess it's possible that the state will oppose it. Then you'd have to make an argument. But I doubt that's going to happen. If they give you any trouble, just call me."

Franklin Lyttle looked like a judge. He had for decades; in his thirties the shock of hair had grayed, the somber lines furled his brow. It had taken much longer to actually get a seat on the federal bench. Lyttle had spent ten years as a U.S. attorney after leaving law school, then moved as a partner into a powerful D.C. firm, where he passed another twelve years before a confluence of timing, connections, and simple luck brought his name up for a vacancy in the Eastern District of Virginia. At forty-seven, he'd been one of the younger appointees, and even now, at fifty-eight, the title of judge still sounded at times more like the law school nickname it used to be than a description of his actual status.

"What do we have on the plate today, Chris?" he asked.

Chris Thomas scanned the docket sheet and looked back at his employer. Chris was one of the new law clerks, fresh out of UVA Law School and eager to get his feet wet. "Discovery motions," he said, apologetically because he was learning. Lyttle sighed. He was a busy man, busier, probably, than he'd been as a practicing lawyer. That didn't surprise him. What had come as a bit of a shock, even after all those years in practice, was the nature of the work. Judges were referees, he had always believed, called in when disputes had reached the stage at which the legal system was the only alternative to violence. They oversaw a game that had taken the place of private force, a contest between the state and an individual, or between two private citizens. They made sure that the rules were observed; when necessary they clarified what the rules meant. Then a jury gave a verdict and everyone went home.

That view, he soon realized, was stunningly naïve. Most disputes never reached trial, which was as it should be, judicial time being a scarce resource. But between the initial claim and the ultimate settlement there intervened a protracted and tedious struggle in which the contending sides used the legal system to beat each other over the head in hopes of adjusting the terms of the foreordained payoff. Mostly this took place in the context of discovery, the process whereby the two sides were supposed to disclose the information each needed to present its case: everything relevant to any claim or defense and unprotected by the privileges recognized by the discovery rules. But discovery wasn't about necessary information, as Lyttle had well known as a lawyer. It was about harassment; it was about threats. A plaintiff suing a corporation would demand disclosure of corporate trade secrets; if the company couldn't fight off the discovery, it would settle rather than suffer the competitive injury. Or, if what the plaintiff sought really was relevant information, unprotected by any privilege, the defendant would still fight it. The request was too vague; it was overbroad; it was unduly burdensome. The plaintiff's lawyers would be forced to go to court to compel disclosure. The dispute went up to the judge; it returned in the form of an order, on which the two sides would fasten different interpretations, and the whole dance began again. What Lyttle hadn't grasped, in his days as a litigator, was the strain this fencing put on the judicial system, which spent most of its resources resolving disputes entirely unrelated to the merits of the cases.

Litigation corrupted, that was what it came down to. It corrupted the parties, who found themselves indulging in the vindictiveness and brutality that law was to banish and replace. It corrupted the lawyers, who might—who, depending on how they understood their duty of zealous advocacy, were required to—bend and twist the law as best they could, run hard upon the boundaries of the bar's ethical norms. And it corrupted the judges, who reacted to such behavior by deciding for themselves what the result ought to be and handing it down like a thunderbolt. Litigation mocked the law, and judges in response became the law and vindicated their own desires.

Some judges. But not Franklin Lyttle. Lyttle was a proceduralist. He had a client, like the lawyers; he had a duty to pursue. The law was his client, the object of his devotion and zeal. The law wanted to resolve disputes, and he sought to help it. But he did not mistake his own desires for those of the law; he did not question the law's ends. He did not judge his client, try to turn it to a higher path. Lawyers who did that were called statesmen, which Lyttle had always found a little ironic. But judges who did it were called activists, and Lyttle was no activist.

"Tell me there's something else," he said.

Chris shrugged. "A new stack of habeas petitions," he answered. "Like every week."

"Any of them have lawyers?"

Chris flipped pages. "No," he said. "Most of them are handwritten. To be honest, they're a little hard to understand."

"Open sesame petitions," Lyttle said. Prisoners who represented themselves typically had only the most rudimentary understanding of the legal system. They tried to compensate by couching their arguments in the most arcane legal formula they could, which only made it harder to figure out if there was any merit to the petition, the arguments cobbled from out-of-date lawbooks and self-educated cellmates. "They think it's a code; if they use the right Latin phrase, it'll work. Habeas corpus, coram nobis, there's no place like home. Say them in the right order and they'll save you. Or like the cargo cults in the Pacific Islands, doing their rituals with bills of lading, thinking it'll bring the planes back. Is that all there is?"

"Well, there's a status conference. New counsel for Wayne Harper."

"Oh," said Lyttle. "Who's he got now?"

"Morgan Siler. There's an appearance filed by someone named Mark Clayton."

Lyttle nodded. He took a sip of the morning's coffee, rolled his shirtsleeves, and picked up the stack of discovery motions. In two hours, the court would be sitting. "Put him first, Chris," said Franklin Lyttle.

Ensconced in the borrowed luxury of a hotel bed, Mark Clayton was feeling fine. He'd never stayed in a four-star hotel before, let alone in a suite, and the novelty added to the already considerable charm. The advantages of big-firm practice, obscure to the young associates toiling in D.C., stood now in sharp relief. Morgan Siler was unable, or more likely unwilling, to distinguish between costs incurred on a pro bono project and those chargeable to clients. So Mark had the same car, the same hotel room, the same meal allowance as a partner down in Norfolk to argue a million-dollar claim. The difference was that his expenses didn't land on any client's bill. Instead they swelled a different ledger, the costs of the pro bono program. Doubtless, the firm would have liked to cut that budget, but putting the pro bono lawyers on a tighter leash would demonstrate that the same, in theory, could be done to paid counsel, raising possibilities no one was willing to contemplate.

Mark's secretary, the formidable Glynda, had arranged everything for him. Mark shared her with a partner, and though that meant that his needs came a distant second, he was realizing that it also meant she was a secretary who could get things done. Reimbursement slips flew through her fingers; car rental agencies, chastised, proffered upgrades. Mark had a Camry in the garage and a two-room suite at the Norfolk Meridian before he knew he'd asked for them. "All you got to do is sign here," Glynda rumbled, pointing a long and lacquered nail. Mark had made the other preparations, scheduling a meeting with Anson Henry and with Anne Brownlee, from the Virginia Capital Defenders Office. He'd driven south on I-95, through Richmond, then headed toward the coast. Past the naval base, hugging the shoreline through Hampton and into Norfolk, which was a nicer town than he'd imagined.

He'd arrived at the hotel in the early evening, treated himself to a steak in the restaurant, and fallen asleep with the TV on. Back in D.C. there were matters clamoring for his attention, but they could wait. Mark was billing eight hours a day to Wayne Harper, and though he wouldn't make up any ground at that pace, he wouldn't fall much further behind either. It'll be like a vacation, Walker had said. Mark stretched, starfished, in the snowy tumult of the cotton sheets. Possibilities of room service turned in his drowsy mind.

John Miller tightened the knot of his dark blue tie. It was tight already, and he knew that his fidgeting hands betrayed a certain degree of nervousness, but he didn't mind. Being nervous in the presence of Caleb Kite was expected, acceptable; indeed, it was almost required. For a young assistant state's attorney like himself not to show some fear would have smacked of disrespect. The courtroom was the place for ironclad certitude, the place where, armored in righteousness, the attorneys of his office stood on behalf of the people of the Commonwealth of Virginia.

Caleb Kite showed no feelings, neither in nor out of court. John Miller was an instrument of the power of the state, but Kite, so far as possible, was its embodiment. The briefs in criminal cases bore the name of the commonwealth, but Kite was the real opponent. The prosecutors and the state's attorneys alike reported to him and sought his approval of all but the most routine decisions. His name appeared on every brief; he exercised at least potential control over every detail of every case. And if a case proved worthy of his time, the control became actual; he would read the briefs, plot the strategy, and personally instruct the lawyers. Though John Miller had no idea why, Wayne Harper had made the grade. He had earned the personal opposition of the senior prosecuting attorney of Virginia.

Kite's head lifted from the newspaper on his desk, deep-set eyes peering down the length of an aquiline and forceful nose. His attention struck Miller like a blow. "You're in court today," he said. "Wayne Harper."

"Yes," Miller answered. "It's a status conference for the habeas petition. He's got new counsel."

"Morgan Siler," said Kite, his voice slow and deliberate. "The lawyer got into town yesterday. Well, we've got a little welcoming present for the new guy. We'll see how he reacts."

17 THE EASTERN DISTRICT
OF VIRGINIA

"**A**ll persons having business before the honorable, the United States District Court for the Eastern District of Virginia, are admonished to draw near and give their attention," recited a blocky federal marshal, "for the Court is now sitting. God save the United States and this honorable Court." Mark tried vainly to straighten a crease in his suit jacket and cursed his garment bag. The courtroom was large and open, with a podium for counsel below the raised chair of the district judge. The back of the room was filled with benches, now crowded with lawyers in the dark gray suits of litigators, there to present arguments at the morning motion call. Some of the people in attendance Mark figured for clients, but it was hard to tell. After a certain number of years, lawyers started to resemble their clients, either in analogy to the pattern of married couples or on the theory that you are what you eat. "Case number 00-5672," the marshal called. "*Wayne Harper* versus *Commonwealth of Virginia*." My God, thought Mark, having caught an unobstructed view of the judge, that man has the largest eyebrows I've ever seen. Belatedly he struggled to his feet and hastened to the counsel's table on the right side of the room. From the other a pale dark-haired young man regarded him coldly. John Miller, Mark assumed.

"You're entering an appearance for Morgan Siler as new counsel for Mr. Harper," Judge Lyttle intoned. "Correct?"

"Yes, Your Honor," said Mark.

"Are you a member of the bar of this court?"

"No, Your Honor."

"Have you been admitted to practice in the highest court of the state of Virginia?"

Mark started to sweat. "I'm not sure, Your Honor." John Miller looked incredulous; Lyttle's eyebrows converged. "I've been admitted to the Virginia bar," Mark offered.

"Raise your right hand," said the judge. "Do you solemnly swear as an officer of the court to conduct yourself uprightly and according to law and to support and defend the Constitution of the United States?"

"I do," said Mark.

"Welcome to the bar of the Eastern District of Virginia," said Judge Lyttle. He seemed half asleep. "Your appearance on behalf of Morgan Siler serves as an appearance for the firm. Other lawyers from the same firm need not make individual appearances in this case. They must, however, be admitted to the bar of this court." The last sentence sounded as though it had not been delivered by rote; Mark, glancing to the side, caught John Miller's smirk. "You are here for a status conference."

"Yes, Your Honor," said Mark. "We will be filing a habeas petition on behalf of Mr. Harper." He paused. "We would like to present evidence on future dangerousness." Like a conductor's arm, Lyttle's right eyebrow arched invitingly.

"The state will request immediate dismissal," said John Miller promptly, rising to his feet. "Any possible arguments about future dangerousness are procedurally barred by the petitioner's failure to present them at trial or on appeal." Lyttle's eyebrows reversed positions.

Mark's mind went blank. Behind him rose a faint susurrus of whispers. "You needn't answer if you don't want to, counsel," Lyttle said gently. "This isn't an argument. But if you choose, you may enlighten the court as to your probable response, thereby facilitating its preparation."

"We will argue," Mark said slowly, "that counsel was constitutionally ineffective for failing to present evidence showing a lack of future dangerousness." Was that comprehensible? Was he even speaking English?

John Miller didn't wait for his cue. "Any ineffective-assistance-of-counsel claims are waived by petitioner's failure to present them on appeal and also procedurally barred."

Judge Lyttle looked at Mark, who looked away. "Thank you, counsel," said the judge. "I will hear argument on the question of procedural bar at four-thirty this afternoon." He paused. "Thereafter, if I deem it necessary, I may call for briefs."

"It sounds like you did fine," said Walker reassuringly. "No, really. It's a good sign. He's just trying to speed things up. If anything goes wrong, we'll get a chance to submit a brief."

"Okay," said Mark, trying to slow his heartbeat.

"You should just go see Anson Henry," Walker continued. "And the Capital Defender people."

"I can't do that," Mark said. "I can't see the Capital Defenders because I'm supposed to be in court at the same time making an argument on something I know nothing about. And I can't see Anson Henry because I need to prepare for the argument."

"What you need to do is relax," Walker said. "This is a preliminary hearing before the district court. There's lots of time to fix any problem. Why don't you see if you can reschedule the Capital Defenders for tomorrow and just talk to Henry before the hearing? It's probably more important to talk to the trial lawyer."

"Okay," Mark answered dubiously. "But what about the argument? What do I say?"

Walker reflected. "Do you have a pen?"

The law offices of F. Anson Henry were misnamed. There was in fact only one office, Henry's, and an antechamber where a bored receptionist inspected her nails. "You go on in," she told Mark. "He's expecting you."

Anson Henry was in his early fifties, Mark guessed, with faint frostings of gray in the longish blond hair that he pushed back from his forehead. He wore a seersucker suit and a white shirt open at the neck. "Mr. Clayton," he said, extending a leathery hand. "That's a fine old Southern name. Do you have family hereabouts?"

He thinks he's Atticus Finch, Mark said to himself. "New Rochelle," he answered uncomfortably. "It's outside New York."

Anson's expression indicated that some things couldn't be helped. He pointed to a chair. "What can I do for you?"

"I wanted to talk about Wayne Harper."

Anson sighed, and a frown settled over his pleasant face. "That was a damn shame," he said. "We none of us thought he'd get the death penalty. Not after pleading guilty. We were hoping for a good institution. They've got one in Hampton. But he caught a bad break with that judge."

"Well, we're going to do what we can," Mark said. "We were wondering about the mitigating evidence at the penalty phase." Anson nodded. "You didn't offer any psychiatric testimony to rebut the future dangerousness argument."

"Nope," said Anson, pursing his lips.

"Why was that?" Mark asked.

"Why was that," Anson repeated. "Well, I'll tell you why that was.

You probably know they'll give you money for your own expert, once they decide to use one."

"Right," said Mark.

"Wrong," said Anson Henry. "They don't have to give you money. They can give you an expert instead. That's what they did to Wayne Harper. And you know who they gave him? They gave him, if you'll pardon my French, they gave him fucking Doctor Death."

"Doctor Death?"

"Roger Mateska, Ph.D.," Anson said, spitting out the syllables. "One of the coldest bastards I've ever seen. He used to be a state expert, before they figured out that he'd be more helpful on the other side. Testified in about twenty capital trials, said in every one that he was certain—one hundred percent certain—that the defendant would kill again if they ever let him out. Two of those guys turned out to be innocent, once they did the DNA. And Roger, he doesn't believe in mental illness, diminished capacity, things like that. There's bad people and there's stupid people in Roger's world, but they get the needle same as you or me. So. That's why it was that we didn't put on any expert testimony. We used the prosecution's report because it was less damaging than anything our own expert was going to say. You want a drink?" Maybe not Atticus Finch after all, Mark thought. Anson read his face. "Too early for you?"

"No," Mark said. "I've got to be in court in an hour or so, though."

Anson looked at him appraisingly. "Doesn't necessarily make it a worse idea," he said. "You been in court much?"

"Just this morning."

Anson nodded. "How old are you?"

"Twenty-six."

"You handling this on your own?"

"No," Mark said. "There's a team at Morgan Siler."

"Of course," said Anson skeptically. "I'm sure they pulled together their top guns for Wayne Harper. Well, I wish you luck. Go tell that court all the things I did wrong."

"Do you have any suggestions?" Mark asked.

Anson Henry laughed. "I wish I could help you. I did the best I could, son. I used all the bright ideas I had."

"How about the Capital Defenders? Do you think I should talk to them?"

"I don't know that they'd be much use," Anson said. "They're aboli-
tionists, which isn't a popular position in these parts. And it means that
they don't care so much about the individual client. They're going after
the whole system. The machinery of death. Unless they can use Wayne
as a test case for some new idea they've cooked up, they won't pay him
much attention. I could tell that from the stuff they filed with the
Virginia Supreme Court. It's good lawyering, but it's all about how the
death penalty is cruel and unusual, arbitrary in its implementation. Lots
of quotes from Brennan and Marshall. They're still refighting *McCleskey*
v. *Kemp*. It's not about Wayne. And it's not going to make any impression
on any of the courts in this state." He sighed. "Sometimes things just
don't go the way you think they will. You got any more questions?"

Mark hesitated a moment. "Did he do it?" he asked.

"The client's never guilty," Anson answered. "Until he pleads guilty.
Of course he did it. He confessed, didn't he?"

"Yeah," said Mark slowly. "Did you think about trying to get the confession suppressed?"

"Wouldn't have worked. Poor boy's so eager to please, they just asked
him a couple questions and he started talking. No way but that it was
voluntary. And it wouldn't have done much good, anyway. There was the
DNA evidence too. No, they had him dead to rights, if you'll pardon the
expression. That's why I pleaded him out, hoping for mercy."

Mark folded his hands in his lap and looked down at the floor. Anson
Henry had all the bases covered. It was hard to see anything he'd done
wrong, much less anything that could change the outcome. "Okay," he
said finally. "Okay."

A red light was blinking on the hotel phone when he got back to his
room. The desk clerk read him a Washington number: Morgan Siler.

"Why don't I have your cell phone number?" Glynda asked.

"I don't have a cell phone," Mark answered.

"Really," said Glynda wonderingly. "Well, I suppose that's one way to
keep them off your back."

"Who?"

"The partners. Harold's been calling for you. And he sent you an
e-mail."

"What does it say?"

"It says you're going to Texas."

"I'm what?"

"You're going to Texas. Tomorrow."

"I see," said Mark. "Does it say why?"

"Hubble Chemical. Does that mean anything to you?"

"Hubble," said Mark slowly. In his mind there flashed an image of the thick complaint, copiously highlighted, half read, sitting . . . somewhere on his desk under the papers from Wayne Harper's trial and appeal. "Right, Hubble." A ball of flame, a deadly cloud, bodies twitching by the fence. "I don't know if I can make that. I have a meeting scheduled tomorrow. I'd better call Harold. Anything else?"

"You got some mail from the Virginia Prosecuting Attorney's Office."

"What is it?"

"I don't know," said Glynda. "You want me to open it?"

"Yes. I'm going to call Harold now. I'll get back to you."

Harold's familiar brusqueness had a harried edge. It was important to push back against pressure, he knew, but it was healthy also to let it flow through you, onto whomever you dealt with. This was his understanding of Buddhism. "Where the hell are you?"

"I'm in Norfolk."

"You like being out of the office?"

"I guess so."

"Then I've got some good news for you. We're going to Texas."

"Right," said Mark. "Well, the thing is, I have interviews I was going to do down here."

"No, no, no," said Harold. "I need bodies there, on the ground. Live bodies, I mean. Who's the partner who assigned you to this?"

"Wallace Finn, I guess."

"Pro bono case?"

"Yes."

"Okay, then. You're going to be on the plane tomorrow morning. I'd love to chat, but I have to go explain to the D.C. District Court why it's cost-effective to cook people who buy cheap cars. Tomorrow morning. Got it?" He hung up, leaving Mark mumbling acquiescence into dead air.

"You straighten everything out with Harold?" Glynda asked.

"I did," Mark said.

"You going to Texas tomorrow?"

"I am. What's the mail?"

"I don't know. It's some kind of a notice. I've never seen one of these before."

"Well, what does it say?"

"You want me to read it to you?"

"Yes," said Mark. "I think I'd like that."

Glynda cleared her throat. "'Please take notice,'" she read, "'that on this the sixth day of October—'"

"When was that?"

"Friday," Glynda said tiredly. "Three days ago. 'On this the sixth day of October, Governor Adam Teasdale signed a warrant for the execution of Wayne Lee Harper, to be carried out by lethal injection, at the Greensville Correctional Facility in Jarratt, in the Commonwealth of Virginia on Wednesday the eleventh of October.'"

Mark felt cold. "But . . ." he said, "but that's a death warrant."

"I guess it is," Glynda answered. "I told you I've never seen one before. Do you want to write them back?"

"No," Mark said. "Just get me Walker."

19 A STAY OF EXECUTION

It's just the coffee, Mark told himself, as he sat in the courtroom waiting for Wayne Harper's name to be called. The reassurance had proved effective many mornings at work. Too much caffeine could produce free-floating anxiety, a sense of creeping dread. Better to attribute it to coffee than to the job, and plausible enough when there were no tangible alternative candidates. But this time it wasn't convincing, not when his client was due to be executed in two days and Walker was nowhere to be found. There was something Mark needed to do, he was sure, some magic phrase that would hold back the forces of the state long enough for him to at least get a hearing. But he had no idea what the formula might be. Nor, to be honest, did he know what he would say at the hearing, even if he got one.

"*Wayne Harper* versus *Commonwealth of Virginia*," the marshal said, and Mark leaped to his feet. He took his place at the counsel's table. John Miller again sat across from him, this time accompanied by two other gray-suited attorneys.

"We're here to discuss the merits of the Commonwealth's asserted procedural bar," said Judge Lyttle. "Is there any new development of which I should be apprised before we begin?"

"Yes," blurted Mark. Judge Lyttle looked at him. "Your Honor," Mark added.

"And that is . . . ?" the judge asked invitingly.

"Your Honor, the governor of Virginia has signed a death warrant for my client."

Judge Lyttle cocked a shaggy eyebrow. "Oh, has he?" he inquired mildly. "And when is the execution to be carried out?"

"This week, Your Honor. On Wednesday."

"I see," said the judge. He regarded Mark impassively.

"Your Honor, there's no way that we can prepare Mr. Harper's habeas petition in time to meet that deadline." Mark heard a snicker from the cluster of Virginia attorneys, and he blushed.

"No," said Judge Lyttle. "Indeed there isn't. Nor could I possibly rule in that time even if you were to submit the petition. Nor would you have time to appeal if I were to rule against you."

"No, Your Honor," Mark agreed. He and the judge looked at each other in silence.

Judge Lyttle sighed. "I take it you are requesting that this court issue an order staying the execution," he said finally.

On the other side of the courtroom, John Miller sprang to his feet. "Your Honor, petitioner's counsel has not made any request for a stay."

"I request a stay," Mark put in quickly, but the judge cut him off.

"Mis-ter Miller," he said sharply. The syllables hissed into the courtroom; silence followed. Judge Lyttle took his glasses off. He breathed on the lenses and polished them with the sleeve of his robe. "I believe the Court was in colloquy with petitioner's counsel," he said meditatively, and replaced the glasses. "Since you seem concerned, however, let me assure you that the State of Virginia will not execute anyone who has a habeas petition pending before this Court." He paused. "Whether I enter the stay on my own motion, or on the motion petitioner's counsel was about to make."

"I move for a stay," Mark said.

Judge Lyttle looked to the other side.

John Miller scowled. "The Commonwealth opposes," he said sullenly.

"Granted," said Judge Lyttle. "Now, where were we?"

Miller's face brightened. "The Commonwealth moves to dismiss the habeas petition as procedurally barred."

"Let's hear it," said the judge.

Miller stepped to the central podium from which lawyers presented argument. He'd stood there only a few times before, in insignificant cases and preliminary motions, but already he was growing used to the thrill that swept through him. And he loved it. He felt poised and lethal, his mind like a razor, all the weapons of law at his disposal. This was combat, and he, the people's champion, took the field to protect them from their enemies. Leslie Anne Clark, he said to himself. Michael Clark. Murdered in your own home. No one was there to protect you that night. But I'm here now, and this is my house.

"Petitioner seeks to use an ineffective-assistance-of-counsel argument to present to this court claims that he waived by failing to present them to the state courts," Miller began. "But that ineffective-assistance-of-counsel claim is itself waived. Mr. Harper expressly informed the trial court that he was satisfied with the performance of his trial counsel, whom he selected himself, and he never sought to present any claims of ineffectiveness during his appeal to the Virginia Supreme Court. Under that court's *Anderson* decision, he cannot now contradict his earlier statements and assert that trial counsel was ineffective."

"*Anderson* is a state court decision, is it not?" asked Judge Lyttle.

"It's from the Virginia Supreme Court," Miller answered.

"But ineffectiveness of counsel is a federal constitutional claim," the judge said. "State courts do not instruct federal courts on the meaning of the Constitution."

"No, Your Honor," Miller responded quickly. He had known this was coming, and he was ready. "But state law may establish procedures that prisoners must follow in presenting their claims. They can't ignore those procedures and save their federal claims for a federal court."

"Indeed," said the judge. "Mr. Clayton, I'll hear from you."

Mark took a deep breath and stood. "Your Honor," he said.

"Come to the podium, please, counsel," Judge Lyttle said. Again Mark heard the Virginia lawyers' incredulous laughter. He gathered his papers and stepped out from behind the table.

"If *Anderson* is a procedural rule," he said carefully, "it amounts to a rule that ineffective-assistance-of-counsel claims must be presented on direct review, during the initial appeal. But in the vast majority of these cases, trial counsel and appellate counsel are the same lawyer. You cannot expect a lawyer to argue that his own performance was constitutionally deficient. As a procedural rule, *Anderson* is simply unfair, and federal courts will not enforce it. Federal courts have, in fact, agreed that prisoners cannot be required to present ineffective-assistance-of-counsel claims on direct appeal."

"Are those Fourth Circuit decisions you're referring to?" Judge Lyttle asked.

"I believe these cases are from other jurisdictions," Mark answered, fumbling in the sheaf of papers in front of him. "I have the citations here for you." Somehow the right pages were failing to materialize. "Well, I can give them to you after the argument." He turned back to his text. "On the substantive significance of Mr. Harper's statement of satisfaction with his lawyer, *Anderson* again means nothing to a federal court. Under the standards set out by the United States Supreme Court, the question with regard to ineffective assistance of counsel is not whether the defendant is happy with his lawyer but whether his lawyer performed within the bounds of professional competence. If you look at the trial transcript, what Harper said was, and I quote, 'He's a good man.' That has nothing to do with how his lawyer performed, and Mr. Harper is in any event not qualified to evaluate that performance. Whether you view the *Anderson* rule as substantive or procedural, it does not justify dismissing this petition without a hearing on the effectiveness of Mr. Harper's trial counsel."

Judge Lyttle nodded. He turned to John Miller. "Rebuttal?"

John Miller truly felt like a man in combat. He knew he'd been hit; he just wasn't sure how bad it was. What the hell was that? he wondered. One minute this guy doesn't know enough to ask for a stay of execution, the next he's coming out with this. Why did I waste my lucky tie yesterday on a motion to suppress? Tentatively, Miller found his feet. "*Anderson* is a procedural rule. The Virginia courts have held that it is. State court interpretations of state law are authoritative. Moreover, the federal district court for the Northern District of Virginia, in an opinion by Judge Lynch, has applied *Anderson* to prevent a habeas petitioner from making an ineffective-assistance-of-counsel argument."

"Thank you, counsel," said Judge Lyttle. Mark returned to his seat at the table; Lyttle paused only a moment. "I'll rule from the bench." Chris Thomas had been busy that day, working through lunch, and half an hour before the sitting he'd given the judge a memorandum on the status of the *Anderson* rule. The memo recommended that the judge rule in favor of Wayne Harper. That meant nothing; Franklin Lyttle would make his own decisions. The important part was that it showed him he had the legal room to do so. He was a custodian of the law, trying not to change its substance but to make sure that it worked in practice, that it allowed for fair hearings and adequate opportunities to present arguments. And in practice, Lyttle knew, requiring a lawyer to argue on appeal that he himself had been ineffective at trial would eliminate the possibility of an ineffective-assistance-of-counsel claim.

"Whether Virginia's *Anderson* rule can operate to bar a prisoner's ineffective-assistance-of-counsel claim is a federal issue," he said. "The decisions of the Virginia courts are not authoritative on that question. The Fourth Circuit has not decided it. And with due respect to the opinions of the Virginia judiciary, I find myself compelled to the opposite conclusion. It is simply unrealistic to expect an ineffective-assistance-of-counsel claim to be presented on direct appeal, and a habeas petitioner's failure to do so will therefore not prevent him from presenting it to a federal court. The Commonwealth's motion to dismiss is denied." He brought down his gavel. "Court is adjourned."

Receiving consoling pats from his colleagues, John Miller felt blindsided. The motions he'd argued before had been easy wins; now he was realizing that his novice status qualified him for the hopeless ones too. Cannon fodder. Mine not to reason why, he thought. Well, let Wayne Harper have his hearing. Miller had reviewed the record in this case, and he was confident that the decisions of the Virginia courts would stand up to federal scrutiny. He looked over at Mark. You've a long way to go before you win anything that matters, he thought.

20 THE MOST DEVOUT PEOPLE THERE ARE

Rebecca Keene was the district court judge presiding over the Carver trial, and she did not like Harold Fineman. That much was plain quite early in the argument. Harold had started from his prepared script. This case isn't about an accident we all agree was tragic, he'd told the judge. It's about whether car manufacturers can be held to a standard much more demanding than what the buyers themselves feel is appropriate. Fifty thousand dollars, that's what car purchasers will pay to avoid a traffic death. Six million, that's what it would cost us. Judge Keene had let him get that far, but it was soon clear that the time to talk hadn't improved his position.

"What are you telling me here, counsel? That Henry Carver thought his life, and the lives of everyone in his family, weren't worth two thousand dollars?"

From her seat at the lawyers' table, Katja could see Harold's shoulders tense through his suit jacket. The argument demanded a certain degree of economic sophistication from the judge, but Harold hadn't seemed to think that was a concern with Keene. It demanded some other things as well, which Katja thought they were unlikely to find in any human being, judge or not. But now Keene was taking them back to the basic nuts and bolts, and Harold scented an ambush.

"Of course not, Your Honor," he said slowly. "When Mr. Carver bought this car, he was making a judgment about the risks that he was willing to take, and how much he was willing to pay to reduce those risks. Two thousand dollars is the amount it would have cost the manufacturer to retrofit a single car. To come to the value placed on life, you need to multiply that by the decrease in risk. That's what gets you the six-million-dollar figure."

"I see. And you say that you shouldn't have to spend six million dollars to avoid killing one of your customers. Make that four of your customers. You say that you shouldn't have to do that because your customers hold their lives less dear. Explain that part again, if you would."

Harold relaxed a bit. "What the studies of consumer behavior show is that purchasers of cars in this price range are willing to pay for increased safety at the rate of fifty thousand dollars per life saved. Obviously, that's nowhere near six million. Now, as a matter of law, a product can't be considered unreasonably dangerous if it costs more to make it safer than consumers would be willing to pay."

A matter of law, thought Katja idly, jotting notes. *Does law matter?* she wrote. *What's the matter with law?*

"What consumers are you talking about? Do we have any evidence at all about what these consumers would have paid to eliminate that risk?"

"Your Honor, we know that they bought the car they did. Anyone who wants a safer car can buy one."

A slow smile spread across Judge Keene's face. "They can, can they?" she asked mildly. Oh, dear, thought Katja. Something's just gone very wrong. She watched Harold's back and shoulders, where defeat first shows itself. "Let me just think out loud about this," Judge Keene continued. "One consumer is willing to pay a certain amount for a safety feature, and another is not. But these are decisions they make of their own free will. If people aren't willing to pay for something, we shouldn't have a legal system that forces it on them. And forcing it on them is the outcome if we hold your client liable, because no manufacturer in his right mind would make these cars if he knew he'd be paying millions of dollars in damages. Yes?"

"Yes."

"Counsel, do you happen to know who buys these cars?"

Harold winced, feeling things unravel. "I'm afraid I don't have that information handy," he said.

"Well, let me put it this way. This is a cheap car your clients made. An affordable one. Do you think that perhaps it's purchased disproportionately by people of limited means?"

"I don't think there's any evidence in the record suggesting that."

"Perhaps not. But as you know, you've brought a motion to dismiss, and in that procedural posture we're simply inquiring whether the plaintiff could possibly prove facts entitling him to relief. So indulge my fantasy a moment and suppose that poorer people tend to buy cheaper cars, which for that reason are less safe. What would you say that means?"

Harold played dumb. "I'm not sure what Your Honor is getting at."

"Then I'll explain. It turns out, we're supposing, that the people who want to pay more for safety tend to be rich, and the people who don't tend to be poor. Someone with five million dollars in the bank will spend twenty thousand for a safer car, but someone with five thousand in the bank won't. What this means, according to your analysis, is that rich people put a higher dollar value on their lives than poor people do. And what you're asking me to do today is to say that the legal system should incorporate that valuation."

Harold sagged visibly. To Katja he looked like a boxer answering the bell for the ninth round, both eyes swollen shut but determined somehow to carry on. That she had never seen a boxing match made the impression no less vivid. "I'm simply saying that we should respect the choices that consumers make in a free market."

"No, you're not." Judge Keene warmed to her task. She'd been an academic before being nominated to the bench, and the colloquy was taking her back. "What we're talking about here is the dollar value of a life. Your clients decided to save money, knowing that it would cost lives, and we're trying to figure out if they saved enough money for that trade-off to be socially acceptable. You're saying that the test of social acceptability should be the dollar value that people place on their lives, as it's expressed in their purchasing decisions. And as a practical matter, you're asking us to say that rich people's lives are worth more."

That's it, thought Katja, oddly thrilled. That's exactly what we're arguing. That's the fundamental premise of this whole theory. Why didn't I see that before? She couldn't see the expression on Harold's face, but his tone suggested that he was completely unfazed.

"I don't think we can use anything else," Harold said. "Not if the law is going to respect individuals as responsible and competent to make decisions about their lives. We won't force someone to pay for an operation he doesn't want, even if it will reduce his chances of dying. We shouldn't force him to buy a more expensive car either."

"You don't want to make any changes to your analysis of consumer choice based on income or wealth distribution?" Judge Keene said.

Harold turned his head to one side, and Katja caught a glimpse of a smile. Doesn't he see what's happening to him? she wondered. He must. "Inequalities of wealth may create some problems," Harold answered calmly. "And if it were possible to do so fairly, they should be eliminated. But the existence of inequalities doesn't mean that we should reject the idea that people are capable of making decisions about their lives."

"Let me see if I can rephrase your position," said Judge Keene gently. "You want the law to respect the values that people place on their lives. And you want to measure those values by how much they'd pay to avoid a particular risk. In a perfectly equal world, this would work perfectly."

"Yes."

"In the world that we have, however, this approach means that the desires of the rich are systematically overvalued. The more money you have, the more you're willing to pay for something."

"I believe that's true."

Judge Keene nodded. "The rich are different from you and me," she said meditatively. "Or from me, anyway, since I'm not a law firm partner. It's not just that they have more money. Because they have more money, they're more important. That's your law and economics conclusion. Now, some people might think that this conclusion recommends a different method of analysis, like letting a jury decide what's unreasonably dangerous. But you don't. That's your argument, isn't it, counsel? Rich people's lives are worth more and the poor get what they pay for?"

"I don't believe I would phrase it that way, Your Honor."

"But from what I've heard from you here, that's what you're offering as the basis for dismissal."

Harold was silent for a moment, collecting himself. "That," he said carefully, "is my client's position."

Judge Keene nodded again. "Thank you, counsel. You can tell your client he won't have to wait too long for a ruling."

Katja spent the remainder of the day hiding in her office, turning aside cheery inquiries with a noncommittal response. "It went okay, I guess." The case had attracted unusual attention, and the inquiries were many.

Tired of repeating the lie, at last she closed her door and tried to study the documents from *Guzman* v. *Hubble Chemical Corp*. Still she could hear Harold repeating his argument. The senseless perseverance of broken things, the faint martyr's smile. At five-thirty she looked longingly at the pile of gym clothes in the corner; at six, unable to stand it anymore, she got up and took her solitary way down the hall to his office.

Harold did not seem surprised to see her. "Have a seat," he offered. Katja hesitated, eyeing the stacks of paper encumbering the available chairs. Cautiously she selected the least official-looking pile and set it on the floor. "You look troubled," said Harold. "What can I do for you?"

"I feel—" said Katja. "Well, I don't know how I feel. I don't know how I'm supposed to feel."

Harold smiled. He gestured expansively, exhaling. "Listen," he said. "Oral arguments go different ways. Sometimes they love you, like you're the star pupil and they want to show off how smart you are. Sometimes they're conflicted. You get a real argument. You make your case. Maybe you change their minds, maybe not. And sometimes they're just against you. That's not an argument, really. It's a torture session. And for a while you think you can still save it; you think, If they stop now, it's still okay. If it doesn't get worse than this, I can survive. But eventually you absorb enough damage that you just start wondering when they'll let you die."

"I'm sorry," said Katja softly.

Harold laughed. "Don't be. It's not really you they're torturing. It's the client. The lawyer's just playing a role. The lawyer's like the actor; he never dies. I could see from the outset that we were going to lose this one. At the end there I was just egging her on."

"Why?"

"Because this is a stupid and heartless argument. I told them not to make it. I told them to settle the case. They barbecued a family of four for two thousand dollars. That's how it's going to look to the jury. But they hired some idiot law and economics consulting firm that thought this was a winner, especially before, as they put it, the economically sophisticated Judge Keene. Well, they'll get their economic sophistication. Right up the ass. If they go to trial, they'll get killed, and they'll deserve it. The plaintiffs' lawyer is going to get up there and wave their memo around and say, 'They knew people were going to die and they decided their lives weren't worth saving. Now you have the chance to make sure this won't happen again. You tell them how much human lives are worth.' But it won't go to trial. Judge Keene is going to write an opinion smacking some sense into them, and they'll settle it. And the good thing here is that after reading Judge Keene's opinion, they're going to be more willing to settle. If they'd just tried to drag this out and starve the plaintiffs into submission, they might have been able to. The problem with our legal system is that it's typically much more trial by ordeal than you might think. You can have the best case in the world, but I can still make things very difficult for you. And very expensive. And very unpleasant."

"Are you happy about that?"

"Happy?" asked Harold. "I'm a lawyer. I have a duty to represent my client. Represent him zealously, fervently. I have to believe in him. Litigators aren't skeptics; they're the most devout people there are. Every case brings a new object of unshakable faith. But there are such things as false gods. Not all your clients are meant to win."

"So what you were saying in there . . ." Katja said, "you mean you didn't believe it?"

"Of course I believed it. While I was saying it. Act, and it will produce belief. That's what litigation is all about." Katja looked stricken, and Harold remembered suddenly what it was like to be young. "Listen," he said. "You're not always the good guy. That's the job. Sometimes you have to be the bad guy. But the bad guy doesn't always win. You have to take satisfaction in that. If you think about it, that's what makes litigation so rewarding."

"Rewarding?" said Katja wonderingly.

Harold was aware his words were having an effect opposite from what he intended. The litigator's instinct propelled him forward: keep moving or die. "Sure. Sometimes you lose when you should have won. That's disappointing, but you can't avoid it. Disappointments happen to everyone. Sometimes you win when you should win. There's nothing better than that. And sometimes you lose when you should lose. You do everything you can to cheat the system, and still the law rises up in righteousness and smites you down. That's the second-best thing. You test the law's virtue with all the wiles the years have trained into you, and it remains true."

"And sometimes you win when you should have lost."

Harold smiled. "There's your keen legal mind at work." He shrugged.

"Sometimes. Depending on how good you are. But that's a win. I mean, if you think about it, representing these guys is a no-lose proposition. Either you win or justice prevails. What is there to worry about? Lots of people in this world go to sleep afraid of the bad guys out there. But if you're the bad guy, what is there for you to fear?"

"But all that," Katja said. "Have you found something you really care about?"

Harold laughed. He stood up and stepped from behind his desk to the window, accidentally kicking over a pile of papers. "Something you care about? Oh, the practice of law is a great way to discover what you care about. In the sense that death is the mother of beauty. Happy lawyers care about the law. They care about their clients. And maybe they care a little about professional organizations. The bar association, that sort of thing. Caring about anything else just makes you an unhappy lawyer. A self-hating lawyer, which lots of us are. There's an incredible amount of denial. 'Oh, I'm a lawyer, but my real passion is the opera.' It's like the waiters who tell you they're actors or writers. But with them, it's temporary. Some of them make it; the rest grow up and go on to some-thing else. Not lawyers. For lawyers, it's just 'Oh, look, I collect model sailing ships.' It's 'Check out these autographed baseballs.' People culti-vate eccentricities to remind themselves that once upon a time they wanted to be something else, to persuade themselves that they still are. It doesn't work. If you commit yourself emotionally to the job, it will give you something in return. But it will consume your life. If you hold back, you may live outside of work, but you'll hate every minute you spend there. You have to give in. This is a big firm. You're in the machine now. It will process you. And when it's over, it won't have mattered if you loved Shakespeare or Coltrane or the Boston Red Sox. What you love doesn't matter to the law. Love is nothing here." He paused, glanced at her, and gave a weak smile. "It's like tennis."

Katja looked at Harold, his piles of paper, his unkempt thinning hair. On the wall loomed a framed poster of Bayreuth's Wagner Festival Theater. You have to give in, she thought. Happy lawyers care about the law. A terrible pity overcame her. "I'm sorry," she said. "I'm so sorry." Without thinking, she rose to her feet, a gentle gliding approach, and kissed his cheek. Harold flinched, and Katja pulled back, as surprised as he was at her body's act. "Should I not have done that?"

Harold Fineman prided himself on his ability to handle the tough questions. What was the justification for subjecting the poor to risks that the rich didn't have to take? Why shouldn't a company be held liable for injuries caused by its products? What was the nondiscriminatory explanation for refusing to hire women who'd expressed an interest in raising a family? He had answers for them all. Now, however, he found himself entirely at a loss. "Hey," he said finally. "Isn't there a firm dinner we're supposed to be going to?"

THE GOOD OF THE FIRM

The annual associate dinner party was a relatively recent addition to the culture of Morgan Siler. Morgan Stevens had not done such things, but Morgan Stevens was no more. Its troubles began, in an unhappy coincidence, at the time of Archie's greatest satisfaction. Peter, returned from Cambridge with a new wife, joined the firm in 1967 and quickly established a reputation as a hard worker. Other lawyers took his eventual ascension to partner as foreordained, but Peter did not, or if he did, it was with a staunch Calvinism, an attitude that said he would not let a little thing like predestination affect the way he conducted himself. Archie was justifiably proud, proud that Peter had chosen Morgan Stevens, and proud that he had evidently chosen it from a belief in its merit and not as the easiest road. Still, he would have liked Peter to accept a little more help, to ask at least for advice. Others did; junior partners and even associates came to the sprawling corner office, sat on the leather couch, and spread their problems before him. Archie looked out the window toward the green recesses of Rock Creek Park and traced his mysterious designs on a yellow legal pad. He liked to advise the younger lawyers. Giving advice, offering sound judgment, that was what lawyers did. But they didn't teach prudence in school — how could they? — and so a man had to pick it up on the job as best he could. To pick it up from his elders.

Archie would be the first to admit that he'd learned a lot from his own father. He'd been encouraged to bring his problems; he'd received advice, money, references. But Peter had always been stubborn about such things. Even as a schoolboy he'd struggle for hours with a trigonometry problem rather than turn to his parents; on the golf course he drove ball after ball into the water despite Archie's urgings to change clubs and lie up. Or perhaps because of them. Archie had told Peter how much he owed his own father, and for a time he'd thought that Peter didn't hear. Now he was starting to think that Peter had heard and chosen not to repeat. The implicit rebuke stung. What was a father for, if not to teach his son how to navigate the world they shared?

But then, Archie was no longer so confident that he knew the answers. That was the trouble. Not long after Peter started work, Archie had received a call from Charles Latham, the president of Glendale Paper. It was a small company but a good client; Morgan Stevens had shepherded it through the first years of its existence, drafted the articles of incorporation, and seen to day-to-day needs. They'd taken it public some years back and Charles and Archie had celebrated over drinks at the club. And now, it appeared, the modest success had put it in danger. "They're trying to take my company away from me, Archie," Charles said. "Someone's buying up my stock. They're going through Goldman Sachs. I don't even know who it is."

A takeover, thought Archie. A tender offer. Those bankers were vultures.

If there was one thing that made Archie glad he'd chosen the law as his vocation, it was the growing rapacity of the investment banks. The country had been through waves of mergers before; the last one had been kind to his father's firm and paid for much of his own education. But things were different this time around. Say what you might about the robber barons, they gave us the railroads. The recent mergers created nothing, as far as he could see, beyond fees for the bankers. And they were accomplished in a different manner—a sudden offer to buy up outstanding shares, a veiled threat that those who held on would be squeezed out at a lower price once the acquisition was complete, the devouring in an instant of a company built through years of toil and sacrifice.

"We'll look into it," he promised Charles. And he did, though halfheartedly. Takeovers were something no self-respecting lawyer would touch. Reputation was hard to come by and easy to lose. For an old friend, Archie made exceptions. He undertook the predictably futile attempt to discover the identity of the mysterious suitor; he sent a dignified letter to the shareholders urging them to have faith in the company's long-term prospects and the wisdom of its founder. All, as expected, to no avail. In a matter of months Glendale Paper was no more. Charles landed on his feet; to Archie's great surprise he'd tendered his own shares and received a substantial premium. But there would be no more dinners at the club to mark the company's achievements.

The loss of a good client was hard enough to swallow; worse was the knowledge that the killer was out there, celebrating his success, emboldening others of his kind. And emboldened they were; the number of tender offers increased. The depravity of the business world—Archie knew it well enough. It was to avoid that maelstrom of cannibalism and ruthlessness that he'd gone into the law, as a place where one could rise through wisdom rather than blind aggression, stand aside from the fray and serve some value other than mere self-regard.

What he hadn't seen was how far the depravity would spread, that the bar was corruptible in a way it hadn't been before. The unspoken understandings that had guided generations of lawyers were unraveling; the bar's attempts at self-regulation were increasingly ineffective. Then discipline was farmed out to the courts, and that, Archie thought, was the last straw. We handed our ethics to the courts, and the courts gave us back law. And who better than a lawyer to get around the law, to exploit the elasticity of a phrase, to dance along the knife edge of the permissible? That was what ethical canons had instructed them not to do, and ethics resisted casuistry—at least, the bar's Protestant ethics did. But law did not; law would never constrain lawyers in the way professional norms had. No rule of professional conduct would tell you not to participate in a hostile takeover. There was only the understanding that such things just weren't done.

And then they *were* done, even by the best firms, and the lawyers of Morgan Stevens began to wonder if they could afford to stand aside. Ridiculous, scoffed Archie. He hadn't declined the brigands' role to make himself their advisor, to do the dirty work for a profession he'd refused to enter for fear of soiling his hands. Others disagreed, and in the space of a few years the disagreements multiplied past the point of settlement.

The litigation department, now an increasing source of the firm's revenues, wanted to grow. "It's where the money is, Archie," said Fred Cox. Archie couldn't dispute the fact; nor could he see its relevance. Cox wanted to recruit more young associates; he wanted to end the practice of lending litigators to Legal Aid, which he apparently saw as Archie's method of enervating the department through controlled bleeding.

"The purpose is to purify," Archie said, immediately regretting that he'd acceded to the metaphor. But there was a point to it. Through their public service the associates were awakened to the ideals of the profession, something Archie was growing aware the law schools were not achieving; they came to see themselves as stewards of the public trust, responsible to society rather than individual clients. Cox shook his head and muttered darkly at steering committee meetings.

Nor was he alone in his complaints. The corporate department wanted litigators who specialized in mergers and acquisitions; they wanted a bankruptcy group. "It's one-stop shopping," Bill Raymond said. "If a company can't get everything it needs from us, it's going elsewhere. And it doesn't help to get a reputation for abandoning clients when they come under attack." Preposterous, Archie thought, but in this as in other matters the world was slowly proving him wrong. The rivals of Morgan Stevens were indeed growing and expanding the range of services offered; increasingly, they were adopting other innovations, allocating profits among partners based on the work they brought in, setting billable-hour targets for the associates to meet.

"It's for the good of the firm," Raymond said, and Archie could have wept with frustration. He didn't doubt his partners' sincerity. They certainly thought they were pursuing the best interests of the firm. And from their perspective, they might even have been correct. But they made a fundamental error, one that Archie would never commit, one that he could never get them to see: when they spoke of the firm, they meant the lawyers. Archie wished his partners well, and of course he had a proper regard for his own financial success. But his loyalty, his love, belonged not to the individuals but to the benign, immortal abstraction he'd birthed, and the idea that they could make more money by changing its nature was as perplexing to him, as barbaric, as if Fred Cox had stood up one day and suggested that they seriously consider getting with the times by throwing a virgin into a volcano.

They'll get over it, Archie thought, and once more he was mistaken. Had it been only their own preferences at stake, Raymond and Cox might have stood pat. They'd spent two decades doing things Archie's way, and their bank accounts attested that those had been good years. But the young partners, the rising stars whose clients and labors would bankroll the founders' golden years, were getting restless. They would be welcome at other firms. Law students raised the subject delicately in interviews. Morgan Stevens was acquiring a reputation as a firm mired in its own traditions, unable to adapt to changing business practices. Is it true, the students asked, that the firm won't work on takeovers?

The rebellion, when it came, began in the litigation department. Archie had long viewed the department as unreliable. Like a troublesome tooth, it offered hot flashes of complaint and sudden sharp pains when pressed. Had he the stomach, Archie knew, he should have drilled it clean, burned out the core, and filled it up with solid material. But he had ignored the symptoms of rot and now faced the prospect of losing the whole thing. And not just litigation. Cox and his subordinates could pack up and leave; the loss would be unpleasant, but not disfiguring. The firm would be less powerful without them, but still presentable. But the decay was widespread. The corporate group, which more than any other was the face Morgan Stevens offered the world, was also expressing concern about his leadership, about the firm's direction. And trusts and estates, the real betrayal, a department Archie had nurtured and championed even after it had ceased to pull its weight. "For the good of the firm," they said.

Archie, forced to take the matter seriously, weighed his options. He dared not raise the question directly with clients, but every indication suggested that if the firm splintered, they would not stay. He considered his scattered fiefdoms; he made office visits. Bert Stevens shook his head. "We need to compete, Archie." There would be no help from the real estate department. In the rebellious provinces, armies were forming. The lack of a partnership agreement made it hard to see how Archie could be deposed, but likewise hard to see how he could keep power. Informal caucuses formed in the hallways; straw polls were taken. At last Cox circulated a draft partnership agreement. Promotion within the firm and partner compensation were to be decided by the steering committee; other matters were subject to a majority vote of the entire partnership. The agreement itself would become effective if endorsed by two-thirds of the partners.

Archie's loyalists remained, some of them, spread across the departments: those he'd brought in early who placed that personal debt first, those who had been his imitators and still believed. For the first time in his career, Archie began to count votes.

He came up short.

He had made two mistakes, Archie thought. He hadn't seen that the corruption of the businessmen could spread to the bar, and he hadn't seen that the corruption of the bar could spread to the firm. That some lawyers would come to admire the bankers, that his own partners would admire those lawyers. And now all the bulwarks on which he'd relied were cast down; the mercenary world whose yappings he'd disdained from the security of his keep was within the walls, and he was powerless to resist.

Archie had one last card to play. The Morgan Stevens partnership track, though it varied for exceptional individuals, had historically been seven years. If Archie shrank it to five, he saw, he could immediately make up to twelve new partners, more than enough to shift the balance of power among the current twenty-three. They would be young partners, so no one could complain that the firm was in the grip of the geriatrics. And they would include Peter.

The invitations to become a member of the firm went out, as always, on Archie's letterhead. In the end, Archie selected nine of the twelve candidates, a higher percentage than usual, but not outrageous. He cut two litigators based on his estimate of where their loyalties lay, and one estate lawyer on the grounds that the department didn't have enough work to keep the existing complement busy. None of those he cut had his own clients; none was such an excellent lawyer that the passing over seemed partisan. As the invitations went out, Archie circulated to the existing partners his endorsement of the Cox agreement. And he waited.

Raymond and Cox recognized the maneuver for what it was, a last attempt to shake up the rosters before the game began. They remained confident; the economics of their position were unassailable.

Archie was hopeful. Peter shared his values; that was certain. He was not the most gregarious lawyer, but there was strength within him. He could become a leader; he could emerge as the guiding figure for his generation at the firm. He could take Morgan Stevens into the future.

Peter Morgan saw his father's letterhead and understood its significance at once. A vast contentment spread over him. All his life he had piled up achievements only to see them discounted by others. No mystery how *he* got into Harvard Law, he'd heard classmates whisper; wasn't there an Archibald Morgan Chair in Legal Ethics? Peter worked ferociously to remove any question as to whether he merited his success, to erase with the sweat of his brow the suggestion of undeserved privilege. And now he had the opportunity to settle the matter at a stroke, to clarify his relationship to the power that had long overhung his future. The old man needed him.

Peter set to the task with his accustomed energy. Time was short; the new agreement called for a general partnership meeting in three months, and Cox had let it be known that he would propose the formal creation of a bankruptcy department. Archie, in turn, had indicated that he would resign if the motion passed. Peter buttonholed the new partners in the halls; he paid respectful visits to the older ones and nodded seriously behind closed doors. What surprised him, in the end, was how easy it all was. It helped that he was tall and his expression grave; it helped that he had a deep and reassuring vertical line between his brows and a measured, sonorous voice. It helped that his name was Peter Morgan; he would admit it. But mostly it helped that he had a vision and a plan for its implementation. Really all one had to do to lead, he realized, was to act like a leader. Peter learned how easy it was to play a role, and then how easy to become the role one played.

There was no regularly scheduled business to conduct at the first partnership meeting of Morgan Stevens. The partners, assembled in a private dining room of the Metropolitan Club, ate an awkward lunch and moved immediately to the consideration of Cox's motion. Archie voted first, a firm and defiant "nay." Bankruptcy wasn't the issue; he understood that, and so did everyone else. It was a referendum on him and his leadership. Raymond and Cox voted "aye," as expected, and Stevens too. Among the preexisting partners, Archie was outvoted fourteen to nine.

Peter's cadre made up the shortfall. They supported Archie eight to one, and as the last, meaningless "nay" came down, Archie looked across the table at his son and beamed. He could have called then for Cox's resignation; perhaps he even had the votes for ouster. But Archie was not a vengeful man. He turned his smile on the rest of the room. "I've always been proud of the firm," he said. "And I'm proud of my partners too. I know we'll move forward together, as we always have."

Later, alone with Peter, he sounded a more somber note. "Legal practice is not what it was," Archie said. "We've done good work here today, but I am not sure what it is that I will eventually hand to you."

Peter Morgan allowed himself a slight smile. Hand it to me, will you? "We should think about that, Dad," he said. "We've got clients that need work done. Why shouldn't we do it for them, regardless of what it is?"

"Clients don't need work done," Archie said. "Clients need counseling. That's what we do for them."

Peter tried again. "But they do, sometimes. They get involved in litigation, or bankruptcy. Or a takeover battle. Why shouldn't we help them out?"

Archie found his pleasure dissipating. "There's work that we don't do because it's all but impossible to do it in the proper spirit. It's nasty, grabbing work. There are other firms for that sort of thing. At least there used to be."

Nasty, grabbing work, Peter thought. Give it to the Jews. Archie might as well have said it. "What was better about that, Dad?" he asked. "Was it better when the Catholics and the Jews couldn't get jobs at a place like this? When we farmed the dirty work out to them? And now we take it because it's a moneymaker, and we take them because we see we're not so different."

"Peter," said Archie sharply. "You know that's not what it's about. We hired Catholics in 1945. Ed Carroll's been a partner for twenty years. Sullivan and Cromwell took a Jewish partner in 1894, for God's sake, and they're the whitest of the white-shoe." His tone softened. "There used to be standards, Peter. That's all. There used to be standards, and now there are only rules. There used to be work that gentlemen wouldn't do. If you don't have that, how can you have gentlemen?"

Archie could see the comprehension breaking over Peter, see it in the pursed lips and slow-nodding head. At last, Archie thought, Peter understands what Morgan Stevens is. The two partners looked at each other gravely, each grasping the enormity of a different problem. We've saved this for the moment, Archie thought. But how much longer can we last?

And Peter: Things are going to have to change around here.

Change they did. The reputational overhaul was accomplished quickly; in a matter of months, the talk in the law schools and the halls of other firms took a different tone. Morgan Stevens was a *young* firm; Morgan Stevens was *aggressive*. The steering committee pushed the partnership track up to eight years; the firm hired litigation associates en masse. Archie watched, bewildered, as the coalition that had ridden to his rescue dissolved. The partners showed no awareness that they were changing sides, that sides existed at all. We're glad the divisiveness is in the past, they said. We're glad to be moving forward as one firm.

The sharp divide no longer existed, it was true. Cox's supporters had faded away just as Archie's had. Cox himself seldom spoke at partnership meetings, and the new proposals came from an array of different partners, in different departments. With no target to fix on, Archie could only sit helpless as the committees chipped away. Partners receiving bonuses for clients they'd brought in, an 1,800-billable-hour target for associates, a bankruptcy reorganization undertaken as an exception for a favored client. Flakes of paint from a frescoed wall, a new image revealing itself underneath.

A stroke felled Bill Raymond two years later. The whole Morgan Stevens partnership, now forty strong, turned out for his funeral, a custom Archie encouraged. Despite his relative youth, Peter took Raymond's place on the steering committee, and Archie was reassured. At sixty-three, he was beginning to slow down, taking longer lunches, lingering at home in the mornings. Peter would look after things.

Peter did. White linen paper went up on the walls, suitable backdrop for the museum-quality art collection assembled by a team of decorators. He commissioned a portrait of Archie for the main reception room. A reminder of where we came from, he said at the unveiling. A head on the wall, some of the other partners joked; a reminder of what happened to those who didn't see things Peter's way. Jokes of all sorts grew fewer as the years passed; crisp professionalism flowed through the corridors like a cooling, impersonal breeze. Peter did away with the custom of daily coffee hours in the library, where lawyers had gathered to share news and anecdotes; instead a firm newsletter was printed up and distributed each week. Peter had two daughters now; he'd joined the Metropolitan Club and advertised the firm with careful asides and the vigor of his person, his starched white shirts and expensive cuff links. Still he spent long hours in the office, leading by example, making constant subtle adjustments to the firm's identity. He could feel it taking shape around him.

Archie never knew, though in later years he must have suspected, what promises Peter had made behind closed doors to lock up the votes against Cox. To Archie's true believers—pitiful how few they were; Peter was almost saddened—he had vowed undying loyalty to the old man's vision. But to the others . . .

A big shakeup will disturb the clients, Peter had said. Let it come gradually. Let it come with a transition of leadership. If Archie resigns in a huff, we'll spend the next three years trying to get back our goodwill.

And they'd agreed. We'll make the vote close, Peter said. Not down-to-the-wire close—don't want to give Archie a heart attack. Close enough that he sees there's a strong movement for change. But he wins; he's happy. And then we start making the changes, slowly at first, and keep reminding him that he's won. He won't even notice for a while, and when he does, there won't be any one thing to single out and make a stand over. If he resigns a few years down the line, no one will make much of it. He's getting to that age anyway.

The end of the 1970s saw the last stages of Peter's grand design. Other firms were getting bigger; Morgan Stevens, barely topping one hundred lawyers, needed to grow. One quick gulp gave them a bankruptcy group. Peter cherry-picked the partnership rosters of other firms, plucking away Harold Fineman, a rising star at Schulman Roth, the brainy but eccentric Larry Angstrom from Jackson Rowe. He leased more floors in the K Street building and approached his ultimate target.

Samuel Siler was a man after Peter's own heart. He'd built Siler & Associates from scratch, creating a highly profitable mergers and acquisitions boutique unique in the D.C. legal community. But he was getting on in years, almost Archie's age, and no established leader in his firm stood ready to take his place.

They met in the Metropolitan Club. Siler was not a member, and Peter felt that this set the appropriate tone. "It's a merger of equals," he said. "We have the greatest respect for what you've created. And of course that will be reflected in the name."

Siler was beyond flattery. More, he recognized a kindred spirit. Peter wanted his clients, his reputation, his corps of disciplined specialists. All those assets increased in value when tied to the Siler name; Peter was doing him no favors. What he did offer was the greater revenues of a larger firm, a substantial increase in income during the twilight of a career. "Really," he said, "what are you proposing?"

Peter lowered his voice to a confidential whisper. "Raymond is dead," he said. "Stevens is irrelevant. Morgan, Siler, and Cox. I've got to keep the old man's name first. I couldn't look him in the eye otherwise."

Siler was amused. "Come on, Peter. That's your name."

Peter shrugged. The thought had occurred to him.

Archie, when news of the merger broke, took the same perspective. But he was getting old enough to be philosophical. It had been hard to watch his firm change around him; in a way, this was a relief. Morgan Stevens was dead; long live Morgan Siler. "Well, my boy," he said, "you've made your own place in the world. May you have better luck with it than I did."

Peter Morgan stretched in front of a full-length mirror in his bedroom. Not too bad, he thought. He was wearing khaki pants and a carefully pressed shirt of midnight-blue linen. Business casual would arrive at Morgan Siler over his dead pin-striped body, but this was a uniform appropriate to the occasion. The vision the party offered the associates was what their lives might be like as partners, and part of that vision was the promise that they need not live in suits. Downstairs, white-shirted servitors passed with calm efficiency through the rooms of his house, bearing trays of tuna carpaccio, miniature crab cakes, and other exotic canapés. His daughter Julie, just out of law school and working at a public interest advocacy job in New York, had returned for a few days to show the guests what had happened to the adorable child in the tasteful photographs displayed on mantel and bureau.

The party was expensive. The hors d'oeuvres and dinner ran fifty dollars a person, the full bar thirty-five; each hour of service by the caterers and waitstaff cost thirty. That fee was almost laughable to a lawyer, when even the lowliest associate billed out at over a hundred an hour. Still, there were twelve of them swarming through the house—Cassandra always seemed dismayed at the way they took over the kitchen, sneering at her flatware—and it would add up. A raw bar, flowers, and valet parking upped the ante even more. But the cost was justified. There was a reason the firm went to the trouble and expense, a reason Peter allowed the use of his Georgetown house, a reason the associates would eventually be invited to see the art collection on the upper floors, taken a few at a time up the narrow stairs to rooms of greater opulence. Keep climbing; a dazzling reward awaits.

Peter Morgan nodded at his reflection. He had climbed, and he had been rewarded. He had worked hard all his life, and his accession to power following Raymond's death did not change that basic trait. If anything, he worked harder. Now the firm was his, and he was working for himself, creating a world that would bear his impress long years after he was gone.

For Morgan Siler, the issue of the 1980s was the competition from the investment banks. Archie had always dismissed the banks, scorned them as dishonorable. Law rules business, he would say, and for that reason lawyers cannot serve businessmen blindly. Peter could rattle off the maxims by heart. *Law is a helping profession, not a facilitating one. The greatest problem is that no one says no anymore. We have to maintain our standards.*

For years Peter had been baffled by these opinions, but he was beginning to understand them. It was becoming increasingly clear to him that what some called honor and probity were second-place prizes, offered to those who could not grasp power. Worse, they were distractions, lures set about the path to success. The weak resented the strong, and called them dishonorable. The weak feared the strong, and tried to tempt them from their strength. Archie had been taken in, taught to despise his potential by those who could not match it. But Peter was undeceived. He admired the bankers, and he had no qualms about working for them. What concerned him was that they made more money than lawyers.

The salary differential drew promising undergraduates into business school; it even drew law school graduates away from the firms. And it undermined his sense of self-worth, for he had decided early that the only true measure of value is what others are willing to pay. That was the only objective metric, the only fact that others could not deny. To maintain the firm's elite status, to maintain Peter's own place in the world, Morgan Siler had to pay more.

Peter reviewed its structure with penetrating eyes. Associates were paid an annual salary, but the firm sold their services by the hour. The key, then, was getting the maximum number of hours out of each associate. There were things other than work in the lives of associates, things that distracted them from the production of hours. Peter swiftly reached two conclusions. It was profitable to have other people do these things for associates whenever possible. And if the associates had to do them, it was profitable to have them do so at the firm.

The secretarial staff expanded to four shifts, supplemented by teams of paralegals, ensuring that assistance was available at every hour. The copy center hummed through the night, a constant rolling thunder; the doors were removed from the library to make plain that it never closed. The firm added a fitness center, a laundry service, a florist, lunch and dinner delivery. It brought doctors, dentists, and financial advisors to the associates' offices; it kept messengers on hand to deliver apologies for broken dates, and drivers to pick the kids up from school. It filled prescriptions, bought groceries, returned videotapes, fed cats, and walked dogs. Rumors spread through the law schools. Morgan Siler would provide a stand-in for jury duty, for your cousin's wedding, for your own. Morgan Siler would provide a roll-away bed for lawyers working through the night. The last made its way back to the firm when a visiting student dared to seek verification. Peter cocked his head, puzzled. "Of course not," he said. "If you're working all night, you don't need a bed." Later he reconsidered, and the Morgan Hotel was born.

But maximizing the individual associates' hours was only part of the answer. Archie's firm had retained a rough balance between the numbers of partners and associates. Peter's acquired a pyramid structure, an army of young associates whose ranks thinned as the years went by, a small cadre of partners who were there for the long haul. No partner, he was proud to report, had ever left his firm for another.

The associates did leave. They left in droves, every year, but every year a new crop came in to fill the gaps. That was as it should be. More associates meant more hours, and more hours meant more money. More profits to be divided among the partners, and more money for associate salaries, in return for which the firm could demand more hours. The formula was simple enough once you saw it. Raise associate salaries and jack up their hours; recruit more to replace the ones who leave. He could push the associates, Peter Morgan realized; he could work them as hard as he wanted. Half of them came in telling themselves that they didn't want to make partner anyway, that they were just there for the experience, and they were surprisingly ready to confuse experience with suffering. Work them hard enough and they would burn out before they ever had to be fired.

Now Peter had the manpower for the biggest deals. He moved the firm aggressively into merger work, studying the latest devices in the battle for corporate control, the technical innovations of the continual arms race between raiders and their targets. He knew he'd succeeded when companies started keeping Morgan Siler on retainer to prevent their opponents from hiring the firm.

Archie retired in 1986, ready at seventy-four to put the law behind him. In his last years he'd spent most of his time talking to associates, wandering from office to office looking for the young men who'd admired him so. Peter's hires stacked books on their chairs to discourage him from taking a seat. Only when they'd decided to leave did they have time for conversation. Archie gleaned what he could of the new world. "You've kept the spirit alive, my boy," he told Peter. "I was talking to this young fellow who's going to the District Attorney's Office. He said he was looking forward to the new job, but he felt bad leaving his soulmates behind." Peter smiled and nodded. He didn't have the heart to correct the old man, but he knew that associate, and he was fairly sure the word had been "cellmates."

Morgan Siler became an immensely profitable firm. Peter's compensation passed the point at which it could be called ample. Still he drove himself hard, acquiring just enough gray hair to prove he wasn't dyeing it. And still he felt twinges of inadequacy when he read about the bankers and the arbitrageurs. In a way, he thought, he had inherited his father's fixation.

Then law exacted its revenge on banking. Rudy Giuliani and the SEC took out the princes of Wall Street with the ruthless zeal of a Mafia hit. Boesky and Milken went to jail; the takeover shops closed. Law stepped further into the world of finance, with Morgan Siler and Wallace Finn leading the way. Junk bonds, Milken's great dream, had been a way of providing access to the capital markets for less established companies, of letting them borrow even if they were poor credit risks. Securitization achieved the same end, but it was law through and through, intellect over economics.

Peter Morgan savored his triumph briefly, one eye always open for the new challengers. In the nineties they came again, this time in the form of the tech companies. Once more rivals siphoned off legal talent, exerted upward pressure on associate salaries. Worse, law firms started relaxing their dress codes to match the upstarts. Morgan Siler offered more money but refused to bend on the suits.

Technology suffused the firms. Computerized research became the norm. The library still had no doors, but now the desks and tables stood empty, where once harried associates had pored over treatises and case reporters. Peter snorted at the claims of increased productivity. He had devoted years to fine-tuning the work environment. The associates might be quicker at looking up cases, but they weren't billing any more hours.

Peter hated the tech companies and he was glad to see them die. The economic downturn hurt the corporate and finance practice groups, but litigation chugged steadily along. Worse times for business meant more things going wrong, more lawsuits. Suits against the failed Internet companies, in particular; suits against the brokers who'd recommended their stock. Once again, law was wreaking its vengeance on the pretenders. And bankruptcy was booming. Morgan Stevens would have staggered, but Morgan Siler thrived. Law was winning, as it had before, as it always would.

Peter Morgan smoothed the front of his shirt and buttoned his cuffs. He was too restrained to smile at himself in the mirror, but he caught the eye of his reflection and winked. I know what you're thinking.

Mark Clayton was furious. He'd driven back to D.C. that afternoon, ignoring a message from Anne Brownlee at the Capital Defenders Office. At the firm he'd found messages he couldn't ignore, from a partner named Lawrence Angstrom wanting to know where he was on the interrogatories he'd been drafting. Mark had been doing no such thing; as he'd explained to Angstrom when the assignment first floated his way, the trip to Virginia had filled his schedule to the point that he couldn't take on more work. "That's fine," Angstrom had said soothingly, meaning, as it now turned out, that it would be fine for Mark to write the interrogatories anyway.

The case was a medical malpractice suit, and Mark was supposed to be writing questions to be submitted to the plaintiff. These were designed to elicit damaging admissions, but since they would be answered by the plaintiff's lawyer, this was unlikely. Instead they would get back a large number of unexplained denials and an equal number of assertions that their client was concealing the information necessary to answer the questions. Mark had done the work hastily, struggling to identify the key issues in the complaint. *Who are the medical practitioners (name, ad-*

dress, and telephone number) with whom you consulted subsequent to your treatment by Doctor Vogel? he had written. *What diagnoses did you receive? Which, if any, medical report a) suggested any present medical complaint is related to the liposuction performed by Doctor Vogel; b) suggested that any treatment is indicated for any present medical complaint; or c) suggested that any aspect of Doctor Vogel's treatment failed to conform to prevailing standards of professional medical care?*

At six o'clock, Angstrom had stopped by his office, toting a copiously annotated copy of Mark's questions. "I made some comments on these," he said.

"Okay," Mark answered. He extended his hand for the papers.

Angstrom pulled them away. "But maybe it's not really worth it to go through them one by one. Could you redraft the whole thing with more of an emphasis on assumption of risk? I know it's kind of a fire drill, but it would be good if we could get these whipped into shape for tomorrow."

Mark wondered whether an explosion of physical violence would adequately convey his sentiments about this proposal. "Okay," he said.

"Hope to see you at Peter's," said Angstrom, loping off.

Did you sign the medical release form provided to you by Doctor Vogel? Mark wrote. *Did you read the medical release form?* Do you think you're making Doctor Vogel suffer for your botched cosmetic surgery? Do you realize he has malpractice insurance? Do you know that the insurance company has a duty to defend this claim? Do you know which law firm the insurance company employs? Do you know who ends up spending his nights writing these inane and pointless questions to inflate the bill submitted to the insurance company? What did I ever do to you? Can't we all get along? Why me, why me, why me?

"Is something wrong?" Katja asked.

Mark lifted his head from the desk in surprise. If crying for no apparent reason counts as something wrong, he thought, then yes. But his innate optimism reasserted itself. After all, hadn't he plenty of reasons to cry? There was his professional incompetence, which seemed only to be increasing with each new challenge. There was the impossibility of finding more than a few hours a night to sleep, and the growing inability to sleep even when the hours presented themselves. There was the tightness in the back of his throat, like the beginning of a cold or the intimation of nausea, which at first had come on only when he talked to partners but was now so constant he almost didn't notice it. There was the chronic and unexplained pain in the small of his back, near what he supposed was his liver, or a kidney, or some other vital internal organ. Those would justify buckets. And the weepiness hadn't hampered him in his work. Usually he found that he could talk to someone else for ten minutes or so before the tears started, and most conversations didn't last that long. Soon, surely, it would all be over. People didn't just go on and on in jobs that made them feel this way. This was a painful apprenticeship, a distasteful learning experience, but soon it would be over and his real life would start. The real life in which he . . . did something else. As usual, it was at this point that Mark's imagination failed him. "No," he said. "Nothing's wrong."

Katja frowned and inclined her head. "I was just heading out to the associate dinner," she said. "I wanted to check if you were going."

"What?" Mark asked. Katja stood in the hallway, one slender hand on the door frame, a tangible suggestion of the alternative worlds that existed outside his office. Worlds he might someday encounter, if he could simply get up and walk over to them. It didn't seem that should be so hard. But student loans bound him to the job, and within the job, assignments bound him to his desk. "Oh, yeah," he said, striving for a casual tone. "I might make it. I have some stuff to get finished here."

"Okay," said Katja. She lingered for a moment in the doorway. "Well, hope to see you there."

Mark nodded. I'm paralyzed, he thought. When he looked in the mirror these days he was always shocked at how young he appeared. In part this was a consequence of spending so much time with middle-aged lawyers, who now set his expectation of what people looked like. But more, it was the psychological effects of the job, the feeling he'd been there for an eternity already. The physical effects could not be far behind. Mark had learned the distinctive physiognomies of the law firm: the solid litigators, big in the shoulders and the belly; the corporate types, who had only the belly; the tax attorneys, rail-thin and burning with intellect. He would become one of them, if he lasted long enough. He wrote out another interrogatory. *Did anyone explain to you the risks inherent in the surgery you elected?* Did you know what you were getting yourself into? Well, I didn't either.

Disdaining the doorbell, Walker Eliot let fall the brass knocker. He smiled generously as the door opened before him, and stepped into the foyer. "Nice," he said appreciatively. The dinner was meant to be impressive, a demonstration to the young associates of what they were working for, what could be theirs. To Walker it was old hat. The firms had shown him everything they could during the recruiting phase, and when you go all the way in the courtship, there's not much room left for surprise. He had taken advantage of them; he was the first to admit it. All his fellow Supreme Court clerks had received similar attention, but he enjoyed it the most, flirting with the firms, pirouetting from event to event. His lunches cost a hundred dollars, his dinners triple that. Still they crowded around; he ate out four nights a week, sometimes five, ordering caviar canapés and hundred-dollar bottles of wine.

The firms accepted this, absorbing the costs with their recruiting budgets. Things would be different, they knew, once he was theirs. There had been a lot of suitors, each with their distinct personality, their selling points. Straus and Ellman, an old and established firm, with a quiet self-confidence suggesting that they didn't need to pursue him, that of course he'd conclude there was no better place. That had almost done it for Walker, the restrained dignity of the partners, the refined grace of the single terminal *s*. Shaw, Morrison, and Blocker, a little insecure, willing to spend more on the dinners, eager to talk about how much he'd make. They'd had no chance. Belknap and Woods, talking down their past conquests to make him feel special: Of course most of the associates won't make partner. We're highly leveraged. But that makes it exceptionally profitable for those who do. And you, of course, you're just the kind of lawyer we're looking for. Sweatshop, Walker thought. And Sullivan Post, the firm where Walker had spent the summer after his second year, like a childhood sweetheart, reminding him of their innocent past. "We still use that memo you wrote about piercing the corporate veil," an associate told him. Juvenilia, thought Walker, youthful love poems, initials carved in an oak. I never promised you I'd come back. He was a Supreme Court clerk now, and prices had gone up. Walker smiled his radiant winner's smile. You can buy my time, he thought. You can have my body. But you will never touch my soul.

"Walker, isn't it?" said Peter Morgan, stepping across the foyer to greet him. "Glad you could make it. I'm hearing great things about the work you're doing. We're very happy you decided to join us."

"Thanks," said Walker. He smiled faintly. He'd settled on Morgan Siler fairly quickly, much more quickly than he'd let on. They were doing well; they had smart lawyers and an interesting caseload; and, most important, they gave him the impression that they'd leave him alone. Reaching a decision had not stopped him from dining with other firms, nor from taking more meals with Morgan Siler to work out the precise details of their offer.

Somewhere in the third week of his protracted negotiations with the firm, he'd met the man himself, lunch at a downtown power restaurant, other diners coming over to the table to shake Peter's hand as if he were a mob boss or the Pope. There were three partners and one associate waiting for Walker when he arrived. A nice gesture, he thought, calculating the intensity of their desire. The lunch would cost the firm a couple of thousand dollars in lost billing time just to start with. Not quite that much, as it turned out. Justice Arlen was out of town, and Walker's casual dress didn't meet the restaurant's requirements. At a nod from one of the partners, the associate surrendered his suit jacket and tie and went back to work.

"Order whatever you want," Peter Morgan said, and Walker felt a sudden echoing unease. He'd had a sledding accident as a child, steered his Flexible Flyer into a car and opened a deep cut beside his right eye. His mother had taken him to the hospital for stitches and afterward, shaking with relief and what might have been, told him he could have whatever he wanted for dinner. Walker, who'd received a home-cooked meal every night of his life, could think of nothing more exotic than a Hungry Man TV dinner.

Walker looked around the restaurant, the white-damasked tables, the dark-paneled walls, the golden bottles arrayed behind the bar. "Whatever you want," he said to himself softly. How cheaply purchased, he thought, how infinitely dear, are the dreams of childhood. Now he heard those words from lawyers, and his tastes were more expensive. What bright unreal path has led me here? "Let me take a look at their whiskies," he answered.

Can he possibly be worth it? Peter Morgan asked himself, following Walker's appreciative eyes around the polished splendor of his house. He could tell already that Walker wasn't a biller. Not for him the dusty hours in the mine, laboring under an invisible whip, hacking the stubborn earth, and sending nuggets of gold to the world above. That was where the money lay. Time, so elusive, was the ultimate currency. And what Peter Morgan sold his clients was his employees' lives.

Walker offered little from that perspective. Some of the clerks did; those who'd made it through dogged determination and were too used to hard work to rest on their laurels. But Walker wasn't that sort, and the firm would be lucky if it made even a small profit on his hours. Even that was a loss, from the proper perspective. Someone else could be filling up that office, someone from a second-tier law school, hungry and with something to prove. But clients liked hearing that there were Supreme Court clerks working on their cases, and it was worth some money to make the client happy. And possibly, Peter allowed, Walker was good enough that he could make a difference somewhere. That too made clients happy. The firm didn't reap the full benefits from winning cases it should have lost; clients didn't usually understand enough to know what should happen with their cases. But they liked winning, and it was possible that Walker would let the firm give them a few more wins than they'd have had otherwise.

Walker wasn't a first-year; he'd come in as a lateral hire, which was also a good thing. It meant that they could bill him out at a higher rate and wouldn't have to spend so much time teaching him law. The partners complained regularly in meetings about associates who'd learned nothing in law school. Peter Morgan let them grumble. The students hadn't been taught the rules, not at the top-tier schools, but they'd been prepared for the firm. They'd been taught the value system, and not to question it. They had learned hierarchy. Courts above courts in an ascending chain of being, infallible at the top simply because no further appeal existed. And likewise at the firm, the senior associates over the junior ones, then the partners, and then Peter Morgan above them all.

This was the service the law schools gave, witting or no, that they taught their students to follow authority and to believe in a legal reasoning that supplanted their intuitions about justice. To use that reasoning in the service of any cause, to argue for positions they despised, which had the inevitable result of cutting them loose from the positions they loved. Act and it shall produce unbelief. The firms provided the training; the firms taught the law. Law school just made students ready to accept it.

"Come out back," said Peter, placing a hand on Walker's shoulder. "The oysters are marvelous." Together they crossed the marble floor toward the garden.

Sipping a glass of chardonnay, Harold Fineman watched the caterers grill. There were five of them, turning steaks of tuna and sirloin, faces flushed with heat. Harold felt the warmth of alcohol rising to his cheeks, the wine loosening and releasing something within him. He didn't usually waste his time on the firm's window dressing, but tonight he felt he deserved it. Getting shredded in court was a draining experience. Whatever you might think privately of the position you argue, having it ripped to pieces and thrown back in your face couldn't be called fun. A few paces away stood Katja.

Peter Morgan drew them together with an expansive gesture. "Katja," he said. "I hear you've decided to leave litigation for corporate." Someone's been doing his homework, thought Harold. "Corporate work gives you a lot of opportunity for creative planning. Litigation is more cleaning up the mess when the plans don't work. But it does bring you face-to-face with some of the interesting policy issues about regulation and loss allocation."

"It does?" asked Katja. "I can't really say that was my experience." She looked about for succor. At the bar she saw Walker, offering an impromptu lecture on the merits of various single malts, and Ryan Grady. Ryan caught her eye and smiled. He asked the bartender for a second gin and tonic.

"Of course it does," Peter Morgan continued. "Look at this case in Texas that Harold's working on. It's all about who should pay for dangerous products. You could impose tort liability on the manufacturers. But then they'll have to internalize that cost. The product will cost more, and some people won't be able to buy it. If you don't make the manufacturers pay, they charge less, and people can use the money they save to buy insurance. And they know much better than the manufacturer whether that's worth it to them. They know about their tolerance for risk, and the scale of the risks they run, and how much insurance they need if something happens. Right?"

Lots of homework, Harold thought. "Of course," he said, "you could also say that it's about a bunch of people who got killed because someone was careless. And they were just people who happened to be in the wrong place at the wrong time. They weren't purchasers. They couldn't insure themselves."

Peter Morgan frowned. "Certainly they could. They'd just be insuring against a slightly different risk. And you have the same question about whether the company should have to pay higher salaries, in which case it would employ fewer people, or whether the employees should insure themselves against the risks of the job." He paused. "But I don't suppose I need to tell you your case."

"No," said Harold. "I don't suppose you do."

For a moment they locked eyes. A young man approached, a drink in each hand. With a nod, Peter Morgan took one and walked away. "What the hell?" said Ryan Grady.

Ryan went to as many firm events as he could. Like riding up and down in the elevators or walking the halls, it increased his visibility. And that, he'd thought, was surely a good thing. Now, however, it was occurring to him that perhaps it was important not merely to be seen but also to make the right impression. He sipped the remaining drink. "Damn, I've been busy," he said. Another thought struck, and he handed the glass to Katja. "Got this for you."

"Thanks," said Katja, seeming unsure what to do with it.

"Don't mind him," said Harold. "I think he's under stress."

"Yeah," Ryan mumbled. "Well, like I said, I've been awful busy."

"I meant Peter. The firm's got a lot going on."

Don't we all, thought Ryan, looking down. The discovery that he wasn't allowed to date paralegals, coupled with a string of embarrassing setbacks in Georgetown bars, had inspired him to seek professional help. He had always engaged in what some called the reading of those publications known as men's magazines. But now the enthusiasm went beyond euphemism. Real magazines, real reading, a real search for answers. At the Safeway near his apartment he'd collected a glossy sheaf. The covers promised revelation: ninety-seven ways to pick up women; a sexual aptitude test; a special section auspiciously entitled "Project Love Machine." The checkout clerk smiled at him. "Heavy reading, huh?" Ryan nodded seriously, fishing change out of his pocket. Back in his apartment he had begun a course of intensive research, and given the volume of literature available, he found it took most of his free hours just to stay current. Indeed, he frequently found himself skipping over the difficult or unpromising articles.

But that was nothing to be ashamed of, he thought, turning his eyes back up toward Katja. He was taking more direct paths. Just now, for instance, he had given a drink to an attractive girl, and surely that counted for something. It was one small step toward making her grateful or drunk, either of which would be progress.

Katja poured a small quantity of the drink into the grass. By virtue of their silence, the three attracted Walker and Wallace Finn, for opposite reasons.

"Good stuff here," said Walker. "Not the usual twelve-year-olds. They've got the fifteens, the eighteens." What a pervert, thought Ryan, impressed. He too had been checking out the caterers. "There's a real difference those extra years make," Walker continued conversationally. "They get a lot smoother." He took a sip and glanced around.

"And legal too," said Ryan sagely. He looked more closely at Walker, noticing the texture of his jacket, the thickness of the buttons on his shirt, the bulky authority of his watch. Dimly remembered images swam through his mind; approving voices echoed in his head. This was someone from whom things could be learned.

Walker hesitated, then forged ahead. "It's really the sherry casks that do it. Some people will tell you that sherry dominates the Macallan, but to my mind they underestimate the strength of Speyside peat."

Katja took advantage of the pause that followed. "How did you get into law?" she asked Wallace.

Wallace started, then recovered. "When I was a boy growing up in Brooklyn," he said, "my parents gave me twenty-five cents for lunch each day. I used to go around the corner from my school. One day there was another boy waiting for me. He was older, about eight or nine. He took my money, but apologetically. He needed to buy medicine, he explained, for his sick mother, and if I returned to the same spot at the same time the next day, he'd pay me back."

"Did you?"

"I did. And he robbed me again. The experience stayed with me. It suggested the need for wise advice. For lawyers as counselors, as statesmen mediating between clients. I know it isn't like that now. You spend more time in the library; you don't see the clients. You work a hundred hours a week until you make partner."

Law's still like that, thought Ryan. You take the client's money and get him to come back and give you more.

"It's become industrialized," Walker said. "I get the impression Peter Morgan wants to put us on an assembly line. He thinks he's the second coming of Henry Ford."

Wallace nodded. "I suppose you have to take it on faith when I say things were different in the old days. Too many to remember now. That's something else that goes."

"Your memory?" asked Ryan.

Wallace nodded again, caught himself, and frowned. "No," he said, "I meant time. Time is what goes, and it's what takes away. Time gives nothing back, and even after you've lost the will to acquire things, it hungers strong as ever to take them from you." He looked into his glass. "Forgive an old man his ramblings. I think dinner's ready."

At the grill, caterers piled food onto the guests' plates. "Have a steak," said Peter Morgan, overseeing the operation. Only Walker accepted. "Vegetarian again, Harold?" Peter asked.

"What you've got there is the only thing that can stop a litigator," Harold answered, forcing good humor. "A steak to the heart." He struck his chest.

"Oh, come on. I remember you with the Cattlemen's Association. Nothing but Black Angus."

"For a two-million-dollar-a-year client," said Harold stiffly, "I'll make an exception."

"And you only eat organic vegetables too, isn't that right? When did that start? Right after we helped out the pesticide producers with their spot of trouble in front of the FDA?" Harold's face reddened to match his hair. He walked away with small, precise steps, and Katja, watching, could almost see the narrow wire beneath his feet, the formless space below.

"So this guy who's interviewing me," said Walker. "Some young partner. 'You get responsibility quickly here,' he says." He gestured and paced as he talked. A clicking noise accompanied his steps. "'You get to take depositions very early.' Like I want to take a deposition."

"You don't?" Katja asked.

"Why would I?"

Katja shrugged. "Sometimes I wonder why anyone would want to do any of it. What's that noise?"

I make diamonds, Walker thought, deciding against voicing this particular insight. I'm not here to mine the coal. Katja's expression reminded him that she had asked a question. "Oh, yeah," he said. "Check this out." He lifted one foot. Just a few weeks after buying the new shoes, he could see signs of wear on the heel. These ones that were supposed to last the rest of his life. The cobbler at Union Station was sympathetic.

"These are really driving loafers, sir. You're not supposed to do much walking in them."

"But what if I want to? There's something you can do to them, right? I mean, these are very good shoes."

"I can give you a heel plate." The man turned and took down a plastic crescent from the wall.

Plastic, eh? thought Walker. I can see where this is going. Planned obsolescence, just like toothbrushes. He gestured to another product on the wall. "What about those metal ones?"

"The taps?"

"They won't wear out so fast, will they?"

The salesman looked at him as though he were a new species of plant or animal. "No, sir. The taps will not wear out."

"Yeah, give me some of those."

"Do you want the toes put on too?"

"Does that cost more?"

"The taps come as a set, sir."

"So I got them all done," Walker announced proudly. "These are going to last forever."

Katja frowned. "Are those even men's shoes?" she asked, happy to see relief arriving in the form of Gerald Roth.

Walker fell silent, considering. "It's a full leather lining," he began.

"Hey," Gerald interrupted. "Any news on Harper?"

Walker looked uncomfortable. "Mark was doing some interviews. And he had an argument down there this afternoon. I helped him prepare; I'm sure it went okay."

"You haven't talked to him?"

"I'm trying to give him breathing room," Walker said. "Let him take on responsibility. That's the point of pro bono, isn't it?"

Gerald's gaze sharpened, assessing Walker's bright eyes, his confident smile. And a shadow that played across his face, a blankness to the features in repose, banished by the smile and then returning. "Aren't you curious?" he asked. "Why there was no psychiatric expert? What happened in the trial?"

"It's not really my thing," Walker said. "I got enough of death work at the Court."

Gerald nodded. "Sure," he said. "You know how it works. So you're not a fan of the death penalty. That should make you want this case."

"That's not exactly it," said Walker. He turned his head away as footsteps approached.

"What's got you so serious?" Peter Morgan asked. For the second time that evening, he put his hand on Walker's shoulder, possessive, almost familial.

"We were just talking about this pro bono case."

"Pro bono?" Peter Morgan sighed. That was not what the Supreme Court clerk bonus was supposed to buy. "You're smarter than that. A good legal claim is worth money. Anyone who has one can at least get a contingency-fee lawyer. What's left over isn't anything you'd want to spend time on. It's only common sense."

"Not a lot of money in getting someone off death row, though," Gerald said.

Peter Morgan looked at him as though noticing his presence for the first time. "Not for us, certainly. When you do pro bono work, it costs the firm money. If you're a partner and you're sharing profits, maybe you can make that decision responsibly. If you're an associate on a salary, I have to say that attitude strikes me as a little selfish."

Gerald's face shifted, retreating behind his beard. "Just thinking out loud," he said. "I'm not doing any myself." He turned to Walker. "Do you know where Mark is?"

Walker shrugged. "Don't think he's here yet."

"Perhaps I'll go look for him," Gerald said.

Dinner was over by the time Mark arrived. Though the circumstances justified a taxi, he'd elected to walk. This decision, coupled with his imperfect knowledge of the geography of Washington, had delayed his arrival to some extent, but the primary blame lay with Larry Angstrom. That was what the law called an unredressable injury, *damnum absque injuria*: hurt without the possibility of cure.

Cassandra Morgan answered the door. At one point, Mark thought, she had probably fit the definition of a trophy wife, but Peter had accumulated his trophies early, and now she was a kindly woman in her midfifties, still attractive but looking tired around the eyes. So do I, I'm sure, Mark thought. "I hope you weren't working this late," she said.

There was what sounded like real concern in her voice, and it gave Mark pause. "I took a while to get here," he said apologetically.

"I'm sure there's some food left," she said. "The caterers really outdid themselves."

"It's okay," said Mark. "I already ate." This was more or less true. Facing the exigency of Angstrom's deadline and his own desire to make it to the party before Katja left, he had slaked his hunger with a goodly portion of the jar of peanut butter kept in a desk drawer for just such occasions.

A glance around the house suggested that better alternatives existed, that they were enjoyed by some on a regular basis. This was another world, opening itself to him again briefly as it had that summer on Nantucket. The community of the rich, of the beautiful; a foreign nation with its own customs and idiom.

"You should at least have a taste," Cassandra said. Why is she hanging around the front hall? Mark wondered. The hovering benevolence brought to mind his own mother, who also urged him to eat more. She collected vintage teacups, a pride in material possession that Mark could understand. Hold fast to what in life is scarce. But what could these people hunger for? More of the same, apparently. Through the glass doors of the patio he caught sight of a group of associates and headed out to join them.

"So you made it," Katja said as Mark took a seat at the table. "What were you doing?"

"Nothing," he said. "I look back at the end of the day, and I try to figure out how I've spent the hours, who I'm going to charge for them, what I've accomplished. It's nothing. And these are the years that are supposed to be such good experience."

"I know what you mean," said Katja. "All the time I ask myself what I've been learning. Is practicing law supposed to prepare you for something, the way people get dogs to practice for having children? I have a plant, but it's not doing so well. It seems to have acquired yellow spots. It makes me think I have no business with children. What would I do if they started to wilt? Or got yellow spots? Dogs, even. What would you do if your dog got yellow spots on it?"

"Shoot it," said Walker. He drained his glass and walked away.

"I've learned stuff," Ryan offered casually.

"What?" Katja asked.

"How to manage time. This billing thing is pretty easy once you figure it out."

"Really?"

"Yeah. We have to bill in fifteen-minute increments, right? So what you do— Oh, hang on a second." He fell silent as Julie Morgan passed by, then rose to his feet. "You know what, I think I'll get another drink before they close the bar."

"What do you think he was going to say?" Katja asked.

"I have an idea," said Mark. He found an unexpected smile rising to his lips. Katja's face was lightly flushed with the heat and the wine; a faint dew of perspiration glowed at her hairline. "It's really quite clever," he said. He lowered his voice, suggesting intimacy. Katja leaned in toward him, likewise. He was acutely conscious of her shoulder touching his.

"Mark, buddy," said Larry Angstrom, arriving. "Glad you could make it. Those interrogatories didn't hold you up too long, did they?"

"I got them done," Mark said carefully.

"That's good. We're going to need them next week."

"Next week?"

"Yeah. Well, I didn't want you to spend too long on them. And I remember from when I was an associate, you always work better with a deadline." He winked and raised an empty glass. "Drink? All set? Okay."

You motherfucker, said Mark Clayton to himself, eyeing Angstrom's receding back.

"Watch your mouth," said Katja, and smiled.

In the kitchen, Cassandra Morgan surveyed the chaos professionalism had wrought. Most of the dishes belonged to the caterers and would be borne away with them at the end of the evening; what was left would be tidied by a maid. She had preferred it, though, when they'd entertained more personally. When Peter was still a young partner, building alliances, there had been dinner parties, and she had cooked and sat at table and they'd talked for hours while dishes soaked in the sink. Now it was a cyclone of caterers through the house, lawyers ambling with plates of food and drinks in hand. Halfheartedly she rinsed a wineglass she recognized as her own and set it on the counter, glancing into the dining room.

A hunched figure was walking slowly around the empty room. Curiosity lit Cassandra's eyes. Wallace the wizard. That was what Peter had called him. She had wondered about him, this man they said was rewriting all the rules, changing the world with the power of his mind. Then, of course, she'd heard of his decline, and the way he looked now suggested the magic was long gone. Wallace paced aimlessly, trailing his fingers over the backs of the chairs. She saw his expression perk up at the approach of footsteps, and the hope drain from his face as a caterer hurried brusquely past. Turning back to the sideboard, he elbowed a decorative vase and stilled its tremble with gentle hands. He's careful of objects, Cassandra thought. It seemed a mark of kindness. But Peter was like that too; perhaps you simply couldn't tell these things until later.

Julie Morgan had grown up in Washington, D.C., and felt she knew it pretty well. It was, admittedly, different to be there when you were over twenty-one and didn't have to rely on borrowing your friends' older sisters' licenses to get into bars. Likewise, it was different to see the city with someone who hadn't grown up there, who brought a fresh perspective and could almost offer you a new city, seen through a new set of eyes. Yet neither of these reasons, nor any one of several others pressed upon her in the study by the oddly persistent Ryan Grady, seemed sufficiently compelling for her to accompany him on a tour of the urban nightspots. "I don't think I should go out," she said. "I'm only in town for a couple of days, and I haven't really had a chance to talk to my mom yet."

"Oh, come on," said Ryan. "She'll understand. Tell her I just graduated from Harvard Law School." This wasn't true, but it had worked for him in the past. Impressive lies could be effective, he had learned, if uttered with sufficient confidence. They were difficult to maintain, and the practice required a good memory, but they were well suited to the one-time conquest.

Julie Morgan had had enough. "Okay, we'll tell her. But let me tell you something first. I just graduated from Yale Law School, and I'm not going anywhere with you."

Ryan cast about in vain for rebuttal. If anything in the magazines explained how to deal with this situation, he had yet to discover it. Peter Morgan's arrival saved him from the need to formulate a response; instead he pointed at his empty glass and headed for the bar.

Peter slipped an arm around Julie's shoulder and kissed the top of her head. She squeezed his thumb in response, an idiosyncratic intimacy that undid him as always. "It's nice to have you back, kiddo," he said.

Julie smiled at him. "Good to see you too." Peter watched the creases by her eyes linger after the smile faded. A stab of pain went through him, a parental presentiment of loss. This was his child no longer, entering a world from which he could not shield her. Adulthood had enfolded him like a cloak, bringing with it power, direction, clarity. What for Julie? Agonizing choices. Women had it harder. She seemed untroubled, dithering with dopey leftist boyfriends and public interest law. Peter did not criticize. He shook the hands that touched her, feeling the weakness in their grip; he feigned an interest in her work. He wanted only her happiness, fearing she underestimated the challenges time held in store. Fearing she'd wake one day dissatisfied and realize it was too late.

Over Julie's shoulder he glimpsed Cassandra, and another pang passed through him. A smaller one, which he quelled. He'd offered her a life, and she had taken it. He had been honest about the life it was; her happiness was not his responsibility.

Cassandra came into the study, touching Peter and Julie. "It looks like most of your guests have left. I'd say it was a successful evening."

"Right," said Peter. "Another success."

Capitol Hill was not the nicest neighborhood in D.C., nor the safest, but it was patrolled by the Capitol police, who took their job seriously. And it offered correspondingly better housing for the dollar; even on his clerk's salary, Walker had been able to afford an apartment he was pleased to come home to. It had been convenient to work, too, which it was no longer, but Walker could take the subway from Union Station and be at the firm in less than half an hour. He let himself in the door and switched on the light.

The apartment was a studio, but a large one, with spacious arched windows looking out onto the street. Two walls held built-in bookshelves, containing Walker's philosophy books from his undergraduate days and the casebooks and treatises of law school. There were dark hardwood floors and out back a small garden in which Walker, had he been so inclined, could have hosted guests and grilled in a modest simulacrum of Peter Morgan's party. He did not; most of his time inside the apartment was spent sitting and reading on a tan couch that faced the windows and a grandfather clock he'd found at an estate sale. Walker looked at the clock, then at an amber stain slightly darker than the couch. His tongue pursued fleeting tastes of the Macallan on his lips; for a moment he felt slightly queasy. He hadn't drunk that Scotch in a while. What of it? Walker thought. So I spent some time with the Islay malts. Good to broaden one's horizons. He felt another quick surge of nausea, a rush of saliva into his mouth.

It had never been clear to Walker why the Court gave so much attention to the death penalty cases. What was presented to the Court, in the last analysis, was a cert petition like any other. True, it had to be acted on quickly; the states would postpone executions for hours while the petition was pending, but they wouldn't wait weeks for the Court's regular conference. But the petitions seldom presented the kinds of issues the Court usually agreed to hear, questions of federal law on which the appellate courts had split, or important questions no court had yet decided. The Court wouldn't typically take a case just because the lower court had erred, and it didn't like to get involved in the facts. Those were standard reasons for denying a cert petition, comforting and familiar phrases to be put in the memos. Error-correction, the clerks wrote. Fact-bound. Splitless. Deny.

There were, Walker understood, two different roles the Court played in the American judicial system. It was the final arbiter for individual cases, the court of last resort. And it was the final answer on the law. History had seen the second role eclipse the first; given the growing volume of litigation, the Court no longer had the institutional capacity to police thousands of lower court decisions for errors or injustices. It existed now to maintain uniformity in the legal rules. As Justice Holmes had said, it wasn't a court of justice; it was a court of law. But death was different; death brought the first role back to life, for here the Court did look for error. Here it was concerned about injustice; here it delved deeply into the facts. This troubled Walker, who had seen even at the appellate level how facts corrupted the law, how they drove courts to bend the law in search of what seemed the just result. I hate facts, Justice Holmes had also said, and Walker agreed.

Eric Tanner did not have what lawyers called good facts. During a three-month span in 1986 he had raped nine women and killed four of them, including an eleven-year-old girl. Walker was glad of this, in a way, for it meant that the execution was more likely to go smoothly. Walker wanted it to go smoothly, because Alabama was one of Justice Arlen's states and Walker was running the execution for the Arlen chambers. There was a long list of things he would rather have been doing, a list that began with working on the opinion he was drafting and went on to enduring dental work, or perhaps a little beyond. But instead he was monitoring the progress of Tanner's appeals through the lower courts, familiarizing himself with the facts and the arguments, assessing the merits of various claims.

From what he could see, Tanner's lawyers had done a competent job at the initial trial and sentencing. That made things harder for the new ones, who at the moment were pursuing an ineffective-assistance-of-counsel argument that Walker could tell immediately had very little chance of succeeding. Still, they were trying, tossing up prayers. They had amicus participation too, the usual anti-death-penalty organizations calling to say that they'd be filing briefs in support. Their arguments didn't add much; sometimes, Walker thought, it was as though they believed constitutional adjudication was a popularity contest, as though the number of briefs filed in favor of a position had some influence on the outcome of the case.

They were going to be disappointed with this one. Walker had talked it over with the other clerks. They were a pretty good group, Jennifer Caputo from the Lambert chambers, a couple of Walker's other friends. Some of them, Jennifer included, were ardent foes of the death penalty, but everyone could see that this wasn't a promising case. Walker took a call from Tanner's lawyers, explaining that they would be filing simultaneously in state and federal court in the early afternoon. He sent an e-mail out to the group of clerks and tried to get back to work on the opinion.

Walker had always been proud of his ability to concentrate, to shut out all distractions. But he was finding it unusually hard to achieve his trademark single-minded focus. Names were passing through his head, imagined scenes, a whole life history. Tanner's trial lawyers had put on substantial mitigating evidence, displayed the variegated horrors of their client's life. Fetal alcohol syndrome, abandonment, violence, abuse. And the courts had been thorough in detailing his crimes. Walker read the trial record, the opinions of the state courts in the initial appeals, those of the federal courts in Tanner's first attempt at habeas relief. The names stuck with him. Catherine Tubbs, Angela Hunter, Lisa Reyes. Misery, thought Walker. Misery. It made it very hard to be passionate about the Framers' understanding of state sovereignty.

At two o'clock he got an e-mail from the Court's death clerk, who kept the law clerks apprised of the status of pending executions. *Tanner has had a stroke and is unresponsive*, it said. *He may die; the execution is on hold.*

Beyond sick, thought Walker, relieved and almost ashamed of it. He turned back to the records of the Constitutional Convention. Another e-mail popped onto his screen. Walker read in disbelief. It hadn't been a stroke; Tanner had taken an overdose of antidepressants. He was coming around; his lawyers were seeking a stay.

The messages continued through the afternoon.

Tanner is awake, but the Governor has granted a 30-day reprieve.

Disregard the previous e-mail. A reprieve was sought but not granted.

Tanner is conscious but not lucid, and the prison officials have decided to hold off.

Good, Walker thought. Someone else is going to have to deal with this. At six o'clock he considered giving up on the hope of getting work done and going home for dinner. Then another message: *The Alabama Attorney General has instructed the warden to go ahead.*

On the phone, Tanner's lawyer sounded breathless. "State and federal court," he said. "As soon as possible."

"Thanks," said Walker. On his computer screen another message had popped up, this one from Jennifer: *What are they thinking? How can they do this?*

I guess we'll find out, he replied.

A Court messenger brought by the first round of filings half an hour later. For people who'd plainly been taken by surprise, Walker thought, Tanner's lawyers hadn't done such a bad job. They were making their ineffective-assistance-of-counsel argument, which Walker would have left out; it was a distraction. But they were also making the right argument, though only in state court: that it was unconstitutional to execute someone who could not understand what was happening to him. It was a straightforward application of a case called *Ford* v. *Wainwright*.

Looks like we get to stop one, Jennifer wrote. *Unless the lower courts do it first.*

The lower courts didn't. Walker understood why the federal trial court denied the emergency motion; there just wasn't anything there. The state court he wasn't sure about. Perhaps Tanner's lawyers hadn't been able to reach a friendly judge; perhaps they'd had to file with someone who wanted no part of this case and preferred to kick it upstairs. The messenger brought another round of filings, for the federal circuit court and the state supreme court. It was nine o'clock. *This is going to take a while*, the death clerk wrote.

Walker went out to get dinner, down the streetlit pavement of First Street to the train station and back. He sat at his desk, still thinking about the names. And thinking about the incongruity of it all. Somewhere in Alabama a man was waiting to hear if he'd live or die, or would have been if he were conscious. Somewhere his lawyers were struggling to find reasons that would keep him alive; somewhere courts were being called into emergency sessions, judges telephoned at home. And as a result of all these frantic maneuvers, back in D.C. inside the walls of the highest court in the land, Walker Eliot was eating take-out sushi from the food court at Union Station instead of frozen pizza in his apartment. It was not a connection he could readily understand.

"Another hour," the death clerk said when he called. Walker went up to the darkened basketball court and shot free throws. His percentage was going up. Back at his desk he played half an hour of solitaire on the computer before the e-mail he was waiting for arrived. *The state and federal courts have denied Tanner's motions. Copies of the orders are circulating.*

Again the messenger made his rounds. At six-thirty, he'd been wearing a suit. By nine he'd taken off the jacket. Now, at eleven-thirty, even the tie was gone. Walker read the orders. The federal court had ruled against Tanner on the merits, which again was no surprise. The state court had also rejected the ineffective-assistance-of-counsel claim. But it had refused to consider the *Ford* argument, reasoning that Tanner hadn't raised the claim in state court before and couldn't present new arguments now. That's not going to stand up, Walker thought. I mean, he didn't have this argument available before today. His phone rang.

"The petition is on its way by courier." Tanner's lawyer sounded tired. Walker wondered how many judges he'd interrupted at dinner that evening, how many conference calls he'd been on.

The messenger's sleeves were rolled up. Walker rose from his computer, where he'd been drafting a memo, and took the papers. There was one petition, asking for review of the state supreme court's judgment. Which made some sense; the federal court's decision presented only one of the two issues. But then there was something that made less sense. Walker turned the pages, frowning. The lawyers were asking for review only of the ineffective-assistance-of-counsel ruling, not the *Ford* claim. An e-mail from Jennifer popped up on his screen: *What the hell is going on?*

Walker picked up the phone. His hand hesitated over the keypad, then dialed Justice Arlen's number. "Tanner's lawyers have filed a petition asking the Court to grant certiorari on an ineffective-assistance-of-counsel claim," he said.

Justice Arlen didn't sound tired, but all the same Walker wished he could be asleep. Important cases were being argued the next morning, and Walker wanted his boss fresh.

"That's all they're asking?"

"Just the one issue," Walker said. "The trial court gave this a pretty thorough going-over. So did the state supreme court. I don't think it's even close."

"I tend to think we should defer on these fact-intensive questions," Arlen said. "And I agree that the lower courts did a complete job."

"I have a memo on this issue," Walker said. It had been part of a longer memo. He read it over the phone.

"Okay," said Arlen. "We'll recommend denial."

Walker sent the memo out as an e-mail attachment and waited for votes. They came in slowly, but they were uniform. *Deny. Deny. Deny.*

At a quarter past twelve he called the death clerk and reported that the Court had denied the petition. Five minutes later he got an e-mail. *Tanner's lawyers will make no more filings. All clear.*

Walker shut down the computer and picked up his bag, his face blank. In the hallway he ran into Jennifer. "What just happened?" she asked.

The messenger bag felt very heavy on Walker's shoulder. "The right thing, I guess," he said.

Jennifer sucked in her breath as though she'd been slapped. "I guess that depends on what you mean by right," she said.

"Legally right," Walker said, thinking: What else is there? "We had to deny that petition."

"I know we had to deny the petition. But that doesn't make it right."

Catherine Tubbs, thought Walker. Angela Hunter. Lisa Reyes. "We're just doing our jobs," he said.

Jennifer shook her head. "Whatever."

As Walker left, the security guard at the Maryland Avenue entrance greeted him by name. Walker had felt a surge of warmth the first time this had happened, quite early in the summer. It was part of being a member of the Court family. But it was also a reminder of his individuality, which at the moment was less pleasant.

In just a few blocks he was home. He poured himself a small glass of the Macallan and settled on the couch, intending to review the memo he'd written for Justice Arlen about one of the cases to be argued the next morning. What came out of the bag instead, to his great surprise, was the full Tanner memo he'd written, recommending a grant on the *Ford* claim he'd assumed would be presented. Walker looked up at the clock. Twelve-forty. *It's over by now,* he thought. *In the time it took me to walk home.* He took a steadying sip of his drink, which had the opposite effect. His throat seemed to close; there was an unfamiliar sensation of pressure at the base of his skull. He squeezed his eyes shut, frowning. Then the glass fell from his hand. He rushed to the bathroom and vomited.

Walker looked from the couch to the clock and back again. He closed his eyes and took three deep and even breaths. "Never again," he said. He turned the cushion over and went to bed.

Ryan Grady was appreciating the increasing marginal utility of alcohol. He frequently drank a beer when he came home from work, and though this night he had come from a party and been drinking a fair amount already, that seemed no reason to vary from the usual routine. Now he was feeling a little bit splendid. I should get drunk earlier in the day, he thought. Have more time to enjoy it, not waste so much happiness asleep. He cast gleaming eyes over his apartment. A box by the door beckoned. With a knife, Ryan broke its seal. "Yeah," he said, extracting compact discs. Only the Internet, Ryan had decided, made the modern practice of law possible. Given the amount of time he had to spend in the office, there was really no way to shop. The city was a world only of surfaces, everything closed in the morning when he went to work, and again when he came home at night. On the Internet, everything was always open, and there was no need even to go outdoors. Of course, there were some things you couldn't do online. And there were some things you could, but not at work. But for the humdrum, the quotidian, the everyday getting and spending, the firm's T1 connection was just fine.

With a smile of satisfaction, he carried the discs to his stereo. There he confronted another cardboard box. It too yielded to the knife, proving to contain more compact discs. Ryan set them next to the first batch and compared the two stacks with a frown. This was the danger of shipping, that the delayed gratification would prompt other attempts to obtain it, all equally successful. "Pfuh," said Ryan Grady. He dropped the discs in a pile on the floor, then picked up the most eagerly anticipated, slit its plastic wrap, and inserted it into the stereo. "Yeah," he said, nodding. "That's the stuff. Good enough to buy it twice."

Ryan retrieved his beer bottle from the kitchen table and upended it. Trickles; warmish residue for the optimistic probing tongue. He pulled another from the refrigerator and sauntered to an easy chair. A pile of magazines awaited, the night's homework.

With the amount of time he spent studying, Ryan thought, he could almost have been holding down another job. And with the effort that he put into it, he almost felt he was. To be fair, it was a better-than-average job, one that could be done drunk and in one's underwear, and in that way it was more like college. But it was still a lot of work. For what reward? His success rate wasn't improving. Julie Morgan would have been a challenge for anyone, but he had to admit that he hadn't come close. Even the easier targets were proving elusive. One of the more attractive caterers had slipped away from his entreaties, offering him only a smile and a business card that proved on later inspection to belong not to her but to Peter Morgan.

The output of intellectual energy with nothing to show for it was bringing back some of the less pleasant aspects of the college experience as well. Picking up girls, which Ryan had assumed was an unquantifiable mélange of intuition, inspiration, and intoxication, turned out to be much more complicated. Possibly, if the magazines were to be believed, it was more of a science than an art. Terrifically difficult if you tried to actually work your way through it from the beginning.

Fortunately, as with calculus, smarter people had managed to come up with formulas that eliminated a lot of the unnecessary effort. But even these were proving more elaborate than Ryan had expected. His brash good looks, six-figure salary, and willingness to accept the occasional embarrassment were only the beginning of the story. Nowadays, the magazines told him, you needed much more to succeed. You couldn't just walk up to a woman and tell her how much you made, what firm you worked for. Well, you could; he had. But what ensued wasn't an experience anyone would want to repeat. You needed a wingman, a teaser line, a closer, and an exit strategy. Further refinements existed if you were willing to spring for them: advertisements informed him of eleven powerful seduction techniques, eight things women looked for in a man, six mistakes he should never make, and one foolproof secret, all contained in two hundred and seventeen pages that could be his for only $39.95.

Ryan shook his head, chastened. He took another swallow of beer. Whatever happened to getting them drunk and telling them lies?

Gerald Roth paced his apartment in frustration. His beard held toothpaste. "Anson Henry," he said. "What were you thinking? Doctor Death, fine, that makes sense. But you don't try to get the confession suppressed. You don't do your own DNA analysis. You don't try to track down this informant. You're not even taking a shot at innocence."

Gerald sighed. He had seen enough death penalty cases to know how they usually came out. To know too that often there was little to be said in favor of the condemned. But Gerald believed in second chances. We are all better than the worst thing we do. Wayne Harper deserved the best defense, and Mark's reports were raising doubts. Questions passed through Gerald's mind, arranging themselves in a troubling pattern. Innocence was always worth a try.

Gerald opened the door to his closet. He looked in on a row of gray suits, a collection of framed certificates piled in a corner. "Something's wrong," he said aloud.

Something's wrong, thought Peter Morgan, lying awake in the cotton swells of his bed. Harold Fineman was an ass, admittedly, and admittedly in questioning Peter's analysis of the case he had been asking to get slapped down. But all the same he was a productive member of the firm, probably the best litigator they had. In court Harold would never give an inch, and wasn't it after all the mark of a good litigator to question his positions, to be able to see what the other side would be bringing? Likewise, the vegetarianism was annoying if an affectation, and worse if a manifestation of principle, but hadn't Harold's lapse shown only that he put the firm first? Hadn't he, in short, been showing that he had the flexibility of a good lawyer, and hadn't Peter essentially rebuked him for not having the rigidity of a good person?

That's not like me, Peter thought. That's not like me at all. Bullying had its place, as a show of power, or a way to enforce professional norms. Gerald Roth, for instance, seemed at times to forget that he was an associate, and Peter felt no remorse for reminding him. But partners knew his power well enough without demonstration, and Harold's professional discipline was beyond question. That left bullying for its own sake, which Peter would be the first to admit was counterproductive. It was, moreover, a sign of insecurity, of unhappiness, of discontent.

Something's wrong. Peter Morgan's mind methodically began chewing away at the possibilities. He skipped past the first two easily. Insecurity was as far from him as Pluto, and he'd sworn off unhappiness when he realized there were better motivators. What could cause him discontent? He had a profitable business, a powerful car, a spacious and elegant home. He ticked off the possessions. A beautiful wife, three admirable daughters.

Children. A twinge of regret flashed within him. Daughters. Had he been cheated by life, betrayed by the machinations of his own haploid cells? Of course he'd wanted a son. Of course he'd harbored dynastic ambitions. Julie, born to them late, had been in part the expression of a hope that after seven years something would have changed in their bodies, become more receptive to the possibility of male offspring. And that after those years something would have changed in the nature of children, or his relation to them, to make the hypothetical son more amenable to following in his footsteps than the first two daughters had seemed. The twins had been nice enough girls, polite, pretty, and respectful. But quite early Peter had seen that that was all they were.

Hence those thoughts of another child, as Peter consolidated his power and Cassandra entered her thirties. Hence those thoughts of a son. But the son had remained hypothetical. Instead there was Julie, crisp and dark-haired. The twins made their debuts and married early, his prophecy proved true. And then they were gone, sucked off to other corners of the country, acquiescing in their husbands' relocations with a deference and calm that made Peter wonder whether he had raised them to be his children or other men's wives. Perhaps, in the end, they simply felt no strong ties to their parents or their home, and that too he had to reckon a failure.

But not Julie. Peter had lavished attention on her, and she had not disappointed him. She was bright and headstrong, with a self-reliance that had pleased him more than any obedience could have, for it showed that his will lived within her. She'd demonstrated an aptitude for analytical thinking, an interest in the law. But then she'd gone to Yale, which by the caliber of its students and faculty would likely be the best law school in the country, were it only a law school. The Yale Theory School, Peter called it in conversations with Julie. The humor had paled for her, but he persisted into her second year. "How's theory school treating you? Learning to think like a theorist?" Predictably, she'd come out of Yale and headed for a public interest advocacy group. I gave my children the luxury of not having to lead the life I did, Peter thought, and they didn't. He'd been given the same opportunity, obviously, the same chance to turn away. But he'd chosen what he had, and they had not.

Peter Morgan shrugged and gazed at the ceiling. Through the gloom he could just make out the lazy turning of fan blades. Unneeded with the air-conditioning, but a nice touch in the older houses. The reminder of a sort of gentility, of Archie's world. But the world moves on. Even if Julie were to come to Morgan Siler, as she still could, what would that profit him? One more generation with a Morgan at the helm, perhaps, but no more. And what were the chances even of that? Julie would not take his path. She bridled even to hear his advice, causing him hurt in proportion to the hurt he hoped advice could spare her. He understood now the pain of rejected support, glimpsed what Archie must have felt, his sins as son visited upon him as father.

I gave my children the luxury of choice, in the hope that they would choose to follow me. I offered them my life and they turned away.

What does it matter? Peter asked himself. He was still at the peak of his powers. His world was in order, the world he had made. He had nothing to complain of. Did he?

He raised himself on one elbow and fondly studied Cassandra's sleeping profile. It wasn't even Harold, he realized. It was that young associate with him . . . it was *that* she was with him, or seemed to be. That was what had inspired him to belittle Harold, as though the two of them were playground rivals sparring for the affections of a bobby-soxer.

Peter Morgan snorted contemptuously and fell back on the bed. As though he could ever be jealous of Harold. As though the girl would ever be interested in that twit. He caught himself. That *was* jealousy, or as close as he'd come in a long time. Peter respected Harold, as someone else who'd sweated blood to make it to where he was. He had brought Harold to the firm, treated him as a brother, gone far toward making him what he was today. There was no reason he should be having these thoughts. Now Peter felt a distinct stirring of unease. Something was definitely amiss. Again he peered at his wife's face. Of course her skin didn't have the same elasticity, the same flush and glow as that girl's. But she was still a fine-looking woman.

Still. It was a word of compromise, of settling, two things he'd done little and enjoyed less. Quietly he got to his feet and walked to the bathroom. Shutting the door, he studied his own face in the glass. He looked good, but he was starting to look good for his age, and that metric was the beginning of the end. Compromise, weakness, the betrayal of the flesh. How quickly time steals your aspirations if you release them for a moment. He could see the signs, the skin sagging below his chin, the carvings of age by his mouth. He looked like a faded copy of himself, the cells renewing themselves toward oblivion, each iteration weaker, as though some anatomical secretary had forgotten to shake the toner cartridge.

Peter switched off the light and stared into the dark. I should have expected this, he told himself. It was bound to happen. Success had never satisfied him, nor was it what he sought. The joy was in the striving, the sense of progress, of victory just around the corner. Success itself was empty; what Peter wanted was to be always succeeding. And that he was no longer. I should have seen it coming, he thought. To fail is terrible, but it allows the possibility of future triumphs. To succeed, to have nothing unachieved . . . that was death.

Darkness enfolded him, pressing in. Peter heard the quiet hum of the air conditioner, a distant rumble of traffic. The tapestry of his life was complete, and now it was shrinking, like the silk scarves folded tiny to show their quality, so sheer they could be wrapped upon themselves and pulled through the narrowest space. In Santorini he'd seen it done, that summer before college when they'd acted out Archie's version of the grand tour. The merchant pulled a ring off his finger and Peter watched as the glorious colors and elaborate designs dwindled to a narrow thread, drawn through a circle of gold.

Through a wedding band.

His wife's sleep-dulled voice rose from the other side of the door, and he made his way across the room, eyes still sightless from the recent glare. "Mmm," said Cassandra. "Honey."

"Here I am," said Peter. She was calling him back to bed. It was a king, the sheets 1,020-thread-count Egyptian cotton, the foot and headboards dark hardwood. They'd bought the house just after he'd made partner, and the bed soon thereafter. He had spent, he thought, close to six thousand nights in this bed, the heart of the familiar domestic world. But there were worlds beyond this one he'd made, worlds unknown and unconquered. He lifted the coverlet and took his place by Cassandra's side, and the thought came to his mind, almost surprising. This is not what I want to do. She reached one arm out across his chest; he felt it come down like a safety belt, her hand curling around his shoulder. To lie motionless in bed, to lie here and empty my mind and wait only for sleep to take me. That, thought Peter Morgan, is exactly what I do not want to do.

Harold Fineman did not think anything was wrong. Like Peter Morgan, he lay awake. But that was nothing new, and hardly a cause for soul-searching. Harold was not, by nature, an introspective man. He was good at justification, at rationalization, at explaining why what seemed like a fatal problem was only a minor hitch. When he considered his life with that advocate's eye, very little seemed awry.

Undeniably, his exercise program had fallen off. The press of business made it hard to find the time; the health club, populated by the impossibly trim, impossibly young, seemed less and less welcoming. He'd let himself go a little; he had to admit it. His ill-fitting suits were fitting worse. The looks that jurors gave him occasionally suggested not trust but sympathy, perhaps even pity. And he found himself out of breath in unaccustomed circumstances. It's all to the good, he told himself. His courtroom effectiveness wasn't suffering; if anything, he was better. And if he panted after climbing stairs, that only meant he was getting exercise without having to look at the twenty-somethings.

So why was he staring at the ceiling? Not a hard question. He was angry, and anger made it difficult to sleep. The answer was not yet a solution; not being able to sleep was a problem, since it threatened his ability to be productive the next day. But the problem had been identified. His anger was now only a difficulty to surmount, and surmounting difficulties was what Harold did. This one simply had to be tackled head-on. Harold frequently had trouble sleeping, and he had a reliable remedy. In boxer shorts and an undershirt he padded from the bed to his living room and poured himself a large glass of bourbon, which he drank quickly. Good liquor, another thing his parents had never appreciated. He put the first *Rheingold* compact disc on his stereo. Forbidden music. The sound swelled softly from his expensive speakers, filling the bedroom with its world-assembling chords, building form from the formless. The primal element, the beginning, a universe limitless in possibility. Harold returned to bed and gave his mind to the music, feeling already a warm liquefaction overcoming him. Release. The problem was solved.

27 WHERE HE WAS GOING

At seven-thirty sharp, Mark piled into a van with eighteen other Morgan Siler lawyers and began the trip to Mayfield. Looking around the interior, he saw some familiar faces. Harold Fineman, Ryan Grady, Katja. Not Walker. Walker apparently had been correct in his assessment of the situation. "Texas?" he had asked incredulously. "I don't think so. They won't use me for discovery. I've never done anything like that before."

"Neither have I," Mark pointed out, but Walker waved a dismissive hand.

"I'm a third-year," he said. "I'm too expensive."

The lawyers clutched the tools of their trade, coffee cups or briefcases, and hunched against the morning chill like paratroopers poised for the drop into the Norman hedgerows. The airport was crowded when they arrived, but the dark-suited phalanx cut purposeful furrows through the waiting passengers, splitting gathered families and interrupting goodbyes. It reminded Mark of something, wolves separating one of their prey from a herd, isolating it, taking it down. He lagged behind, stumbling over an unlaced shoe, feeling awkward and vulnerable. A lawyer with a broken wingtip.

On the flight, Mark found himself next to Harold. He gazed longingly toward the back of the plane, where Katja and Ryan sat. "Have you done any document production before?" Harold asked when they were airborne.

Mark looked out the window, following the Potomac as it wound through the city. Small sails moved on the river, scraps of white against the glassy blue-green. Flying is amazing, he thought, but we take it for granted. It's an inconvenience. "How much do you think people would have paid just to get up here a hundred years ago?" he asked.

Wonderful, Harold thought. Another one of those reflective types. Probably a philosophy major or something. We should pay more attention to undergraduate degrees when we're hiring these people. Law school can only do so much. He'd studied philosophy himself, of course, but he'd overcome it. Those days were past. Harold considered the back of Mark's head, where the airplane seat had called a defiant cowlick to life. A nice kid, but not enough aggression. Not enough focus. He hadn't made the transition. Perhaps he couldn't; perhaps he lacked what it took to immerse himself in the job, to get inside it like a diver's suit. "Are you listening to me?" Harold demanded.

The plane banked and began its westward progress; Mark glimpsed gentle scalloped waves of coastline, the site of childhood vacations. He thought of the ocean and the beach, sands that advanced and receded, those who fought them and those for whom they fought. He turned back from the window. "What?"

"Forget about it," Harold said. "I'll explain what to do when we get there." He fished a compact disc player from his briefcase.

"Okay," said Mark. He closed his eyes and tried to nap, but inactivity bred unease. I used to be able to nap. When did that stop? When did I forget how to relax? "What should I do now?"

Harold rifled through silver discs. "You can do some work, if you like," he said. "For another client. If it's Hubble, you'll have to pretend that you did it later. We're already billing the flight as travel time, and you can't raise the rates. Of course, billing work to one client while you're traveling for another is considered bad form. It's what they used to call double-billing. But I won't tell if you won't." Satisfied with his selection, he closed the player and raised a pair of expensive noise-canceling earphones to his head.

"What are you listening to?" Mark asked.

Harold looked briefly annoyed, then relented. "Wagner," he said. "*The Ring*. People need a conceptual framework to organize experience. If you're a lawyer, you could do worse than pick *The Ring*. It's got your themes right there. The lust for gold, the renunciation of love." He paused. "The dragon."

"The dragon?"

Harold's annoyance returned. "If you think you don't know who the dragon is," he said, "you're kidding yourself. You met him your first day on the job."

Mark looked out the window again. "Should the wing be shaking like that?" he asked.

"Don't worry about it," said Harold. "If you die during litigation you go straight to heaven."

"Why's that?"

"It's like battle." He pointed at the CD player. "*Ride of the Valkyries*. Hoyotoyo. The bravest men are tapped on the shoulder, called away to live with the gods. Anyway, it's not going to happen. We're too important for a plane crash."

Harold put the headphones on his head and lost himself in the music, letting his thoughts roam free. He and his band of warriors, riding to the rescue on sky-devouring jets, bringing their swords and shields to bear in the affairs of mortals. It worked. The firm as Valhalla; that worked too. The abode of the gods, built from law. Built too on a broken promise, a primal betrayal. Harold knew the history; he had been there. But he loved the firm. It had made him what he was.

Harold had grown up in the Borough Park section of Brooklyn, a third-floor walk-up crowded with family. His father was Orthodox, a dressmaker who bought five tickets to baseball games, the empty seats around him warding off the possibility of physical contact with women. Harold had never believed. Perhaps in the mist of childhood, with a child's superstition. But looking back now he could remember no trace of religious sentiment. It was simply a faculty he lacked.

His father demanded conformity with ritual nonetheless, took him to shul, davened each morning. Act and it will produce belief. Harold wanted none of it, neither the belief nor the acts. Without a god behind it, ritual had no point. He wanted to be free, not to tie himself to traditions for which millions died. This is America, he said. Why reforge the ancient fetters, build the old world in the new?

America *ganif*, his father said darkly. America the thief of values. Harold went to Yeshiva University high school and summer camps in the Catskills and Poconos; he recited the Sh'ma Yisrael prayer. He studied philosophy at City College and reached his own conclusions. Faith was not the solution, Harold decided. Faith was the problem. Certainty led to catastrophe, faith to crusades. Faith should be opposed—not with faith, for that was war, but with doubt, the ability to see other perspectives.

When his father died, in the spring of his junior year, Harold felt the first stirrings of liberation. He was under no one's control now. But soon he realized that command was not the only bond. His younger sisters were still unmarried; with his mother, they had kept the books for his father's business. With the dress shop in new hands, they'd be paid a salary. The family could live on those earnings; they could live without any earnings, borne up by the tight communal webs of their neighborhood. But he could not leave them to do that.

Harold turned from philosophy to law, enrolling at Columbia. It was a compromise, but not a bad one. Law valued perspective too; the ability to see all sides of an issue was what his professors demanded. Harold excelled, studious and thoughtful. He took a room in Manhattan, amassing student loans, and seldom crossed the river. His mother's face lit up when she saw him, but to Harold the smile was a demand and, when in his mind he refused it, a rebuke. There was something he must do to deserve it, he was sure, and whatever it was, he declined. When the smile persisted, he felt a debt unpaid and came less often. There were others in the small apartment, his sisters, loud uncles who visited. She was not alone.

The others rebuked him more openly. Harold cut his curls short and polished his diction, rubbing the rhythms of Brooklyn from his voice. His hair was fair and reddish, his eyes a sharp green. "What, you think you can pass?" an uncle demanded. Harold was stung. He wasn't trying to pass. He wanted no more to be thought of as a Christian than as a Jew; he wanted only to be himself, single and unique. Any community, even two people, bound its members with concerns and traditions, a shared history. But one person could float free, an atom, without ties or allegiances or responsibility, able to take on any role.

There were few jobs available when he graduated. Harold was near the top of his class, but his name was Fineman and his résumé still listed Borough Park as his permanent address. Again he struck a compromise. He would work to support the family, but from afar. He joined the litigation department of Schulman Roth in Washington. Litigation suited Harold; it was, he often thought in those days, what he'd been born for. Clients brought their problems to the firm, and Harold contemplated them from every angle, assessing the possible arguments. He advised the clients, offering a skeptic's assessment of their claims; when necessary he fought for them with an advocate's zeal. Doubt and certainty intertwined, mutually reinforcing, mutually constraining.

And most of the time, he won. Harold's courtroom presentation was impeccable, his demeanor calm, his logic precise. He knew that he started from a disadvantage; Schulman Roth was an outsider's firm. Judges and juries expected a fast-talking shyster. They were taken aback by this serious young man, and then they were won over. In the courtroom, preconceptions dropped away and Harold was nothing but himself. It was what he'd been seeking all his life. Work had made him free.

It was after Harold won a trial against Fred Cox that Peter Morgan approached. Cox was getting old, on the downward slope of his career, but the win was impressive. And if Cox was on his way out, it was that much more important to stock the next generation with talent. Peter knew potential when he saw it.

Harold found the decision easy. Morgan Stevens was an established firm, with resources that Schulman Roth couldn't offer and compensation that it couldn't match. Harold moved in laterally as a partner and sent larger checks to Borough Park. He realized soon that things had changed. On a motion call one day he asked for an extension of time, the supporting arguments carefully marshaled in his mind. The judge granted the request without discussion. After Harold came Nathan Meyer, one of his friends from Schulman Roth, with an identical request that met a fierce interrogation. Nathan had never been as assiduous as Harold, and eventually he was reduced to splutters of indignation. "But you just gave him an extension without any questions."

The judge frowned down from his perch. "When Morgan, Stevens, Raymond, and Cox seek an extension of time," he said, "I can be quite sure that they have a good reason."

Leaving the courtroom, Harold could see the fury on Nathan's face, and he shrugged apologetically. They were in different worlds now, playing by different rules. Peter Morgan was a valuable resource in those early days, explaining to Harold how this world worked and what his role in it would be. Judges and juries had different preconceptions now, and different means were required to combat them. Once again, Harold changed. He bought his suits off the rack, the pants a few inches short. He strapped a cheap plastic watch over the sleeve of his jacket and let his curls bloom. He abandoned the hard-won precision of diction; he turned himself into one of the rude uncles he'd promised never to become.

And it worked. He went up against the best that Washington's established firms had to offer, the prep school products in their Brooks Brothers and Polo, and he crushed them. Juries trusted Harold, knew that he wouldn't try to pull a fast one. He crossed his ankle over his knee at the counsel table and a white patch of shin winked from the gap between sock and cuff: I have nothing to hide.

Opponents were incredulous. They dropped oblique references to the resources behind him, the teams of associates whose nights of research uncovered the cases he reeled off as though struck by sudden inspiration. The jurors nodded sagely. All that, and he's keeping it real.

There were other changes too, though these took longer to notice. Morgan Stevens, and more so Morgan Siler, was not in the business of giving advice. The clients wanted certainty; they wanted to hear that they were right. Realism was appropriate in predicting outcomes, for there was always a chance the judge would make a mistake. But a Morgan Siler client was never on the wrong side of the law.

Thus said Peter Morgan. Harold heard and obeyed. He was inside the firm now; the job was his armor, his might, and his protection. For a while he felt he was again a child in Brooklyn, reciting formulas without conviction. But his father had been right about one thing. The assertion of certainty carried certainty in its wake; the acts produced belief.

Harold shifted in his seat, glancing past Mark to the plane's small window. Litigation at least was less constraining than Orthodoxy. He still had his freedom. But here his thought paused. Freedom to do what, exactly? To listen to forbidden music, to eat what he chose, to work or drive a car on the Sabbath. To drive a Volkswagen or a BMW, even. But these were ordinary things. Not a life's definition. Not the freedom he'd imagined. He had wanted the chance to choose his own identity, and he had won it, but as he considered his life, it occurred to him that he'd never quite gotten around to making the choice.

Harold switched CDs in his player. He was nearing the conclusion now, shadow falling on the gods. All were dead at the end. That was a relief. Death allowed a fresh start, free from the entanglements of the old order. Harold did not miss God, or his father who had spoken for Him and demanded obedience. He missed his mother, though she had burdened him too, and it was her voice he occasionally heard in what he thought of as religious moments. Jell-O and tapioca she had made for him. They had not seen each other much those last years, but he had provided; he had taken care of her. Or the firm had; he was too busy to be personally involved with the details when his sisters married and moved out, when her health began to fail. The firm had found her a home, engaged a nurse. But he had loved her, and she had loved him, and wanted only the best for him, and struggled to understand why he did what he did. And through it all, she was proud of him, no matter what his father would have said. She believed. If you do it, it must be right. That trust was what she owed his father's God, Harold thought. Why should she give it to him, who was only her son? Like love, the faith of others was a terrible thing. It brought with it the demand that it be deserved; it raised questions he would rather not ask.

Her death had been in some ways almost a relief, a release from the need for self-scrutiny. Harold did not like to interrogate himself. Everyone was culpable if you looked deeply enough. Any witness could be discredited; everyone had something to hide. Harold tried to avoid weakness through simplicity. He was an effective lawyer; he had never sought anything else. He had taken on the roles he had to. He was a dutiful lieutenant, leading his forces into battle. Why were they not pleased with him? Why had Peter Morgan rebuked him at the dinner party, assailed his inconsistency, which was no more than faithful service?

Harold frowned fiercely. He had dealt with this question, in his fashion, the night before, with bourbon and music. It was not supposed to return, and the recurrence itself was a worrisome symptom. Harold's control was weakening; the things he pushed from his mind did not stay gone. He no longer chose what he thought about, and that, he had read, was the very definition of insanity.

Dispassionately, Harold reviewed the evening. The truth was that he had provoked Peter. The question was why. And the answer was Katja, another thought he could not banish. Had he wanted to redeem himself for the Carver fiasco, demonstrate his ability as a litigator? No. He had wanted to convey something to her, to show her something, certainly. But it was not that he was right. It was that she was.

Harold's inchoate thoughts coalesced into a single proposition. Katja saw something in him, believed in it. Like the beliefs of others, hers was a demand. But he found it was not one he wanted to refuse. He wanted to justify her belief, to make it true. He did not want it proved false, both for what it would say about him and for what it would do to her. He did not want her to become the kind of person who believed in no one, who found certainty only in roles. That was the threat he had seen from Peter Morgan, that he had risen to resist. Doubt opposing certainty, as it had not for years. But opposing certainty this time in the service of belief. He didn't want her to lose her faith.

Harold's frown deepened. He didn't want her to lose her faith. If that wasn't a sign of incipient madness, what was? Hurtling through the sky toward Texas, he wondered for the first time where he was going.

28 THE LITIGATION EXPRESS

Texas was hotter than D.C., hotter than Mark expected any place to be in October. From the Brownsville airport, a chartered bus took them to Mayfield. Mark studied the landscape as it rolled past outside the window: flat, empty, with clusters of scrub pine hugging each other against the blankness of the plains. "That's a sweet gum," said Harold, twisting and peering over his seat back to address Mark. "Or maybe cat's-claw." Mark said nothing, looking for tumbleweed. "Texas has more than five hundred different kinds of grass," Harold commented. "Buffalo grass, bluestem, grama." He flashed a guidebook. "I'd advise you to get your sightseeing done now."

Two hours into the trip, black thunderheads massed and the sky darkened over them. They drove through sheets of rain and emerged on the other side of the storm as into a new day. The Redbird Hotel in Mayfield was not what they had selected but rather all that the town had left to offer. The plaintiffs' lawyers, as Harold had explained, were already there in force, and Mayfield was not used to welcoming so many.

"I think this is more properly described as a motel," said Katja, stepping from the bus. The parking lot was mostly empty, despite the promises of a buzzing sign: CABLE, AIR, POOL. The last of these was visible, drained and leaf-ridden, the deflated corpse of a beach ball its only attendant.

Ryan Grady paced increasing circles, eying his cell phone with disbelief. He held it high in the air and frowned. "I'm outside the network," he said. "I'm going to have to use analog roam the whole time we're here. That's going to cost a fortune." He turned to Mark. "Do you have a signal?"

"I don't have a phone," Mark answered.

Ryan looked at him pityingly. "You don't have one? What's wrong with you? Girls love cell phones. Especially the little ones. Little phones, I mean."

Mark smiled knowingly. "Keeps you on a short leash, though, doesn't it? I like to be able to get away." Inspiration struck. "Cell isn't just short for cellular."

Ryan looked at him with new respect. "Yeah," he said. "I guess that's cool too. But I have Web access and instant messaging."

"Get unpacked," Harold told them. "Clock's running. We've got a meeting scheduled in half an hour." He surveyed the small crowd, his index finger floating like a sniper's rifle. "You," he said to Katja. "You, and you," to Ryan and Mark.

Ryan and Mark were sharing a room, again not by choice but because the influx from Morgan Siler had overwhelmed the Redbird. There were no hangers in the closet, and Mark's shirts remained as they'd traveled, tripled in a garment bag beneath the jacket of his other suit. Ryan dumped the contents of a duffel bag on the floor. "What a shithole," he commented amicably.

Mark stared nonplussed at the room. There was a television, a dented table with two chairs, and a bed whose comforter featured the same floral pattern as the curtains, amplified by a faint lattice of indeterminate stains. "That's a double bed," he said at last.

Ryan shrugged. "Don't be a pussy," he said. "I don't find you attractive." A crafty smile spread across his face. "Unless you turn out to be a pussy. Come on, let's go." He cuffed Mark on the shoulder.

"Ouch," said Mark.

Ryan shook his head. "Pussy."

The plaintiffs' lawyers had set up camp closer to the factory, in Mayfield's larger hotel, and the only one with a conference room. The invisible hand of Morgan Siler had procured several cars, and Harold drove the four lawyers over. Guidebook splayed on his lap, he disdained directions, and several times barricades and yellow tape forced them to turn around.

"Why are all these roads blocked off?" Mark asked.

Harold reversed the car into a three-point turn, injuring bushes on the shoulder. "That's my boy," he said. "Totally unnecessary, I'm sure."

He put the car into drive. "Completely safe," he said. "Nothing to worry about. Roll up your window, by the way."

"Oh," said Mark. He peered past the tape, glimpsing a black expanse where white-suited figures moved.

"My God," said Katja softly from the front seat. "They did that?"

"We did," Harold corrected absently, accelerating down the road. "The client is us. Their interests are our interests. Shit, I'm lost again."

"Seriously," said Mark. "That looks pretty bad."

"Of course it's bad," Harold answered. "They wouldn't need us otherwise. They're in big trouble. The lawsuit is a train bearing down on them. The litigation express."

"So we cut them loose from the tracks?" Ryan asked. "Or are we tied to the tracks too, seeing as how the client is us?"

"Your quick wit will make you quite a lawyer," said Harold. "Except that someone's going to kill you first. Where the fuck is the fucking hotel?" He passed the guidebook to Katja.

"Next left," she said promptly.

"Nice work," said Harold. "You'll be a good lawyer too. No," he continued, "we're not tied to the tracks. And we're not going to cut them loose either. Once in a while you can do that, but not often. And not this time. We're not the hero here." With a sigh of satisfaction he turned in to the hotel driveway. "What we are is another train, bigger, meaner, faster, and headed the opposite way. We're here to apply pressure. Show them that if they don't settle cheap there's going to be a hell of mess. Show them the client will go bankrupt paying our legal fees before the plaintiffs see a cent. That's why I brought three of you to this meeting. Macey will sit there with us and see the money available for settlement trickling away at a thousand bucks an hour, and he'll know that Hubble's willing to go down fighting. And then we can buy him off and the client's happy." Harold paused. "Either that or he tries to play hardball and we really will drain off all the assets in legal fees." He looked at Katja. "Win-win situation. By the time he gets to the client, there won't be anything left. Because he's not the real litigation express. We are."

"Now *this* is a hotel," said Katja, getting out of the car.

Tanned and jocular, Robert Macey did not look like any lawyer Mark had ever seen. Not for him the armor of worsted wool. His suit hung silky from his shoulders; a bracelet glinted on one wrist. A pallid, serious associate restored an air of normality.

"We meet again," said Harold, extending his hand.

Macey shook it. "I'm like a bad penny," he answered with a smile.

Harold's eyes flicked to the corner of the conference room, where a video camera stood on a tripod. "Nice toy. You can't tape this."

"I like to have a record for the judge in case there are any disputes," Macey said, still smiling.

"Local Rule 27(a) permits videotaping," the associate put in.

"Only for depositions," Harold answered smoothly. "And not without notice. The judge will never see it. But go ahead if it makes you happy."

Macey shrugged. "I assume you got our document requests," he said.

"And you, ours," Harold answered. "We did indeed. That's why we're here. We've got a team assembled, and we're going to go through every file. But you understand, there's a whole warehouse of them. Several warehouses, in fact. We'll make a preliminary assessment of relevance and privilege here, then we'll photocopy everything that might be a candidate for disclosure and take it back to D.C. Then we'll go over all of those again. Morgan Siler at your service. It might take a few months. How about your experts' reports?"

"They take time too. But we've got one here for you now. Professor of biochemistry from Texas A&M." He looked at the four of them, then slid a folder across to Ryan, who opened it curiously. "You'll find a description of the properties of various chemical agents being stored at the site and an analysis of the burn residue." He looked again at Ryan, who was bending closer to examine the contents of a plastic bag. "And a sample."

Ryan jumped back from the table. "You maniac," he shrieked. "What are you trying to do, kill us?" Mark flinched. He looked at Harold, who sat calmly, then at Ryan, who had removed his jacket and was wrapping it around his face.

Harold shook his head. "Each time I see you, I think you'll have grown up," he said. "But I'm getting used to the disappointment." He picked up the bag and inspected the crumbs. "What is this, your lunch?"

Macey shrugged. "I had a brownie. It was a spur-of-the-moment thing. You never know what's going to come in handy." He turned to his associate. "You can stop the taping now. So, where were we?"

"Depositions," said Harold. He twisted in his chair and regarded

Ryan. "Sit down, you moron." He slid a paper across the table to Macey. "This is a notice for the deposition of Felix Guzman."

"What for?"

"He's your class representative," said Harold. "We need to know if he'll adequately represent the interests of absent members. We need to know if he's subject to any unique defenses that might distract him from their cause. And we need to know how he found you. Or the reverse. There are rules about that, you know. No, of course you don't. They're ethical rules."

Macey's eyes flashed annoyance, though his face remained impassive. "Knock yourself out. If he's not a good representative, there's lots of others."

"Oh, cut the crap, Robert. He's your representative, and if he goes, you're not lead counsel anymore. I'm sure justice will still be done if you're sitting on the sidelines, but it won't be going into your pockets. And you're not going to be able to get the class certified anyway. This is a mass tort, and it presents all sorts of individualized questions. Can't be tried." Harold paused and steepled his hands. "Now, if we were talking a settlement class, that would be different. That might get approved."

Macey shook his head. He tilted his chair back and put his feet up on the table, revealing a pair of soft and glossy shoes, an absence of socks. "I don't think you have the authority to offer anything we'd be interested in. We're not just suing Hubble, you know. Parkwell's a defendant here."

"Piercing the corporate veil," said Harold. "Last refuge of the plaintiff's lawyer. Sorry, pal; it's not going to happen. We've got a Supreme Court clerk writing a motion to dismiss Parkwell right now."

"Good for you. I've got three hundred potentially exposed people here, and a judge who can still smell the smoke."

Harold shrugged. "We'll see. Anyway, that's not going to help with your class certification."

"I don't even really care about that," said Macey. "I can bring these cases one at a time if I have to. We'll photocopy the complaints and fill the names in on the way to the courthouse. You can get it over cleanly, or you can die from a thousand cuts."

"Again," said Harold, "they won't all be your clients. I hear Addison and Bain has been rounding up quite a handful. Anyway, I think we'll take the thousand cuts." He smiled. "You're not the only bloodsucker in the room, you know."

Robert Macey took a sheet of paper from his briefcase. "We've got some depositions scheduled. Here's a list. Some executives, security personnel, anyone who was on duty that night. You know they locked the workers in."

"For their own safety," said Harold equably. "It's a rough town. Wild West and all that."

Macey nodded. "You've still got it, Harold. You look good. Have you lost weight? Or is it just your soul?"

Harold shrugged. "I can sleep with myself."

"You can sleep with yourself?" Macey asked. "Sure. If you ask me, you can fuck yourself."

"I think that about does it for this meeting," said Harold. "We'll see you in court." He stood and gave Macey a valedictory nod. "I never get tired of saying that."

"Yeah," said Macey. "Well, one of you's got to be back here tomorrow morning for the first deposition."

"Son of a *bitch*," Harold exploded. Mark stood apprehensively in Harold's hotel room. It had twin beds, he noted, but now seemed an inopportune time to mention that. Mark had never seen Harold angry before, and he was frightened. "Mother*fucker*," Harold continued. "*Mother*fucker. Motherfucker, motherfucker, motherfucker."

"What is it?"

Harold thrust a sheet of paper before his face. "Look at this." He pulled it away, leaving Mark to goggle at empty air. "I can't believe this crap."

"What?"

"These depositions. They've got the supervisor who fielded the first distress call. They've got some fencewalker who made it, probably because he was taking five in the cactus cantina. They've got the guy who designed the storage facility. The guy who oversaw the placement of the barrels of ammonium nitrate. The guy who checked on them. They've got everyone."

"Is that improper?"

"No, it's not improper. It's perfectly appropriate. It's exactly what they should do. And it should never happen. These people should be in Sierra Leone. Or Paraguay. Or Uzbekistan. Hubble's got worldwide operations, and if it doesn't, Parkwell does. These people should be drawing nice fat paychecks, learning foreign languages, and forgetting English. Never to be heard from again." Harold took a deep breath and exhaled. "I thought old Robert was looking a little smug. Not easy to tell with him, of course."

"He's got a real poker face," said Mark.

Harold snorted. "Oh, it's been poked. You noticed he didn't show much expression?"

"Yeah."

"Botox. Very popular with the trial lawyers now. Some witness drops a bombshell on you in court and the jury won't see any reaction. It stops sweat at the hairline, too. It's a little creepy going up against those guys. Like the fucking Terminator or something. The only plus is that if they try to look happy or sensitive it comes across as fake." He shook his head. "Anyway. Someone dropped the ball on this, but it doesn't really matter. It's probably not going to make a difference. We're going to defend all the depositions; we're going to make a lot of objections; we're going to bill a lot of hours. It's just that this is a pretty big fuckup, and you want to do everything right. Dot all your *i*'s, cross all your *t*'s, make sure all the witnesses are unavailable."

"Can you do that?"

"Well," said Harold, "not on purpose. But sometimes it happens. This is scorched-earth litigation we're doing here. God, I've got to stop saying things like that." He took a folder from the table, seemingly at random, and consulted the label. "You got Martin Jessup," he said, handing it to Mark.

"Great," said Mark, striving for a positive tone. "What do I do?"

"You know," said Harold. "Defend the deposition. Isn't that what all the young associates want to do?"

"I guess," said Mark. What he really wanted to do, he realized, was get on the next flight home and fall asleep watching television. Practicing law had made his aspirations simpler, if no more attainable. "So what does that entail?" And when, he wondered, did I start saying "entail"?

"Didn't they give you a litigation manual when you started?"

"No." Mark hesitated. There had been a lot of literature handed out those first weeks. A directory of health care providers, 401(k) plan selections, instructions on claiming reimbursements, phone directories. For months he'd received intermittent calls and e-mails admonishing him for failing to return various essential forms. "Maybe."

Harold twisted one side of his face, presumably to convey indifference. "You're a learn-by-doing kind of guy anyway." Mark opened his mouth; Harold raised a hand. "Of course you are. Just get some sleep. I'll give you a couple of pointers at breakfast."

Mark spent a sleepless night in Room 208. The mattress was lumpy; the air conditioner, like the pool, existed but did not function. Ryan mumbled and moved in ways that made Mark first doubt, then hope, that he was asleep. "You won't believe the dream I had," Ryan said in the morning.

"I need a shower," Mark said.

Harold had beaten him to the breakfast buffet and presided over a plate of eggs. Other lawyers hunched at other tables, their dark suits suggesting an assembly of crows. "Dining out on the firm," Harold said. "Help yourself. It's all good. Or all of the same quality, anyway."

Mark selected a dispirited wedge of cantaloupe, a blob of yogurt, the sausage that least plainly advertised its animal antecedent. "You're a lucky boy," Harold said. "Most of your friends are stuck with document review. So you've never done one of these?"

Mark shook his head.

"Well, don't worry about it. The Hubble lawyers are going to prepare the deponents. They'll be saying what they were told to say. You can object if the other side asks something privileged, but I don't think Martin knows any trade secrets. There's going to be some damaging testimony, probably, but we can figure out a way to keep it out of the trial if things get that far. Just make a couple of objections to keep them on their toes."

"Okay," Mark said. A troubling thought entered his mind: this isn't yogurt.

"I mean it," said Harold. "Don't worry. It'll probably seem pretty bad, because, let's face it, this isn't a pretty situation. But nothing that happens in your deposition is going to make a difference. The Parkwell people who are directing the litigation are talking tough for now, saying they want to go to trial, but they'll settle in the end. With the facts they've got here, they'd be crazy not to. Hubble got into some dispute with its disposal subcontractor; they were just letting this stuff pile up. Anyone could have told you it was going to blow eventually. So the worst that could happen is something comes out that helps the plaintiffs' bargaining position. But Martin doesn't have any smoking gun either. He's just the guy who happened to be on duty that night."

Mark chewed a small resilient piece of sausage, trying to decide what to do with it. Harold belched; encouraged, Mark spat carefully into his hand and placed a knobby white lump of gristle on his plate. "So this is going to be settled?"

"Always is," said Harold, wiping his mouth. "It's an interesting calculation, though. The plaintiffs could insist on going to trial. That's their right. Given the way things look, they'd have a good chance of winning. I wouldn't want to go to a jury on these facts. And if they won, they could probably wipe out Hubble, get all of its assets. But from that you'd have to subtract the litigation costs, ours and theirs, which of course are going to be substantial because we're the litigators. And because the lawyers are on a contingency fee, they don't want to spend any more time on this than they have to. Unlike us. The wild cards are their idea that they can pierce the corporate veil and go after Parkwell too, and the possibility that we can defeat class certification. So those are going to be decided in court, and then we'll know what kind of settlement we're looking at. That's the real legal action. What we're doing here is just going through the motions. Expensively. It's like a striptease."

"So you don't have any specific advice?"

Harold considered. "You know those travel mugs they have for coffee, with the little lids on top?"

"Yeah," said Mark. He realized unhappily that his attention had wandered from the plate; his fork had again picked up the gristle and returned it to his mouth.

"Never buy one of those. People are going to give you like fifteen over the next couple of years. The firm, the litigation department. You'll get one for doing pro bono. Clients like to hand them out too. I wish someone had told me that when I was your age."

Mark swallowed uncomfortably and grasped the wisdom of his prior decision.

Harold sighed expansively and set his half-empty plate on an adjacent table. "I think I need a do-over. That's the beauty of the buffet. You can go home again. A new plate, a fresh start. Learn from your mistakes; change whatever you want. This time, I'm not going to get anything runny. That's more advice."

Mark felt an unpleasant swelling in his stomach. The sausage was re-minding him that the past cannot be erased.

"But the reason we're really fucked here," Harold said as he returned to the table, "isn't the dead people. The workers, you know, that's fairly straightforward. They're settled in their lives; they've got an earning stream we can calculate and pay off. Discounted to present value, of course, minus expenses. The problem is that Macey's got these environ-mental scientists talking about harm to children in the area. Children, all bets are off. Juries love to sock it to you if you've injured children. Say one of them's brain-damaged. They'll hit you with medical costs, lost wages, anything the plaintiff's lawyer can dream up. Will they deduct the costs of education, complicated toys, all the things the doting parents will never have to pay for? No. Even bring it up and they'll think you're a monster, slap on a couple of extra million. Why do you suppose that is?"

"Well, I guess it seems heartless."

"That's true," said Harold, chewing. "But heartless is okay in most contexts. Heartless is the standard in litigation. Educate the jury enough and you can get them to be about as heartless as you want. But not with children. Because that's what you have faith in. You invest yourself emo-tionally in your parents. They die. Same with your friends, your spouses. They die, and you know they'll die, and you know that you'll see them die, if you're lucky. But children. They'll outlive us; they'll carry on into the future whatever values we place in them. That's what people think." Harold paused for a bite of toast and continued, chewing again. "Also, they believe in us. When we were children, there was another world above us, the grown-up world. It was hard to understand; sometimes it was unfair, but it was there and it took care of things. And we thought that when we became older, we'd be grown-ups too, and we'd know how to take care of things. But that wasn't what happened. What happened was that we got older and suddenly there weren't any more grown-ups. There were only us and people like us, trying to muddle our way through. And then there were children again, and they gave us our authority. That's why juries fixate on them. Try to get them to be rational about children and they act like you're crucifying their god."

"Do you have children?" Mark asked.

"Me?" said Harold. He sounded surprised. "Not that I know of. Hate the little buggers. They're a crutch, I told you. A false idol. Besides, I'd probably have to be married. And women, well, you know women."

"Sure," said Mark doubtfully. "I think I can probably find my way back to Macey's hotel."

Martin Jessup looked surprisingly young, younger than Mark. He wore khaki pants and a blue-and-white-checked flannel shirt. Mark wore his second suit, distinguishable from the first in that it had acquired fewer wrinkles during the trip. He was relieved to see that Robert Macey's associate matched him, gray for gray. "Tom Peters," the associate said, extending a hand. Mark shook it.

"Mark Clayton."

"Well, let's get this show on the road." Peters turned to the court reporter. "Nice to see you again, Caroline."

Caroline, young and attractive but apparently intimidated, blushed and mumbled a response. Mark's anxiety ratcheted up a notch. Peters had evidently done this before, perhaps many times. Maybe the best thing to do would be to object to the first question, just to throw him off his game. "Do you swear to tell the truth the whole truth and nothing but the truth?" Caroline asked Martin, as though reading from the back of a cereal box. I'm not counting that one, Mark told himself.

"Yes."

"Okay," said Tom Peters. Mark tensed. "Please state your name for the record." Maybe not the first one, Mark thought. For almost an hour, Peters asked Martin about his educational background and work experience. When they broke for lunch, Mark was relaxed to the point of boredom. This is easy, he thought, heading to the hotel in hopes of scrounging a sandwich.

"Am I doing okay?" asked Martin, who had trailed behind him unseen.

"Oh, yeah," said Mark. "Nothing to worry about."

"They told me just to answer all the questions the best I could."

It struck Mark as an unconventional strategy. "Right," he said. "Well, that sounds reasonable." The hotel restaurant was deserted, and he looked vainly about for a greeter. Martin approached a girl busing tables; they spoke and she went to the kitchen.

"Jeannie went to high school with me," he explained, as she returned with sandwiches.

"You grow up here?" Mark asked.

"Yeah. Started working at the plant right out of high school. Lots of us did. I figured I'd spend the rest of my life there. But now . . . well, everyone's getting laid off. I didn't even want to stay. They kept me around." He gave half a laugh. "Spend the rest of my life there. I guess I should be glad I didn't. Lot of people did."

"How old are you?"

"Twenty-one. Like I told the lawyer back there."

"Right," said Mark. "Of course."

Tom Peters had a different air when they returned. "I'm going to play a tape for you now, Mr. Jessup," he said. "I'd like you to tell me if you recognize it."

"I object," said Mark.

"What grounds?"

"No one said anything about playing a tape."

"I just did. Let's mark this plaintiff's exhibit one. The record will show that it was obtained from Hubble Chemical's director of security. Now, Mr. Jessup, if you'd listen, please." Martin looked at Mark, who nodded. Tom Peters placed a tape recorder on the table and pressed play. Mark heard a young man's voice.

"Jessup here. There's a problem at the plant."

Peters paused the tape. "Can you identify the speaker?"

Martin looked paler. "That's me," he said.

Peters started the tape again.

An older voice answered. *"What kind of problem? Worth waking me up for?"*

"And that speaker?"

"It's Roger Allen."

"Who is he?"

"He's my supervisor."

"Is he the person you were supposed to notify in the event of an emergency?"

"Yes." I should have objected to that, Mark thought.

"And is he the person Hubble has chosen to handle its on-site emergencies?"

"Objection."

"What grounds?"

Mark thought. "Mr. Jessup has no personal knowledge of what Hubble has chosen Mr. Allen for."

Tom Peters nodded thoughtfully. "Do you know what Mr. Allen's title is?"

Martin hesitated; Mark shrugged, then caught himself and nodded reassuringly. "He's the emergency containment coordinator," Martin said.

"Thank you."

"*It sounds that way, sir. There's a fire, and some sort of toxic smoke.*"

"And that voice," said Tom Peters calmly.

"It's me again."

"*I see.*"

"And that one."

"Roger Allen."

"*What should I do? Should I call Disaster Response? The state people?*"

"Who is speaking here?"

Martin gave Mark a harried look. "Why does he keep asking me that? There's just the two of us. Me and Roger."

"It's okay," said Mark. "We're prepared to stipulate to the identities of the speakers."

Tom Peters raised one eyebrow. "That's very generous of you."

"*No, no. Call Morgan Siler. And the local counsel. Weiland Hart. They're our guys on the ground. And the in-house people.*"

"*Who? I'm sorry, but aren't those—*"

"*Yes. They're our lawyers. And that's who you call. Get on it now. That's the first thing you do. You call all the lawyers.*"

"Now, Mr. Jessup," said Tom Peters. "How did you learn about the fire?"

"I got a radio call from Janette Guzman."

"Who was Ms. Guzman?"

"She was a security guard."

"Did you know her before the events of that night?"

"Yes."

"How did you know her?"

"Well, we worked together. We saw each other sometimes."

Tom Peters frowned thoughtfully. "Did you know her before you started working for Hubble Chemical?" he asked.

Mark's sense of control over the proceedings, tenuous since the lunch break, was starting to slip away altogether. "Objection," he said.

"Grounds?"

"Why does it matter if he knew her before?" Tom Peters tilted his head to the side but said nothing. "Relevance," said Mark.

"You can only object to the form of the question," Peters said gently. "Relevance is an issue of admissibility, which will be resolved at trial." He turned to Martin. "You can answer."

"Yes."

"How did you know her?"

"We were in high school together."

"And what did she say on the radio call?"

"She said—" Martin stopped. He seemed to have difficulty forming words, as though the memories of the night had gathered in his throat. "She said—" He stopped again.

"Let the record show that the witness's answer is delayed."

Mark was suddenly furious. Martin was his witness, and he wasn't about to sit by while Peters bullied him. "Let the record show the witness is crying."

"Objection," said Tom Peters. He pursed his lips. "No, I think I'll let that stay. Let's move on. Mr. Jessup, what did you do after your conversation with Roger Allen?"

Martin swallowed. "I did what he said. I called the lawyers."

"Did any of your supervisors later criticize or question your actions?"

"No. 'You did everything right, Marty.' That's what they kept telling me." He stopped and swallowed again. "But, you know . . . ?"

"Yes?" Peters inquired.

"If I did everything right, how come they're all dead?"

Tom Peters smiled a cold smile. "Objection," said Mark, which even he knew was futile. Perhaps Harold would be too busy to get around to reading the transcript.

Katja Phillips was starting to sweat. Harold hadn't, as she'd hoped, been joking about the warehouse of documents, or enjoying a figure of speech. Instead there was a literal warehouse, tin-roofed, dusty, and poorly lit. And there were documents. There were, more precisely, boxes of documents. Boxes of documents and shelves of boxes. Shelves of boxes and rows of shelves. Quite likely, Katja thought, Hubble had other warehouses with other rows of shelves squatting out in the desert somewhere, with other dry-rotted boxes of documents that had similar peculiar smells. Other corporations in the state, other states in the country, other countries in the world. That was the numerology of discovery, its units of measure, its segmentation of the universe. And it all came down to documents, the essential, the indivisible unit. Documents all the way down.

But not all documents were alike. There were, first, the standard legal dichotomies. Relevant or irrelevant; privileged or unprivileged. The plaintiffs asked for everything that was relevant and unprivileged; the defendants fought over the definitions and over which documents fit in which category. At least, that was the way it usually went. "But we," Harold had said, grinning as he stood with her and Ryan outside the warehouse, "are going to subvert these dichotomies." Getting no response, he tried again. "Taxonomy is a creative project." Dust blew around his feet. "Come on," he said. "Surely one of you was a humanities major." He sighed. "Trying to make things a little more interesting. But never mind. Here's the drill. We have slightly different categories at Morgan Siler, and we use them in a slightly different way. First, you decide whether something is relevant or irrelevant. If it's irrelevant, then you decide whether it's unprivileged. If it is, it's discoverable. We send the plaintiffs everything that's irrelevant and unprivileged."

"Everything?" Katja asked.

Harold looked at the warehouse. "You're right," he said. "You're right, I'm getting too enthusiastic. Just pick out some stuff that's complicated. Hard to understand. Illegible. As long as it's clearly not relevant. We'll give them a couple thousand of those. Maybe ten thousand. Maybe fifteen. No, that's probably sanctionable. Well, we'll give them a good lot. Then we take the irrelevant and privileged documents, and we withhold them on grounds of privilege. Send the plaintiffs a note, saying what lovely little documents they are, but we won't turn them over. Pique their interest, get them to make a motion to compel, litigate it for a couple of months, and then if they win they can have them."

What is that? thought Ryan Grady, looking back at the car in which Harold had driven them, by his customary circuitous route, to the warehouse. Is that a lizard? It is. There's a fucking lizard by the car.

"And what about the relevant documents?" asked Katja.

"This is where it gets good," said Harold excitedly. "You take the relevant documents. Find a couple that are clearly, absolutely, one hundred percent ironclad privileged, and we'll toss them in the privilege log with the rest of the junk, just to show that we're playing fair. But most of them, the ones that are unprivileged, the ones you're not sure about, we get them together and we . . ." He stopped; a small giggle escaped. "Guess what we do with them."

That's like a fucking iguana, that's what that is, thought Ryan.

"What do we do?" said Katja.

"We send them to Canada. Hubble has operations in Canada, and Canada has better discovery rules. It's our fortress of solitude. The real land of the free. It's where our dear little documents go to escape the net of discovery. Our poor draft-dodging documents, finding foster homes in the Great White North." He paused and looked at them. "Last shot. Information wants to be free. You've heard that, right? That's what we're doing here. We're letting these documents go. Be free, little files!"

"That," said Katja, "is not at all what it means for information to be free."

Harold looked crestfallen. "Just trying to give you a little inspiration. Get to work. I've got other people to supervise. This isn't the only warehouse. It's a good one, though. Tony Streeter picked it out himself."

The problem with our legal system, Katja thought, *is that it's typically much more trial by ordeal than you might think. You can have the best case in the world, but I can still make things very difficult for you. And very expensive. And very unpleasant.* Someone had once said that to her, someone who hadn't, at the time, seemed to think it an unalloyed good. What happened to that man?

I wonder where that iguana went, thought Ryan Grady.

Katja pulled the collar of her blouse away from her neck. Documents lay piled around her. A few feet away, Ryan sat on a box, surrounded by similar, though smaller, piles. *If she had no head,* he thought, *I could look right down her shirt.* "Got anything interesting?" he asked.

Katja looked at the papers in her hand. *A true sale opinion, a sale and leaseback, the charter of an SPV. I know what these are,* she thought. "No," she said. "This is just the corporate structure. Hubble's been securitized. It sold its assets to a holding company and leased them back."

"Ah," said Ryan wisely. *There's something sexy about girls who talk finance,* he thought.

"This is a waste of time," Katja said. "None of this is relevant." She sighed. "I guess it's a good source of paper to bury the plaintiffs under, though."

"Bury their lawyers," Ryan corrected. "The plaintiffs are in the ground already. Sorry," he added, seeing Katja's expression. "That's just Harold rubbing off on me." Katja looked no happier, and he changed tack. "You must be tired. Take off your glasses for a minute." She did. "You look better without them," he said softly.

Katja considered. "So do you. Look, I'm going to take a run to clear my head."

"That's probably a good idea."

"So I need to change. Could you go outside?"

Another good idea, thought Ryan, *and then a bad one.* "But the sun's so hot outside," he said. "And I saw a big lizard. It might be poisonous."

How did I get stuck with this cretin? Katja wondered. *Why were men so difficult?* Jason still called her on occasion; Harold was acting increasingly odd. *Sympathy is an error of judgment. Keep your eye on the ball,* she told herself. *Professionalism could still save her; immersion in the* work. "Okay," she said. "Could you go off somewhere else in the building or something?"

"Sure," said Ryan. "Of course I respect your privacy. And your, you know, individuality or whatever." He ambled to the other side of the warehouse, considering his options. He wasn't going to look at her; that was beneath him. But if there happened to be a mirror of some sort . . . well, it wasn't his fault where light chose to stray. Investigation soon turned up a likely candidate: a janitorial closet with a window in the door, backed by a dark blind. Katja's pale image moved within the glass, and Ryan Grady smiled. It was not a perfect solution, he realized; he was now standing directly in her line of sight. But if he opened the door and left it slightly ajar . . . Ryan nodded to himself, calculating the angle. And if he went *inside* the other room . . . Cunning glee suffused his features. He tried the door but found it locked. Well, thought Ryan Grady, *that's not going to stop me*. He fished a credit card from his wallet and jimmied the lock. No problemo. The closet contained the expected complement of brooms and buckets, also more boxes of documents. Ryan took a seat on one of the boxes. Yeah, he thought. That's more like it.

On the other side of the warehouse Katja took off her blouse. Nice, thought Ryan appreciatively. Lacy. But you're not going to run in that, are you? You need to take that off and put on something else. Katja reached into her briefcase and his spirits soared. What you need is, yes, that's it, a sports bra. That's my girl. Katja glanced over her shoulder and unhooked her bra. Ryan convulsed. God, he thought, that's really not fair, now, is it? I mean, girls don't earn their breasts. One absentminded hand strayed to his own chest. Feel that. Hours in the gym, sweating, suffering. That's how I got these muscles. And what did she have to do for those? It's like, it's like . . . Katja undid the waist of her slacks and a longunused constellation of synapses in Ryan Grady's brain fired to life. It's like free grace compared to salvation by works, he thought.

Katja stepped out of the pants and Ryan, stunned by revelation, managed nonetheless another thought. Thank God for the thong. His patient study of the women who passed into view at work or during his morning commute had taught him little of women's fashion, chiefly how much you could divine of nipples through different sorts of shirts and bras. But the ubiquity of thongs was a development hard to miss. Everyone wore thongs these days. Fifteen-year-olds, crossing guards, library ladies. The point, he'd heard, was to eliminate the panty line. Ryan didn't really understand why they would want to do that; he'd always found the panty line quite appealing, its visible demarcation of the body's zones. A panty line was almost as enticing as a tan line, which likewise advertised the distinction in covering, though with the added benefit of emphasizing that what had once been covered was now exposed. But these days he looked for the panty line and saw just the tiny triangle diminishing down from the small of the back. And that was sexy too. Just about everything girls did was sexy. Especially taking off their pants. Free grace, he thought again.

Katja's footsteps approached, jolting Ryan from his reverie. "Where are you?" she called. Ryan hastily tore open a box. He tossed his jacket to the side and rolled up his sleeves.

"I'm in here," he answered. "There's some more stuff I was looking at."

Katja switched on the light and regarded him suspiciously. "You might find it easier if it's not so dark," she said. "Well, I'll be back in about half an hour."

"Yeah," Ryan answered unthinkingly. Free grace and salvation by works, he mused. Where the hell did that come from? He took a handful of documents from the box. These look good, he thought. Incomprehensible, anyway. He put them in the litigation bag for transport back to Washington.

Some distance down the road, Harold Fineman sat in a parked car, looking past an orange barricade. Something was definitely wrong; he realized that now. Harold was starting to remember his dreams, which he hadn't for years. They were more pleasant than they had any right to be, but they found pleasure in things and people he had barred from waking life. And even if he wasn't much for introspection, he could watch his own behavior. He was alert to unease, expert at detecting a guilty conscience, able to read a witness through one quivering eyebrow or a single bead of sweat. He had assessed himself with an advocate's eyes in the past, of necessity, for he had no others. But he had always taken his side in the matter, placed things in their best light. And now, with one simple change, the shift of perspective that had once been habitual, he was seeing it from the other side. The picture was not pretty; when he looked at himself, he saw a man who was coming unglued.

The signs he was giving off weren't particularly subtle, more galling still. There was the professional hyperaggressiveness, for one thing, the laughing will to push the boundaries of acceptable litigating behavior. In the past he might have taken that as merely a sign of high spirits, which on some occasions it had been. But now it was paired with solitary moments of painful remorse, self-doubt, anxiety. That had never happened before; the sword does not question what it cuts. Uncertainty meant that he was no longer the pure advocate he had been. Part of him clung to that role, more fiercely than ever, but part was now divested, living outside the arena and trembling to watch.

So I'm overcompensating, Harold told himself. That stuff about sending the documents to Canada. I'm disparaging what I don't have. That ridiculous rant about children, like auditioning to play Herod. I've been a little excessive in some ways. Why does that mean anything?

The rhetorical question did not console, for Harold knew quite well what it meant. The witness asserts himself more forcefully because he doesn't believe what he's saying. Push him a little more, drive him to a grosser exaggeration. Make him say something he can't stand to hear, and he'll crack. He'll recant it all. And the jury in the courtroom sees what the jury within has pronounced, what the heavenly jury has always known. The starry sky above and the moral law within, the immanent and the transcendent. They will not be thought away. Something had tracked him to this stretch of highway: the doubt he had lived by and lost, the doubt that had been his earliest faith. It had come back, a part of himself long put aside and now returned to judge what he'd become in its absence.

That's it, Harold thought. It's finally happened. They warn you that law will divide you from your family, your friends, your hobbies. He had avoided this by having none. But no one tells you that it will divide you from yourself, that it will fracture you, one half horrified by what the other does. That's where I've come. Where the path of the law leads. This is splitsville.

Nor was there much of a mystery how it had happened. Work had called to him in the mornings, sweet with the promise of struggle. He enjoyed it all, arguing motions, writing briefs, giving commands to his legions, crushing opponents with resources they couldn't match. Even filling out time sheets, recording his battles, tabulating his worth. Now he was growing deaf to that voice, and Katja was what he thought of, her querulous smiles, her brave resolve. He had used her for her fresh eyes, but what she showed him had become more than a datum for the litigator. There was something unbearably moving about the world she lived in, its beauty and innocence and vulnerability, the blue-green pearl of the earth seen from space. He longed for it like all he had set aside, and he longed for her as its embodiment and bearer. Fitful connections kindled within him, the agony of sea on a lonely shore.

All this was deeply irksome to Harold, who'd consciously set himself on a narrow path. His basic thesis had been that everyone was an enemy.

Some were provisionally on your side. They were your partners, your associates; they played on your team. But they were still rivals against whom you had to strive, the partners competing for the same points, the associates fighting to keep a life beyond the job. Harold had been alone all his adult life, but he had never been lonely. What he had failed to anticipate was her kindness, that sudden unexpected shower. It seeped into him like water into a rock, and in the chill of the night it bloomed into ice and split him from within.

Harold watched a small figure grow in his rearview mirror. The heat laid illusory puddles across the road, bending the light in unexpected ways, and she danced through them as though flying. I shouldn't have brought her here, he thought, shouldn't have involved her in this. Bad for both of us. Katja rapped on the car window and he lowered it.

"What are you doing?"

Harold gestured at the map. "I thought I'd try deciding where I was going before I got there," he said.

Katja laughed and leaned in through the window. "Need help?"

I certainly do, Harold thought. Her sudden appearance took his breath like a pack-a-day habit. He felt a tumult of possibilities, a speechless upheaval within him, an urge to lay his lips in the hollow of her neck. "No, I think I've got it figured out." He paused. A longing for the kiss, a dim apprehension of what that kiss would mean. "Go back to the warehouse."

"Don't worry, Harold," she said. "I'm going to bill ten hours today."

"That's not what I mean," Harold told her, suddenly in pain. "You shouldn't be out here. In this." He gestured toward the blackened plains beyond.

Katja lost her smile. "You mean it's dangerous?"

"Just go back," said Harold. Katja stepped away from the window, lips slightly parted, hands on her hips, her chest rising with the even rhythm of her breath. God in heaven, thought Harold. I'm falling in love. What else can go wrong? He gunned the car to life and accelerated savagely away.

31 THE NEEDLESS GRIND

Back in Washington, Peter Morgan and Anthony Streeter faced each other across Peter's mahogany desk. "Well, Anthony," said Peter. "What's the good news?"

Streeter looked gleeful. The expression did not suit him, as Peter's frown advised. Quickly Streeter recomposed his features into a mask of bland satisfaction. "It's done," he said. "All the filings, all the notices, all taken care of."

"Wonderful," said Peter. "Now, what is it, exactly, that's been done?"

Despite himself, Streeter let a bit of glee slip through. "We've securitized Hubble."

"And you really think this is going to work?"

"Well," said Streeter, "no one's tried it before." He paused modestly. "I don't think anyone saw the possibility of this particular application. But how can they stop us? It's a true sale. The assets are gone. The law's on our side."

"That's good work, Anthony," Peter Morgan said appreciatively. "What happens now?"

"Like I said, the documents are there. Our litigators are probably turning them up right now. I saw to that myself. Then we give them to the plaintiffs, who'll kick up a fuss when they realize what it means. But I don't think there's much they can do about it. Securitization is a multitrillion-dollar industry. If you call it into question to satisfy some plaintiffs' lawyers, the whole world economy will shake. So I expect that after a while they'll give up."

Peter felt a paternal warmth. "Excellent," he said. "I think our clients will be very pleased." Streeter left the office and Peter watched him go.

This was groundbreaking legal work; they were doing something new. The firm was still progressing, still moving. That part of his life was in satisfactory shape. As for the rest . . . He sighed. The rest needed a bit more thought.

Peter met Cassandra in law school, toward the end of his first year. He'd applied to several schools—Yale, the University of Chicago, even Stanford—and been admitted by all. But the Harvard acceptance letter came with a card to be returned and a choice of two boxes to check. Not "I accept" or "I decline," but "single" or "double." Peter liked that confidence. And he liked Harvard Law School. As an undergraduate he'd watched the law students bustling across the campus in coats and ties, freighted with an importance the undergrads lacked. He checked the box for a double room.

It was the roommate who was responsible for their meeting, in fact, ginger-haired Roger Hanson, gone west after graduation and not seen since. "Mixer at Harkness," he said, splashing on cologne in front of a mirror. "You should come. Even Friendless will be there."

Peter looked up from his Property casebook, then down to the leather-bound notebook in which he inscribed digests of the weekly reading. He scowled. "That's not his name."

Roger whistled tunelessly through his teeth. "Sorry, pal," he said. "Didn't know you cared."

Peter shook his head. Roger knew well enough how he felt about the nicknames. Three students in the class of 1967 were known as the Grinds, viewed as siblings for their long hours in the library together. Hopeless was Paul Sowell, a blond and affable Iowan. How he'd gotten into the law school in the first place was a mystery, for he collapsed under pressure. He was backbenching by the second week of classes, taking refuge from his assigned seat in the anonymity of the back row. Every so often, after heroic preparation, he'd return to flush and stammer in response to even the simplest question. "It all goes out of my head when I hear their voices," he explained sadly. Eventually the professors began ignoring him, even when he raised his hand. Hammond, in Contracts, invoked him occasionally when the other students struggled, wondering aloud why they had turned into a class of Sowells. As everyone expected, Paul failed the first-semester exams and wasn't there for the spring.

Adam Singer was Friendless, a Jew from New York, dark and intense, ferociously prepared. He did extra reading; he'd worked in a law firm for two years before coming to Harvard and when outflanked by a line of questioning he'd invoke the experience that few professors had. Or he used to; three months in, Hammond cut him off. "When you're back in your beloved law firm, Mr. Singer," he said, "assuming you graduate, which is by no means certain, I'm sure you will find ready ears for your practical wisdom. At the moment, however, you are in my classroom and I would like an answer drawn from the law."

The third was Peter. His inclusion in the group explained part of his distaste for the nicknames; the one he'd received did the rest. The Needless Grind, they called him, asking only half in jest why he had to take one of the top places in the class with a job waiting for him already. "Some of us actually need to be on *Law Review*."

For Peter it was not a joke at all. Without the possibility of failure, there was no such thing as success, and they were stealing that from him, undermining his efforts as surely as the rabid competitors who ripped crucial pages from the library books. Peter respected those people, whoever they were; they knew what they wanted and were willing to take risks to get it. For the rest of his classmates he felt very little. Adam Singer came closest to inspiring affection; he was smart and could have coasted, but chose to work instead. Most of the other students shunned Adam, and not just because he embarrassed them in class.

"Some of my best friends are anti-Semites," Roger remarked carelessly after Peter started eating lunch with Adam. Archie might have smiled at the line, Peter thought, but not he. He did not object to anti-Semitism on principle. From a certain perspective, in fact, he was glad of its existence. Prejudice was an inefficiency, and inefficiencies could be exploited. Peter would be happy to hire good lawyers on the cheap; his eyes were clear. His annoyance with Roger had a different source. Though he hesitated to admit it, there was an emotional aspect to his analysis.

Peter felt solidarity with his Jewish classmates, obsessed with proving themselves against a world that devalued their accomplishments and refused to see them as individuals. He was with them in the library late at night, long after the other students had gone, still working because nothing they did was ever enough. In this way, he understood their lives. Not what it was like to be discriminated against, but what it was like to be judged on attributes beyond your control. When people looked at him, he knew what they saw. Prep school, an Ivy League education, a firm that bore his family's name. He knew what they thought, and to some extent they were right. His grades wouldn't matter; the doors were open for him. Adam's grades wouldn't make a difference either; some firms would be willing to hire him and some would not. They were on opposite sides of the fence; their nicknames alone made it clear. But there in the library they occupied the same small space, the same small group, the only elite that Peter Morgan ever believed in. The people who would always have something to prove.

He had worked hard, that first semester. As exams approached, the tension increased. Hopeless Paul Sowell was taking pills to wake up, pills to fall asleep, pills to keep him calm while he studied. When panic and claustrophobia made the law school unbearable, Peter took something else, a motel room in Cambridge where he cloistered himself with his books. Then, amid the clattering of typewriters in an overheated room, while his classmates wept and swore around him, he calmly poured out his hard-won knowledge, returning to the sea of law as many of the memorized rules and exceptions as time allowed.

And he'd succeeded. When first-semester grades came out, half the class gave up. The remainder had their faith renewed. With three A's and two A-minuses, Peter relaxed, though only a bit. He was well on the way to *Law Review*; even a mediocre performance in the spring would get him over the bar.

He could afford to go to the party, he thought. The Property reading was almost done; his outline was in good shape; and Adam had agreed to study with him. But what was the point? Roger sensed his hesitation. He shrugged into a jacket and inclined his head toward the door. "Come on. There'll be Wellesley girls."

Peter raised his eyes. He'd made it through college with very little time wasted dating. Girls were a distraction. But that stage of life was passing, and for the future he imagined, girls were, or at least one girl was, a necessity. A family gives you something to work for, Archie had told him.

"Okay," Peter said.

The Harkness Commons was just a short walk from their dormitory, Holmes. They could have gotten there without going outside, following the covered pathway lined with lockers that connected the dorms to the dining hall. But it was April, and the campus was starting to warm, the ground releasing the scent of damp earth and growing grass. Peter felt a promise in the night air, the mercy and reprieve of spring. When they walked in, a band was playing and students clustered around a punch bowl or shifted awkwardly from foot to foot in the center of the room. He saw her immediately, standing amid a small group of friends. They looked familiar to him, these girls in their A-line skirts and matching sweaters, their low-heeled shoes. Familiar, almost interchangeable. But only one had her graceful carriage and silky blond hair; only one had sun-kissed skin and wide-set, intelligent blue eyes. Peter walked straight over and held out his hand. "I'm Peter Morgan."

She took it, the blue eyes regarding him with faint amusement. Her hand was smooth and cool to the touch. "Cassandra Lake."

Peter wouldn't have called it love at first sight, but from their first conversation he knew she was what he wanted. She'd grown up outside of Philadelphia, in Ardmore on the Main Line, taken a Thoroughbred hunter with her to the Ethel Walker School in Connecticut. She had poise and polish and an appreciation of what he offered. And she had personality and independence, though not too much. "I'm not going to sit at home darning my husband's socks," she told him on their second date.

"When I get a hole in my sock, I throw it out," Peter said. That silenced her, though not for long.

She had some silly romantic Harvard boyfriend too, some kind of graduate student, but she soon stopped mentioning him and was available whenever Peter called. They met for study dates in the libraries, usually hers, as she had to be back in Tower Court by ten; for a break they'd get coffee at the Howard Johnson's in the village. On weekends they took picnics to Singing Beach in Manchester, where he read her poetry on the sand. And they went to the parking lot at Alumnae Hall, where the Wellesley girls and their dates negotiated over articles of clothing like nations poised on the brink of a terrible, half-desired war. Peter didn't push Cassandra. He respected her; he could wait until they were married. A different conquest was driving him. The body he dreamed of mounting was neither corporeal nor female; it was corporate and immortal. In those melting moments when fantasy came, just before sleep, he saw himself sprawled victorious atop a large organization.

He proposed one year after they met, on Tupelo Point, looking out over Wellesley's Lake Waban. Peter was a second-year then, third in his class, and in line to be executive editor of the *Law Review*. He dropped to one knee and took her hand; she caught her breath and said, "Oh, Peter," and "Yes," as he'd known she would. They were married shortly after her graduation and spent his third year in a small Cambridge apartment. Living together took away the pressure to go on dates, which Peter appreciated. The *Law Review* demanded his time. It had its own building, Gannett House, which came to feel like a home; most nights found him there or in the library. Cassandra baked cookies and carried them over, or sometimes she'd go to enrichment classes at the Cambridge Center for Adult Education where broken-down old professors lectured, pastured racehorses trotting circles, still feeling the track.

Some of Peter's classmates joined the Peace Corps after graduation; some went south to try voting rights cases for the Justice Department. He went south too, but only as far as Washington. Cassandra came to the firm from time to time, draping herself over the couch in his office and suggesting that they sneak out for an hour, or just lock the door. To get the work done he'd taken to arranging for his secretary to call or knock for him after fifteen minutes. But most nights Cassandra stayed in the small Georgetown house. Sometimes Peter was home for dinner; sometimes he brought guests: clients, or partners from the firm. The twins were born when Peter was a third-year associate, and they kept her busy. Then he made partner, and their house was larger. Peter's hours were still long. Once she'd complained about them, he remembered, and he'd explained that he wasn't working for the client or the firm but for her, for their family. And she'd made some silly joke about wishing she could be the client instead, and they'd made up tenderly.

He'd been more involved with Julie, and that had led to more time with Cassandra. They ate dinner as a family; they went to museums on the weekend. He'd even made it to a couple of the Madeira field hockey games. Those had been the best years, Peter thought, the years of shaping, when he'd molded the firm in his own image. And Julie too. He'd given her his confidence, his self-reliance. It had been seven years since she left for college, and they saw her infrequently, but in that assertion of independence she was more his child than ever.

The marriage had been a success, Peter thought. They had accomplished things together. Hosted dinner parties, raised three children, established themselves in Washington society. But the dinner parties were catered now, the children grown, the circle of familiar faces starting to shrink. There was a stale air around the house, a sense that nothing was left to achieve. Cassandra was turning outward; she spent more time riding and took classes on Renaissance architecture at Georgetown. Once, last year, she'd spent a week in Italy without him, touring Palladian villas with friends. It was awkward, in some ways. There were spaces people fit in your life, and growth disrupted order. Their marriage was a partnership, built on certain understandings. He would provide; she would be beautiful and supportive. That was the bargain they had struck, so many years ago. But without a partnership agreement, things could change.

He couldn't blame her, he decided. Their work together was done. He still had the firm, a child that would never leave and continued to grow. It was only to be expected that she'd find her own interests. And together they had stability, a counterbalance and anchor against the uncertainties of the world. They had a life together; they had their own lives apart. It was a new bargain, but a fair one. Still, Peter thought, those terms were by no means fixed. Without a written agreement, things could change. They could change on both sides.

Three doors down, Walker Eliot scowled at his computer screen. As he'd started writing the motion to dismiss Parkwell from the case, he'd looked over the list of plaintiffs' counsel. Macey's firm was there, of course, but they'd enlisted public interest groups to help: MALDEF, the Sierra Club Legal Defense Fund, Earthjustice. The names caused Walker a momentary pang. Nothing personal, guys, he thought. It's just business.

Now, halfway in, he was realizing that the most straightforward understanding of the law was against them, and that hurt more. Not because he thought it damaged their chances of winning. He didn't care what happened to Parkwell, and anyway, he was confident he could find a way around the problems. He could call the needed law into existence, do it with nothing but ink and imagination, like a cartoon character who sketches a door on a blank wall and ducks inside. But there were some costs to reshaping the world like that. And anyway, he asked himself, what's the point? I find some esoteric reason why this case doesn't quite fit into the doctrinal category it seemed to, and the law becomes more complicated, more intricate, less able to guide behavior. His argument would be correct, of course. The professors would enjoy it; it would provide grist for law review articles. But Walker was beginning to suspect that complexity for its own sake was not a virtue. There was, he thought, little beauty in it, and it was with a smattering of distress that he turned to the task. This suggested that happiness might require something more than nice shoes. "Gah," said Walker, who loathed epiphanies.

He steeled himself. It's just business. I am an advocate. I do not appear here as amicus curiae. I am no friend of the court.

"Hey," said Larry Angstrom, knocking on the open door by way of introduction. "Congratulations. You did it."

"What did I do?"

"We won *Vendstar*. Unanimous." He waved a sheaf of papers. "The slip opinion's just come out. Your brief, buddy. Your brief is now the law."

Walker brightened. "I'm sure it was your masterful oral argument," he muttered, that being what one said in such circumstances. He took the opinion and began to read, and what had been a bad morning became worse.

Walker had been happy with the *Vendstar* brief. It had been a true test. Jennifer Caputo, whose presence he had sensed in the ranks of the opposition, had come back with the arguments he'd expected. Morgan Siler filed a reply; battle was joined. The minds of the former clerks struggled for mastery, feinting, parrying, conjuring cases to do their bidding. It had been exhilarating, the most intellectually demanding project Walker had worked on. And if his position hadn't been the most obvious, that only added to the challenge, like dueling left-handed, or running a race with weights tied to your ankles.

That he had actually prevailed, Walker thought, was a testament to the ingenious subtleties of his argument, its ability to beat back every objection. But as he read the opinion, he realized that something quite different had happened. He and Jennifer had been fighting it out in the rarefied air of theory, and the court was writing doctrine. It had taken Walker's argument, but without the grace and intricacy. What had been an elegant reconceptualization of the cases, a dance across perspectives, had been condensed into a flat statement of the law. And put that way, Walker had to admit, it was far from convincing. Law could bend, and often enough to support any outcome in any particular case, but only if you were very careful with your words. One misstep, and what was going on was more than bending.

Walker spread a hand in the air, regarding his fingers. The law of class actions was beautiful in its complexity, studded with dusty gems like the wings of a butterfly, and he'd enjoyed exploring it. He'd even enjoyed his artful refinement. But this result—he wasn't enjoying it at all. His touch, which had been healing, was now destructive; he saw jeweled powder on his fingertips, the law limping and damaged.

Idiot judges, thought Walker, writing something like this. Idiot law clerks, misunderstanding the brief, not doing the research themselves.

Idiot Larry Angstrom, arguing it the way he wanted and not the way I wrote it. All of them doing their jobs, and I mine, and what's the result? This wound on the body of law, which once I swore to protect, this crack in the doctrinal edifice. The sort of mistake I used to spend my time fixing.

What would Harold say? That the law did not exist itself in any way he need worry about. It existed only to serve human interests, and he'd made it a little bit better able to serve the interests that were ultimately paying for his shoes. Walker shook his head.

"Aren't you happy?" Angstrom asked.

"This isn't what I wrote," Walker said.

"It's better."

"It's not. There's an integrity to legal materials. You can't just do what you want with them."

"Looks like *you* can," Larry Angstrom said. "You can change the law."

"I don't change the law," Walker said. "I just give you a path to a particular result. What I wrote was right. It was good law. What the law wants to be."

Angstrom laughed. "Good law for the client, maybe. It's what you want it to be."

"No," said Walker, but he doubted. Had he imposed his will, however unknowingly; had he convinced himself of an untruth? Had he forced himself on the law?

He put the thought from his mind. Maybe the court was right; maybe it was taking the law in a better direction. Well, there'd been a gap in the published opinions. The Fifth Circuit hadn't yet decided this precise issue. But he heard Justice Arlen's voice. *There are no gaps in the law, only answers we have not yet found.* The opinion could be called clever, but it wasn't beautiful. It didn't cohere with the rest of the doctrine. It didn't show the law in its best light. In the last analysis, Walker had to admit, it just didn't ring true.

No. His argument had been ingenious. As phrased, it could have been reconciled with existing law. A strain, a sprain, the sort of thing that could be walked off in subsequent cases. The ice of a sober second look would bring down the swelling. And that, he realized now, was what he'd been hoping for. But the way the court had written it, this was a break, no doubt about it. A clean split from the other federal circuits. This would require professional treatment, attention at higher levels.

Cert bait, his clerk's mind said. This one's going up. And Arlen would see it, would see what he had become. Shame overcame him. Oath-breaker, Walker thought; defiler. And more: criminal. I broke the law.

Walker looked at his shoes. He pulled one foot free and, frowning, examined the sock. There at the heel, bare skin was showing through the cashmere. "Gah," he said again, this time with feeling.

33 ONE OR THE OTHER

Harold pulled the car into the gravel driveway of the Guzmans' ranch house. "Now you're going to see how to do a deposition," he said. Inside, Felix Guzman sat on a couch in the living room, Robert Macey and Tom Peters at his side. A wicker chair held the court reporter. No provision had been made to seat Harold, who began a professorial pacing. Mark stood uneasily in the corner, looking around the room. Janette Guzman, he thought. Who had she been? Framed photographs answered: a smiling dark-haired girl, clutching a diploma or a friend's shoulder, posing with classmates in front of the Capitol, with her parents beside a weathered car. Once, made up and gowned, her escort ill at ease in a rented tuxedo. Marty, Mark realized, and looked away.

"Okay," said Harold. "Mr. Guzman, let me extend my condolences for your loss."

Felix Guzman said nothing, deep-set eyes fixed ahead of him, face impassive. "That's not a question," said Macey. "Let's get to what you're here for, Harold."

Harold nodded. "Okay," he said again. "Mr. Guzman, could you tell me how you came to be represented by the firm of Macey and Schiller?"

"Objection," said Tom Peters promptly.

"What's wrong with that?"

"Representation is a legal relationship about which our client is not qualified to testify. Moreover, the process by which it was created is shielded by the attorney-client privilege."

"How did you first hear about this firm?"

Felix Guzman said nothing. "You can answer," Peters told him.

"I was looking for a lawyer. I found them on the Internet."

"Do you have a computer in this house?"

"No." Harold raised one eyebrow. He opened his mouth, then closed it again. Tom Peters cleared his throat. "I went to the public library," said Felix Guzman. "I used the terminals there."

"Please let your client decide for himself when he's finished his answer."

"What are you insinuating?"

"I'm asking the questions. Let the record show that Mr. Peters is prompting the witness."

"The record shows nothing of the sort," said Macey. "Come on, Harold, let's keep it moving."

"Okay," Harold said.

Felix Guzman interrupted. "You think I can't go to the library? We used to go there a lot. You don't know me. You don't know Janette."

Mark bit his lip. The line about the computers sounded like an agreed-upon fabrication, but this one rang true.

Harold dipped his head toward one shoulder, then the other, eliciting faint crackles of vertebrae. "How did you decide to become a class representative?"

"Objection. Please try to speak English."

"Mr. Guzman," said Harold. "Are you aware that you are pursuing claims on behalf of a number of injured parties other than your daughter?"

"Objection. They're not injured, Harold; they're dead. Let's be straight about this."

"Are you aware that your suit presents the claims of other deceased persons?"

"I want justice," said Felix Guzman. "What they did, they did to a lot of people. They should pay for everyone they killed."

"Could you tell me why you feel that you should present these claims instead of allowing the other representatives to sue individually?"

"My lawyers are good lawyers. Not like you. They will hold these men accountable. They will bring justice."

"Could we strike . . . Forget it." Harold ran a hand over his face. "Have your lawyers consulted with you about the possibility of a settlement?"

Felix Guzman shook his head. "You know what they gave me, the men from the company? A box of dirt that they said was my daughter.

Now you come here, into my house, throwing more dirt. You think I want a settlement? You think you give me money, everything's all right again? You want a settlement, you give me back my daughter, my Janette."

"What is the fee arrangement you have with Macey and Schiller? No, strike that." Harold paced and frowned. "What's that on the wall?" he asked. Macey and Tom Peters turned their heads; Mark looked up at the framed paper, read Janette's name. A diploma?

"It's a stock certificate," said Felix Guzman. "Janette, she was proud of her job. Proud of the company. She took her first paycheck and bought stock. What did they do? They locked her in like an animal and burned her to death." He paused. "You got any more questions you want to ask me?"

"You know what?" said Harold. "I think that'll do. I thank you for your time, Mr. Guzman, and again, let me offer my condolences." Felix Guzman shook his head angrily. Harold made as if to offer his hand and reconsidered. "Let's go," he told Mark, and they left the house. "So," said Harold, starting the car. "As I was saying, that's how to defend a deposition."

Ryan Grady lifted a pair of pants by the hems and shook them. He laid his suit jacket flat on the bed and patted it down. He looked around the motel room in panic. I know it was in my pocket, he thought. I know because I was checking e-mail this morning. And then we went to the warehouse, and then I came back here and changed, and where the fuck is my phone? Okay, he told himself. Calm down. Take a deep breath. Have a drink. Or take another deep breath. There's something you do in this situation. Remember the crucial things. Free grace and salvation by works and how to find your missing phone. Oh, yeah.

He picked up the motel phone and stood with it for a moment in his hand, gazing about the room. You're here somewhere, baby, and I'm going to find you. He dialed his number, waiting to hear the familiar electronic rendition of "Für Elise." Three rings from the cradle in his hand, and silence in the room. Did I leave it on vibrate?

The voice in his ear surprised him so much he almost dropped the receiver. "That's a very annoying ring you've got there, buddy," it said. "Who is this?"

"Who is this?" Ryan repeated, incredulous. "It's the guy who owns that phone you're holding. Who are you?"

There was a pause. "I'm the guy that's got your phone."

"Yeah, well, you'd better give it back. I'm a lawyer."

Another pause. "What have you been up to, lawyer?" the voice said. "Looking at things you shouldn't have been?"

"No," Ryan said reflexively. Then he remembered Katja. What the hell? he thought.

"Oh, I think you have been, lawyer," the voice said. "Did you see anything that interested you?"

Ryan shuffled through possible responses. Perhaps there was a strip club nearby, or someone running an escort service. "What business is that of yours?" he demanded finally.

"It's our business, lawyer. I suppose you don't understand, not being a businessman. But that's exactly what it is."

Aha, thought Ryan. Things are looking up. "I might be interested in your business. If you're discreet."

The chuckle on the other end did not indicate amusement. "Think you're going to come in here with your pals and then do a little freelancing, is that it? See something you like, you think you can just have it? You leave your phone so we can get in touch? You're a smooth one, aren't you?"

Freelancing, thought Ryan. That's a nice way to put it. What did you do last weekend, man? Oh, a little freelancing. How about you?

"I don't think so," the voice continued. "I would advise against it. You're in over your head just talking to me, lawyer. I don't think you'd have the faintest idea what to do, out on your own without your buddies from the firm."

Ryan collected himself, insulted. "Look, you fucking psycho," he said. "Maybe I don't care about your business after all. That's not what I came for. I'm not on vacation. I'm just here to do a job. Maybe I'll just concentrate on that. So why don't you stop hassling me and give me back my phone?"

"Sure," said the voice. "I'll do that. Why don't you tell me where you are?"

"The Redbird Hotel," Ryan said. "Room 208. When are you coming over?"

"It's a motel," said the voice. "And you'll know." The line went dead.

"So," said Mark. "How was your day?" He hung his suit jacket in the closet, atop the other jacket, and began to change.

"Sucked," said Ryan.

"Yeah," said Mark. "Mine too. You want to go out for a drink? I ran into Katja, she said she saw some little bar down the road."

That's the first sensible thing I've heard you say, thought Ryan. "Can't," he said sadly. "I have to meet someone here."

Mark pulled on jeans and a T-shirt. "Hot date?"

"I wish. No, it's a long story. Maybe I can catch up with you guys later."

Katja squeezed a wedge of lime into the beer bottle and tilted it toward her lips. "So," she said. "How was your day?"

Mark shook his head. "I don't know. I do these depositions, they almost have me in tears. And I don't know when to object." He consulted his own bottle. "But I went to one with Harold today and he got crushed too. So I feel a little better."

"I've seen that happen," Katja said. "How did he take it?"

"He told me that I was learning how to defend a deposition."

"Yeah. But did he seem upset about it? Or do you think he was maybe a little relieved?"

"Relieved? No, he was just Harold. You know, kill them and eat their babies." Katja leaned back. She's disappointed, Mark thought. "Well, I don't know," he said. "We were talking to this girl's father, the lead plaintiff. They set it up for us, had us go to his house, pictures of her all around. You could see it was staged. But I think it got to him a little bit, even so. I mean, he felt for the guy. I could tell." Katja sipped and nodded calmly. Whatever emotion Mark had detected was hidden again. "How was your day?" he asked.

"Well, I was in a warehouse for most of it, going through boxes with your pervert roommate. Then I went for a run, but I had to come back because I realized I'd forgotten my gas mask. Have you noticed that the air around here smells funny?"

"I thought it was Ryan," Mark said.

Katja rewarded him with half a laugh. "I don't know," she said. "It's just, at times it all seems unreal. If you'd asked me a couple of years ago what I'd be doing now, I couldn't even have imagined this. I mean, is this why you joined a firm? Why you went to law school?"

"I don't know," he said. "Mostly it was for my parents. So I could give them something back. Why did you?"

"To do something with my life. To have a career. My mother never did. Well, you'll laugh at this, but she was an airline stewardess when she met my father. Lufthansa. It was more glamorous back then."

Mark shrugged. "Mine's a secretary. And what did she do after?"

"Nothing, really. Social stuff. My father probably didn't think I was going to work either. But I had all these opportunities and I didn't want to waste them. I wish he was still here to see what I've done." Mark said nothing; Katja closed her eyes for a moment and continued. "But is this really what it's all about? Working harder to have less freedom? You give up half your life to get good grades so you can get that top-firm job, then as a reward you get to give up the other half. And then if you're lucky someday you bail out and go work as in-house counsel to some corporation so you can get a little bit of it back. Who told us that this was what we wanted?"

"Who said we get to do what we want?"

Katja shrugged. "If we don't, who does?"

"I don't know," said Mark. "I think it's different when you get a little more seniority."

"Yeah," said Katja. "You'd think so. Or that's what they tell you, anyway." She paused. "I turned up some interesting documents today."

"Did you send them to Canada?" He got a full laugh this time, but not a happy one.

"You heard that speech too?"

"Just the highlights. What did you find?"

"Securitization," said Katja. "It's a financing technique. It means that Hubble doesn't own any of its assets."

"How can it not own its assets?"

"That doesn't matter. It doesn't own them."

"So?"

"Well, it didn't hit me until later, because I was thinking about it in terms of financing. But what this means is that there's nothing there. The plaintiffs can get their judgment, but Hubble just slips into Chapter 11 bankruptcy, discharges the debt, and comes back out. They never have to pay anything. It's like one of those toys you can't knock over."

"That's good," said Mark. Katja looked at him. "Or not," he said. "Or not good."

"One or the other," Katja said. "But doesn't it make you wonder what we're all doing here? I mean, the plaintiffs' lawyers are gearing up for a big battle; we're here doing all this preparation for defense, but we're fighting over nothing. It's an empty shell. Once Macey and Schiller figure that out, they'll just pack up and leave. There's nothing in it for them if they get a judgment they can't collect. So why didn't Hubble disclose the securitization immediately?"

Ours not to reason why, Mark thought. "I don't know," he said.

"I don't know either. But it makes me curious. Don't you wonder?"

"Yeah," Mark said. "I do." How had he come to this place? This town, this bar, this green-eyed girl. "Do you have any guesses?"

"Not yet," said Katja. "Maybe something will turn up." She drummed her fingers on the table. "But so that's not going to make more sense when I've got more seniority. I get these projects, you know, and I immerse myself in them, and it seems like I'm doing something. But then I take a step back and it's all canceled out. It's like you're swimming in a river, and you can feel yourself moving through the water, but then you look up and it's the same bit of shoreline."

"Or you look up and get clocked in the head by a log," Mark said. What she was describing sounded like a substantial improvement over his experience. "You should try pro bono."

Katja nodded. "I admire you for taking that on. I don't know how you find the time."

"I don't either," Mark said. He didn't have the time, if he thought about it realistically. There was no way he was going to make the annual target of two thousand hours chargeable to a client. But thinking about things realistically was proving to be a recipe for depression. Perhaps that was the value of law school, that it taught you how to rationalize away what happened to your life when you became a lawyer. He looked down at the table, studying knife-etched graffiti in the dark wood. At the moment the billables didn't seem all that important.

"I guess it helps that you can have the firm do your shopping for you," Katja went on. "Isn't that crazy? Before you join the firm you have this normal life. Then all of a sudden half of what used to be your life is taking place inside the firm. Your meals, your exercise. And half of it is still taking place outside, but the firm is doing it for you. It's like a fairy world. You eat one meal with them and suddenly three years have gone by outside."

"Yeah," said Mark. "Funny, they didn't play that up so much in the interviews."

"What if they had?" said Katja. Her face had grown more animated. "Can you imagine what the interviews would be like if they told you the truth?"

Mark smiled. "'Don't worry if you don't like the associates you meet,'" he said. "'They'll all be gone by the time you get here!'"

"Right," said Katja. "And when they talk about the classes you should take. 'Forget Bankruptcy. I highly recommend Proofreading. And Document Review. And Staying Up All Night Because a Partner Called You at Seven.'"

"Really, they shouldn't have interviews," said Mark. "They should just bring us all in and see how long we'll hold our hand over a candle flame. Last thirty get the job."

"Oh, it's not just a job."

"It's an indenture?"

"It's a lifestyle."

"It's two or three really terrible jobs all stuck together is what it is," Mark said.

Katja laughed, pushing her shoulders forward, deepening the hollows under her collarbone. She shook her bottle by the neck: empty. "Your round, isn't it?"

She watched Mark walk away, shaking her head. Affection leads to distraction; distraction to errors of judgment. How many times would she have to learn that? She was window-shopping something she could not afford, not while the consequences of earlier mistakes pressed upon her. What had she been thinking?

Nothing; that was the problem. She hadn't been thinking at all. And even as she saw the first changes in Harold, she'd let herself imagine they were just parts of a more general transformation. Fairy-tale kisses turned beasts to men, brought statues alive. But Harold wasn't showing many signs of recovered humanity. Only one, in fact, and it was one that Katja tended not to connect with humanity at all: he was starting to look at her *that way*.

It had been clear when she stopped by his car that afternoon. Clear earlier, if she hadn't been trying to avoid the knowledge. She'd seen that look often enough, and she knew what followed. A week or two, maybe a month, of great solicitude, then the distant reproach of wounded dignity, the snide comments behind her back. As though something had happened that was her fault; as though she should be blamed.

She did blame herself, this time at least. It was how the fairy tales went, after all. Harold was just following the plot. But why was it that men had to take any gesture of kindness as an indicator of sexual availability? Perhaps because, coming from them, it was. Still, you'd think they'd learn from experience. Though likely Harold's experience of kindness was small. Katja clenched her teeth against a surge of pity, summoning frustration in its place. Why couldn't she find someone normal, someone she could talk to, someone . . . She raised her eyebrows, surprised at the thought. Someone like Mark.

Mark walked toward the bar, keeping his eyes down. The floor was speckled with sawdust and peanut shells. The Cactus Cantina was small and dark, and though a sign outside had advertised nightly battles between man and margarita, most of the patrons sat quietly sipping beers. Mark and Katja had entered to near silence, no one meeting their eyes. Now he could feel a few stares directed his way. "Two more Coronas," he told the bartender.

"Where you from, buddy?" one of the men at the bar asked.

Mark kept his head down. "Washington," he said.

"Nice place, ain't it, that Washington? Nation's capital and all."

"It's okay," Mark answered. He collected the bottles and overtipped.

"Surprised you don't miss it more," the man said. "But I guess you'll be going back soon enough. Just visiting our little town, aren't you? Come to see the sights."

"Yeah," said Mark. "I guess." He turned back toward the booth where Katja waited, took two steps, and abruptly found himself on the floor, having tripped over an outstretched leg. He grabbed for a rolling, foamy bottle, hearing laughter.

"Careful, there, Washington," the man said dryly. "Lots of things to stumble over out here. You don't watch where you're going, you might even run into a fist or two." Mark got to his feet, sudsy and glowering, the bottles wet and half empty in his hands. "You lookin' to have a conversation about something?" the man asked. "Me and the boys, I don't know if we're up to your Washington standards. But the way you lookin' at me, makes me come over all chatty. Makes me think I might take you out back and conversate you a good one."

Mark dropped his eyes and shook his head. Watching the floor, he walked back to the booth. "I'm afraid it doesn't count as your round if you spill the drinks," Katja told him.

"I think we'd better get out of here," Mark said.

"What," Katja asked as they trotted back down the road, "they were going to fight you? All four of them? That doesn't seem fair."

"I wasn't concerned about the numbers," said Mark, holding his breath as headlights rumbled by.

"Really?"

"Well, when you have my degree of experience in bar fights, it really doesn't matter how many of them there are."

"I see," said Katja. "What you mean is that you've never been in a fight and any one of them could have kicked your ass by himself."

"You could put it that way," Mark said. The fear past, he was beginning to realize that certain kinds of unpleasantness could be enjoyable in retrospect. "Won't Ryan be sorry he missed the excitement."

"I'm sure he will," said Katja. "I bet he didn't come half as near getting stomped to death as you did. I'm feeling a little jealous myself."

"I guess I'm just lucky," Mark said, and laughed. The night was crisp with oncoming fall, the stars bright overhead. Katja had been right; there was still a chemical flavor to the air, borne on the breeze from the wreckage of the Hubble plant. But the stars were luminous and distinct, and Mark felt a sudden eerie slippage, as though the true map of the universe were emotional, time and space folded upon themselves to bring distant points together through the power of common feeling. He had come again to the Nantucket night, the wonderment and longing, the possibilities looming in the vast unseeable future. The sense that darkness was a gift, a curtain behind which anything might await: the girl on the other side of the fence, all the unknowable treasures of the world. But now there was a girl at his side, close enough to touch. Mark cast a glance at

Katja and it all returned, the smell of red clay and seaweed, the wooden decks as they dried in the sun. The hedge clippings in the road and the steady thwack of a ball against racket strings. Wonder stirred within him. Why not? Katja's sleeveless shirt showed smoothly muscled shoulders; her dark hair hung in a long ponytail. She looked like a tennis player. Maybe something had indeed brought them back together.

Mark opened his mouth, hesitating. Katja turned her head toward him, eyebrows raised, the beginning of a smile on her lips. The girl on the other side of the fence. The wind shifted; the breeze brought poison. Janette, Mark thought. She would have grown up with these stars; to her they would have seemed normal. And then she died under them, because she was on the wrong side of the fence.

He closed his mouth and looked down at the road. Luck, he told himself. You could grow up behind any number of fences, or you could walk around them looking in. It just depended on where you were born. And that was what had brought him here. His luck, Janette's lack of it. He wondered what the air had smelled like when she was a little girl.

Soon the lights of their motel appeared. Mark opened the door to his room and turned to Katja. "You want to come in?" Her face registered shock. "I mean just to talk," he explained quickly, alarmed. "I'm sure Ryan's here."

"He's here, all right," Katja said, her voice grown suddenly small. Mark turned back to the doorway and felt momentarily abashed. The room hadn't been tidy when he left it, but now it was a scene of mayhem, clothes and papers scattered, the mattress torn off the bed. Then understanding's chill alchemy turned embarrassment to dread, as his gaze followed Katja's to where Ryan Grady lay motionless in a small pool of blood.

Ryan's evening had never held much promise, and soon it soured completely. Alone in the room, he tried first to locate the motel's movie channel, then a decent cable movie, and finally a game, or even a game show. His peregrinations yielded nothing better than scrambled porn, and that gave him a headache after half an hour or so. He switched back to a replay of the 1973 Super Bowl. I could be drunk right now, he thought with a pang of regret. By rights I should be. Instead I'm waiting for some freak who may not even show up and has probably spent the day calling Tanzania on my dime anyway.

With a sigh, Ryan reached into his bag and withdrew a well-thumbed magazine. After a few weeks of study, he believed he was making progress. Magic tricks, he had learned, could be performed with bar materials and were good icebreakers. These would be useful, surely. All across the country, he thought, men were doubtless getting laid courtesy of the levitating olive, the exploding straw. Making fun of her drink, apparently, was also a simple introductory device. And he had learned some basic principles that would stand him in good stead. Pale gray suits looked cheap; shoe shines were essential; video games helped concentration. Ryan absorbed this wisdom. One to two drinks a day were said to aid memory; white wine was recommended to avoid sulfites. Ryan drank beer in larger quantities and soon forgot this one. Women taking birth control pills preferred more masculine-looking men. Ryan nodded sagely. But what was the use of that?

There was a disturbing amount of information that was irrelevant or simply unhelpful. Ryan didn't care about the twenty-five greatest movie scenes. He had no interest in readers' stories of embarrassment; he had enough of his own. He had neither the time nor the inclination to learn the distinctions between various shoes and the occasions they fit. And some of it was worse than irrelevant; it was dispiriting. The magazines didn't just want to help him pick up women. They wanted to help erase his flaws.

This was puzzling. Ryan seldom thought about his flaws, and when he did it was with the kind of affectionate indulgence afforded the miscreants among a beloved flock of grandchildren. The magazines, however, were concerned with things Ryan had never considered. There was, for instance, the matter of the nasolabial fold. Before the magazines had instructed him to the contrary, Ryan hadn't known he had a nasolabial fold at all. It sounded like something a girl had, which one might admire surreptitiously from appropriate angles on the beach, and later, if lucky, be allowed to kiss or lick or fondle. But the facts were other. The nasolabial fold, he had learned, was the crease running from the nose to the corner of the mouth, and he did have one, or would in a few years, and then would apparently have to pay to have it eliminated via laser resurfacing. This was daunting news. At times Ryan thought that whatever expertise he acquired from his study was unlikely to be enough to balance out the erosion of his self-confidence.

He shook his head and set the magazine aside, lamenting the absence of a minibar. More reading of strategic literature was not the answer. There had to be a simpler solution; even in the complicated exile that was post-collegiate life, there had to be a better way. Something like the clever method he'd used to locate his lost phone, a strategy he felt it was past time to try again.

He walked to the desk and picked up the telephone. Distracted by the noise of the television and the effort of remembering his number, he didn't hear the door open. "Where are you, you son of a bitch?" said Ryan Grady.

The familiar tune sounded directly behind him. Huh, thought Ryan, perplexed. What followed was a very strong blow to the back of his head, but Ryan didn't experience it that way. For him, it was a burst of light and a sudden, brief moment of extraordinary alertness. As his legs buckled under him, he had the curious impression that things were moving unusually slowly. This allowed time for another thought, which would likely have been expressed as "What?" or even "Fuck!" But as it happened, it wasn't expressed at all, for Ryan was out well before he hit the floor.

He awoke to Katja bending over him, her hand on his neck feeling for a pulse. Also to significant pain. "Fuck me," said Ryan sincerely. He collected himself. "But maybe not tonight. I have a headache." He smiled at his remarkable composure. Then he moved his head, and the room moved back, and he decided it might be better just to lie still for a while.

"It sounds like he'll be okay," Katja said, her eyes following the ambulance out of the motel parking lot. "They'll probably keep him overnight for observation, but we'll have him back first thing tomorrow." She turned to Mark. "Who do you think could have done that?"

"I don't know," said Mark. "I'm getting the impression that Hubble's lawyers aren't too popular around here."

"Yeah," said Katja. "But I don't think that was it. Someone really went through your room. Someone who was looking for something."

"Ryan said he was meeting someone," Mark remembered. "And Macey's firm knows we've been doing document review. You don't think they could have had anything to do with it, do you?"

"I doubt it. They're plaintiffs' lawyers, which I know makes them the scum of the earth from our perspective, but they are lawyers. I think our discovery tactics are pushing the bounds of what a court will accept. They couldn't very well think they'd get away with beating someone up, even if it was Ryan. Anyway, if they wanted documents, they would have gone to Harold's room. That's where the files are. Someone was really interested in yours."

"I don't know," said Mark. "Nothing in it has impressed me so far."

"Yeah," said Katja. "Well, anyway, you'd better be sure to lock the door."

"You're on the next flight home," Harold told the assembled group the next morning. "All of you."

"What about you?" Katja asked.

"I'm going to wrap things up here. I'll be back in a week or so."

"Is it safe?"

"Evidently not," Harold said sharply. "That's why you're going home."

Katja sighed. Despite himself, Harold felt a surge of happiness at her concern. Ryan Grady gingerly touched his bandaged head. Some vacation, he thought. Well, I'm damn sure billing the client for last night. Time and a half, probably. Combat pay, isn't it?

35 **LIFE IN EQUIPOISE**

Alone in his apartment, Mark Clayton took stock. He had a studio in Woodley Park, near enough to Connecticut Avenue that the buzz of traffic and revelry kept him up weekends. He had a couch, a television, a table, two chairs, and a bed. And he had a bicycle locked up downstairs in the garage. It was, he thought, not a lot to show for eleven months at a hundred twenty-five thousand a year.

Of course, he had savings too. As the firm's orientation materials had advised, he was investing. The firm retained a team of consultants to help the associates build their portfolios; the first time they called, Mark had thought they were partners discussing an assignment he'd forgotten about and tried to play along. But now he was well under way. Mutual fund prospectuses arrived in his mailbox like letters from a wise uncle; they lay splayed across his bed like porn magazines. He was making sound choices, the prospectuses told him. He was doing the right thing. Mark was not entirely convinced; as best as he could tell, the approach his private banker had suggested was perfectly suited to the preceding ten years. In the present it was not working quite so well; so far he had lost approximately twelve thousand dollars. The advisor remained upbeat. Markets were cyclical, and if he had the discipline to follow the correct strategy, eventual wealth was all but guaranteed.

Neither the current losses nor the promised bonanza moved him much. Mark had never been able to attach much reality to the figures in his accounts anyway, and whether they were slightly larger or slightly smaller seemed mostly irrelevant. What he enjoyed about investing was the feeling that he was making choices, exercising power.

That was also what he enjoyed about his evenings, the feeling of power over himself. It wasn't freedom, not quite. He still had to go to work the next morning, and the morning after that, a succession of bright unpleasant dawns stretching ahead as far as he could bear to imagine. But power over himself, that had been restored, if only for the moment. The flight from Texas had arrived midafternoon. No one expected him back for a couple of days at least and, feeling reckless, he'd headed straight home.

There he confronted the fact that when work occupies eighty percent of your waking hours, the rest of your life is bound to wither. There were no hobbies to turn to, no friends to rouse on short notice for a movie or a couple of beers. He carried his dirty clothes to the laundry room and put them in a washing machine. He made himself a dinner of frozen chicken tortellini and pasta sauce from a jar. High-quality sauce, handmade, identical, the label said, to that served in a famed New York restaurant. Expensive too; the kind of indulgence that fit his lifestyle. He transferred the laundry from washer to dryer, watching the clothes of his co-tenants spin behind the glass doors, vaguely envious when he noticed panties and boxer shorts together in the whirling heap. To do laundry together, that would be nice. To wake up next to someone else.

He sat on the couch in jeans and a T-shirt. I can make myself do whatever I want, he thought happily. I can watch TV. I can read a book. The possibilities are limitless. Why, if I wanted to, I could bake a cake. Mark smiled to himself. Now I will go to bed. Not because I have to but because I will it.

Arranging the covers around him, he lifted the *Times Book Review* from a stack of yellowing papers. A girl from the class behind him in college had published a collection of short stories that the reviewer likened to a series of perfectly executed dives. Is this what I wanted to do? Mark asked himself. No, but I didn't want to do anything else. Legal education promised flexibility, which in theory he still had. And that was what there was to say for it. Law is what happens when you have no other plans. He closed his eyes and sleep came on him like a heavy thing.

On the subway the next morning, Mark tried without success to plan out the next step in Wayne Harper's habeas case. In part, the difficulty was that he simply had no idea what to do. They'd beaten back the state's initial attempt at dismissal, but the conversation with Anson Henry had given an adequate explanation for the failure to offer expert testimony in mitigation. Beyond that, he could see no grounds on which to attack the conviction.

The other difficulty was that this failure troubled him only slightly. He had slept almost nine hours, and he felt good all over, almost stupidly happy, capable of feats in fields unrelated to the law. The everyday wonders of the world pressed upon him, urgent marvels almost painful to contemplate. Across the train, a girl read a novel, blond hair tucked behind her ears. Girls! With books! Of fiction! How beautiful life was. The Hubble case, from what he could tell, was not going well. Wayne Harper's petition would almost certainly be denied. But in moments like these he could glimpse a world in which such things mattered little. A world in which he had a life outside of work, in which his clothes didn't lie on the floor for weeks at a time, in which his silverware matched. I could write a poem, he thought. I could take guitar lessons.

"Peter Morgan wants you," Glynda said as he passed her station on the way to his office. Her cubicle bore the usual secretarial decorations, the greeting card depictions of angels, the troll dolls and fluffy animals. Also a block-lettered sign reading DON'T RUSH ME, I GET PAID BY THE HOUR. Mark's unaccustomed energy transmuted swiftly to fear, a more familiar feeling and oddly reassuring for that reason.

"Why?"

"I'm just the secretary," Glynda said, waving a hand. "They don't tell me what it's all about." She turned back to her telephone conversation. "So he says he spent the night at a friend's house? Girl."

Peter Morgan's office was large, but it was crowded to capacity and beyond. Mark recognized the other members of the Hubble discovery team, some crushed together on a leather couch, others standing aimlessly in the center of the room. Peter Morgan surveyed them from behind his desk, fine features crinkled in a concerned frown. "Apparently something unusual occurred during our conduct of document review in Texas," he said. This ought to be good, Mark thought. "I gather we don't know exactly what happened, but I've received some disturbing reports from the client. Don't worry; I'm not interested in assigning blame. At this point. But let me emphasize that our role as counsel for a corporation, even counsel supervising the discovery process, does not give us unlimited license to examine corporate records. There are documents that a client may withhold after consultation with partners. There is no need, and in fact no justification, for associates to examine those documents."

This is about something else altogether, thought Mark. I guess that's not surprising. Maybe I should take a vacation this year. I could go to Florida, or the Bahamas.

"I'm sure I don't need to remind you that this is a sensitive case," Peter continued. "It has received substantial attention in the national press. What we do is likely to be closely scrutinized."

Or France. I could go to France. I've got the days saved up. I could spend like five days in France and then go to Italy.

"It is because we are a firm with a national reputation that our advice is sought in such cases. Our reputation is perhaps our greatest asset."

And after Italy, Greece. And maybe Turkey. I could see the Bosporus. And the Strait of Gibraltar. No, that's somewhere else, isn't it?

"Its importance transcends any particular case. It would be a sad irony if misplaced zeal in one case led us to compromise that reputation or to do anything that might cause other clients to hesitate before calling on us."

Oh, damn, thought Mark. I left my clothes in the laundry room again, didn't I?

"I would ask you all, in this matter in particular, to consult with your supervising partners to make sure that you understand your assignments precisely. And I believe it goes without saying that there is no room for freelancing. You are Morgan Siler lawyers because we believe that you will live up to, and indeed embody, the high standards of this firm. What any one of us does reflects on us all. You are as much a part of this firm as I am, and I hope that you are just as proud of what we have created here, and just as committed to see that our traditions are upheld."

Mark shook his head. At least they made it to the dryer. Someone would have taken them out, someone who needed the machine. He'd done this before, several times, and usually found his clothes stacked in a disorderly pile on the ironing board. Once on the floor. But once folded, which he'd liked. It seemed a wink from the world, a promise that compassion and affection existed out there somewhere, nudging him playfully and slipping away unseen. Maybe they'll be folded. But no wonder I keep losing socks.

Gerald Roth was standing outside Mark's office when he returned. "Got a minute?"

Mark looked around apprehensively. "I guess so."

Gerald waved him inside and closed the door. "I've been thinking a little about the Harper case. Something's bugging me about it."

"What?"

"Well, a lot of things, actually. But there's a pattern." As Mark watched, Gerald's face shifted, his eyes brightening, his features sharp with concentration. He looked almost like a different person. "The defense never really put the prosecution's case to the test. It's not that this guy Anson Henry abandoned Harper, or even that he's a bad lawyer. But there are a bunch of things you always do, even if you're going to plead the client out. You challenge the admissibility of the confession; you make the state turn over their evidence; you check out anything that might be exculpatory. It didn't happen, and I can't figure out why."

Mark racked his brain. The lapels of Anson Henry's seersucker suit appeared in his mind, followed by the man himself, holding a glass of bourbon that Mark suspected was a fabrication of memory. "If he was guilty, though, and they had the DNA evidence, wouldn't it have made sense to cooperate and hope for leniency?"

"Maybe," admitted Gerald. "That's why we can't make anything out of it at this stage. It's not ineffective assistance of counsel; it's a strategic choice. And they did get blindsided at the penalty phase, getting Doctor Death as their expert. But it's still odd. It's the sort of thing I'd like to understand better. Did you talk to the family?"

"I didn't have time. I got sent to Texas. It cut my Virginia trip short."

Gerald rubbed his beard thoughtfully. "Do you think you've got the time to go back down there for a little while?"

"Yeah," Mark said. "I do." He hesitated. "Can I ask you something?"

"What?"

"Why are you so involved in this?"

Gerald shrugged. "Death penalty litigation is an interest of mine. From before. I used to be a journalist; I covered a bunch of executions. Then I did a little here while I was getting a night school degree; they gave credit for clinical work. I ended up going the transactional route once I became a lawyer because I didn't like the feel of big-firm litigation. Not enough good guys. So they won't use me on pro bono projects anymore. It's training for the litigators. I try to follow along, though, as best I can. It's good to have a hobby."

"Yeah," said Mark. It struck him as a morbid hobby. "I'll talk to Wallace about making another trip."

The associates gone, Peter Morgan sat alone in his office. He was, he thought, having a bad day. Early that morning, he'd received a phone call from the Parkwell general counsel. The man was an old friend of Peter's, but the conversation had been far from pleasant. There had been vague but outraged complaints about the scope of the document review the associates had conducted, and more specific demands for a comprehensive list of everything now in Morgan Siler's hands. Worse, there had been a distinct lack of enthusiasm for Streeter's creative solution, and pointed remarks about the need for lawyers to focus on the job they'd been given. This stung Peter, who preferred an expansive conception of his role. He never would have presumed to question his clients' goals; he was their lawyer, not their judge, something Archie had never understood. But he believed that some degree of freedom in pursuing those ends made him more effective. Still, the bottom line was the bottom line. Parkwell was a significant client, and Morgan Siler could ill afford to lose their goodwill. There were things to be done to address that particular issue. The meeting with the associates from the Texas discovery team had been the first step. Streeter would see to the rest.

But solving Parkwell's problems in this way did not help Peter's. In fact, it made them worse. Talking to Streeter weeks ago, laying out their strategy, he had glimpsed a new future for the firm. Securitization as a defense to liability—no one else had thought of it; no one else would know how to do it. Morgan Siler would be again at the forefront, possessed of a singular expertise. But Parkwell had rejected their innovation. It would not let them grow; it wanted only the familiar services to which it had become accustomed.

Peter's thoughts turned to Cassandra. She was finding novelty, cultivating her own interests. In a way, he admired her for it. He was realizing how hard it was to maintain a life's momentum, how easy to submit to the web of convention that strangled the great. But if she could, why not he?

Cassandra was easily satisfied, of course. She always had been. That was the difference between them. For Peter Morgan, it would not be a matter of taking up hobbies, of dabbling in fly-fishing or portraiture. He needed a real challenge, a new world to conquer or create.

There was the rub. Society frowned on the wholesale reorganization of personal lives; it tied him with the tiny threads of custom and duty. As Morgan Siler was bound to its clients, Peter was bound to his family. And yet, he thought, there *was* a difference. The firm could not defy its clients' wishes. It would starve without them, and its obligations were rooted in contracts that could not be shrugged aside. He, on the other hand . . . Parkwell was irreplaceable, but Peter could find a new wife. A new child, if it came to that. Maybe—why not?—a son.

There would be social costs, of course. There would be talk at his clubs; he would lose some friends. Cassandra and Julie would wield the weapons of intimacy. But those costs he could bear. Relationships could be broken; they constrained only those who agreed to be bound.

Peter stared into space, feeling his life in equipoise, balanced like a coin on edge. He could do it, he realized. He could do it easily. Bargaining, his law school professors had told him, occurs in the shadow of the law, meaning that what someone will agree to depends crucially on what will happen in court if negotiations break down. But it wasn't just bargaining, not anymore. Law's reach was broader now, its influence more pervasive. As older forms of social ordering receded, relationships that had been personal became legal. One day, Peter thought, there would be no other kind, nothing but the clean efficiency of statute and rule. That day was yet to come, but Peter knew how close it was and charted its advance. He watched law grow, swelling beneath the surface, filling the interstices, forming the omnipresent backdrop, the invisible architecture of the world. Peter watched and understood what most did not: that we live all our lives in the shadow of the law.

Armed with that knowledge, he had been able to structure a great many things. The finely ordered lattice of legal relations that made up his life gave him not only order but flexibility. It insulated him from what otherwise might have been the costs of certain choices, including the one he was making now. The preparations had been laid: the prenuptial agreement, the careful reservations of title. Not with this moment in mind, but there was a special delight in adapting old forms to new purposes. It was as Streeter had said. *How can they stop us? The law's on our side.* Peter Morgan allowed himself a smile of satisfaction. He punched his speakerphone to life and began making calls.

Wallace Finn was reading the paper when Mark walked in. He stirred as if mildly startled. "What can I do for you?"

"I've been thinking about the Harper case," Mark said. "I didn't get as much done down in Virginia as I'd hoped."

"No?"

"I got called back for this Hubble Chemical thing. Had to go to Texas."

"Oh," said Wallace. "Hubble." He folded the paper and laid it on his desk, then marked a story with a forefinger. "You see this about Parkwell?"

"No," said Mark. "I didn't see it. What's the story?"

Wallace shrugged. "Parkwell made a bad bet on interest rates," he said. "Trying to hedge some of their trading exposure, but it went the wrong way. Probably they didn't quite understand what they were getting into. That's what happens with derivatives. So, suddenly they're looking at billions in liability, which they may not be able to cover. The rating agencies don't think so, anyway."

"That's too bad," said Mark, bemused.

Wallace nodded. "It looks like their debt is going to be downgraded, which will trigger default provisions in the swap agreements they still have open. That's going to saddle them with more liabilities, which they definitely won't be able to pay. It's like a run on a bank. That's what kills you, when people stop believing. There's not a corporation out there that can survive a loss of confidence. The whole thing comes down like a house of cards. Not that Parkwell was any more unstable than any other corporation, but all of them live on public faith. This is going to make Hubble look like small potatoes."

"Well, at least no one's died."

"That's one of the nice things about corporate law," Wallace said. "You never have to think about dead people." A wave of his hand took in the Lucite blocks on his desk, the black leather-bound volumes on his bookshelves. Mark peered at the legends on the thick spines. *An Offering of Convertible Debentures by Rossman Incorporated. A Sale of Substantially All the Assets of Leftronic Corporation.* "That's twenty years of my life right there. A lot of it was for Parkwell. Tony Streeter and I spent the better part of two years setting them up in the early nineties. That was one of the last deals I worked."

"Right," said Mark, feeling a need to reassert control over the direction of the conversation. "So as I was saying, I think there's some more work that needs to be done in Virginia. I'd like to take a look at some of the state's evidence, conduct a few more interviews."

Wallace nodded. "Go ahead, if you've got the time. Do you think you have anything?"

"I don't know," said Mark. "At the moment, all I have are questions."

"There are always questions," Wallace said, his smile commiserating. "I've seen a lot of these cases, and almost every one of them has had real questions. What's harder to find is a judge who cares what the answers are. Most of the time, you just never find out. You understand that, don't you?"

"Yeah. I was just thinking I might be able to turn up something."

Wallace nodded encouragement. "Do it," he said. "Go there. Talk to people. Just don't expect too much. If you put too much of yourself into this work, it rips your heart out. Makes me long for the days when my clients were immortal."

"What?"

"You know, corporations. That's one of the basic corporate attributes. Infinite life. We used to joke about it in law school. If the state can make corporations live forever, why can't they do it for the rest of us? I suppose you have different jokes now."

Mark thought. Nothing occurred to him, then something about a blonde in a convertible. If the state can make corporations live forever, why is it in such a hurry to kill Wayne Lee Harper?

"I guess I've come full circle," Wallace said. "Now I'm doing pro bono and all my clients end up dead." He lifted his head. "See what you can do. And good luck."

Mark shut the door behind him; Wallace looked back at his paper. Idly he drew from his vest a pocket watch on a gold chain and consulted the dial. The watch had stopped years ago, but he still looked at it from time to time, curious as to how far wrong it was. Twice a day it was right, but he'd yet to catch it. Nine in the morning was no longer within his working hours; nine at night found him in bed. In the midafternoon heart of the workday the hands seemed almost ludicrously out of step. Still, Wallace thought, it was almost certainly past three. The worst was over for the day; the watch was getting better, slowly approaching its moment of perfection.

He wished he could say the same for himself. Parkwell was in crisis, blood in the water. Infinite life didn't really make corporations immortal; it just ensured that they didn't die of natural causes. When they grew too weak to carry on, they were torn to pieces by creditors. Ten years ago, maybe even five, he'd have been the first person they called. Now no one called; now he sat in his office and waited for associates to update him on the progress of their hopeless cases.

It was a circle, in a way. Securitization had been law's response to the end of junk bond financing, another way to make borrowing easy for less established companies. It was his response, his brainchild, and as they plotted out those first deals, unsure whether any of it would hold up in court, he'd felt a more than mortal power. Redistributing risk, that was one way to look at it. Aggregating risks that had been distinct, yoking lives together. Separating those that had been linked, dividing the company from itself with the blade of law. He'd carved with a surgeon's precision, spinning fates from his hands. Cheating death, that was another. Bankruptcy liquidation was what the lenders feared, all the company's assets pooled to satisfy overwhelming liabilities, no creditor receiving close to what was owed. But if you could separate assets out, prevent them from being drawn into the bankruptcy process, the threat was less awful. Lenders would be indifferent. Death, where is thy sting?

Perpetual motion was what it seemed like to the captains of industry, a foolproof way to add value to their companies. Wallace knew that wasn't true. Some people were made worse off, those who had claims against the company but hadn't been able to negotiate them. Involuntary creditors, people whose rights were the product of accident rather than bargaining. Still, those were heady days. The practice took off, and perpetual motion was what it felt like to him, struggling to cope with demand no other firm yet had the expertise to fill.

He didn't know what Mary thought of it, until she left. That showed him clearly enough. And that was when Wallace had understood that you can't cheat death. You can't eliminate risks. You can only shift them around. You can decide what you will lose and what you will keep.

He'd made the choice, not knowing he was making it. And he'd tried to carry on with what was left, even after the heart attack, after the doctor's orders cut his hours. He'd taken dancing lessons by himself for a while, reaching out for a new life. But the lessons started to seem pointless; the new life eluded him and was now beyond his grasp. He was not the man he'd been. Age saved itself up and came at you in a rush. He still dressed carefully, more from habit than anything else, but he missed things a wife would notice. His tie outside his collar, his socks not matching, a belt that skipped two loops. He'd discover them in the bathroom mirror at midday; sometimes his secretary would make a cautious gesture.

You can't decide what you will keep, he was realizing now. You can decide only what you lose first, for in the end you lose it all. Pain and infirmity waited in the future, with the patience of the ineluctable. A package with his name on it, a label. Do not open until . . . when? It could come any day now.

Even the memories were less comfort as the years went by. Securitization had been a clever creation, but Wallace wasn't sure he deserved credit for it. The firm itself had shown him how it was done. It took the bright young lawyers and walled them off from the claims of society. The world was safe for business, with its guaranteed access to the best minds. Come what may, the corporations would not lack for legal advice. And who was worse off? Who bore the risk? Someone always did, and since he'd been placed in charge of the pro bono practice Wallace had realized who it was. The people who hadn't negotiated their interaction with the legal system, who were caught up in it against their will. They were the involuntary creditors of the law, and they had no one to turn to.

That was the circle, and at times he saw some humor in it. For what he was doing now with the pro bono practice was a piecemeal unlocking of the structure the firm had created. He sent lawyers out into the world. He made them available to everyone; he exposed them to risk.

The firm was unenthusiastic. Peter Morgan would have called pro bono a necessary evil had he been convinced of its necessity. The associates resisted too, understandably. Lawyers were notoriously risk-averse, and they had billable-hour targets to meet. And Wallace wondered sometimes whether action on such a small scale could make any sort of difference. Most likely it couldn't; that was why they'd put him in charge. An old man, a succession of hopeless cases. He looked once more at the watch in his hand. Getting better, he thought, but still such a long way to go.

37 WHATEVER YOU WANT

Ryan Grady wondered if he was getting smarter, if that knock on the head had jolted back into alignment some bruised pieces of mental machinery, casualties of his youthful athletic career. Since returning from Texas he had thought differently about the magazines. Their advice, he had noticed, was not always consistent. Should one approach women with a pad and pencil, pretending to be conducting a survey on the best or worst lines heard recently? Some authorities considered this a high-percentage play; others scoffed, holding that the best technique was a simple "I just wanted to tell you I think you're very pretty." There was a lack of consensus, likewise, on such basic issues as which drink one should order for an attractive stranger, the proper amount of hair gel (some even recommended skipping gel entirely and substituting moisturizing lotion), and whether a suit jacket could be paired with a T-shirt. Ryan surveyed his conflicting texts with dismay. They were as bad as the law, full of irreconcilable precedents, a tangled web of rules and exceptions and fact-dependent balancing tests. And no duty of advocacy to bring clarity, no final authority, not even a magazine to tell you which magazines to read.

Then came the inspiration, the eureka moment. There might not be magazines that told you what lines would work, but there were magazines that *made* them work. Magazines that did not reveal the truth but shaped it, that determined, by fiat, what women would go for.

Women's magazines.

Like all great ideas, it seemed obvious in retrospect. Why waste your time reading the same advice that every other guy in the bar could get for four dollars, or pick up and scan for free while awaiting a haircut? Why try to master the complicated systems, the contingencies and fallback plans? There was a shorter route. For while he read these magazines and absorbed their wisdom as gospel, across the city, girls were doing the same thing. They had their own instruction books, their manuals for life, which told them what to wear, to drink, to say. Probably the magazines told them which lines they should fall for, which should elicit a light flirtatious laugh and cause them to press a hand to their neck, which deserved only a blank stare. All he had to do was read the same magazines and he would know too. There, in the glossy pages amid the perfume samples and subscription cards, in the template and crucible of their desires, he would learn what women want.

The cold enthusiasm of the secret agent burned inside him. He was going behind enemy lines. In the grocery checkout line he clutched his *Cosmo* like blueprints to the hostile base. Which it was, of course; that was exactly what it was. The salesclerk's eyes held greater skepticism. "For the girlfriend?"

"Yes," said Ryan. For the girlfriend. For *all* the girlfriends. In his apartment he fanned out his acquisitions. The pile was thicker this time, but the women's magazines contained a higher percentage of advertisements, and probably many articles he could safely skip, personality tests and reviews of the hottest bras for fall. Ryan felt his excitement building. This would be quick, easy, effective. No more struggling with complicated systems, no more self-improvement tips to remind him of all the things he should change but didn't have the time, the money, or the fortitude to address. This would be *efficient*. Now we're getting somewhere, he thought. Now we're on the same page.

Walker Eliot was checking the performance of his mutual funds on the Internet, hardly the worst of the things he did on the firm's time, but still he started guiltily when Harold's head poked through his office door. "Hey, wunderkind," said Harold. "Big couple of days for us."

More of my briefs come home to roost, thought Walker, unsure at this point whether good news or bad was more to be feared. "What's the word?" he asked.

"Parkwell's out," Harold told him jubilantly. "Dismissed from the case. The judge loved your motion. Ate it right up."

Ate it up, and in the manner of judges produced . . . what? "What was the reasoning?" Walker asked apprehensively.

Harold smiled. "Worried about an appeal? I think we're pretty solid on this one. There's no opinion; he just ruled from the bench. But it was what we said. Piercing the corporate veil requires more than the prospect that a plaintiff won't be able to get a full recovery. You showed that there was no abuse of the corporate form, and that's that."

Walker nodded, cautiously pleased. "That sounds okay."

"Okay?" Harold asked. "It's huge. You should be very happy about this. I'm not sure how we're going to do on class certification. Judge Preston is a split-the-baby kind of guy, and he might feel he needs to give the other side something."

Walker frowned. "Class certification? But that's the one we really should win. You can't certify a mass tort."

"You know how judges are," said Harold, shrugging. "Preston, it's a good day if he zips his robes. And listen to this. The day I go into court to argue class certification, there's another Hubble case on the same motion call. Right before me. It's a wrongful discharge claim. They fired someone for refusing to clean the inside of one of their tanks. And why did he refuse? Because a couple of years ago some poor fucker *died* doing the same thing. I had to twist some arms to get rid of that one. Pay him off, I told Hubble's guys. Kill him; I don't care. But don't do anything to make your company look like the evil bastards you are right before I have to get up and argue for you." He laughed. "So they did it."

Walker was genuinely distressed. That matters?

Harold read his expression. "Don't worry, they didn't kill him. He got a nice settlement. And don't worry about class certification either. Getting to Parkwell's assets is the biggest issue here, and we nailed them. You should have heard Macey spluttering. He's up there talking about how many people have been hurt, and the judge just cut him right off. 'Counsel, I don't see how that can be relevant if you don't show me that Parkwell exerted an improper degree of control over its subsidiary's operations.' Stopped him in midsentence. After that, he almost has to go against us on class certification." Walker shook his head wonderingly, and Harold's tone softened. "I know, what *about* all the people who were hurt? Don't worry, they'll get something. Hubble's not going to get off scot-free on this one. The facts are bad; I'd be the first to admit it."

Harold paused for a moment. The facts *were* bad, and the more he saw of the files his team had brought back from Texas, the worse they got. Whoever had been in charge of waste disposal had been unimaginably reckless; whoever had left the paper trail documenting the recklessness, unimaginably stupid. "I understand that a case like this can cause you to doubt yourself," he said. "As a lawyer, you'll get called in to deal with a lot of bad situations. But we're just trying to make sure that the outcome is fair. After all, what sense would it make to ruin all the people who invested in Parkwell when it didn't have anything to do with how Hubble stored its chemicals?"

"Right," said Walker, thinking: The world's gone mad. The trouble with being a lawyer, it was becoming clear to him, was that it required you to think about people instead of the law. For a moment he envied Mark, hunting facts through the wilds of Virginia, taking the case law as he found it, never worrying about the precedents he might create. Never dreading that his touch would change what he sought. His touch, his very glance. I was wrong in *Vendstar*, Walker thought, even the way I wrote it. I believed I was right, but I wasn't. The admission shook him; it woke the fear that something had gone unalterably wrong within him. That his mind had lost its clarity, some neutrality of vision that, like innocence, could not be restored. That he would never again look upon the true law. Walker was having trouble sleeping, waking nights now from dreams in which clients came to him in a larger office, one that in some versions had much the feeling of an upscale shoe store, asking what the law was. And he answered with the affable indifference of the heretic and the whore: *The law is whatever you want.*

The Parkwell brief had been right, though. It had taken some fancy footwork, but his argument had been sound. He clung to that thought, though it gave diminishing comfort. He was no longer sure he could trust his judgment, and anyway, virtuosity was less than virtue. There must be something I can do that I'd actually feel good about.

Walker's concentration blazed to life and Harold, noticing, backed away. "Well, I can see you've got other things to think about. Just wanted to congratulate you." Walker nodded, unhearing. Maybe there was something to this Harper case after all. His mind accelerated; his face assumed an expression of monastic peace. Walker's attention was given to few things, but it was given to them entire, and it consumed them completely.

Reentering the Norfolk Meridian, Mark felt like a long-lost son who'd returned to the bosom of his family. The hotel staff did not recognize him as the person who'd been there weeks before, but they recognized him as a Morgan Siler lawyer, and that justified a welcome. Pocketing a tip, the bellhop talked of conference rooms and data ports. "I think I'll be okay," Mark said, wondering. His status as a lawyer hadn't gotten him better treatment before. Indeed, at Morgan Siler itself he some-times felt worse off than the support staff, who pulled overtime for working late and, if they'd put in his hours, would likely have ap-proached his salary. He flopped on the bed and clicked on the televi-sion, where plucky upstarts proved their mettle. In two hours he was due to meet Wayne Harper's family; after that, he was expected at the Capital Defenders Office. But for now, there was time to lie on a queen-sized bed in front of a twenty-seven-inch television screen and let his mind go completely blank.

The Harpers' house showed signs of a hasty cleaning, as did Earl Harper. His wife, Beth, who'd answered the door, did not; she seemed by contrast habitually scrubbed. "We appreciate you taking the trouble to come down here, Mr. Clayton," she said.

Mark fought an impulse to look around for his father. "It's no trouble."

"And taking on Wayne's case. We used all our money on the trial. Do you think you can help him?"

"I'll certainly try," said Mark. "But it depends on whether we can identify mistakes in the trial."

"I'm sure he didn't know what he was doing when he killed that woman," Beth Harper said. "He's a sweet boy, really. You should have seen him when he was a baby. Just a darling little thing, like an angel with his blond hair and his blue eyes."

The same scene, thought Mark. The lawyer, the parents, the lost child. Over and over again it replays itself, with different people and different settings and always the same plea: Give me back my baby. His eyes scanned the room. No pictures of him this time. No pictures of anyone. And just one lawyer. Well, that's pro bono for you. "Can you tell me anything that might be helpful?" he asked.

"I don't know," said Beth. "We didn't realize there was anything wrong with him until he was about six. Just figured he was a little slow. We couldn't afford any expensive schools or programs. We knew he wasn't going to amount to much. But he was sweet and gentle. Just a big child, really." She paused, tears welling in her eyes. Earl's jaw twitched. He stared stolidly at the floor, making no move to comfort her. Beth shook her head. "Excuse me," she said. "You know, he still likes stuffed animals." She looked Mark in the eyes, forcing a smile. "That's what he asked for, in prison. I think he must miss them."

A sinking feeling in his stomach informed Mark that his problems were multiplying. This is excruciating, he thought. This is something I'm never going to be able to forget. "Mr. Harper," he said. "Do you know anything you think might be useful?"

Earl scowled. "Can't say as I do," he pronounced slowly. "Can't say as I do."

"Can you tell me what happened after the crime was committed?"

"Well, we heard about it the day it was discovered," Beth said. "Everyone did. Just a terrible tragedy. But we didn't think Wayne had anything to do with it. Not until the police came here and took him away. Even then we couldn't believe it. But he confessed. You know that, don't you?" Mark nodded. "We got him the best lawyer we could afford. He even lowered his usual rates." She smiled. "Anson knew my parents. He thought that pleading guilty would give Wayne a good chance of avoiding the death penalty. And it should have. Maybe he made one mistake. Who hasn't? He doesn't deserve to die for that."

Two mistakes, thought Mark. Two murders. "Would you have thought that Wayne might ever do something like this?"

"Of course not," Beth said. "He's a sweet, sweet man. Anyone who knows him will tell you that."

"Do you think he did it?"

Beth looked at him blankly. "Well, he confessed, didn't he? And there's that DNA evidence. But I'm sure he wasn't in his right mind. Maybe he's got some other mental defect we don't know about."

Mark nodded again. "The problem there, Mrs. Harper," he said, "is that I don't think we can really relitigate the penalty phase. When the death sentence was imposed, I mean. The state provided Anson Henry with an expert, and he chose not to put on expert testimony."

"That man's not an expert," Beth said angrily. "He's an executioner."

"I know," Mark told her. "I know that. But legally, Anson made a strategic choice. Without new evidence, we can't challenge his decision. The only way to get a new penalty hearing would be to get a new trial. So we'd have to find some grounds for withdrawing the guilty plea and starting over. At the moment I'm not sure how we can do that."

"But he doesn't deserve to die," Beth said. "Can't you just show them that? He doesn't deserve to die."

Mark found himself unable to meet her eyes. "Mr. Harper?" he asked. "Do you think your son is guilty?"

Earl's smile was bitter, showing nicotined teeth. "My son did it," he said, slouching deeper into the couch. "Yes, indeedy." Beth's eyes darted to him, and he looked again at the ground. "You're wasting your time talkin' to me."

Mark swallowed a sigh. "I'll do what I can," he said. "There are some odd things about the state's case. One of them might give us something to go on. But I don't want to get your hopes up. Very few death penalties get reversed at this stage."

He stood; Beth Harper grabbed at his hand. "Please, Mr. Clayton," she said. "Promise me you won't let them kill him."

Earl Harper snorted. Mark forced a smile. "I promise I'll try." Outside, a dispirited patch of flowers baked in the sun. An aging red Camaro slowed as it passed; the driver gave Mark a hard look. I guess I don't fit in too well outside the office, he thought, and quickened his steps to the firm's Camry.

"I've been trying to reach you," Anne Brownlee said. "Is your firm taking this seriously?"

Mark was taken aback. "Of course we are," he said. Anne was redhaired and slender, about Mark's own age, he guessed. So were most of the members of the Capital Defenders staff. And most, like Anne, wore blue jeans and casual shirts. Their office was about the size of Anson's, but far busier. Ten or fifteen young lawyers crowded three rooms, some carrying folders and passing information, some bent in concentration over piles of documents.

"Timmins denied our stay request for Garland," a bearded young man told Anne.

"Big surprise there," she said. "What are we, one for twenty with him? Are the appeal papers ready?"

"We're going to file this afternoon."

Anne nodded quickly. "Okay," she said. "Run it by Steve first. He's the *Brady* expert." She turned back to Mark. "So where have you been?"

"Texas."

"Find any exculpatory information?"

"No," said Mark. "It was another case," he admitted.

Anne gave him a pitying look. "And I thought you were tracking down the real killers. It's too crowded to talk here. Why don't we go outside?" Two blocks down the street they found a coffee shop. "I know it's not your fault," Anne said. "I'm sure you've got partners breathing down your neck. But it drives me nuts when the big firms come in with all this talk about how great their resources are and then they dump a capital case on some first-year with thirty hours to spare." She paused and looked at him more closely. "No offense intended. But you are a first-year, aren't you?"

"Yes. But we've got other people on this."

"Who?"

"Well, there's the supervising partner, Wallace Finn."

"Who's supervising every one of your pro bono projects, I expect."

"And Walker Eliot, another associate."

"Walker? Walker took a death penalty case?"

"You know him?"

"Yeah," Anne said. "Walker was running an execution last year." She stirred her tea and took a small sip, frowning. "I mean, it was from one of the states in Justice Arlen's circuit, and he was the clerk assigned to it, so he was handling the communication with the guy's lawyers. We were there as an amicus, so I talked to him once or twice. It turned into a big mess. Must have been upsetting for the clerks to see it go wrong. I ran into Walker again at a reception that summer, after he'd finished clerking, and he said he'd never get involved in death penalty work again. 'I'm through tinkering with the machinery of death.' Quoting Harry Blackmun."

"Oh," said Mark. "Well, he's working on this one."

"Good for him," said Anne. "What do you have?"

"I don't know. Probably nothing, unless we can withdraw the guilty plea. We're not going to bring down the death penalty, if that's what you're wondering."

Anne frowned. "What do you mean by that?"

"I think all we can hope for is something specific to this case, something that might help Wayne Harper, if no one else. Probably nothing you'd be interested in."

"You don't think we'd be interested in saving his life?"

There's been a miscommunication somewhere, Mark thought. "Aren't you more focused on, you know, systemic reform?"

"So we don't care about Wayne? How can you think that? Of course we want the death penalty abolished. We want it abolished because we think that killing people is barbaric and wrong. And we think it's wrong for Wayne Harper as an individual. We'd do whatever we could to save his life."

"But all you argued for him was that the death penalty is unconstitutional."

"What are you talking about?" Anne asked.

"With the Virginia Supreme Court," Mark said. "When you guys were representing him. You argued that the death penalty was cruel and unusual punishment."

"That was one of the arguments," Anne said slowly. "But we hit every point they let us. We went over the facts. We rechecked the DNA analysis, as much as we could."

"What do you mean?"

"I told you they threw out the crime scene sample as soon as the direct appeal was over. The state wasn't relying on it, since Wayne pleaded guilty. But it seemed like it might be worth a shot. So we got a swab from Wayne and checked their HLA DQa analysis."

"And?"

"Well, their test got him right. No way to tell about the crime sample. But with a guilty plea we were mostly looking at the penalty phase, anyway. We were challenging the death sentence. But not just on constitutional grounds. Mostly we were trying to use *Atkins*."

"*Atkins?*"

Anne looked almost surprised. "You don't have a lot of experience with defense work, do you?"

"Most of our litigation is on the defense side," Mark offered.

"Not for people, though," Anne said. "*Atkins* v. *Virginia*. A very recent Supreme Court case. It says that executing the mentally retarded is unconstitutional. That's what Anson was relying on in pleading guilty, I assume. It would have looked like a sure thing going in, until the state appointed Mateska as his expert. That pretty much shut the door. We still thought it looked good enough to try again. We got our own expert, some affidavits from Wayne's teachers, pulled his educational records. Unfortunately, Virginia responded to *Atkins* by getting pretty strict about what you need to show for mental retardation. And unfortunately, you can get passed through this school system if you sit still and keep your mouth shut. Wayne had a solid 'satisfactory' record as far as he went. And 'very good' for effort." She stopped. "Who told you we only argued the constitutional issue?"

"Anson Henry," said Mark. He considered. "Well, that's what he suggested, anyway."

Anne shook her head. "That guy pisses me off. Oh, he acted like he was cooperating, but he didn't like us questioning anything he did. Didn't want us to try to withdraw the guilty plea. We went to Wayne's parents, asking for permission, but his mother wouldn't hear of it. Said it would just make the judges angry. I tried to tell her that things couldn't get any worse, but I couldn't reason with her. She kept talking about what Anson Henry had said. Which might have made sense as a strategy going in, but not after Wayne had already gotten the death penalty. How much worse can it get?" She paused, as if expecting an answer.

"Right," Mark offered.

"Obviously we would have tried to withdraw the plea if we'd found grounds for it. But we didn't have a chance to go into his facts. Did you talk to his parents?"

"Just this morning."

"And?"

"Well, they didn't seem very focused on the mechanics of it."

"So see if you can withdraw the plea. Look at the prosecution's evidence. They'll have to turn it all over if you ask. If you can show that Anson Henry was ineffective in advising Wayne to plead guilty, you can get it thrown out."

"Yeah," said Mark. That much he knew. "But the evidence seems kind of overwhelming. What would show that pleading guilty was ineffective assistance? I mean, you just said it made sense going in."

Anne frowned again. She bit down on her plastic straw. "That's what you have to find out. I'm not saying it's going to be easy. Face it, we don't win a lot of cases. But this one did seem a little off. Maybe you should try to talk to the father by himself."

Mark remembered Earl's nicotined smile. "He didn't seem all that helpful."

"Maybe you should talk to Wayne."

"Really?"

Anne smiled. "No one suggested that to you, did they? That's the big-firm style. It's a training opportunity. A case, not a person. And you said we didn't care about him as an individual."

"Will they let me see him?"

"Of course they will. You're his lawyer. But to be honest, it's probably not worth the time. I expect you're on a short leash. And he won't tell you anything useful. I spent half a day in Waverly. Learned a good deal about Beanie Babies. Wayne's memory's not so good for things that happened a year ago and he gets confused easily. Plus you couldn't use anything he tells you now to argue that Anson shouldn't have pleaded him out back then."

Mark felt relief, then shame. The prospect of meeting Wayne Harper filled him with terror. Just seeing the parents, he was realizing, had already made the case infinitely more difficult for him. Boxes of documents, those he could deal with. Those he would not be thinking of years later. "I think I'll focus on the evidence."

Anne dropped the straw into her cup. "It's your baby. Give me a call if there's anything we can do. And tell Walker I said hi."

Just wanted to check on the Harper case, Gerald said to himself, approaching Walker's office. No, that's not right. *Just wanted to say hi.* Implausible, but not impossible. It's an opener. He peered through the doorway.

Surrounded by stacks of paper, Walker Eliot was working, as hard as he had worked in his life. For days now he'd been turning down projects, apologetically at first, then curtly. This is important, he thought. This is what I was made for.

Gerald felt like a parent checking on a sleeping child. Walker's expression was perfectly blank, the serene intensity of a man at prayer. His hands flew over the keyboard, paused to extract a printout from the pile on his desk, clenched and flexed in thought, weaving form into the air. That's right, Gerald thought. That's what we need more of. There were things about the case he could tell Mark did not yet understand, but Walker would take care of it. Why can't all the associates be like this? Treading softly, he continued down the hall.

In a dim corner of his consciousness, Walker heard the footsteps. He turned his head toward the door. No one. Walker rubbed a hand over his face and gathered himself. Okay, he thought. This is going somewhere. This is going to work.

In the state's attorney's office, John Miller tightened his tie. The cubicle wall behind him held two framed diplomas and a photograph of the governor, the desk in front of him a pile of motion papers, printed cases, and notes for oral argument. He was due in court in half an hour to argue preliminary motions in a felonious assault charge. It was nothing glamorous, barroom posturing and a couple of lucky punches, but it was a felony, and it was his. The defense was trying to exclude prior convictions, and in a way, Miller almost hoped they'd win. Success on the preliminary motions would make them more likely to turn down the plea bargain, and he'd yet to first-chair a trial.

Flipping through the police reports, he tried to work up sympathy for the victim. It wasn't so easy in this case. The man was in the hospital, and the admitting physician's statement suggested that his jaw was unlikely to be the same again. But as Miller had looked into the facts, the story became more complicated and less clear. There was drinking; there was provocation; there was a history of bad blood between the men related to unproved charges of sexual assault committed by the victim against his assailant's sister.

John Miller wrinkled his features in displeasure. There were injury and injustice enough to go around; he knew that well enough. But not all of it was illegal, and of what was illegal, only a small fraction could be proved beyond a reasonable doubt. The prosecutors couldn't fix everything. They couldn't fix anything, in fact; all they could do was punish. But punishment was justice, or as close as they could come. It was the will of the people.

That too was part of the problem in this case. The prosecutors represented the people, and part of that representation was the decision of whether or not to file charges, the exercise of discretion. The prosecution in this case, however, was being driven in large part by the noisy insistence of the victim, and the victim, Miller was certain, was simply seeking vengeance. But justice was not vengeance, and the prosecutors were not simply victims' lawyers. In court, the state was not just another gladiator. It had a duty to ensure that the outcome was correct and the process fair; it was required, for example, to provide the defense with all possibly exculpatory evidence. It served broader interests. It served the public good.

Their opponent in this case was the Public Defender's Office. As always, the name stirred vague annoyance in Miller's mind. He was the one defending the public; the people on the other side were doing something very different. Still, there were worse names to see. The public defenders were underfunded; game and experienced, but stretched very thin. There was no danger of being swamped by resources.

Not like the Harper case. That one worried Miller, worried him every time he looked at the files and saw the name of Morgan Siler. He imagined a skyscraper, a bustling hive, an army of gray-suited lawyers with laptops and briefcases and paralegals. And then he looked around his own office, seeing the two printers shared by forty attorneys, the single balky copy machine. They ran out of coffee by noon every day.

The prosecutors handled the unending stream of cases; they tied loss and violence and terror into neat packages and bound society's wounds with the threads of the law. But they were barely keeping up with the caseload, and their ability to do even that depended in large part on the fact that they were regularly matched against the public defenders or local sole practitioners. A single partner at Morgan Siler took home a salary as large as their annual budget. Caleb Kite's team was good. They were smart lawyers, there because they believed in what they were doing, and Kite himself was a legend in the office. He'd never lost, Miller had heard. He had turned down a judgeship to stay with the prosecutors; the offers from firms had ceased because there were none left he hadn't rejected. But Kite couldn't be everywhere at once, and his team couldn't afford to fight a war, or not many of them. They had to pick their battles.

Harper was a good case, Miller thought. He would go to the wall on that one, do without sleep, put in unpaid overtime. It was a good case because the victims were dead. That was good because it meant the stakes were higher. Miller was happy to be involved in a capital case, even if he was only doing the mopping up, protecting the conviction. But it was also good because it made the issues much clearer. Nothing justified murder, for one thing; no prosecutor would ever decline to bring charges because the facts were murky. And more importantly, there was no need to deal with the victims.

Living victims made things more difficult, even if they weren't simply seeking to have the state take their side in the continuation of a barroom brawl. More often the problem was the opposite; the victims wanted the state to step back. They were struggling to negotiate an uncertain future, to piece together the torn world. They had conflicting desires, the parents robbed by their addict children, the battered women refusing to testify; they had wants Miller could not fulfill. The trembling hope in their voices made him cringe. He could prosecute or drop charges; he could not repair their lives. But with the dead there was no such worry, no sense of inadequacy. The dead were past repair, and when Miller heard their voices in his mind, they asked for only one thing. They asked for justice, and he could give it to them.

Fortunately, Kite seemed to feel the same way. He wasn't taking a prominent role; he seemed to want to avoid the attention that would come if it were known he was personally involved. But he was committed to fighting this one, and Miller was grateful, even if he didn't quite understand. Here he could commit himself wholeheartedly; he could promise the victims that justice would be done. The state came on the scene late, as it had to, but it came in power and righteous rage, stalking like a father drawn by the cries of a child. You took my boy's football? You bloodied his nose? You murdered a couple in their own bedroom; you raped a daughter of the commonwealth? Now it's our turn.

With an effort he brought his mind back to the assault case. He glanced at the motion papers, rehearsing his argument. "It goes to intent, Your Honor," he said quietly. The telephone cut him off.

"Miller," he said. "Oh, yeah. Of course we will. Just give me a list." He hung up and, motion papers forgotten, jogged down the hall to Caleb Kite.

Mark lay back on the hotel bed, staring at the television. What do I want to see? He consulted a notepad. *Psychiatric expert,* it read. *DNA test. Anonymous informant. Confession.* To these he added, *Atkins?* The issue wasn't really on the table anymore, not at this stage. But it troubled him that Anson Henry hadn't even mentioned it. It would have looked like a sure thing going in, Anne had said. A sure thing for what? Life in prison? Maybe an institution. Was that better than what his parents could offer him at home? Not from Wayne's perspective. Maybe it was close enough that they could live with the guilty plea. But what about the guilt? Unease stirred inside him, vague memories of his meeting with Anson. *I pleaded him out, hoping for mercy.* He could hear the solemn regretful tones, the faint lilt of the Virginia coast. But if Anson had thought there was no chance of the death penalty, what was the mercy he was hoping for? What could be important enough that he wouldn't take the chance of arguing Wayne's innocence?

The telephone rang. "Hello?" Mark said.

"Mr. Clayton?" The voice was deep and unfamiliar.

"Yes."

"Caleb Kite here, state's attorney. I understand you're asking for some of the papers on our boy Wayne Harper."

"Yeah," said Mark slowly.

"How can we help you?"

"Uh," said Mark. "How about the psychiatric examinations?"

"They're all in the trial court record," Kite said. "You have that, don't you?" The record, thought Mark. The boxes in his office. "Right," he said. "Of course we do." I'm sounding like an idiot. The DNA analysis must be there too. But what if it isn't? He pitched his voice lower. "One of my associates has been going through the record," he said. "I haven't had a chance to look at it myself yet. Is the DNA analysis there too?"

Kite chuckled. "No, Mr. Clayton. The record contains the material presented for the court's consideration. Since Harper pleaded guilty, the DNA report was never presented to it."

"Oh," said Mark. "Well, we'd like that."

"I'm afraid I don't see how it's relevant at this stage. You can't relitigate a guilty plea."

Fuck you, Mark thought, senior prosecuting attorney or not. "Well, we'd like to take a look anyway."

"I suppose that's your right. We'll send it to your hotel."

"How about the confession?"

"We'll send a copy of that too."

Mark considered. "Wasn't the interrogation videotaped?"

"I expect so," said Kite. "We don't have the tape, though. Could get it from the police, but it'll take a day or more. How long are you planning to visit with us here?"

Mark hesitated. He'd been thinking he could drive back that evening. Larry Angstrom, evidently believing Mark had proved himself by meeting the fabricated deadline for the interrogatories, had offered him the opportunity to draft a motion to dismiss. Mark didn't like the idea of working with Angstrom again; more simply, he didn't like Angstrom. But it was more responsibility than anyone else was giving him. It was a good chance to start doing real work. Another day in Norfolk would mean missing the meeting they'd scheduled, which would undoubtedly erase whatever good impression he'd created. And what was there to do, waiting at the hotel for Kite's messengers?

I could go to Waverly, he thought suddenly. I could see Wayne.

The prison housing Virginia's death row was called Sussex I, in distinction to the adjacent Sussex II. It would be little more than an hour's drive, west toward Petersburg. A total of two hours in the car for an interview that probably wouldn't help at all, then the drive back to D.C. in the evening. He could bill all the time, but they were pro bono hours, essentially meaningless. No one would question him if he went back now. Not Wallace, whose primary concern seemed to be that Mark not come to care too much about a hopeless case. Not Walker, whose indifference to all things factual would surely extend to an interview with a marginally competent client. Not Peter Morgan, who'd warned him off the case; not even Anne Brownlee.

But maybe Wayne, if he understood what was going on. Oh, hell, Mark thought. He's my client. I didn't ask for this, but I can't abandon him. Who else does he have?

"I'll be around until tomorrow afternoon," he said. "Can you get it to me by then?"

Kite sighed. "Suppose so," he said. "Just trying to save you some time. You want it sent over?"

"Might as well," Mark said nonchalantly. "Got to keep the associates busy." He thought he heard a chuckle on the other end of the line. Of course he knows who I am. "What about this informant?" he asked.

"Who?"

"The person who tipped the police off about Wayne's involvement. Can you tell me who that was?"

Kite boomed a deep laugh. "I'm afraid that's not our end of things, Mr. Clayton. Police work. Possibly someone in the department could help you. But again, you know, it doesn't have any relevance to anything that happened at trial."

"Right," said Mark. "Well, why don't you just send me what you've got now. The tape can wait a day."

"Pleasure to be of service," Kite told him. The line clicked dead.

Twenty minutes later Mark opened his hotel room door on John Miller's earnest face. "Here you go," he said.

Mark took the package. "Thanks."

"Nice place you got here." Mark watched Miller's eyes scan the room.

"Yeah," he said apologetically. "It's the firm's regular hotel. Not exactly what I'm used to." He smiled.

John Miller gritted his teeth. "Change of pace for you, huh? Nice to get out of the office?"

Mark found himself wishing the television were slightly smaller, or that he'd turned it off before answering the door, or that it wasn't tuned to Cinemax. "Well, it's nice to feel like I'm making a difference. Helping someone, you know?"

Miller looked stunned. "Helping someone? Is that what you think you're doing?"

"Doing pro bono, I mean. Having a client who's a person instead of a corporation."

Miller shook his head. "You don't get it, do you? For a little variety you come in here, get some good experience, screw up our cases over technicalities, and go back to your corporations and your hundred and fifty thousand a year. You're on the wrong side. You're not doing good here. Evil subsidizing evil. That's what pro bono is."

"Oh," said Mark. "I never really thought about it that way. I mean, I can see how from your perspective it might look like that. But—"

"Forget it," Miller interrupted. "I shouldn't have said that. Enjoy your espresso maker."

Mark watched the door close behind him, nonplussed. *I guess it would look that way to him. But how does it look to Wayne Harper? I'm just here to do a job*, he thought. He opened the package Miller had brought.

The DNA report, as he'd expected, meant nothing to him. From what Anne had said, there was nothing to be done with it at this point anyway. The confession was neatly typed and signed with an illegible scrawl. In detail it described the crimes already familiar to Mark from the Virginia Supreme Court's opinion. In detail, and in complete sentences. Wayne hadn't written it; that much was clear. Mark shook his head. There were plenty of questions, just as Wallace had predicted. Everything he turned up was troubling in some way. But none of it seemed to offer an opening for the habeas petition. He picked up the phone and called the Sussex State Prison.

Outside Norfolk, Interstate 264 turned west through the coastal plain. Mark drove through flat stretches of farmland, past wooden stores with signs advertising fireworks. He caught occasional glimpses of horses and cattle, deep black earth and tobacco plants. Far to the west he could see rolling forested hills and the hazed mass of the Blue Ridge Mountains. He found a classic rock station on the radio and read the names of passing towns with mild curiosity. Algren, Sunray, Nansemond. They sounded like interesting places but didn't look like much from the highway. Near Suffolk he merged onto 460, turning northwest. These town names were even better: Zuni, Isle of Wight. The prison itself was on Musselwhite Drive, an appealing enough address unless you knew what it was.

Nearer Waverly there were signs by the roadside. STATE PRISON. DO NOT STOP FOR HITCHHIKERS. Mark smiled. They should have some of those around Morgan Siler. LAW FIRM. ENTER AT YOUR OWN RISK. He was enjoying the feel of the open road, the sense of freedom that came with driving. Waverly itself was bigger than most of the towns he'd passed through, a consequence of prison jobs. A large blue sign standing in a circle of flowers identified Sussex Prisons I and II. It would have been hard to mistake them for anything else, Mark thought, the squat concrete buildings surrounded by guard towers, the high fences topped with gleaming razor wire.

Mark pulled into a small parking lot by the guardhouse. It too was concrete and boxy, flying an American flag. Inside, Mark produced identification and signed in. He underwent a perfunctory search and surrendered all possessions other than a legal pad and pen. The guards expressed surprise at his lack of a cell phone and sat him in a plastic chair to wait while Wayne was brought out. Mark looked around the room. There weren't many visitors, maybe fifteen. Half he took for lawyers, older and in suits; the others seemed to be wives or girlfriends, some with children in tow. All looked equally tired of the wait.

Eventually the guard at the desk called Mark's name. They walked him through a metal detector and put a stamp on the back of his hand to be read under ultraviolet light on the way out. It was invisible to the naked eye, and Mark had an anxious moment imagining what would happen if it didn't show up when he tried to leave. A bored guard led him through a series of thick metal doors that resembled airlocks and operated similarly, each one closed and locked before the other could open. The locks were operated from some distant command center; the guard identified himself and his visitor through a walkie-talkie, facing a video camera as he requested each door to be opened. In the visiting center Mark waited again before being shown to a small room bisected by a wall of the same dull concrete as the rest of the prison. In the middle of the wall, halfway up, the stone yielded to a gray metal screen with a slit large enough for papers.

Mark took a seat in the plastic chair in front of the screen and watched the door on the other side of the wall. The first person through it was a young and muscular guard, somewhat more alert than those in the exterior guardhouse. The second, in an orange jumpsuit stamped INMATE—VA DOC, was Wayne Harper. Alert though the guard was, he didn't seem to be expecting any trouble from Wayne; as they entered, Mark heard the guard say something indistinct and laugh in friendly tones. Nor could Wayne have given trouble even if so inclined; a chain around his waist led to shackles on his wrists and ankles. The shackles gave him a hesitant, mincing gait; he smiled a slow, puzzled smile as the guard led him to his chair.

"This lawyer's going to talk to you for a while, Wayne," the guard said. "Don't go confusing him with your big words." He laughed again and went out the door; Mark heard a bolt click shut as it closed.

Wayne peered through the grille with an expression of mild curiosity. "Who're you?"

"My name's Mark Clayton," Mark said. "I'm a lawyer with Morgan Siler in D.C. We're representing you on your habeas petition."

Wayne's reaction suggested a lack of interest in his representation and his habeas petition alike. "Is my parents here?"

Oh, God, thought Mark. I wish I'd thought this out better. I wish I'd thought it out at all. He'd felt so good after making the decision to visit that he hadn't planned the interview. It had seemed like something that could be done in the car. But then the liberation of driving, with the windows down and the radio up, the scent of earth on the warm breeze, the lulling simplicity of the landscape. "No," he said. "It's just me. I have a couple of questions I'd like to ask you, Wayne." The hope drained from Wayne's face, leaving it impassive and agreeable. "Do you know why you're here?" Mark asked.

"That lady," Wayne said, his eyes shifting down toward his hands.

"Leslie Clark," Mark said. "What do you know about her?"

Wayne's face turned serious. "She dead."

"Do you know how she died?"

"Something bad," Wayne said. "I seen it."

"You saw it? What happened? What did you see?"

"I don't remember," Wayne said. "You got to tell me, then I see it."

Mark's excitement faded. For perhaps fifteen minutes he tried different ways to phrase the question.

Wayne repeated that he couldn't remember and soon seemed tired of the conversation. He shifted uncomfortably in his chair. "Is my parents here?"

This is going nowhere, Mark thought. He looked at the metal grille between them, dividing Wayne's face into diamonds of pale flesh. "No, Wayne," he said. "It's just me."

"My dad don't like it here," Wayne said, looking sorrowful. "He cried. My mama says if I'm good they won't keep me long."

She got that right, Mark thought. Good or not. In a matter of weeks, unless he could come up with something, they'd transfer Wayne to Greensville, where the death chamber was waiting.

"When're they coming?" Wayne asked. The beginning of a whine was in his voice.

"I don't know," Mark said. Wayne's face twitched, and Mark felt an answering twinge in his chest. He stood and waved for the guard waiting behind his door. "Maybe soon."

The signs advising against picking up hitchhikers were still there on the drive back, but Mark didn't smile this time. Everything about the case was depressing. When would Wayne's parents visit? He hadn't seen his own since Christmas. But he was a competent adult, a lawyer working on important cases, drawing a fat paycheck. That last was beyond dispute, if nothing else. They'd been protective when he was a child, holding his hand on the sidewalks, warning him not to stray into the street. And he'd delighted in doing it anyway, or threatening to, dangling from tree limbs, leaning out over the white wooden sill of his bedroom window. He did it because he wanted the rescue, because he never felt so safe as when the strong hand pulled him back from danger. And that, he thought, is what it means to be an adult. You're on your own now. No one will save you. There, at least, he and Wayne Harper had something in common.

At the hotel the desk clerk held a package for him. Mark carried it up to his room, ripping open the envelope, and popped the videotape into the hotel's VCR.

The camera appeared to have been wall-mounted, shooting over the head of one of the officers. Wayne Harper, hands cuffed in front of him, sat across from the interrogation table.

"What do you have to tell us about what you did that night, Wayne?" a voice said. Mark couldn't tell who was speaking, or see Wayne's face as he answered.

"I done it," Wayne said thickly. What's that tone in his voice? Mark wondered. He's not unhappy. He sounds relieved, almost eager.

"Let's start at the beginning. Did you go to the house?"

"Yeah."

"And then what?"

"I went inside."

"How did you get inside?"

Wayne paused. "Through the door."

"How did you open the door?"

There was more silence. "I . . . I opened the door."

"The door was locked, Wayne, remember? So how did you get it open?"

"I, uh, I broke the lock."

"What did you break it with?"

"A stick or something."

Mark heard a muffled consultation.

"Okay," the first voice said again. "And then you went inside. Now I want you to see yourself inside the house. What did you do?"

Mark stopped the tape. He pulled the Virginia Supreme Court's opinion from his bag and quickly scanned the pages. *At 7:30 a.m., the detectives falsely informed Harper that his fingerprints had been found in the victims' residence.* This is bullshit, he thought. What had Wayne said? *You got to tell me, then I see it.* This is outrageous. They told him he was there, and they got him to repeat the story back to them. Well, we'll see about that. He ejected the tape and began packing. Evil subsidizing evil, Miller had said. The nerve of that guy. Mark jammed clothes vehemently into his suitcase, feeling the courage of a man who knows his cause is just.

Ryan Grady felt the courage of a man who has mixed alcohol and painkillers. He rode on the current of a steady imperturbability, a defiant nonchalance, a sense that things were drastically wrong coupled with an inability to understand why, exactly, that should bother anyone. His workload had dropped dramatically since the return from Texas; partners seldom called him and, when they did, prefaced all requests with disclaimers that he shouldn't take on anything he didn't feel up to. They're worried I'll sue, Ryan decided eventually, and accepted the invalid's role gladly.

It was a welcome change. The partners had been making his life difficult for a while. They might have been good lawyers, but they weren't very good at taking no for an answer. He'd tried to let them down gently, making excuses about other projects he'd been assigned. "That sounds great," he'd say. "But I'm really kind of swamped right now." They didn't get it; they'd ring back the next day, sometimes the next hour, wondering whether his schedule was clearing up. Ryan took to screening his calls, asking his secretary to tell people he was in a meeting. He waited several days before calling back; he maintained a three-to-one ratio between the pink message slips and his responses. All to no avail. Nothing dampened their ardor; they kept after him.

His practice of walking the halls had only made things worse. It wasn't even flattering, Ryan thought, the way they'd stop him to offer assignments. He knew they didn't see him as a person. Just a producer of billable hours, one of many, interchangeable object of undifferentiated desire. Some kinds of attention, he was learning, were worse than being ignored. At first he'd tried to show them how wrong they were, projecting an air of intense concentration, toting a notepad or a stack of books. I'm a good associate, his serious frown asserted. Not someone you can grab for whatever monkey work you can't lay on a paralegal. Nothing changed, and lately he'd taken to hiding in his office, almost wishing for a way to become invisible, to make them pass his door without even glancing in. Now he had it, a set of foolproof, can't-miss lines that did not attract but repelled.

He deployed them liberally. I've been having difficulty concentrating, he told the partners. I might take a little longer on that memo because I've been getting these blinding headaches. Concern bloomed in their faces; they raised open palms in acquiescence, surrender. These were more than just good lines, Ryan thought; they were almost like hypnosis. No more cursing and yelling at him, as that lunatic Harold had once. No more throwing papers in his face; no more chill statements about observing the standards of an elite law firm. My short-term memory isn't quite what it was, he said cheerfully. I need to make time to see some neurological specialists.

Many evenings now he left work early, roaming the streets of Georgetown. There were specialists aplenty in the bars and clubs, not neuroscientists, to be sure, but perhaps more helpful for a man in his condition. And things were going better with the women too. Ryan had devoted more hours than anticipated to reading his new stock of magazines, but it was time well spent. There was something to be picked up on almost every page, if you knew how to use it. The tips on the kinds of guys to trust and to avoid; those were the mother lode, the pure stuff. But the sex pointers would surely come in handy. The readers' stories of what boyfriends had done that made them feel beautiful or ugly, appreciated or neglected; those were good too. The advice on makeup and fashion let him get inside their minds. Even the advertisements helped fill out the picture. Ryan pored over the pages with a cryptographer's eye. He could feel knowledge swelling inside him, connections forming within his brain, patterns emerging. For the first time, he was starting to understand what it was all about.

So why this sense of looming disaster?

Ryan glanced around the bar. His afternoon had begun as most did these days, with him staving off some hopeful partner, this time Larry Angstrom. Angstrom was one of the more skeptical of the bunch, and he required the heavy artillery. With a little practice, Ryan had developed the ability to keep the left side of his face immobile while smiling with the right. This technique, coupled with protestations of enthusiasm and a pronounced limp, was almost too effective, and he reserved it for the most serious occasions. "Interrogatories?" he slurred from the side of his mouth. "I'd love to handle those. Get back in the swing of things. Would you believe some people don't want to give me work?"

Angstrom narrowed his eyes in concern. Ryan put his right hand on the desk and pushed himself upright, threw in a quick facial tic, and began a hideous, lurching progress across the room. "Got the file?" he croaked, dragging the left side of his body behind him and working the half smile. Angstrom's frown gave way to an expression of frank terror, then a less than fully successful attempt to hide his pity and revulsion.

"You know, actually it's not that urgent. I should probably think a little more about what we're looking for before anyone does any drafting." He backed out of the room.

Ryan's smile resumed its normal dimensions. He turned to his time sheet and made a quick entry. *Conference w/ LA re: interrogatories—.25 hours.* He turned off his computer and swallowed one of the Norco pain pills the firm's doctor had prescribed. Then he limped down the hallway and out into the evening.

On the sidewalk, moving away from the firm, Ryan watched the pedestrians. It was only a little after six, and the people leaving work now weren't the high-powered ones. There were many secretaries on their way home, also some older established types who no longer had anything to prove. Gradually, glancing about for Morgan Siler employees, he eliminated the limp from his gait; he straightened his shoulders and shot his cuffs. The George Washington campus spread itself to the south, and on K Street he encountered the occasional stray coed to favor with an inviting smile. They walked by without looking, in sweatshirts and jeans, apparitions of a world now drowned in his past. College, thought Ryan. Atlantis, lost paradise. He took deep breaths of the cooling evening air. A crisp, metallic taste summoned memories of burning leaves, intimations of snowfall. He crossed Rock Creek Park and headed into Georgetown.

Ryan had not yet decided on a favorite bar. None had proved especially reliable as a place to meet girls, and at some there were regulars or waitresses who remembered his visits from the earlier, less informed days. Chadwicks was off limits for that reason, likewise Third Edition.

The place he'd settled on this evening was more upscale, less of a college watering hole, with countertops of luminous granite and some kind of undersea theme he couldn't quite figure out.

A cute blonde at the bar attracted his attention. Her hair was glossy, her build slender and boyish. Appropriately, she had chosen jeans with flap pockets on the back to enhance the appearance of curves. Good for her, Ryan thought. But was it good that he was noticing this? He delved into his repertoire and insulted her drink. The stratagem proved a failure; she defended its Brazilian origins with a vociferousness that went beyond the playful. Perhaps she was Brazilian herself; perhaps she had simply read the "Guys Talk" section where some tool had offered the insight that men appreciated being put in their place on occasion. Ryan didn't appreciate it at all.

Ryan settled himself at a corner table with a beer. Across the room he saw a girl with dark curly hair looking at him. She was wearing the colorful eyeliner *Glamour* recommended to brighten up fall evenings. Meeting his gaze, she gently bit the inside of her lower lip and looked at the ground. Good, thought Ryan, good. But she had chosen the wrong jeans for her body type, tapered legs that thickened her waist; worse, they were cropped above the ankle, a serious mistake for a short girl. Even from a distance her curls looked stiff, the result, he surmised, of an alcohol-based hair spray.

Ryan shook his head. He sipped his beer and was again assailed by the impression that something was deeply amiss. Something was happening to his sense of the world. It was not, as he'd initially thought, simply that he was becoming more perceptive. He had learned a lot from the magazines; there was no doubting that. He read them cover to cover, the beauty tips and the advertisements, the sex surveys and the makeovers. And now, as he looked around the bar, he knew that the research had paid off. He had been reading about the women there, or they had been reading the same things he had, and he could see what they had done, or, if not, imagine it: how they were trying to make their teeth whiter, their tans darker, their legs thinner, their cleavage deeper, their hair thicker and shinier, their tired eyes perky.

Free grace and salvation by works. The phrase entered his mind again, as surprising, as unbidden, as it had been in Texas. It had seemed like an inspired analogy at the time. He worked hard to make himself attractive to women; they were attractive to him without even trying. But they did try, and now he could see their effort. He could see the successes and the failures, the ones that didn't need it and the ones that would never pull it off.

It was like reading their minds, like having broken the code. And it had, he was sure, given him an edge in the bar pickup scene. But the knowledge came at a cost. Increasingly he found himself musing over the questionnaires in his magazines. Would you date a divorced man? What's your girlfriend style, your ego health, your sexual temperature? He was starting, there was no other way to put it, to see things from their perspective. It was inevitable, when you thought about it, like the CIA moles who gained sympathy for the Russians. Living in deep cover, absorbing their world, as he had been, he couldn't help but start to internalize their values.

And that was not helpful; it was not helpful at all. In fact, there was something discouraging about it; there was something almost heartbreaking. Ryan was beginning to understand the psychology of the defector, the double agent. Knowing your enemy may help you in the struggle, but it may sap your will to fight too. For you may come to discover that your terrible enemy isn't so terrible after all; that in fact she's confused, insecure, human like you. This was terrifying disequilibrium for Ryan, who had no faith in God and the Devil, or West and East, but had seen the world defined by the eternal struggle between those two great antagonists, Man and Woman, and now was realizing that there were people out there who weren't women by choice, who'd fallen into it as much as anything else, not seizing the power to crush his heart but having it thrust upon them, and unsure what to do with it. That, perhaps, among the ranks of his great adversary there was no one but such people, getting their marching orders from the same magazines that sent him out into the field with his hair gel, square-toed shoes, French blue shirts, and arsenal of silly lines.

Not the same magazines, of course, but their counterparts. Close enough; probably they all worked together. Reading both sets at once had built the suspicion in Ryan's mind that the men's magazines were not truly on his side, nor the women's against him. Instead, he thought, the magazines were on the same side, their own, setting up complicated sets of mutually reinforcing insecurities, reasons to seek next month's guidance. The editors doubtless got together at rooftop parties in Manhattan to look out over the darkling plain and laugh, planning reciprocally outflanking maneuvers for their ignorant armies.

If the magazines were in it together, what did that mean for men and women? That they too were on the same side, or at least in the same boat? Ryan hadn't liked the reminders of his imperfections, the models he resembled less every day, and he was sure the women didn't either. The advertisements alone were enough to induce some sort of complex: the shampoos that moisturized, colored, enhanced curls, conditioned, detangled, purified. The menstrual heat patches, the fat burners, breast adhesives, masks of mint or egg; the body washes, controlling underwear, depuffing eye gel, and renewing night cream; the removers for shine, eye makeup, polish, scars, and stretch marks; the pore minimizers and brow tweezers; the skin-firming moisturizer and odor-absorbing tampons. So many things to fix, so much to worry about.

And what was it that made a reader feel beautiful? That a boyfriend had told her she looked good when she was dirty from doing housework; that he'd shaved his head in sympathy when she had chemo; that he'd taken her to a model search for plus-sized women. Such simple things. That's your free grace, Ryan thought; quite likely that's all the grace there is.

He finished his beer. The bar looked suddenly grotesque, a collection of mannequins and advertisements come alive, confused alarms of struggle and flight. What have I done to myself? Ryan wondered. He didn't want these thoughts. He didn't want this knowledge, this multiplicity of perspectives, this world shifting beneath his feet. He wanted a drink. In fact, he wanted many drinks. All problems were soluble in alcohol, he'd heard once, and that seemed like the kind of bedrock truth on which one could build.

Crouched over the toilet some hours later, Ryan wiped his lips with his sleeve. Chunky vomit laced his shirtfront; the hammering on the stall door felt like it was inside his head. "Closing, buddy," someone called. "Time to go home and sleep it off. You'll thank me tomorrow."

Ryan had wit enough to recognize that for the snare it was. Let tomorrow deal with tomorrow. He was re-creating himself this night; he was constructing identity from the ground up. Sleep was a distracting temptation, and he would not leave the work unfinished. "You got any coffee?" he asked as the door burst open.

"Right outside," the bouncer said, taking Ryan by the collar and dragging him across the tiled floor. "Check under the lamppost; the light's better."

"Hold on," Ryan protested, as the man thrust him roughly outside to collapse in the leaf-strewn street. Shapeless thoughts winged through his mind, obscure and vengeful. Something important had happened, but he no longer remembered what. Or even to whom. There was some significance to that. He frowned. "Do you know who I am?" The bar's door shut. He fumbled in his pocket, feeling the business card the caterer had given him at the associate dinner. That had been a neat trick, he thought, and he had carried the card with him since then in the hopes of offering it to some sufficiently credulous undergrad. Now its shape and texture brought a flash of clarity. One particular thought assumed a definite form, pressed its way to the front of his consciousness. "I'm Peter Morgan," he said, enthusiastic, authoritative. "I'm the managing partner of Morgan Siler." A few passersby favored him with quizzical glances. "Don't you get it?" Ryan cried to their blank faces. "I'm Peter Morgan. Don't you know who I am?"

Nothing happens in the future, Ryan realized upon awaking. Everything happens now, in the eternal, the inescapable present. It was now when you woke up this morning; it will be now when you fall asleep. It will be now when you die. And now, Ryan was thinking, now I have one hell of a headache. Normally Ryan valued hangovers. He saw them as badges of courage, as present reminders of past enjoyment, like the muscle aches you got after a workout, the nail scratches and bite marks from vigorous sex. Still, he was beginning to concede that it was possible to have too much of a good thing. Last night, he could tell, he'd had too much of something, good or otherwise. The idea of letting the future look after itself, which had seemed such profound wisdom scant hours before, made less sense in the light of dawn. It's not like you miss these things, he thought painfully. You still have to go through them, and not later either. You have to go through them now, here. But where was here?

An office, but not the sort he was used to; this was larger and better appointed, with windows on two walls. A corner office, Ryan realized. But whose? Innately optimistic, he tried to reconstruct a sequence of events that could plausibly culminate in his installation in such opulence. The venture foundered on the difficulty of explaining his presence under the desk, also the photographs and diplomas on the wall. Peter Morgan, Ryan said to himself. I know that guy.

Ryan cradled his head. He had given the firm's address to a taxi, he deduced, which was not all that surprising under the circumstances. Arguably it had been a sign of devotion, or an attempt to get an early start on the day's work. Perhaps that was the plan worked out by his unconscious mind, but Ryan was beginning to find that he didn't much trust his unconscious. He was beginning to fear, in fact, that his unconscious had it in for him.

Resolving to salvage the situation, he looked about for something that might be of use. Peter Morgan's office was the font of power; surely it held information that might be helpful. The desk offered papers aplenty, and Ryan indulged in a brief perusal. Filings with the Texas commercial registry. Notice of transfer of assets. Tedious things, but linked undeniably to this room and the life its occupant led, a life whose advantages he had seen. Perhaps, Ryan thought, his unconscious *was* trying to tell him something, to give him a vision of a future that might be his. He fingered the business card in his pocket, vague memories roiling his mind.

"I think I've got something," Mark said excitedly. Walker cocked an eyebrow. "Wayne Harper's confession," Mark said. "I don't think he was really confessing."

"What do you mean?" Walker asked.

"I watched the interrogation tapes. They gave him a story about how he committed the murders. They told him to imagine it was true. And then they got him to say it back to them. He was just doing what they asked. He wasn't saying that he really did it."

Walker tapped a pencil speculatively against his chin. "And this helps us how?"

Mark was baffled. "Well, it shows that the confession's not real."

"Maybe," said Walker. "But it wasn't coerced or anything. It would still have been admissible for the jury to consider if Wayne had gone to trial. And he didn't. Anson decided to plead him out. Maybe you think the confession's bogus and the jury wouldn't have convicted, but Anson saw the tape too, and he decided not to risk it. Maybe he thought seeing the confession would make a jury more likely to impose the death penalty. You aren't doing anything to show that the decision to plead guilty was ineffective assistance."

Mark's face fell. "I guess not," he said. "But it shows that the government wasn't playing fair. Doesn't that count for something?"

"No," said Walker. "But the case has gotten me thinking. There's definitely something interesting about it."

"What?"

Walker offered a cryptic smile. "Something I've been working on. I haven't thought it all the way through yet. I'll let you know. You should get to work on the habeas petition."

"Okay," Mark said doubtfully. The impression grew on him that his presence was no longer desired. "Anne Brownlee wanted me to say hi for her," he ventured.

An indeterminate emotion passed over Walker's face. "Yeah, I remember her."

"She talked about an execution you ran," Mark pressed. "Said she didn't think you'd be doing death penalty work after that."

Walker smiled grimly. "Tanner," he said. "That's right. She told you why, I expect. Because it was such a miscarriage of justice? He had a good claim but the lawyers didn't make it?"

"Yes."

"Did she tell you about what this guy did?" Walker asked.

"No."

"Rape and murder. A lot of it. Young girls, teenagers. I read all the trial papers several times. The execution was scheduled. It looked like it was going to go smoothly. He didn't have any arguments. We were expecting one round of filings, a quick vote, everyone goes home by ten. Then Tanner gets his hands on the pills. And I thought, Fine, it'll be put off. Comes back in a couple weeks and a different clerk gets it. Not my problem anymore. We didn't learn they were going ahead until about six, neither did his lawyers. And when they did find out, they panicked. Couldn't get their claims straight, couldn't figure out where to file. They made it to us around eleven-thirty, with half an hour to spare. Tanner was already in the chamber, waiting. Not that he knew what was going on, of course. Apparently he'd lose consciousness if he wasn't propped up at a forty-five-degree angle, so he was out when they put him on the table.

"It took us maybe fifty minutes to get the votes in. Justice Lambert was in Louisiana; Friedman was at some reception. I called Justice Arlen at home and woke him up. But it was an easy vote. Hunter's clerk had told me they were going to vote 'deny' before I even sent around a memo. Of course, Hunter's chambers did that a lot. I don't think the clerks even talked to him about the filings, just followed their standing orders. The state waited for us. They do that; very embarrassing if they kill someone and then the Court says they can't. I phoned it in at twelve-fifteen. And that was that." Walker fell silent.

"So that bothered you?" Mark asked.

"No," said Walker. "It didn't. Usually it's harder when the executions run late, because then you know it's happening as soon as the voting's done. You're turning off your computer, packing up your bag. And while you're doing it, you think, Now they're strapping him down. Now the needle's going in. Now the sodium pentathol is flowing; now the Pavulon; now the potassium chloride. There are three different solutions, you know, one after the other. So I thought that: *Now it's happening*. And then I thought something else: *I'm glad*. If you'd read the trial papers seven times you would have been glad too. I still remember those girls' names."

"Oh," said Mark.

Walker looked at him, considering. "There's one more thing," he said finally. "I got the petition at eleven-thirty. But the clock wasn't really running out. The state was waiting; they would have waited longer. We held them up past three sometimes. I got the petition and I realized immediately that they'd left out the *Ford* claim."

"So?"

"So I could have said something. It wouldn't have been proper, of course. And it wouldn't have made a difference in the long run. But I could have done it. Given him a couple more weeks or something. I was on the phone with Tanner's lawyers about their filings; I could have called them up. 'Does this mean you're going to argue *Ford* in a separate petition?' That would have done it. If I'd said anything, he wouldn't have died that night. But I wanted him to. And that was all I was thinking about."

Walker looked down at the floor, then back up. "The death penalty's a great equalizer, if you think about it. Not in the sense that it's going to be applied to you or me or anyone we know, of course. How many murderers do you think had happy, normal childhoods and grew up to be productive members of society? Not a lot. It's an unusual person who'll actually kill another human being in the ordinary course of events. But the death penalty brings us a little closer to them. It spreads it around. Innocent or guilty, the jurors are just finding facts and then the law tells them what to do. Life or death, that's something else. It's an individualized determination. The law can't require that the death penalty be imposed the way it can require thirty years. All it can do is give you the opportunity. So it's not society that says the defendant should die; it's not the legislature; it's not the law. Some individual ends up making the decision, a holdout juror, a judge. And the law says, if you think it's appropriate, if you want to, you can kill this person. Some soccer mom from the suburbs, some college student, some bank teller. If you want to, you can kill. Some law clerk. You'd be surprised who ends up grabbing the chance."

You'd be surprised who ends up grabbing the chance, Mark thought, staring at his computer screen. The screen stared blankly back. *Wayne Harper v. Commonwealth of Virginia*, he typed. John Miller didn't seem to mind. And Walker perhaps was seeking absolution. For his own part, Mark was coming to regret that he'd ever gotten involved. The confession was staged. The psychiatric expert had been Virginia's pawn. But none of that mattered, apparently. He needed to show that it had been objectively unreasonable to plead guilty. And just how, he asked himself, am I going to do that?

Caleb Kite leaned forward and splayed his hands on John Miller's desk. "Did he give any indication of what strategy he was planning to pursue?"

"No," said Miller uneasily. A wedding band and a heavy gold signet decorated Kite's fingers; from his cuffs emerged a silver watch and a profusion of wrist hair. "We didn't really talk."

"Right," said Caleb. "Well, we can assume he'll watch the tape. That ought to pique his curiosity. Might be a good thing if he focuses on the confession."

"Yes," Miller agreed, uncomprehending. Kite pursed his lips and nodded thoughtfully. "I'm sorry, sir," Miller said at length. "But I don't really understand what's going on. This is just a habeas petition. Why are you so interested in this case?"

Kite took his hands off the desk and folded them behind his back. "We represent the people of Virginia," he said. "We bring to justice those who harm them. And by doing so we protect the people from further harm. That is the mission of our office, and it is a noble one." Miller nodded, having heard much the same speech the day he started work. "Of course, the servants of the people are not infallible," Kite continued, and Miller raised his eyes, sensing something new. "Mistakes are made. Sometimes serious ones, that rightly call into question the soundness of a conviction. And we recognize that. We do not exist simply to win convictions. We exist to convict the guilty. We do not bring prosecutions unless we are convinced that we have the right man. And if we discover that we have made a mistake, we admit it."

Again John Miller nodded. "But there are those who have a different view of the process," Kite said, his voice falling. "Who see it as their mission simply to oppose us at every step. To protect the guilty as well as the innocent. Now, I don't argue with their right to do so. That's what it means to have an adversarial system of justice. But the fact remains that we go up against people who are not constrained by any sense of the public good, who exist only to stop us by any means possible."

That's right, thought Miller approvingly. That's what I was telling that firm punk in his four-hundred-dollar suite. "I was just thinking that," he began, but Kite continued without pause.

"We can't let those people take advantage of our mistakes to stop us from achieving our purpose. When we've won a conviction, when we have the right man, we must protect it. Protect the conviction, protect the people of Virginia. That's why I'm here."

Miller tilted his head in puzzlement. "Was there a mistake in this case?" he asked.

Kite scowled. "Of course not. Have you been listening? We own up to our mistakes. But we won't let the existence of those mistakes overturn convictions that are sound."

"I don't get it."

Kite's expression softened. "Here's what the problem is. Do you remember Roman Fleischer?"

"Fleischer?" Miller asked. "I remember reading about him."

"An embarrassment for us," Kite said. "A serious one. But one that we owned up to and remedied. Not a get-out-of-jail-free card for people who weren't affected."

Miller looked troubled. "Wasn't there a court order?"

"Harper doesn't get a new trial," Kite said, shaking his head. "He didn't have a trial in the first place. He pleaded guilty. Don't worry about it. This one's solid." He clapped a hand on Miller's shoulder.

Mistakes, thought John Miller. Innocent mistakes shouldn't interfere with the conviction of the guilty. But there were some things that weren't innocent mistakes, that were at best misplaced zeal and at worst . . . well, at worst, they were criminal. "Okay," he said.

"There's nothing to worry about," Kite said reassuringly. "Just don't talk too much about the DNA. The smartest lawyer in the world couldn't find grounds to withdraw this plea."

Mark Clayton was feeling like a world-class idiot. Three hours had brought him nine more words: *Wayne Harper's Petition for a Writ of Habeas Corpus.* Beyond lay uncharted wilds. Ineffective assistance, he thought. It has to be ineffective assistance. But how? Every start led to a dead end. There was nothing to be made of the confession; even he saw that now. Likewise the psychiatric expert. He'd called the Norfolk Police Department, seeking the identity of the informant, only to be told that they had just the telephone number from which the call had come. And that, he thought, looking at his legal pad, is pretty much all we had to go on. He frowned. *DNA test* was also written there. But what was there to say about that? Nothing, not with the guilty plea and the crime scene sample already discarded.

"Hey," said Katja, leaning halfway inside the door. "Do you have a second?"

"Sure."

"You were doing discovery in Texas, weren't you?"

"A little," said Mark. "Among other things."

"Did you see these papers?"

Mark gave them a brief glance. "I have no idea. What are they?"

"Fund transfers. Parkwell put some operating capital into Hubble a couple of weeks before the accident."

"How much?"

"About five million."

"So that's good," said Mark. He paused. "Or not. Depending on which side you're on."

"No, no," said Katja. "It's good. The plaintiffs get something. It's nowhere near what their claims are worth, but they'll get something. And it's enough to keep their lawyers interested, so they won't just drop the case. It's just that . . ."

"What?"

"I've never seen these before. I can't figure out where they came from. I mean, I know there were lots of different people doing discovery over there, but I looked at plenty of financing statements and I should have seen the transfer."

"Why does it matter?" Mark asked. "The plaintiffs get something, everyone's happy."

Katja raised an eyebrow. "Happy? Well, they'll get some money. Unless Harold sends these to Canada. What are you doing?"

"Defending murderers. Just one, actually. And it's not so clear that he's a murderer. But it doesn't seem to matter. I'm not making very much headway. How would you find out who made a call if you only had the number it came from?"

Katja looked puzzled. "Is it an unlisted number?"

"I don't know. The number's all I have."

"But what do you get from a reverse listing search?"

"A what?"

"It's called the Internet," said Katja. "It's got more than porn." She glided to his desk and tapped keys. "What's the number?" Mark brushed her hair away from his face, inhaling floral scents. There was a tightness in his chest, a sudden buzzing in his ears. He spoke; she typed. "Okay," she said a moment later, "it's unlisted."

"You and your Internet," Mark said. "'It's got more than porn.'"

"Well," said Katja, "why don't you just call the number?"

"From here?"

"Sure. It'll just show up as the firm's switchboard. No one can trace it to you."

"Okay," said Mark. "Maybe I will."

"Good luck," said Katja, and walked away.

Mark watched her, his mind gone blank. Slowly it filled with memories, stars in the black sky, dark hair through the hedge. Someday, he thought, I'm going to ask where she spent her summers. After a moment he picked up the receiver and dialed. The phone on the other end rang for what seemed like a long time. Eventually a man's voice answered. "Hello?"

"To whom am I speaking?" Mark asked politely.

"To whom are you speaking? Who are you?"

I should have thought this through better, Mark realized. "I'm calling . . ." he said. Why? To offer you a new long-distance service? To involve you in litigation? Because I'm out of other ideas? ". . . to let you know that your phone number has been selected in our grand-prize drawing."

"Is this a joke?"

"Of course not, sir," Mark said. "All I need is your name and address."

"The address for this phone number, right?"

"Yes, sir."

"Well, that's gonna be a little bit of a problem."

"Why is that?"

"Well, see, you called a pay phone. But I answered it. So it is my number right now. I still get the prize, don't I?"

A pay phone, Mark thought. Of course. "Could you tell me where the telephone is?"

"Don't you want my address?"

"No," said Mark. "You see, what we have to do is send our prize patrol to where the telephone is." Hey, he thought, that's not bad.

"Oh, sure. I'm on State Street, right by the corner of, hold on, the corner of Oak."

"What city is that?"

"Alanton. And I'm wearing a red baseball cap, okay? So your guys can find me. I'll be standing right by the phone. What did I win, anyway?"

Mark felt a sudden surge of regret. "I'm sorry," he said. "I just checked with my supervisor and I'm afraid we can't give an award to a pay phone."

"Aw, come on. I was just using it. It's like my phone. I don't even have a phone at home. How can I win when I don't have a phone?"

"I'm sorry. I don't make the rules."

"Look," the man said, "I got a buddy with a phone. How about I give you his number and we cut you in?"

"It's all done by computer," Mark said, wondering at his sudden creativity. "I can't select the numbers. Otherwise there'd be too much risk of abuse." The computer prints out the numbers, and they're brought to me by a team of genetically engineered monkeys. Perhaps I'm even a robot myself. The possibilities are endless.

"You know what you are? You're an asshole." The spell broke, and Mark hung up. State and Oak. Not especially helpful. What else is there?

Walker picked up the telephone. "Yeah," he said.

He sounds distracted, Mark thought. "Is this a bad time?"

"No, it's fine. What do you want?"

"I'm not really getting anywhere with this habeas petition."

"Okay."

"So I thought I'd ask what you'd been working on."

"Oh," said Walker. His tone warmed. "Yeah, it's actually very interesting."

"What?"

"Well, you've got a guy filing a habeas petition, right? Saying that something was wrong with his trial."

"Right."

"So what happens when there's a Supreme Court decision that comes after his trial but before his habeas petition, a decision that sets out some new requirement that wasn't followed at his trial?"

"What do you mean?"

"Well, say it's *Miranda*. Before *Miranda* the cops don't have to read you your rights. Afterward they do. Suppose you have some guy arrested before *Miranda*, who doesn't get the warning. That's okay at the time of his trial. But then *Miranda* comes down and suddenly the law's changed. Then he files his habeas petition saying, 'Hey, I didn't get my *Miranda* warning.' What do you do?"

"I don't know."

"It's a hard question, isn't it? Because if you say he should get out, then everyone's getting out. But if you don't, it looks like you're ignoring a constitutional error."

"I don't think I understand."

"No one does," said Walker gleefully. "The current approach is totally incoherent. Everyone thinks about this in terms of retroactivity: whether the new decision reaches back and changes what the law was at the time of the petitioner's trial. But that's not a workable solution. In fact, it just makes the problem worse. What I figured out is that Justice Harlan, back in the sixties, had the right idea. You have to realize that a habeas petition is not the same thing as an appeal. Then it all falls into place, and you don't have to use the concept of retroactivity at all."

"No," said Mark. "I mean I don't understand how this helps us. What's the new decision?"

Walker paused. "Oh," he said. "Well, there isn't one. So it doesn't help us in this case, really. It's for an article that I've been working on."

"You're writing an article?"

"I know, I know. In the old days they'd hire you on the strength of a clerkship and some good recommendations. But nowadays you've really got to publish before they'll look at you. Or at least have some project you can describe in a job talk."

"Who won't look at you?"

"Law schools. This is for the teaching market. You didn't think I was going to stay at a firm, did you?"

"I didn't really think about it," said Mark. "But what about the habeas petition?"

"I can't," Walker said. "I thought I just told you that. You get into those things and you stop caring about the law."

"I guess I missed the point," Mark said. He was starting to get it now. It wasn't the execution of an unconscious man that had upset Walker, as Anne Brownlee had thought. It wasn't even that Walker regretted the choice he'd made, felt guilt for his part in sending Eric Tanner to the death chamber. It was that he'd made a choice at all, acted on something other than the eternal logic of the law. "But you agreed to do this case."

Walker sighed. "Well, I didn't check it out quite as thoroughly as I should have. But it's good experience for you."

"Except that the client's going to wind up dead."

"It's pro bono, Mark," Walker said gently. "No one expects you to win. You're supposed to get some experience, which is what you're doing. And even if he does end up dead, John Harper will have been lucky to have had you representing him. Otherwise who would he get? No one. The states don't even appoint counsel for habeas petitions."

"Wayne," said Mark. "His name is Wayne. And I think he'd be better off with you."

Walker nodded to himself. "Did you know that something like half the guys on death row are named Wayne?" he asked. "It's uncanny."

42 ZEALOUS REPRESENTATION

Norfolk again. The hotel staff was as ingratiating as ever, and by this time they remembered his name. Big-firm clout, thought Mark, spreading his papers on the bed. It brought his insignificance into sharp relief. The might of Morgan Siler. A plush suite at the Meridian, a Camry with new-car smell. Four hundred lawyers, about that many support staff. An annual income that had to reach the hundreds of millions. And Wayne Harper was getting him and a twelve-page habeas petition that hadn't a chance in hell of working. The state's response had made that perfectly clear; reading it, Mark had almost heard John Miller's voice setting out the irrefutable logic of their position. Nothing established that the decision to plead guilty had been objectively unreasonable. Still, Miller was flattering himself if he thought he was fighting it out against a big firm. There could have been fifty associates breathing down his neck, pummeling him with document requests, a parade of expert witnesses, endless motions for change of venue, subtle outreaches to the governor's office. But instead there was Mark Clayton. I can't win this, he thought. And no one expected me to. No one even cares.

Walker Eliot paced behind the closed door of his office. "We invented the concept of retroactivity to deal with the problem of what happens when the law changes," he said, gesturing expansively. "But that concept is itself the source of our difficulties. Eliminating the concept will allow us to achieve intellectual coherence." A moment's break allowed for applause. "I will now take questions." He pointed at an imaginary audience member. "Am I saying that forty years of Supreme Court decisions are conceptually confused? Yes, I am. Do I expect that my solution will be adopted? Well, not in the near future. Would I like to accept a teaching job as a reward for brilliant and useless scholarship? Why, yes, I would. I believe that concludes the presentation." He permitted himself a short bow.

What does this do for Wayne Harper?

Walker sat, frowning. It wasn't really a fair question. He wasn't, after all, a defense lawyer. Guilty or innocent, that came down to the facts, flotsam and jetsam in the eternal river of the law. And Walker was not a fact guy. Let the river flow, pure and unending, carrying us all to our appointed destinations. He would chart its forks and bends; he would guide it, smooth its path, cabin it within the banks of his mind. What floated and what sank, what bobbed past on its way to the sea—why was that his proper concern? Walker selected his words carefully. "I'm afraid I don't see how that's a *legal* question," he said.

"Am I interrupting?" Katja asked. "I thought you should see this."

"No, it's fine," Harold said. "What is it?"

"Are you sure? You seem preoccupied."

"Just thinking some things over," said Harold, embarrassed. "Wasting time, actually. It's good you came by. What do you have?"

Katja approached his desk and laid down a sheaf of papers. "These are from the Hubble discovery file, what we brought back from Texas."

"Okay. What are they?"

"Financing statements. They show that a couple of weeks before the accident Parkwell made a capital contribution to Hubble. About five million dollars."

"Okay," said Harold, nodding. "Well, that's good news for the plaintiffs. Turn them over."

Katja blinked. "Really?"

"Sure." He looked at her. "You're surprised."

"Well . . ." said Katja. "Well, I just thought, after what you said in Texas . . . I mean, we could make an argument that they're not relevant. They don't relate to a claim or defense."

"You thought I was going to tell you to send them to Canada." Katja was silent. Oh, God, thought Harold, she's blushing. Don't do this to me.

He cleared his throat. "You know why they're relevant. If the plaintiffs' lawyers think there's no money in Hubble, they'll just drop the case. No one sees a dime, and Hubble gets away with it."

"Isn't that what you want?"

"What we want," Harold said. "No. Look, I think I've given you the wrong impression. You have to understand what the world is like for corporations. They're the deep pockets out there, so when something goes wrong, everyone comes after them. Even when what goes wrong isn't their fault, even when it has nothing to do with them. Juries don't like corporations. And the plaintiffs' lawyers have gotten pretty good at making them out to be the bad guys. It's not that hard. So you get a lot of frivolous suits, people looking for quick settlements because no corporate general counsel wants to risk going in front of a jury. If he pays off a couple of meritless claims, no one cares; if he loses a big case he's out of a job.

"That's where we come in. A corporation retains Morgan Siler and the plaintiffs' lawyers know that we'll fight. No easy bucks for them. And the general counsel can sleep easy because even if something goes wrong, he's done his job. He got the best defense possible. So we protect them from intimidation, from extortion. We're like bodyguards."

"We're mercenaries."

"You're making it sound worse than it is. You remember the plaintiffs' lawyers in Texas. You heard what they said. They're like the Vikings, pulling up in their limos and demanding tribute. Pay up or we'll burn your town. It's the Danegeld all over again."

"The Danegeld," said Katja.

"Tribute," Harold explained. "Protection money. And you know what they say. Once you pay the Danegeld, you never get rid of the Dane."

"As a matter of fact," said Katja, "I'd never heard that particular saying before."

"You're teasing me."

"Maybe."

Harold smiled. "All I'm saying is that when you have money concentrated in one place, like a corporation, people want to take it. We stop that from happening."

"For a modest fee."

"Yes. But they only pay us if there's litigation. And if there's litigation, it means the plaintiffs' lawyers think they have a good case. Maybe our client did do something wrong. What we're there for is stopping the frivolous suits from being filed. Once you get to the real lawsuits, it doesn't matter so much if we win or lose, as long as we fight the good fight. And we do that within the rules. Like I told you before, not all your clients are meant to win. It doesn't mean they're bad guys. It's easy to think about litigation as good versus evil, especially when you're on the side of good. But it's not really like that. Life calls you to make plenty of hard choices. Good versus evil, that's an easy one. You should be so lucky to encounter evil. Evil lets you be good. To be good in the absence of evil, that's the challenge. To make yourself by affirming, not rejecting. There's evil in the world, certainly, but it's unnecessary. A lagniappe. You get plenty of bad things happening without any evil at all. Law straightens them out. And we help it along."

Katja nodded.

"Okay?" Harold asked.

"Okay."

"Good," said Harold. "Let's get the discoverable materials together and see if we can get them out by the end of the week. No sense in dragging it out, right?"

"I suppose not," said Katja, regarding him quizzically. After a moment she turned and left.

I should have told her, Harold thought. She thinks I changed my mind, that I'm speeding it up. And she approves, because it's what she wants to do, to get everything out in the open instead of holding her shield before anyone the firm picks. He understood the desire; he felt it himself. But he wasn't sure what he would have done had the Parkwell lawyers not unaccountably instructed him to make a full disclosure, to accelerate discovery. Well, he'd said that life was more complicated than it seemed. And there were lots of things to tell her. Maybe that one could wait. Where was I? he thought. *I know this isn't really appropriate. I try to tell myself that it would be the same with someone else. There are other people in the world. I could fall in love with one of them. But right now . . .*

What would fifty associates be doing? Mark asked himself. Researching the issues exhaustively. Writing a better petition. Conducting lots of interviews. These were beyond him. But they would also certainly be checking out the intersection of State and Oak. There were two hours before the hearing. Zealous representation, he thought. Might as well give it a shot.

State Street was familiar. Mark knew he'd driven it before. Oak took a little finding, but once he'd figured out which direction to head, it had no chance of eluding him for long. And there on the corner was a pay phone, thankfully unaccompanied by any hopeful face under a red cap. A partner couldn't have done it better. I know this place, Mark thought. That bookstore, that diner, that building with the little white sign out front.

LAW OFFICES OF F. ANSON HENRY.

What the hell?

Mark hit the steering wheel, sounding the horn; startled pigeons took flight. Something's really wrong here.

"What do you want?" asked Earl Harper.

"I've got to talk to you," said Mark. "It's about your son." Earl looked at him suspiciously. Mark pushed the door wider, forgetting even to marvel at his boldness. "Let me come in for a minute. It won't take long."

The living room had reverted to what seemed its usual disorder. Earl fell back on the couch and indicated a chair; Mark removed a beer can and sat. "You figure something out?"

"I don't know," said Mark. "But listen to this. I talked to the police. I got the number that called in the anonymous tip. I ran it down and it's a pay phone outside Anson Henry's office. Something very strange is going on with this case."

"Huh," said Earl. He rubbed a hand across his chin. "Pay phone outside Anson's office. Well, that's something I didn't know. Figured them cops started looking this way on their own." He shook his head and laughed. "Always used to say Wayne was good for nothing. Guess she changed her mind. Pay phone outside the lawyer's office. Don't that beat all."

"Do you know what's going on? If there's anything you can tell me, it's got to be now. I'm going into court in an hour and a half, and if I lose it's all over."

"Beth's not one to leave much to chance, is she? Two birds with one stone, she must have been thinking. That's a smart girl I married. Above my station, her folks said."

"What do you mean? Do you know who called in that tip?"

Earl's head drooped. "Hell," he said. "You understand, we none of us thought he'd get the death penalty. Anson was talking up this institution they got, made it seem like a real nice place. Better than anything we could give him."

"Did Beth make the call?" Mark asked. "I don't know what you were thinking, but right now Wayne's going to die. I think there's real doubt about his guilt, but the way things stand, there's not much I can do."

"Real doubt," said Earl. "That's a good one."

"Do you think he did it?"

"You say you went to law school?" Earl asked scornfully. "Of course he didn't do it. He was here at home. He don't go out much. Not really one for the nightlife. You talked to him; I'd have thought you figured that out."

"So you can give him an alibi? I need you to sign an affidavit. I can write it out right now." Mark fumbled in his pockets, looked around the room. "Just give me a piece of paper. Anything."

Earl shook his head. "'Fraid I can't do that."

"But why not? Surely Beth realizes Wayne's not going to end up in an institution now. I can't get you that. If we don't withdraw the plea, he's going to die. Why wouldn't she want you to save his life?"

"Why wouldn't she? You still don't get it, do you?"

"What don't I get?"

"I can't help you," Earl said. "Beth'll be back soon. You'd best be going."

"I'm not going anywhere until you tell me what's going on."

Earl's expression darkened. "You ain't in your office now, son. When a man tells you get out his house, you get." Mark stared at him. "Get!" said Earl loudly. Mark flinched. He looked at Earl a moment longer, then rose from the chair.

"I have a duty to your son," he said. "To do everything I can to save his life. I'm going to go into court and tell the judge exactly what you just said. I don't think it's enough, but I'll do it. Because I'm his lawyer. And you—you're his father, and you won't sign a piece of paper."

Earl nodded approvingly. "You got some spine. You're a good man, and I mean that. There's the door."

———

Earl barely had time to open a beer and resume his place on the couch before his wife returned. "That lawyer boy came by," he said.

"What did he say?"

"He had some doubts that Wayne was the right guy. Said there was something strange about this case."

Beth's eyes narrowed in suspicion. "What did you tell him, Earl?"

Earl took a drink. "Turns out whoever told the police Wayne did it was calling from outside Anson Henry's office. What do you make of that?"

"That's over and done," Beth said. "Now what did you tell him?"

"I told him Wayne didn't go out too much."

"What are you thinking, Earl? We talked about this." Beth's voice was rising, and Earl shrank inside himself.

"Don't worry," he said. "I didn't sign anything. He wanted me to." Beth looked at him coldly. "It's not right," Earl protested. "You know it ain't."

"You think Wayne's going to take care of us when we get old?" Beth asked. "You think he'll provide?"

"You think anyone else will?"

"You shut your mouth," Beth told him. "You do one damn thing for this family and maybe then you can talk to me about what's right. He's your goddamn son. If you'd been more of a father maybe he wouldn't have done it."

"My son," said Earl. "Got my name, anyhow. Sometimes I think he looks like a lawyer I know."

Beth's smile showed malice. "I would have thought the DNA test set your mind at ease."

"Yeah," said Earl speculatively. "You were always wondering why they couldn't be more alike. Like enough, it turns out. 'Cept Wayne's no killer."

"It's done," said Beth. She forced a warmer tone. "That Mr. Clayton seemed like a bright young man. I'm sure he's got some good ideas."

Forty-five minutes to the hearing. Stretched on the hotel bed, Mark scribbled desperately. *Mr. Harper stated that Wayne Harper was at home at the time the murders occurred.* Got to dress this up somehow. *Mr. Harper testified.* No, he wasn't sworn. *Mr. Harper stated on the basis of personal knowledge that Wayne Harper was at home at the time the murders were committed.* That's better. *He further stated on the basis of personal knowledge that Wayne Harper did not commit the murders and is factually innocent of the charges against him.* What else is there to say? *Mr. Harper refused without explanation to sign an affidavit.* Should that go in? Lyttle seems like a decent man. It'll have to do.

But of course it wouldn't. There must be something else, Mark thought. Something more to say. Earl all but told him that Beth had made the anonymous call. Why didn't I at least ask the cops if it was a woman or a man? Maybe they taped it. But did the prosecution rely on the call? He consulted the papers on the bed, looking for the Virginia Supreme Court's opinion. He rummaged inside his bag, then threw it across the room in frustration. Why can't I just be halfway competent for once in my life?

Mark looked around the room. High-speed Internet access, he thought, and picked up the phone.

"Room service."

"I need a computer."

"I'll transfer you to the business center." The voice was amused; Mark was not.

"Business center."

"I need a computer. Right now."

"We have a number of computers available for our guests."

"Can you send one up to my room?"

"Are you one of our corporate guests?"

"I'm with Morgan Siler," said Mark emphatically. "I need a laptop and Internet access in the next five minutes. It's extremely urgent."

"Of course, we'd be happy to accommodate you."

"Here you go," said the bellhop two minutes later. "Just plug it in."

"Thanks," said Mark. He extracted a bill from his wallet without looking and pressed it into the man's hand.

"Are you working on a big case?"

"No," Mark said absently. "Small case. Death penalty."

"Just asking," the bellhop protested. "Don't have to be rude about it," he continued, but Mark didn't hear.

The Westlaw.com site didn't run quite as fast as it did from the Morgan Siler computers, but Mark's watch promised him half an hour. More than enough time to pull up the case, if he knew the citation, which of course he didn't. It's okay, he told himself. Search the database of Virginia cases. *Title=Harper*, he typed. Seventy-five hits, far too many. What narrows it? Something about the facts, something distinctive. They found something at the crime scene. *Title=Harper and "handkerchief."* Three hits, all *Harper v. Commonwealth.* That's it, Mark thought. One of these is the direct review. One is the review of his state post-conviction proceedings. And the third . . .

Mark looked more closely. *Harper v. Commonwealth.* It was dated 1993. He clicked the file open. *Earl Harper, Jr., v. Commonwealth of Virginia. Appellant was convicted of forcible sodomy and second degree sexual assault,* he read. He skipped to the search term. *The intruder left a **handkerchief** at the scene. Tests on the **handkerchief** revealed the presence of . . .* What is this? Earl Harper? But why would he tell me those things? No, Earl Junior.

Mark fell back in his chair. What did Earl say that first time? *My son did it.* That's it. My God, that's it. They weren't just trying to get Wayne into an institution. He's got a brother.

43 A CHOICE ALREADY MADE

"*Wayne Harper* versus *Commonwealth of Virginia*," the marshal called. Mark gathered his papers and made his way to the counsel's table. Across the room John Miller acknowledged him with a calmly confident nod.

Judge Lyttle arranged a stack of papers in front of him. "You're seeking to withdraw the guilty plea, is that right?"

"Yes, Your Honor."

"And you're arguing that trial counsel was constitutionally ineffective for making the decision to plead guilty."

"That's right."

Lyttle extracted one document, then another, and examined them. "I've read your petition," he said. "And the state's response. I've read them carefully. I don't want you to think that I'm prejudging the issue. I'm ready to listen to you. But on the basis of the arguments presented in your petition, I'm having a hard time seeing how I can grant it. Trial counsel made a gamble, and obviously it didn't work out the way he'd hoped. But nothing here really establishes that his decision was unreasonable. So what I'm saying, I guess, is that if you have anything beyond what you've presented so far, I'd be interested in hearing it." Mark nodded. John Miller smirked. "Do you?" Lyttle asked.

"I do, Your Honor." Mark pulled out a paper, savoring the expression of surprise on Miller's face. "I have an affidavit I'd like to submit."

John Miller rose to his feet. "That's improper," he said. "The petitioner can't spring this on us now. It's an ambush."

Lyttle waved him down. "Your objection is noted, counsel. If you feel it necessary, you'll be able to make an additional response. Whose affidavit is it, Mr. Clayton?"

"It's mine, Your Honor." Judge Lyttle looked perplexed.

Miller stood again. "Counsel can't be a witness."

Lyttle raised his eyebrows. "This is unusual, Mr. Clayton. What is the substance of the affidavit?"

"It attests to Wayne Harper's innocence. It's an alibi."

"An alibi?"

"Yes."

"Do you mean to say that you personally know where Mr. Harper was at the time of the murders?"

"Not exactly, Your Honor. What happened is—"

Lyttle's raised hand cut him off. It rotated; the fingers beckoned. "Let me take a look at this."

"I'd like to see it too," said Miller, still on his feet.

"Approach," said Judge Lyttle. Mark handed him the original and gave John Miller a copy. Lyttle scanned it rapidly and set it down, waiting.

"This is hearsay," said John Miller. "It's completely inadmissible. And a habeas petitioner can't present new evidence anyway unless he can show grounds for not discovering it earlier."

"Well, let's think about this," said Judge Lyttle. "If the argument is that counsel was ineffective for failing to investigate or present an alibi defense, then I believe it's proper to offer the evidence that he failed to. But I'm afraid I have to agree with the state that this affidavit is hearsay. I don't see how I can consider it. And frankly, I'm troubled by the lack of explanation for why Mr. Harper's father refused to sign an affidavit."

Mark took a deep breath. "I think I can explain that, Your Honor."

"Yes?"

"Wayne Harper has a brother, who was previously convicted of a sex offense. I believe that the brother committed these crimes and that the family remained silent in order to protect him." This was the version he'd settled on during the drive to the courthouse. It was simpler, and it was all he could substantiate. But in his mind he saw something else. Earl Junior would have gotten the needle without a doubt. Death for one child, a life sentence for the other. An institution. He could hear their father's voice. *Better than anything we could give him.* Beth would have made that choice without much hesitation. *Two birds with one stone, she must have been thinking.* And then when they saw it was one death or the other . . . That would have been harder. No wonder she cried with me. No wonder Earl cried with Wayne. But at that point it must have seemed a choice already made.

"Oh, come on," said John Miller. "This is entirely speculative."

"There's a record of the conviction, I assume," said Judge Lyttle.

"Yes, Your Honor. I've got the case right here." Mark lifted the print-out he'd received from the business center.

"And it would be permissible for me to take judicial notice of that conviction, as a public record."

"Yes, Your Honor."

John Miller had the sense that matters were spinning out of control. "That doesn't prove anything except that it runs in the family," he said. Lyttle gave him a severe frown. "Your Honor," Miller amended. "The only question is whether it was objectively unreasonable to plead guilty. The state's evidence against Wayne Harper was overwhelming. There was a confession, there was . . ." *Don't talk too much about the DNA.* He collected himself. "It's not ineffective assistance not to pursue every theory Morgan Siler can dream up after the fact."

Judge Lyttle's eyebrows slowly ascended his forehead. "It's my impression," he said, "that the state's case was indeed quite strong."

Mark pressed forward. "But Your Honor, if you look at the confession—"

Again a raised hand silenced him. "However, that's not what's troubling me." Mark and John Miller looked at him, waiting. "What you're saying, it seems to me, is that the family was less than fully cooperative."

"Yes," said Mark.

"That they may actually have hindered the lawyer."

"Yes."

"Well, that's a problem for you, isn't it, counsel?"

Uh-oh, thought Mark. *I should have realized I can't just say yes to everything.* "I'm sorry?"

Judge Lyttle looked disappointed. "It's one thing if the state withholds evidence," he said. "They have a constitutional obligation to turn over everything exculpatory. So if the state's efforts frustrated trial counsel's attempt to put on a defense, that would be a constitutional violation. But here you're saying that some other private parties—in fact, petitioner's family—did so. Doesn't that theory just make it more likely that counsel's performance was objectively reasonable, given the circumstances he faced?"

"That's exactly right, Your Honor," John Miller interjected.

"Thank you, counsel," said Judge Lyttle dryly. "Mr. Clayton?"

I was expecting to lose, thought Mark. But not like this. How did I end up arguing for the other side? "Your Honor," he said, "if you look at this case, the brother's conviction, it's just too similar to be a coincidence."

"There's a family resemblance," said Miller happily. Judge Lyttle's face made him regret it.

"So what you're arguing," Judge Lyttle said, "what I think you have to argue, is that the mere fact of this brother's conviction creates reasonable doubt about Wayne Harper's guilt. And trial counsel acted unreasonably by failing to discover it and proceed to trial on that basis."

It sounded very little like a question, but Mark answered anyway. "Yes."

"I'm willing to believe that there are some similarities. But this was, after all, a murder trial and not simple sexual assault. I was never a defense lawyer, but I think I would have hesitated to go in front of a jury with nothing more than that case."

"But Your Honor," said Mark, "it's the same neighborhood." He flipped through the pages, seeking resemblances. "It's the same MO," he said. "It's . . . it's even the same lawyer."

The effect was remarkable. John Miller's head whipped toward Mark. Just as quickly, his eyes flashed back to the judge. Slowly, with studied nonchalance, he turned his head forward again. Judge Lyttle was motionless. "This is a distraction from the real issue," Miller said.

"That's enough," said Judge Lyttle. "Give me the case." He looked quickly through the pages, then consulted a document from the stack in front of him. Lyttle closed his eyes, looking pained. He removed his glasses, polished and replaced them. "Your theory, Mr. Clayton, is that this brother was the real culprit."

"Yes," said Mark.

"And in his prior conviction he was represented by F. Anson Henry, who was trial counsel in Wayne Harper's case."

"Yes."

Judge Lyttle drummed his fingers. "Would that make it difficult for him to show undivided loyalty to each client?"

"Yes," said Mark. His head was swimming. Of course they couldn't have done it by themselves. They would have needed Anson Henry. Perhaps it had been his idea. What had Earl said? *Anson was talking up this institution they got, made it seem like a real nice place.* He saw it now, the fact that made all the difference. The machinations of the family were nothing to the Constitution. But once they involved a lawyer, once an officer of the court was corrupted . . . Lyttle appeared to be waiting for something. "There was a conflict of interest," Mark said.

"That argument wasn't presented in the petition," Miller said cautiously.

"All the relevant facts are subject to judicial notice," Mark retorted.

"All right," said Judge Lyttle. "I see an actual conflict of interest here. A defendant is entitled to conflict-free representation."

"But there's no evidence that it affected the outcome," John Miller protested. "The evidence against Wayne Harper was overwhelming. There was a confession. There was DNA evidence."

"Yes, about that DNA evidence, counsel." John Miller winced. "I've been a judge here for eleven years. I'm quite familiar with the procedures of your office. And the DNA evidence I'm called on to review is usually somewhat more precise. Your test found a marker possessed by seven-point-eight percent of the Caucasian population. Where is the standard test?"

"I'm not sure, Your Honor," said Miller. "I don't know that it was done. Since Mr. Harper decided to plead guilty, they may have stopped the lab work." He paused. "I'll certainly look for it."

"Do that, counsel. You may have use for it in the future. I'm setting aside the conviction. The plea is withdrawn. The commonwealth is instructed to initiate new proceedings against Wayne Harper or to release him within twenty days."

44 NOTICE OF APPEAL

Mark walked into the Morgan Siler lobby with a spring in his step. I won, he told himself. Not quite the way I planned it, but taking advantage of unexpected opportunities is one of the most important things to learn. I went into court, I stood up and made an argument, and I won. What does that make me? A lawyer. Okay, a lucky lawyer.

Glynda turned her attention from the telephone long enough to acknowledge his wave with a smile. A fingernail decorated with golden glitter pointed at the stack of memos that had accumulated in his absence. Her cubicle had a new sign tacked to the wall. I CAN ONLY PLEASE ONE PERSON A DAY, AND THIS ISN'T YOUR DAY. Mark nodded absently. I can deal with whatever comes along, he thought. More important, I can deal with it later. Now is the time to enjoy the success.

"Congratulations," said Wallace Finn. "That's a great achievement. I have to tell you, we don't win a lot of pro bono cases. Especially not in Virginia. How did you do it?"

Mark smiled modestly. "Well, I just kept pushing at the weak points. Eventually everything fell into place. It almost seemed to happen by itself."

"Still," said Wallace. "It must feel good. You saved a life."

"Yeah," said Mark. "It does."

Wallace nodded. "Looks like I did too. In a manner of speaking."

"What do you mean?"

Wallace gestured at the paper on his desk. "Parkwell's going to weather this storm. It's standing on its securitization. The creditors will have to let them work something out. There's nothing there otherwise."

"How can that be?" Mark asked. "Don't they own lots of other companies?"

"No," said Wallace. "The special-purpose vehicles own them. The SPVs borrow against the assets and pass money on to Parkwell as it's needed. But if anything goes wrong for Parkwell, the assets are protected from that exposure. Parkwell's creditors can't reach the assets held by the SPVs. That's the whole point of securitization."

"But doesn't Parkwell control the SPVs?"

Wallace smiled. "You're just humoring me, aren't you? Well, I'll take the opportunity. Parkwell controls the SPVs. It could get the assets back if it wanted to. It could unlock the whole securitization. There's always a key, some sort of convertible stock with the voting power to undo the SPV structure. But it's held by some subsidiary, and it can be destroyed. A creditor would have to find out which subsidiary that is before it could even hope to force Parkwell to unlock. And if Parkwell gets pressed, all it has to do is throw the sub into bankruptcy. The stock converts and the key's gone. They've probably done it already, to be on the safe side."

"Oh," said Mark. "Can they just do that? File for bankruptcy whenever they want?"

"Not exactly," said Wallace. "They'd have to really create a liability the subsidiary can't pay. But that's not too hard. They could do it with nothing more than clever accounting. Restate their earnings and what looked like a solvent corporation goes up in smoke. Everyone's been overstating for years; it's easy enough to do it in the other direction. Of course, it can't look too contrived or they'd just be calling attention to it. And it can't be reversible or something a creditor's likely to forgive. They've really got to kill the subsidiary, which is expensive. But it saves Parkwell, and that's where the real money is."

"Oh," said Mark again. "Excuse me for asking this, but is that a good thing?"

Wallace considered. "Well, the bankruptcy of a major corporation isn't a good thing. Very messy, very inefficient. It's probably better if Parkwell survives. And all of this gets taken into account when people are bargaining in advance. I have to admit I actually never thought of using securitization to defeat liability like this. But the market understands."

"Yeah," said Mark. The market understands, he thought. Where have I heard that before?

Wallace reached across the desk. "Let me shake your hand. I know you don't want to go around crowing about your win. I'll get on the horn and make sure everyone hears."

Mark felt vaguely disappointed. "Thanks," he said.

John Miller felt terrified. For fully three minutes he had sat motionless in Kite's office, watching the man pace. Kite's deputy, Alex Reiner, quietly grim, occupied another chair. "Well, Caleb?" Reiner asked at length. "What'll it be?"

Kite turned to face them, hands linked behind his back. "We'll appeal," he said.

Based on what? John Miller wondered. "Based on what?" Reiner asked.

"The DNA evidence," Kite said.

Reiner looked alarmed. John Miller was merely puzzled. "What do you mean?"

"The other test," said Kite slowly. "Judge Lyttle asked for it. And now we have to give it to them."

"Caleb—" Reiner began, but Kite silenced him with a look.

"So there is another test?" Miller asked.

"Oh, yes," said Caleb Kite. "There certainly is."

I know this isn't really appropriate, Harold said to himself. *I try to tell myself that it would be the same with someone else. There are other people in the world.* His mouth formed the words, feeling their shape and cadence. *I could fall in love with one of them. But right now . . . right now it's you that I love.*

Not bad, he thought. And perhaps that was as far as the script needed to go. Harold had prepared a lot of oral arguments in his time, and generally he liked to have a full presentation in his pocket. You never knew when the bench would be cold, the judges uninterested, the questions desultory or simply not forthcoming. His first solo appeal, they'd let him go all the way through without a word and he'd ended up saving most of his time for rebuttal. But sometimes the case was such that you simply couldn't predict how the judges would see it, which issues they would fasten on as decisive and which they would disregard. Then the full speech was useless; you had to tease out their thinking. Say something suggestive, something provocative . . . and be poised to respond.

That was a matter of working through the issues and having the relevant authority at your fingertips. Harold tapped his teeth with a pencil. Issues. What were the issues? The preparation was causing him unexpected difficulty. There were moments, in fact, when he started to doubt that the matter was best approached as an oral argument at all. There were precedents in his favor, of course. The books were full of them. What was a volume of poetry but a collection of authorities? But it was hard to know which of them would be persuasive. Perhaps the best way to tackle it was to start with the arguments for the other side.

Those were easier to identify. Love means nothing here—he'd said so himself. And what he'd said was true enough, but it could be distinguished away. It was not the rule that governed his case. For what he'd meant was just that other enthusiasms distracted from work, weakened the wholesale commitment he'd cultivated so carefully. Now he saw that there was another possibility, another way of looking at things. The shift of perspective, which once had been effortless, which she had given him back. Look at it from a different angle and you'll see that love can add to work.

Love, or what love brings, Harold thought. It could make him stronger. His performance was slipping; he could see that. He had the aggression, still, but he was losing the delicacy needed to make aggression work. He was becoming rash, heedless, as if hoping to be called to account. As if willing his own destruction, seeking in battle the end to all battles. He had felt the touch on his shoulder, the call to another world, and he was half gone already.

He wasn't grounded; that was the thing. There was something he lacked, and for the first time he knew what it was. Freedom was a fine thing, but it was a negative, the absence of constraint. Harold wanted constraints he chose for himself, a framework, a tether. A life. He longed for connection, as he never had before. And love could give him that, a quiet certainty, a reservoir of strength and assurance to support him in desperate hours.

It was a policy argument he was making, he realized. But that was okay. Policy arguments were often the most effective tack when doctrine was unclear. Judges were never blind to the consequences of their decisions. What he was suggesting here would make him a better lawyer. What could be a stronger argument than that?

I'm going to win this one, Harold thought, his excitement building. He caught himself. Make your arguments like an advocate; evaluate them like a skeptic. Am I overreaching, making extravagant claims? That kindness could have a place in this world, what's so impossible about that? Surprising, admittedly; counterintuitive, perhaps. But impossible? No. In fact, he rather liked the idea of an enclave of tenderness. Wall it off from the rest of your life, guard it as a treasure, a private storehouse of affection and courage. Like the best arguments, it had an elegance that lent a ring of deeper truth.

Nor is the proposal difficult to implement, Harold thought, warming to his task. One of them would have to leave the firm, presumably, but lawyers changed jobs all the time. It needn't be her, though that made more sense. He nodded, humming softly to himself, and jotted a note on his legal pad.

Mark hadn't even made a dent in the backlog of memos when Glynda appeared in his office doorway. "Messenger just brought this over," she said, offering him a paper. "Figured you'd want to see it right away."

Mark tilted his head in concern at the suggested urgency. He hadn't, to be honest, been working especially hard. True to his word, Wallace had spread the news, and Mark had fielded nearly a dozen offers of congratulations. Most had come from people he knew. There were phone calls from Harold and Katja; Gerald and Larry Angstrom had stopped by in person, the first eager to learn the details, the second shopping requests for document production that Mark had forcefully declined. There also had been e-mails from partners he'd never spoken to, whose names were only vaguely familiar. Even one, which Mark suspected was automatically generated, from Peter Morgan via his secretary: "Congratulations on your impressive victory . . ." That was a distraction. Then too, he'd been feeling competent and successful, even capable, and it seemed justified to luxuriate in the sentiment rather than ruin it by attempting to tackle something else. "What is it?" he asked.

"Notice of appeal," Glynda rumbled, receding.

Mark nodded, scanning the sheet. *The Commonwealth of Virginia hereby appeals from the district court's order in* Harper *v.* Commonwealth, *Number 00-5672*. Go ahead and try it, he thought. Let's see what you've got. I have this one under control. I'm not worried. On second thought . . .

"Hey, congratulations," said Walker. "I've been meaning to call you."

"Thanks."

"Honestly, I'm impressed," Walker continued. "I didn't think you had a chance. That makes you look really good. Winning the unwinnable case. It's what every litigator dreams of. Shows that you're not just a technician. You can do magic, upset the natural order of things." He sounded almost suspicious. "How did you do it?"

"Conflict of interest," said Mark. "It turned out Wayne's lawyer had represented his brother in a previous case and there was some reason to think the brother might have been the guilty one here."

"So you won on the facts," said Walker, relief in his voice. "That's even better. Makes it more likely to stand up before the appellate court."

"That's what I was calling about, actually. I just got the state's notice of appeal. I was wondering if you could talk it through with me."

"Hey, you just won this all on your own," Walker said. His upbeat tone was sounding forced. "What do you need me for? And you're defending what's basically a factual finding. Lyttle's a well-respected judge. The appellate court's not going to want to reverse him on that."

Mark felt his buoyant mood evaporating. "Come on," he said. "I don't have any experience with appeals. That's your specialty. And I understand that you don't like death penalty work, but you signed up for this."

"Yeah," said Walker. "Really, it's not that. I'd be happy to help. But the truth is I'm probably only going to be with the firm for another couple of weeks, and I'm pretty busy right now. I've got job talks lined up, and I need to prepare for them. It's a little more complicated than I'd realized. You really have to be familiar with the academic interests of everyone who's interviewing you so you can make them think that you care about what they think is important. Compliment them on their contributions to the scholarship and so on."

"I see."

"Thanks for understanding," said Walker. "And one more thing. I haven't really told people that I'm leaving yet, so I'd appreciate it if you could keep it under your hat for a little while."

Strolling the corridors of Morgan Siler, Harold Fineman exuded magnanimity. The best way to test an argument is to see how it plays in different contexts, to check your view of the world in other settings. This works, he thought, offering friendly nods to the harried associates hustling past. Of course it makes sense. They'd be more effective with a wellspring of private joy. He called to mind a roster of his married partners. They are the better lawyers, aren't they? Distracted, sometimes, but they work with greater dispassion, greater detachment. It's so simple. No fear of losing, not because you think your client should lose, but because in the most important sense you've already won. You can risk things that would annihilate someone who had nothing but the struggle.

It was there in *The Ring*, Harold realized, staring him in the face all this time. A slightly different angle, but the same connection. The man without fear wins love, wakes the Valkyrie maiden where she sleeps fenced in fire. The free agent born to redeem the old law. He paused. There were a lot of divorces among the partnership, of course. But perhaps that just proved the theory: they needed something more to generate the same sense of security, to keep them fearless as the stakes rise. Think what I could accomplish as that kind of lawyer. Dark-suited Siegfried, a man invulnerable.

He glanced inside Mark's office. There's a winner for you. Takes an impossible case right out of the box, nails it. Very different from how he seemed in Texas. "How's it going?" Harold asked. He ambled through the door without waiting for an invitation.

"Okay," said Mark.

"Nice work on that pro bono case. We need to get some of your magic for the paying clients."

"Thanks."

"Have you recently started dating someone?"

"What?"

"Oh, I was just wondering," said Harold. "Don't mean to pry."

"That's okay," Mark said. "But no, I haven't." Harold's face fell. "The job keeps me pretty busy, actually. I just got a notice that the state's appealing."

Harold considered. Maybe it was the other one. "Walker did a lot of work on that case, didn't he?"

"What do you mean?" Mark asked.

"Nothing," said Harold, realizing the slight. "Something's been keeping him from doing much for me, though." He circled back. "Does he have a girlfriend?"

Mark looked baffled. "I have no idea. Why do you ask?"

"Just wondering where his time goes," Harold said. This at least was true. "So is he taking the appeal away from you?"

"Hardly," Mark said. "I think I'm going to need help from someone else, actually, if you have any suggestions."

A light flashed in Harold's brain. "He's leaving to teach, isn't he?"

"I probably shouldn't say anything about that."

Harold laughed. At times he almost envied the associates. They were mortal; they could be fired, while partners could not. But with mortality came the freedom to choose. Associates left the firm; no partner ever had. They could attach themselves to things outside his world. Another source of security: there it was. "Oh, don't worry," he said. "No one's going to be surprised. We all knew Walker was going to leave. It was just a question of when."

"You knew he was going to leave?"

"With his résumé? Absolutely. To be honest, I don't know why we hire Supreme Court clerks at all. They never stick around, and they don't do much for the firm when they're here."

"Why not?"

Harold shook his head. "They don't have a very good grasp of the nature of legal practice, to be frank. Give them a research question and they come back with a new theory of constitutional law. Like that's going to impress a state court judge. And they're too fucking smart, never spend enough time on anything. Associates like that make the client unhappy with everyone else—he wants to know why this brief is costing him three times what the bright boy did the last one for. Smart, efficient people aren't meant for law firms; they just make the rest of us look bad."

"I'll keep that in mind," Mark said.

Harold smiled at him, feeling his soul enlarge. "You know, I can help you out on the appeal if you want."

"Really?" asked Mark. "I mean, yeah, that would be great."

"Sure," said Harold. "We've got to protect our win, right? If you don't want the glory, I'd be happy to argue it."

"I haven't even been admitted to practice before the Fourth Circuit."

"Well, we could take care of that if we needed to. But if you don't want it, I'm your man."

"That would be great," Mark said again. Everything was falling into place. He wouldn't see Virginia's brief for another two weeks, but he couldn't imagine they'd have much to say. And if Walker was abandoning the case, Harold was surely a more than adequate replacement. Wayne Harper had finally gotten a break.

John Miller dropped a forensic report on his desk. The record in Wayne Harper's case lay strewn around his office. For an hour he had pored over the papers, at first casually, then with the haste of mounting panic. Now with the unthinking languor of shock.

It felt like getting kicked in the stomach. Or so John Miller supposed; that had never happened to him. The closest match in his actual experience was the sensation of being dumped. It was not a bad comparison; there was the same sense of unreality, of emptiness, the pain at once distant and internal. The sense of something wrong at the core of his being, the loss of what had been his comfort and his strength. Then too, there was the wondering what the other person was doing. Many nights he'd sat around imagining what the girls were up to. In this case he needed no imagination to conjure the circumstances of the two people responsible for his current dull ache and enfolding anxiety. One of them, he knew quite well, was sitting in a Virginia prison. The other was in the office down the hall.

A sea of paper spread across the floor of the conference room, lapping at Harold Fineman's feet. He was paying a price for his exuberance. Collecting large numbers of irrelevant documents to turn over to the plaintiffs' lawyers had seemed a good tactic; indeed, it was one he'd used with success before. Apparently, however, they'd cast the net too wide. Somewhere among the piles, Peter Morgan had told him, were papers that absolutely did not belong in the discovery trove, papers from a locked room in a warehouse the team had entered only on Streeter's instruction. Parkwell would not identify them; instead the general counsel had demanded a list of everything in Morgan Siler's possession. And since this was for some reason not a task to be entrusted to associates or paralegals, it had fallen to Harold to wade through the waves of paper he'd raised up to break over the enemy.

It was a punishment out of Dante, and imposed for no reason Harold could fathom. Clients had no secrets from their lawyers, not if they were smart. But there was nothing about Parkwell's conduct of the litigation that Harold would call smart. In addition to struggling through the irrelevant documents, he'd been ordered to turn over the relevant ones. That too had a ring of divine comedy to it, being forced to litigate a case with a client constantly demanding that he play it straight.

Harold shook his head. Going through the chaff was bad enough, but the relevant documents were almost more than he could stand. Not only should the other side never see the files he had assembled; they never should have come into his possession in the first place. There was room for misunderstanding, of course; he'd seen it happen. He'd represented clients against regulatory agencies, knowing that the government couldn't make its case without the information locked in their cabinets. You couldn't tell the client to destroy documents; that was obstruction of justice. So you asked them some questions. *Do you still have all those files? There's no law that says you have to keep them, you know. Storage space must be getting tight. Well, we'll be stopping by in a couple of days to see what you have to turn over to the investigators.* And he'd show up as promised and there the damning information would be, the equivalent of a confession, and the general counsel sweating bullets over how to keep it out of the government's hands. But he had expected more from the Parkwell lawyers.

What's the story we're going to tell? That was the litigator's first question. There were no facts proof against redescription, no set of circumstances that couldn't be massaged into a better tale. But there were, all the same, more and less plausible stories. The one confronting Harold, the plausible one, was not one he wanted to hear in court.

Hubble had gotten into a dispute with its waste disposal subcontractor. They'd made no alternative arrangements while renegotiating contract terms; they'd just let the chemicals pile up. That was negligence, enough to sink them, but as Harold read through the time sheets and duty rosters, other possibilities suggested themselves. Admittedly, not much was going on in the summer; admittedly, telecommuting was increasingly effective. All the same, the staffing levels seemed unusually low. The workers on site at the time of the accident were what, in happier days, he'd have called a skeleton crew. Middle management hadn't been in for a week.

That went beyond negligence; that suggested they'd known of the risk and simply disregarded it. Or shifted it onto people deemed expendable. This was not something he wanted the plaintiffs to know; it was not something he wanted to know himself. Harold sorted the documents on the table. He was still a lawyer. Staffing levels weren't relevant, not as long as the plaintiffs were only arguing negligence. These ones weren't going out.

In the antechamber to Caleb Kite's office, John Miller was twitching with nerves. Disturbing Kite unbidden was not a pleasant prospect unless you had very good news to report. What Miller had was not news, really; neither was it good. The secretary finished her study of the switchboard and raised her head. "He's off the phone now. You can go in."

Caleb Kite did not lift his eyes from the papers in his hands. "What is it?"

"I've been working on the brief," John Miller said.

"Good."

Miller waited, but Kite had no more words for him. His own came in a rush. "I won't make this argument. And I don't think we should be bringing this appeal."

Kite sounded mildly curious. "And why is that?"

"I think you know why."

"No," said Kite. "I don't know why. We have a guilty defendant here. A murderer who confessed, who was implicated by a reliable DNA test, who was properly convicted and sentenced after he pleaded guilty. And his high-priced lawyers have gotten that conviction set aside because of some supposed conflict of interest that had no effect on the outcome. Why don't you tell me why we shouldn't be bringing this appeal?"

John Miller swallowed with difficulty. Kite's certainty was something he had admired, his forcefulness, his lack of doubt. The man was the ultimate wrathful father, the terrible angel wielding a sword of justice. Of course you couldn't do the job unless you believed in your cause. Miller did; he never doubted that he was in the right. The defendants were bad, and the prosecutors were good. But his belief that he stood for justice came from the knowledge that he stood within the law, and Kite's belief, he was realizing now, had a different source. "Maybe I'm out of line here," Miller said, "but it seems to me that we should be more concerned about that court order. I mean, I believe this guy's guilty. I believe he's bad. But we don't punish people for being bad. We punish them for breaking the rules. And how are we justified in doing that unless we follow the rules ourselves?"

Kite looked at him as though struggling with a difficult thought. "You're absolutely right," he said at length. "You are out of line." He looked back down at his desk. "An oral argument in front of the court of appeals is the sort of thing that could be very helpful to your career," he said placidly. "This one especially. But if you don't want it, no one's going to force you. You just do what you're told." He punched a button on the phone. "Get me Reiner." At last his eyes turned to Miller. "Why are you still here?"

Miller left without a word. The turmoil within him was giving way to resolution. The state is not just another litigant, he thought. We protect the innocent; we do not bring a case unless we are sure of the defendant's guilt. But is it enough to be sure? The things we cannot prove but are sure of nonetheless—those things are simply unproved to the courts. The courts tell us who is innocent; they tell us what we must do, and we obey. John Miller clenched his teeth. I serve Caleb Kite, he thought, and Kite serves the state. And the state serves the people through the laws they have enacted and the courts declare.

My duty is to the law.

I'll do what I'm told, he thought. And maybe a little bit more. I'm taking my name off that brief, for one thing.

Brief for Appellant the Commonwealth of Virginia, Mark read. He studied the blue-bound volume carefully. John Miller's name was absent; instead the brief listed Alex Reiner and Caleb Kite as its authors. He flipped it open and began to read. *Let's see what they've got.*

For almost four pages, Mark felt untroubled. A conflict of interest, the brief explained patiently, was not a Sixth Amendment violation unless it had an actual adverse effect on the quality of representation. But Anson Henry's decision to plead guilty, it went on, was in fact the only reasonable option under the circumstances. The Commonwealth's evidence was irresistible.

I think we know how far that gets them, Mark thought scornfully. *Walker was right. We're defending a factual finding by a respected district court judge. This is going to be easy.*

The district court, the brief continued, was unaware of the full power of the Commonwealth's case, because not all of the evidence was placed in the record. In addition to the DNA test establishing an HLA DQa match, a test was performed with results that decisively established Harper's guilt. The chances that someone else had been the source of the samples recovered from the crime scene were somewhat less than one in ten billion.

Mark's eyes widened. With a tone of deep regret, the brief went on to note that the new team of lawyers brought in for Harper's federal habeas proceeding failed to perform an adequate investigation of the evidence against their client, squandering the resources of the federal judiciary and the money of the Virginia taxpayers on this frivolous petition.

Mark sagged back in his chair. Taking responsibility for a case, the great allure of pro bono, no longer seemed such a prize. There was frustration at being merely a cog in the machine, but there was safety too. The world lets you pass in anonymity, tender in its indifference. The spotlight of individuality offers no such shelter. The lance from the dark will pierce uniquely you.

Wayne Harper's going to die, he thought. And me. I should be disbarred.

"Relax," said Harold. "It always feels that way when you read the other side's brief. It looks official. You think they're honest men. For a moment you believe everything they're saying. But it isn't and they aren't. They're lawyers, same as you or me, and they're just out to make their case. And presenting new evidence on appeal? That's not going to get them anywhere unless it's extremely persuasive."

"I think you'd better take a look," said Mark.

Twenty minutes with the brief changed Harold's tone. "Okay," he said. "That's pretty persuasive. Did they include the test?"

Mark flipped to the back. "It's in the appendix. I can't understand it, though."

"We'll get someone else to check it out," Harold said. "But you know, it may be that they're right. You've got to allow for that possibility."

"But his father said Wayne was home that night," Mark said. "I really thought he was innocent."

"He wouldn't sign the affidavit, though, right?"

"Yeah."

"Maybe that was because he knew it wasn't true."

"But why would he say that Wayne was home?"

Harold sighed. "You see a lot of strange things, litigating. I represented a guy once, in jail for rape. He was a DNA match, but he filed a habeas petition arguing that the real rapist was still out there. He was the one-in-a-million false positive."

"So?"

"So his point was that another rape had been committed after he went inside, same DNA. I checked it out, and yes, there was a rape reported, and the DNA matched the sample that put him away."

"Did he get his petition granted?"

"No. Turned out he'd smuggled out semen during a visit, had a female friend, you know, insert it and then claim to have been raped."

"Oh," said Mark.

"You never know who's telling the truth," Harold said. "Maybe Anson Henry came up with the idea of a conflict of interest after Wayne got the death penalty. They couldn't have told you about it straight out; if the parents knew about it, it would look like they'd consented to the conflict, which would waive the argument. So they led you in that direction, made it seem like they were hiding something, gave you a reason to look for it."

It almost seemed to happen by itself, Mark thought. He shook his head. "I can't believe this."

Harold put a hand on his shoulder. "I can do the argument," he said. "I'll take the hit for you. You'll still have a perfect record. Look at it that way. You can tell people I fucked it up." Mark said nothing. "Or we could get a miracle," Harold offered. "This is a pretty good panel. Loomis is a hard-line conservative, but Pilcher is as liberal as they get, and Townsend is fair. If we can come up with something, they'll listen to it. Maybe we just need a fresh pair of eyes. Why don't you have Katja take a look at the brief?"

"Should I give her my copy?"

"The Fourth Circuit requires electronic filing, don't they? Just give her the disk they submitted. Or give it to me. I can take it by." That's right, Harold thought. It looks hopeless now, but maybe Katja will see something in it. It's worth taking a shot. Everyone deserves a chance.

Katja's office door was closed, and when Harold knocked he heard flustered activity within. "Just a second," Katja called. The opened door revealed her in athletic clothes and running shoes. She blushed. "I had to come in early today. I was hoping to get a quick jog in during lunch."

"Of course," Harold said. "I was just talking to Mark about his pro bono case. We were wondering if you could maybe take a quick look at the state's brief. Help us brainstorm." He laid the disk on her desk.

"Sure," said Katja. "Do you mean right now? I could do it right now. I don't need to go running."

"There's no hurry," said Harold. "We've got a couple of days before the argument. Whenever you have time." An idea struck. "You know, a run would do me good. I didn't get much of a chance to exercise in Texas. Mind if I come with you?"

Katja's stomach tightened. She could imagine few things less desirable. The looks, the work more properly given to a litigation associate— those things added to the worry she ran to quell, but they were manageable. They could be ignored. The prospect of Harold's company suggested crisis. It made her want to bolt from the office, dash down the hall without looking back. "Sure," she said.

Harold's running costume consisted of a golf shirt and shorts bearing the Morgan Siler logo. The absurdity increased Katja's apprehension. "Where do you usually go?" he asked.

"Down to the mall," Katja said. She headed down K Street, anxiety quickening her pace.

This girl's quite an athlete, thought Harold, struggling to keep up. You can't even hear her feet hit the ground. Beside her he felt hulking and awkward, a cave-dwelling monster scared into the light of day. Inappropriate, he breathed to himself. Well, that's the theme. Press on.

They passed through the crowded downtown, making their way amid the lunchtime swarms. Constitution Avenue offered more space; federal buildings surrounded them. The dome of the Capitol beckoned, the narrow silhouette of the Washington Monument. Katja ran faster, pulling ahead of him. The ponytail bobbed on her shoulders, tracing through the air a sideways eight, an infinity sign. Harold started to feel a little better. He pushed harder, noticing the breeze on his face. Running together, he thought. Flying through the air. This is what I wanted.

By the Reflecting Pool she paused. Harold, breathing heavily, came to a stop beside her. "Are you okay?" she asked. "You look like you could use a break."

Harold put his hands on his knees. "I'm fine," he said. "Winded. Just a little out of shape, I guess." Not looking my best, probably, but that shouldn't matter. Katja jogged uncertainly in place, trying to keep her pulse up. "I've been meaning to talk to you," he began. Katja stood still. "I don't know quite how to say this." Small beads of sweat stood on Katja's forehead; he could see a faint dusting of freckles across her nose. All of my life spent answering the hard questions, Harold thought, and in the end there are only two that matter. Is it now? Is it you?

I can't let this happen, Katja thought. I have to stop him. "I know what you're going to say," she burst out.

"You do?"

"It wasn't appropriate. I understand," said Katja. "It was a mistake, and I apologize."

I know this isn't really appropriate, Harold thought. "What?" he asked.

"I've heard that it happens a lot," Katja continued, fear lending fluency. "People work intensely together and confuse their feelings for the project with feelings for each other." Of course, she thought, I was feeling mostly revulsion about that particular project, but still. "I was way out of line. I'm sorry if I made you uncomfortable. But I understand. We can just forget it ever happened. We can be professional." Harold looked at her. "That's what you were going to say, isn't it?

"Not really appropriate," Harold managed. He stopped. Judges ask you this question all the time, he thought. And the right answer doesn't depend on whether it was or it wasn't what you were actually going to say. It's just a question of whether they're on your side or not. If they're friendly, then they're trying to help you, and you say yes. If they aren't, you say no. And now . . . He looked at Katja's earnest young face. "Yes," he said. "Of course. I'm glad that you see it that way too." His smile did not look like a smile.

Katja felt a small stab of pain in her stomach. "I'm going to do another lap," she said, and turned.

"That would probably be good for me," Harold said, forcing himself to follow. A general sense of unwellness passed over him in waves. Discipline, he thought. Push through it. Like a shark. Keep moving, or . . . or what? Pain that would not be ignored brought him up short. Katja doubled back, coming to a full stop. "I think I need to sit down," Harold said. He felt a shortness of breath that breathing did not cure. Something was happening inside his chest. He reached for a nearby bench but missed. The sky filled his vision.

"Harold?" said Katja faintly. "Help!" she said, more loudly. Her face moved erratically above him, swimming in and out of focus, dancing through the air. Then her hands were on his chest, her lips pressed against his. Murmurs and cries reached him as from a distance. Hoyotoyo.

Of course, Harold thought. Riding with the Valkyries has its price. I knew that all along. I hear the call, he thought. I am ready. With this touch, with this kiss.

Kneeling by his side, Katja continued chest compressions, already beginning to suspect they were futile. The litigation express had reached the end of the line.

In the Wisconsin Avenue Whole Foods, Cassandra Morgan studied the glazed purple surface of an Italian eggplant. She went grocery shopping every Tuesday afternoon, and it reminded her, as chapel never had, of how much there was in her life to be grateful for. Organic produce, imported cheeses, delicately flavored olive oil. She had never lacked for material comforts, and she had Peter to thank for that.

Not that she had no money of her own. Not that her life had been deprived before they met. She'd grown up in comfort; she had still a trust fund, a gift from her father, intended to pay for her children's education but never touched. Peter took care of everything. That was what she had sensed the first time she saw him, that here was the promise of stability, a solid footing in the world. That was what her friends at Wellesley had wanted; that, in part, was what school had trained them for. They dressed in skirts, stockings, and heels for dinner, in white gloves for weekly chapel or formal mixers with the Harvard men. Fundamentals of Movement, one of the required freshman courses, taught them how to enter and alight gracefully from various vehicles, how to stow a bag in the overhead compartment of a train—or to look fetchingly helpless and entice a man to assist.

She'd learned other things too, of course. A round bald professor impressed upon her a bit of physics, a tall gangly one with an Abraham Lincoln beard somewhat more of English poetry. Among her classmates were girls who won Fulbright fellowships, others who went to graduate school, a few who even entered Harvard Law. A fellowship or an engagement ring by senior year; those were the peaks to aim for. Her friends had set their caps for the latter. And when all those around you want something, Cassandra thought, it's easy enough to believe you want it too.

Want it or not, she'd been an indifferent student of the road to matrimony. Until she met Peter, her only boyfriend had been Timothy Phelps, a graduate student in the Harvard English department who postponed his oral exams out of certainty he'd fail and supplemented his teaching assistant's salary by drawing flowers for the margins of weekly magazines. The sketches bought her countless cups of coffee, and real flowers on rare occasion. Cassandra could have been happy with a professor, she thought, though her friends disapproved. In Tower Court they compared the dates they'd been on, the restaurants and Harvard formals. Sometimes, after a few glasses of wine, they compared the ones in the parking lot.

Cassandra had little to report. Timothy couldn't afford to take her many places, and though she could have paid, she had sense enough to know he'd resent it. Little from the parking lot too. Some of her friends went all the way, gave themselves to their beaux and giggled about it afterward. But they did other things Cassandra would never think of, smoked cigarettes between classes, drank themselves to fits of wild laughter, sneaked out after hours. Cassandra was a good girl, happy enough wandering around museums or sitting through cheap matinees at the Brattle Theater.

But then Timothy had summoned the courage to take his exams, and to fail them as he'd predicted. It was a liberation, he said afterward, a gleam she'd never seen before in his eyes. Now he was free to do what he'd always wanted, to teach in a high school. Cassandra was shocked. A professor's wife, that was one thing. But a high school English teacher? They were walking around Lake Waban, heading for Tupelo Point, and an awful suspicion grew within her of what Timothy's freedom was leading him toward. "It's gotten so cold," she said. "Let me go back for a sweater." Once in her dorm room she remembered a physics assignment and sent him home.

Peter had no idea how lucky his timing was when they met that weekend. Her friends were delirious with envy, and Cassandra found herself ready to agree. Peter was tall and handsome, well bred and well spoken, clearly a young man of promise. He bought her dinners and took her to the symphony and the ballet. When they found themselves on Tupelo Point a year later, the sense of inevitability was too strong for doubt, too strong for any but the briefest flicker of curiosity about where Timothy might be now. She looked into Peter's deep blue eyes and thought, I have found my rock.

The marriage was not easy, but she had not expected ease. She knew she would have to compete for his attention, and she did. First with the *Law Review* and the library, battles she had lost. She brought him cookies she'd baked, and he seemed appreciative. But everyone else looked up with stern expressions at the noise of her heels on the floor, and soon she found herself unable to run that gauntlet of gazes. And then with the firm, the long war for which she had steeled herself from the beginning. She'd lost that one too, in the end; neither her preparations nor her experience made a difference. In the early days she'd almost enjoyed it. She would go to his office and act the seductress, while he acted the busy young lawyer. It was all she could do to keep from giggling. But their skits always ended the same way, a few stolen kisses and the phone would ring, or there'd be a knock at the door and they'd spring apart.

She understood the source of her defeats after a while. It was a simple thing, a lack of allies. Frequently Peter came home after she was asleep, even after the twins were born. Perhaps more, then; she'd seen the disappointment in his eyes when the doctor announced girls. Once she tried to call him on it, to ask where the reinforcements were, the cavalry riding to her rescue. "You don't have to work this late," she said, switching on the light after he'd slipped into bed. "You're going to make partner."

Peter tensed. Work had given him a perpetual frown, worse at the end of the day. Worst in the early morning, worst now; his expression was almost frightening. "Why will I make partner, if I don't put in the hours?"

The unsayable hovered near. "I didn't mean it like that," Cassandra said.

"How did you mean it, then?"

"I mean you're doing a good job. Everyone says so."

"I'm doing a good job because I'm putting in the hours," Peter said. "I'll repeat the question. Why do you think I'll make partner without that?"

Cassandra shut her eyes in frustration. "I wish you'd stop talking to me like a lawyer," she said.

"I wish you'd stop talking to me like a silly little girl." Cassandra burst into tears. Peter's voice softened. "Come on, sweetie. You know I'm doing it for you. For us, for our family. But clients have deadlines, and I have a duty to the client."

"That's just it," said Cassandra, sniffling. "You and your clients. You and your duties. You say you're working for me, but then you talk to me like I'm on the other side. Why can't you be on my side? I'm the one you swore to love and cherish. Why isn't that a duty that matters? Why can't I be your client?"

Peter Morgan looked puzzled. "But honey," he said slowly, "you don't pay me."

Cassandra fell back on the bed. She had no answer for that, not even tears, which had long been her strongest rejoinder. Peter turned off the light and reached out for her, a sign that in his estimation he'd won the argument. She felt his hand settle on her breast, and she lay still. Soon enough his breathing turned regular and slow, but for hours afterward Cassandra lay awake, feeling his arm across her, watching distant head-lights cast faint patterns on the ceiling.

He had won, or the firm had; that night Cassandra conceded defeat and began to sketch the terms of her surrender. The armistice was not unfamiliar. Her father had been a strict and unyielding man, accepting nothing from the world and happy to give the same in return. Only his final illness had robbed him of that self-reliance, forced him to receive the kindness of others. That, Cassandra thought, was perhaps the cru-elest part of it, that when disease broke down his defenses it thrust upon him, undeniably, the love of his family and the knowledge that love had circled him for years, baffled and muted but seeking him ever.

I've married my father, she thought. But I won't be my mother. Peter would never guess, if he was lucky, what he had sacrificed for his ambi-tions. She pitied him for that, all the kindness he could have known. But she would not beat her wings against the glass. She would love him, as she'd promised, but she would live too.

The twins were still young, still enough to take all her energy. But as they grew older and started school full-time, she began to recover what she'd set aside. She bought a horse and stabled it in Virginia. At Ethel Walker's she'd ridden every day, and when the school had staged a car-nival, the tenth-grade fortune-teller solemnly predicted she'd canter to Olympic gold. That future was gone, but there was still a satisfaction in working her bay, teaching the tempi shifts, the flying change. Satisfaction too in volunteer work at the public library, the animal shelter on New York Avenue. Peter didn't mind; frequently she thought he didn't notice.

Julie had disrupted those plans, bringing them together in a way she'd almost ceased hoping for. But Julie grew too, and went away to college. The firm stayed. It became bigger, more efficient, more Peter's creature, almost his other self. Cassandra learned these things dimly, as if by osmosis. All she cared was that it was an unending source of fascination, a rival that grew only more attractive as her charms faded. She was becoming invisible to him, she thought, too familiar to register as anything more than one element of the constant background.

Cassandra added the eggplant to her cart, beside the vine-ripened tomatoes and the goat's-milk Brie. So much to be thankful for. The free-range chicken breasts, the Alaskan sockeye salmon. Some of her remained within Peter's focus. He was aware of her face. He critiqued her hairstyle when they had company; he noticed, usually, if her expression was happy or sad. And other parts of her body still received his attention, though not as often, and not as much. But her hands, her feet. Her clavicle, her hipbone. The nape of her neck, the backs of her knees. Those places where once his fingers had traced patterns, his lips left kisses. They were inessential, no longer in play; they might as well not exist for him. I could grow an extra toe, she thought, and it wouldn't make a difference.

It's not as though this is a surprise, she told herself. I knew what I was getting into. And there had been good years. There might be good years ahead, when the work was done. It's too bad we didn't have a son, another Peter, someone to push him out and take his place. She had waited for him to come home, waited until she could wait no longer. And then he had, to Julie and incidentally to her. Now she was waiting again, but not idly. There was no more time, she had realized, to say she'd do it later. Things put off now were put off forever. And so there was another horse; there was her work at the hospital. There were Italian sunsets, and the wines of Veneto in the company of her old friends. This is a good life, Cassandra thought, carrying the bags to her car. She could have done worse. Some of the friends had; they'd found philanderers, alcoholics, rocks indeed on which to end their maiden voyage. Peter was solid; he was reliable. And in the end he would come back to her. What else could he do?

Cassandra pulled her car into the driveway and went to unlock the door. The key fit grudgingly and did not turn. She'd taken the keys out of her purse at the checkout counter; had she picked up someone else's by mistake? No, of course not; the car key was on the same ring. She bent closer, inspecting the lock. It was new, glistening clean but for the scratches she'd left. Well, now, Cassandra thought. This is a fine mess. Peter would know what to do.

"I know this isn't really appropriate," Peter Morgan said. He gathered his features into an expression of thoughtful sorrow. "I try to tell myself that it would be the same with someone else."

Cassandra frowned puzzlement. "I don't know what you're talking about, Peter," she said. "Didn't you hear what I said? Someone's changed the locks on our house. Some sort of practical joke. But I've got groceries in the car."

"My house," said Peter Morgan thickly. "I changed the locks on my house."

"What?" asked Cassandra.

Peter bit his lip. Maintaining composure was costing him effort; he felt off balance, almost panicky. He had imagined this conversation taking place over the phone, which would have allowed him to use his notes. He hadn't expected her to show up. And if she had shown up, he expected it to be in a rage that would preclude talking, the sort of thing that would undermine her credibility in any subsequent court fight. *And how many officers were required to escort her from the building?* But that she would turn to him for help, that she simply wouldn't understand . . . it brought back memories of Archie, trapped in his vision, unable to see how things had changed around him. Unable to grasp that he'd been betrayed. And now Cassandra too. Peter was growing tired of the vulnerability of others, tired of their unthinking trust. It was a weakness, certainly, but such a weakness as to make him ashamed of strength.

I will not be compromised, he told himself. Thus I willed it. "You can check the papers if you like. It's all in order."

"I don't care about the papers," Cassandra said, baffled. "What are you talking about?"

Peter recomposed his face. "I try to tell myself that I'd come to feel the same way about whomever else I was with. But the fact is that right now it's you."

Cassandra took a step back, into a cold dawn of understanding.

"You're leaving me? Is that what you're saying? Is there some other woman?"

"No, it's not like that at all. You must understand that. I'm not leaving you for another woman." Not at all, Peter thought. That was tawdry, the sort of thing lesser men did. "I'm leaving you for every other woman." Except, he admitted to himself, the older ones. "For the future. Listen, here's a poem by Philip Larkin. It's called 'To My Wife.'" He picked up a piece of paper and cleared his throat. "'Choice of you shuts up that peacock-fan / The future was.'"

Cassandra's eyes widened. "You've lost your mind," she said.

"No," said Peter Morgan. "I'm thinking very clearly about this. 'Matchless potential! but unlimited / Only so long as I elected nothing; / Simply to choose stopped all ways up but one.'"

Cassandra batted the paper down. "Talk to me, Peter," she said. "Talk to me yourself."

Peter thought longingly of the lines ahead. *No future now. I and you now, alone.* How can you argue with that? "I don't want my life to stop," he said finally. "But with you it has. Everything is settled. That's what people fear. That's what they regret, the loss of possibility, the choices drowned in the irretrievable past. It's not that there's something better out there. Just that there's something else."

"Just that there's something else," Cassandra repeated.

I should have stopped with "irretrievable past," Peter Morgan thought. He summoned a thrum of urgency to his voice. "We have to go our separate ways," he said intensely. "Don't you see? That's the only way we can continue to live. Together, there's nothing for us to do but die. But we can go on living. There can be more to the world. More variety." Damn, he thought, I did it again.

Cassandra heard his voice coming from a very long way away. What a misunderstanding, she thought. Peter might be having fantasies about a new life with some other woman, but fantasies were all they were. It would be the same with someone else; he was right about that much. He was right about what it would be, and she was wrong about what it had been. She could see that now. The way I acted the seductress; the way he acted the busy lawyer. The way I pitied him, for all the kindness he could have known. It almost made her laugh. I was wrong about everything.

Of course, there had been signs. Not the hours at work; any man might be ambitious. But the tone of his voice, that should have taught me something. The way he sounded on the phone.

She'd been shocked by the coldness in his voice when she called him at work those early years, the flat and affectless way he announced his name into the phone. She'd told herself it was a role that he had to play. He was trying not to sound human, because that was what clients wanted: a lawyer, not a person, not a friend. Not a lover, not a husband; not the man who was hers. Still it was disturbing; she started calling his secretary instead so that he'd know it was her before he said anything. So that he'd say "How's my baby," in that gentle lilt, not "Peter Morgan," in that awful bark. So that he could be himself. And that was where she'd been wrong, she realized, to think the gentle voice was the real man. It was the gentleness and warmth that had been the role; the cold and unfamiliar voice was the man she'd married, liberated by the firm from the scruples and politesse of the world outside.

What a waste, Cassandra thought, all those years imagining that he'd come back when the work was done. In reality it was always the other way around. He wasn't acting at work; he was acting with me. My rock was a mirage. And now I'm done, and he's going back to work.

"I once thought," she said, "that I would enjoy growing old with you." Her voice had changed too, she noticed. "I see that I was mistaken."

Mark Clayton gazed listlessly out his office window, trying to organize his thoughts. Katja's voice echoed in his mind, a dried-out husk. He had been the first person she called from the hospital, a fact that might in the future give him some happiness. Right now he was finding it hard to feel much of anything. There had been a firmwide e-mail breaking the news, then another, more narrowly targeted, reshuffling assignments. No mention of Wayne Harper.

He couldn't blame the firm for that; in all likelihood Harold had never gotten around to filling out the forms necessary to add Harper to his case list. All the same, Mark felt cheated. It was astonishing how completely his victory had collapsed.

That wasn't what he should be thinking about, he knew. Not himself, not Harold, not Katja. He should be thinking about Wayne Harper, who still faced execution, about the oral argument that would determine his fate, only weeks away now. About the brief due in two days.

Mark closed his eyes and tried to focus. Concentration on the task at hand was what Harold would have wanted. Would he? The world rests on convenient fictions. In any event, Mark was still Wayne's lawyer, honor-bound to fight it to the end. At the least, there had to be an argument that they shouldn't consider new evidence for the first time on appeal. Let the district court sort it out. It wouldn't be a win, exactly, more a delay of the inevitable, but it was worth a try. He began typing.

"How's it going?" asked Gerald Roth.

Mark looked up. "How do you think?" he said.

"I know," said Gerald. "I heard about Harold. I'm sorry; he was a good man. But you're still going to win this. Walker's been burning the midnight oil on it, hasn't he?"

Why does everyone say that? Mark wondered. Can't they accept that I won it on my own? I won by myself, and now I'm going to lose by myself. "Not exactly," he said.

"But I saw him working."

Mark felt near tears. "He wasn't working on this, okay? He was writing an article or something. He never did anything on this. And now there's no one to do the argument, which doesn't matter all that much because there's no argument to make."

Gerald sat on the corner of Mark's desk, his face creased with concern. "He was writing an article?"

"Yes. So he could get a teaching job and leave the firm. Which means that I don't have a whole lot of help right now. Unless maybe you'd like to handle the oral argument."

Gerald stood abruptly. "Oh, no," he said. He lifted the lapel of his jacket. "See this? Blue suit. It means I'm a transactional lawyer. I can't go into court. I'm not even admitted to practice before the Fourth Circuit."

God, that's right, thought Mark. That's another thing I need to worry about. "I'm not either," he said. "So things aren't looking so great. Unless you have some advice, I should probably get back to the brief."

Gerald nodded. "Of course," he said. "Look, I'll see if there's anything I can do. Maybe I can turn someone up for you."

Mark didn't look up. "Whatever," he said.

In the twelfth-floor bathroom, Ryan inspected his reflection. He had stopped reading the magazines after that unsettling night; instead he had been doing some serious thinking about his life. He'd been on the wrong track, he could see that. Memorizing pickup lines, chasing after girls in bars—that was fine for college, but he was a lawyer now. He had chosen a path, and it was time he got serious about it. That was what Harold had said, after all, in the interview. *"There are rewards commensurate with devotion."* Ryan remembered his sharp green eyes turning out the window, losing their focus in the vacant sky. *"If you give yourself to the job, it will give you something in return."*

Ryan's hand strayed to the business card in his pocket, as it did frequently these days. Destiny had spoken to him in the form of that caterer; it spoke to him still through the fine ridges of embossed letters spelling out Peter Morgan's name. He could see what the firm offered more clearly now. There was the money, of course; there was the cycling certainty of litigation, the license to advocate free of doubt. But more, there was identity complete at a stroke. The firm would embrace him, encompassing as the oceans that wrapped the earth. It would be his whole life, if he let it.

Ryan practiced an array of smiles in the mirror. One scared him, and he stopped. That's it, he thought. That's the look of a partner.

"**W**e gather in sorrow," said the Right Reverend Andrew Simmons, "but sorrow is not the final word for us." The reverend was a small and pink-complected man, with a face that seemed to call the word "cherubic" irresistibly to others' minds. Many times on such occasions he had explained patiently that the cherubim were not winged infants but fearful warriors, but the correction did not take. Nor could he do anything about those who applied the term out of his earshot, and eventually he'd given up and decided to accept it as a compliment. Harold Fineman, the reverend thought, seemed a man to whom the description would better apply, but he had resisted the temptation to make that point in his remarks. The temptation had been real, for little else was offered him. His custom was to speak to the bereaved, to offer support and take in exchange bits of information that could be blended into his homily. He did this not merely to personalize his remarks but to make them a representation of the transition over which he presided: the Church's message of comfort and hope wrapped personal reminiscence just as God's love enfolded the soul of the deceased.

That had proved difficult in this case. Those facts of Harold's life he knew, he had gathered mostly from the firm's promotional biography, and they were but the trappings and carapace of the man himself. Still, even cast-off clothing retained impressions of its wearer. Even shrouds permitted surmise. "Strength," said Reverend Simmons. "Strength such as Harold had, such as we must try to have without him, comes not from despair, nor from personal power, but from committing ourselves to the incomprehensible mystery of life and death. From the hope we have been given, that death is not an end but the door through which we pass into grace and reunion with the one who loves us best of all." His voice was somber and reassuring, but he felt a momentary flicker of annoyance. This is what comes of pandering to the alumni, he thought. I don't even know when the poor man converted.

Harold's funeral was a small affair. It was not intimate, though, not when almost everyone in attendance was a lawyer. The whole Morgan Siler partnership turned out, marching two by two into the chapel and making a full circuit before taking their seats. The ritual procession, called the Morgan walk, was performed for each fallen partner. "It's right that we should be there, right with the family," Peter Morgan had once told a curious journalist.

Indeed, it is right, he thought now, seated in the wooden pews. One of us is gone, and still the firm endures. But where was the family? His eyes scanned the small audience. There was no one at all, as best as he could tell, from outside the firm. No wife, no children, just lawyers in their dark suits and Harold's secretary, her tears suggesting an unglimpsed devotion. Plenty of flowers, to be sure; the firm could do that much. But it couldn't provide mourners.

Well, it *could*, Peter thought. Perhaps it should. He fingered the cue cards in his pocket and considered making a note of the idea. Most of the organizational demands had fallen upon him, or his secretary, and he felt he'd risen to the occasion. He'd prevailed upon his prep school to allow the use of their chapel, a small and tasteful building in the shadow of the Washington Cathedral. It had proved impossible even to locate a friend to speak, so Peter himself had taken the responsibility of saying a few words before yielding to the reverend. He'd done it without consulting the notes, which pleased him, though in truth they contained precious little. "The firm will miss a great litigator," Peter had said. "And we who knew him will miss Harold Fineman." That was workmanlike, but appropriate. He'd considered opening with a joke about how it was usually only plaintiffs' lawyers who showed up at funerals, but in retrospect he was glad to have omitted it. Harold deserved better. The firm would miss him, that much was true.

But with no complementary family presence, the Morgan walk had a different significance. The ceremony showed nothing, except that the firm continued. It did not commemorate Harold so much as deny him; deny that he was essential, deny that his death could change things. And for those in attendance, thought Peter Morgan, that should be a potent reminder. Live all you can. There would be more people at his own funeral. The children, certainly. Maybe a wife. Maybe two.

"Death is not the final word on the human condition," Reverend Simmons said. "The resurrection is. Our lives do not end as we leave this world. They change, and change into something better." Peter Morgan bowed his head to hide a slow smile. He was accustomed to taking the words of religion figuratively, if at all, and when properly interpreted, the message today was apt indeed. Things end; arrangements change. But life goes on, as long as we have the will to believe, as long as we have the strength to take.

"Amen," said Katja softly, glad it was over. The service brought back her father's funeral, his illness before. She had been six, young enough to think that love or promises could save him. In the church she'd kissed his cheek, almost surprised that he didn't awaken. She had felt guilt then too, but this time she deserved it. This time the childish impulse had been rewarded, but it had only made things worse. And then she had run too fast, feeling herself in danger, letting reflex substitute for thought. There was a lesson there, the same lesson, the one it seemed she couldn't learn.

You'd never know anyone was missing, she thought, watching the partners parade out. If Harold were there, he wouldn't even look like he belonged. Involuntarily she was remembering the peculiarities of his gait. His tightrope walker's pacing; how the heels of his shoes had worn down, no longer touching the floor, and how this had made him appear to rise perpetually on his toes, an eager child seeking approval.

Now he was gone, and the gray ranks had closed over the gap. Interrupting Harold had seemed the safest thing to do, avoiding the risk that she would hurt him with rejection, the risk that he would try to hurt her in return. But those things seemed less terrible compared to the total erasure she was seeing now. There was a lesson there too, a new one. This is what happens to the risk-averse.

———

"Amen," echoed Mark beside her.

"This is unreal," Katja said. "Couldn't they find anyone who knew anything about him?"

"I guess not," said Mark. "All I really knew was that he liked opera." And that stuff about children, he thought, which probably didn't bear repeating. That line about the travel mug. What a horrendous set of memories to leave behind. There was a little bit more. Once, he recalled, Harold had told him a story that centered on a sandwich containing an unexpected complement of jalapeño peppers. Perhaps that had been his way of reaching out.

"And this chapel. Can you believe it?"

"I thought it was nice."

"No," said Katja. "Can you believe it didn't occur to anyone that he was Jewish?"

Mark tilted back a bottle of beer and took a reflective swig. He didn't usually drink in the evenings, but it seemed to be what people did when they were troubled, and after a couple of beers he was starting to see why. A pleasant dullness enfolded his senses, the sort of relaxation that would let you fall from a second-story window and rise, unharmed and vaguely puzzled, while those who went rigid with fear shattered their bones on impact. You needed that, he was realizing; you needed something to take the edge off. Life doled out experience in inhuman portions, as though it expected us to be able to take much more, as though in some distant past our souls had greater compass.

It had done that to him with happiness once, in the nostalgia and folly of incipient college graduation, when he'd spent the remnants of a May night in the bed of a girl he'd long admired. Six hours or so, his arms wrapped around her naked body, his hands on her breasts while he thought, Too much, too much. I can't absorb more than about ten minutes of this; I don't need it more than every couple of months. Properly paced, the happiness of that night could have lasted him until their fifth reunion, when they'd greeted each other with the calm enthusiasm of old friends and she was engaged to someone else. But rapture was not to be rationed; it overflowed to meaninglessness and was gone.

Then with boredom, in his time at the firm, great waves of tedium coming one behind the other and long after his initial enthusiasm had drowned. And now it was catastrophe's turn. The ruthless generosity of the world, that always gives us more than we bargained for.

So it all falls apart, he thought. All my work is for nothing because there was some other test that I didn't ask for explicitly enough. And Walker leaves, and Harold dies, and I'll go into court and take the hit for some guy who, it turns out, is actually guilty. Nothing to get upset about. It's just the reality of big-firm practice.

The conclusion didn't ring entirely true, but it seemed possible that another beer would convince him. He rose and padded in stocking feet to the refrigerator. I'm open to all reasonable arguments. Let's see what this bottle holds.

Wallace Finn placed a leather bookmark between the pages of Gibbon and pushed his glasses up on his forehead. He'd had more time, these past years, so much more that he'd struggled to find ways to fill it. Books had been a blessing, an antidote to the evening, companions to take away the quiet hours.

He doubted he needed them now. The hours seemed to go so quickly. The years had grown shorter, celluloid flickers of night and day. It isn't really fair, Wallace thought. Not only do you have less time left, but it goes by faster. And what at the end? Wallace looked at his bedroom window, which reflected a wall of books. Dark was coming, turning glass to mirrors, infinite vistas to solitary reflections. The yearning possibilities of the night were waning, its promise of a permeable future turning ominously solid. The threat was real now, as the black wall approached each evening: this time there may be no other side.

Nothing to fear, he supposed. We've all known oblivion before. Not death, quite, but unbeing, the same absence from the world. That sleep, rounded with a birth.

But we didn't know that we knew it. We didn't anticipate it, late at night, alone.

I don't want to be left alone, Wallace said quietly to himself. At his age, he found, that was all one ever thought about. His wife had remarried; his children had grown. The people in whose minds he'd lived were gone, lost to the years that bore them ever further away. It would be easier, wouldn't it, with someone else? Someone to validate the hours that pass, to mark and measure transient time. Someone who knows who you used to be, who holds what trace you leave in this world, passes that blind impress on. None of that for Harold, who like an expert diver broke the plane without splash or sound.

It could all be different, Wallace thought. He shook his head. That's what's unfair, the persistence of hope. It clamors: Just one person. Just one other and life is boundless. Even now, so late in the day. Power wanes, not the ability to feel. Wallace studied his hands, the skin thin and spotted, the bones moving beneath. A bag of sticks, roped with vein and tendon. The body ages, we all understand. But the heart stays unforgivably young.

Mark Clayton cradled his head in his hands. This seemed to be something people did when they suffered from hangovers, and he could see why. But he was rethinking the wisdom of following convention. Listlessly, he surveyed the brief he had written. It might buy Wayne a couple of weeks while the court wrote an opinion. And to a condemned man a few weeks were surely priceless. He scowled, unconvinced. If Wayne even understood what was happening to him. They were going to lose this appeal. Then, presumably, the state would set an execution date, and he'd file some last-minute motions, and the clerks at the Supreme Court would report the votes and sit around waiting for the all-clear. Mark opened a bottle of aspirin. All suggestions welcome.

It was hardly a surprise to see the familiar concerned face at his door. "I thought you might want to talk about the panel," Gerald said.

Mark shrugged. "I've got half an hour before I have to leave for court," he said. "Why not?"

Katja cast her eyes over the boxes of documents on the floor of the conference room. Fortitude and dedication were what she'd always had to offer, and now the firm appreciated them. It had told her so, in person, or at least through the person of Peter Morgan. He had told them all. It was a critical time, an unsettling time, but above all an opportunity to show their clients how Morgan Siler lawyers responded to challenges. Katja felt an astonishingly forceful indifference to the firm's reputation. Let's get them out by the end of the week, Harold had said. She would.

She lifted a document and inspected it. "Discoverable," she said, placing it in a pile. "Privileged." Another pile. "Irrelevant. Why did we bring this back?"

Ryan Grady looked up from his seat on the floor. "I don't know," he said. "Part of Harold's bury-them-in-paper strategy, I guess."

Katja bit her lip. Her mind betrayed her, as it did so often now, returning against her will to Harold's earnest sweating face, the sudden pain in his eyes. She'd known what he was going to say, all right. Known and felt she had to stop him, because she saw danger to herself. But what was it she had fled; what had she outrun? Harold was, in what way he could, however vain or awkward or inappropriate, trying to make a connection. To become human again, to live outside the law. To which she had said: It's not us, it's the job. There is nothing but the job, not for you, not anymore. And this Harold knew, or suspected, and at any rate could not bear the confirmation. That was the truth he had lived by, the truth that had killed him. She could have given him hope; she could have acknowledged his struggle. She could have let him say it.

She shook her head more vigorously and picked up another sheaf of papers. "Discoverable," she said. She paused. In her hand were the records of Parkwell's five-million-dollar capital contribution. "Have you seen these before?"

Ryan Grady looked them over. "Sure," he said. "They were on Peter Morgan's desk."

"What were you doing in his office?"

Ryan hesitated. "Well, I kind of woke up there. It was an act of God."

Katja snorted. "Yeah," she said. "Bacchus, I bet. But you saw these on his desk?"

"Definitely," said Ryan. "There was a memo too," he offered. "More like a note."

"What did it say?"

"Just to put them in the discovery file. It was to Anthony Streeter. Do you know who that is?"

"He's a partner," Katja said, distracted. "I did a securitization deal with him once. We went over budget and he made me write off my hours." Annoyance surged at the memory. "It was his fault. He was doing some higher-profile thing and I had to basically run the deal myself. Of course, it took me longer. So I work hours I can't bill and he gets on 60 Minutes."

"Partners make the calls," said Ryan. "They have to keep the clients happy."

Katja closed her eyes and breathed evenly. "Why don't you finish this? I'll check it over later. I have something else that needs to get done today."

"You're not senior to me," Ryan said. "But if you have other work, you can go. I have this under control."

Katja nodded, unconvinced.

Back in her office, she inserted the disk with Virginia's brief into her computer. She stared at the screen, frowning. *This means something.* But what? It didn't matter at this point anyway. Mark had driven across the river to Arlington to wait for his case to be called, looking approximately the way she felt. But Harold had asked her to take a look at the brief. It was a meaningless gesture at this point, and she was starting to think that as gestures went, throwing herself into work wasn't the most appropriate. But it seemed to be all that was left.

"How's it—" Gerald began, and caught himself. "What are you working on?"

Katja turned her head. "*Harper*," she said. "Harold . . . Harold asked me to take a look at the electronic version of the state's brief."

"How does it look?"

"There's something I can't figure out. The program their forensic expert used has all this metadata in it, tells you who wrote a document, when it was changed, what the earlier versions looked like. Some firms got very embarrassed by it a couple of years ago, so now there's a privacy feature you can use to strip it out. One of those upgrades the tech support people inflict on us to prove how much we need them."

"So?"

"So the DNA report has it all in there. It was even highlighted when I opened the file."

"You mean the test was changed?"

"No, it's all the same. Wayne's a match. But the date is different. The first report was prepared before the HLA DQa test, the one that got the seven-point-eight percent match. Now it says it was done afterward. And the author is different. The original one was written by someone named Roman Fleischer."

"What?" asked Gerald.

I don't think I've ever seen anyone actually go pale before, Katja thought.

Gerald opened his mouth, then closed it. "I've got a little bit of a science background," he said. "Why don't you let me take a look?"

51 ARGUMENT

The United States Court of Appeals for the Fourth Circuit sits in Arlington, Virginia, just across the river from Washington. Mark sat there too, feeling the sting of sweat on his fresh-shaven neck, watching the argument that preceded his. Gerald's take on the panel was proving accurate. Loomis and Pilcher clearly despised each other, and Townsend, the senior judge, had difficulty keeping them in line. One of them was bound to be on Mark's side. Probably not Loomis. Conservatives didn't always favor the government, Gerald had advised him. They loved authority, but it was a complicated relationship, and they could turn brutal if disappointed. Still, Mark didn't have the facts to make Loomis think that the state had let him down. That meant he'd have to angle for Pilcher's support. But at best that was one vote, which meant absolutely nothing. Mark squinted with unhappiness. It was easier to be fatalistic about these things when they were days away, rather than minutes. And he would get to start the argument by telling them he wasn't even admitted to practice there. He ran a hand across his forehead and frowned at the result. His palms were sweating more than his face. He looked at the cluster of Virginia attorneys. None displayed any evident signs of anxiety. Unless they'd all been Botoxed, which Mark had to grant was unlikely, the plausible conclusion was that they expected to win.

Standing in his underwear, Gerald Roth surveyed his closet. The row of gray suits, the framed certificates. I doubt they'd even fit. A poor excuse. There were duties that would not be denied, duties to others, perhaps to himself. He had known criminal defendants in the past. He had been their hope, wanting to give them another chance, a first chance for those who had never had one. Some he had saved from the wrath of the state, casting their lives in a new light. Some he could not; they were who they were.

He walked to the bathroom and picked up a set of clippers. He examined his reflection, thinking of a day ten years ago when he'd stood in front of the mirror with a razor at his neck. He'd had his second chance, his new life. He had put the old self aside. But some truths would not be thought away. Some people were who they were.

Gerald ran the clippers experimentally over his beard. A large clump of hair fell into the sink. He looked at the bare track on his cheek. No going back now.

"May it please the Court," said Alex Reiner. "The district court in this case granted a writ of habeas corpus on the grounds that Wayne Harper's trial counsel faced a conflict of interest. We don't contest that conclusion. But a conflict of interest warrants relief only if it had an actual adverse effect on the quality of representation. And given the evidence that the state has presented, evidence much of which was not called to the attention of the district court, the guilty plea was the only reasonable choice."

"And whose fault is it that this wasn't presented to the district court?" Judge Pilcher asked. Mark nodded. As expected, Pilcher was looking for an angle.

"We don't think it's necessary to assign blame, Your Honor," Reiner answered smoothly. "Mr. Harper's lawyers requested the evidence referenced in the trial court's opinion, and we provided them with that evidence. We agree that the proceedings would have gone more smoothly if Mr. Harper's lawyers had seen this test, and we should have offered it to them at the beginning. Our office faces a serious burden of inmate litigation, however, and because this test was not performed until after Mr. Harper expressed his willingness to plead guilty, our lawyers were unaware of it." He looked briefly at John Miller, seated by Kite's side at the counsel table. Miller looked away.

"Well," said Judge Pilcher, "was Harper's trial lawyer aware of it?" He consulted the briefs in front of him. "Anson Henry. I mean, if you're arguing that he performed reasonably, don't we have to decide that based on what he knew?"

Reiner hesitated for a moment. Mark felt a stirring of hope. Judge Loomis leaned forward in his chair. "Conflict of interest is just an ineffective-assistance-of-counsel argument, isn't it?" he said. "And ineffective assistance of counsel requires a showing that the outcome would have been different with an effective lawyer, doesn't it?"

Pilcher shot a nasty glance down the bench at his colleague. "I'd like him to answer my question, if you don't mind."

"Oh," said Loomis, "I think he's about to."

"Please," said Judge Townsend. "Answer Judge Pilcher's question, counsel, if you would."

"Mr. Harper must show that the outcome would have been different without the conflict of interest," Reiner said, sounding embarrassed to be spoon-fed. "To determine what the outcome would have been, the court has to consider the actual case the commonwealth could have presented, not the lawyer's impression of it."

Pilcher leaned back, silent. That's it, Mark thought. For another couple of minutes, Reiner drove home his points, uninterrupted. "I'd like to reserve the remainder of my time for rebuttal," he concluded.

"Thank you, counsel," said Judge Townsend. "Mr. Fineman."

Mark shook his head. Another mistake. I didn't even tell them he wouldn't be here. He felt a hand on his shoulder and looked up into an unfamiliar face.

Who is this guy? Mark wondered. Gerald must have found someone to do the argument after all. Then recognition dawned. Gerald looked different without the beard, certainly, but there was more to it than that. His whole demeanor had changed; he was sleeker, sharper, lethal. "Jeremy Rothbardt for Wayne Harper, Your Honor," said Gerald. "Admitted to practice in the Eastern District of Virginia, the Fourth Circuit, and the United States Supreme Court. I'll be presenting argument." Mark's confusion returned. Jeremy Rothbardt? Who is this guy?

"We didn't have any notice of this," Alex Reiner said. "We've never heard of this guy."

"I'm with Morgan Siler, Your Honor. Once the firm has entered an appearance, it has done so for all its members. Separate notice is not required."

"Very well, counsel," said Judge Townsend. "We'll hear from you."

Gerald cleared his throat and stepped to the podium. It'll come back, he thought. You never forget. "As Mr. Harper demonstrated to the district court, his trial counsel suffered from an actual conflict of interest, having represented his brother earlier on similar charges. That conflict of interest tainted his representation of Mr. Harper, in violation of Mr. Harper's Sixth Amendment right to counsel."

"What about the DNA evidence?" Judge Loomis asked. "If you can't attack that, don't we have to uphold the conviction?"

"The test that the state offered was an HLA DQa analysis that excluded all but seven-point-eight percent of the Caucasian population. It is quite likely that Wayne Harper's brother falls within the seven-point-eight percent not excluded. Any reasonably competent lawyer would have investigated that possibility."

"No, no, no," said Judge Loomis. "Not that test. The other one."

"I'm glad you brought that up, Your Honor," said Gerald. Like riding a bicycle, he thought. "The state represented today that a test performed after Mr. Harper agreed to plead guilty offered more conclusive proof of his guilt." He paused. "That is a lie. The state has perpetrated a fraud on this court and it has done so in knowing reliance on the work of Roman Fleischer, a state medical inspector who is currently imprisoned for his falsification of test results."

A babble of confusion broke out at the Virginia prosecutors' table. Reiner rose excitedly to his feet. "Your Honors, there is not the slightest shred of evidence in the record to support these accusations, which the appellees have moreover not mentioned in any of their briefs to this Court."

"Sit down, Mr. Reiner. You've had your turn. You may await your rebuttal." Judge Townsend turned his attention back to Gerald. "The question is, however, a valid one. These are disturbing allegations, to be sure, but you know that we cannot look outside the record. Where is the record support for your claims?"

"It's here, Your Honors," said Gerald. "In the commonwealth's appendix to its brief, the forensic report."

"Well," said Judge Loomis, "you must have a different version of the brief. Because I read mine, and I don't remember seeing anything like that."

"I do have a different version, Your Honor. We were able to recover an earlier version of the commonwealth's report, which reveals not only that the test the commonwealth now relies on was done before Mr. Harper agreed to plead guilty, but that it was done by Roman Fleischer."

Loomis looked skeptical. "How is this in the record?"

"It's on the disk the commonwealth submitted pursuant to this court's electronic filing rules. And the Court can take judicial notice of the fact that Roman Fleischer was convicted of defrauding the state of Virginia by falsifying forensic results, that he is currently incarcerated, and that the Virginia Supreme Court ordered new trials in every case in which his analysis played a role."

For a moment no one spoke. Loomis pursed his lips and nodded. Reiner whispered furiously to John Miller, who offered in response an innocent shrug. Kite sat silently, lost in thought, staring at Gerald. He wrote a note on a slip of paper, looked at John Miller, and handed it to another one of his aides, who left the courtroom at a run. "Unless there are questions, I have nothing further," said Gerald.

"Rebuttal?" asked Townsend. Alex Reiner did not look happy. He had been chewed out by judges before; as a young lawyer, he had been given his share of unwinnable cases, sent out as a sacrificial lamb. But he had never seen an appellate panel that looked quite as menacing as this one. He cast his eyes around helplessly and got to his feet.

"First, Your Honors, these claims are being presented for the first time during the oral argument. That is an unfair surprise to the commonwealth—"

"And yet it seems, Mr. Reiner, that the commonwealth has been concealing these facts," Judge Loomis broke in. "Doesn't that seem a slightly more significant unfairness?" Mark felt almost delirious with relief. Conservatives, he thought. They want to believe in the government, but if you get them angry . . .

"Even if the court were to consider this argument, there is nothing in the record to support it. Whatever the defense has done to that file, it did in the privacy of its own law firm, with no sort of supervision and no observation to be sure that no improprieties occurred."

"That's true enough," Loomis said. "Of course, we have the same disk you gave to them. Are you willing to go on the record as telling me that if we perform the same reveal-changes operation on that file, we're not going to find anything like what they've suggested?"

Reiner paled. "I'm not in any position, Your Honor, to make representations about the content of that disk."

"I didn't think so," Judge Loomis said scornfully. "Not that it matters. If what they say is true, you're all facing sanctions. I won't even mention the possibility of a civil suit by Mr. Harper." Reiner opened his mouth, then shut it again. "Now, then, counselor," Judge Loomis continued. "Is there anything you would like to go on the record with?"

Kite's assistant had returned with several sheets of paper. During Reiner's immolation, Kite had scanned them hastily, and now he stood up, putting a hand on the shoulder of his subordinate. "One thing, Your Honors. The commonwealth requests that this court enter a default judgment vacating the order of the district court."

At the appellee's table, Mark looked at Gerald. A default judgment was entered only if one side failed to appear for argument. The remedy in that case would be to vacate the lower court's order. It wouldn't be reversed, but it would be set aside, a nullity. Wayne Harper would go back to jail, the death warrant that had been suspended would issue—and it would be too late to do anything about it. Mark shook his head violently. "That can't happen. Where is this coming from?" Gerald took a deep breath.

Judge Loomis was incredulous. "You'd better have something good here, counsel," he said. "I've got some rulings coming to mind, and let me tell you, default judgment for you is not one of them. Why would we do that?"

"Appellees have presented no argument today. This man"—Kite gestured to Gerald—"was disbarred by order of the Virginia Supreme Court ten years ago. His license to practice in the state of Virginia was revoked, and his admissions to the bars of the federal courts were likewise." He allowed himself a smile. The names of the jurisdictions tasted sweet on his tongue. "United States Supreme Court, Eastern District of Virginia, and . . . the Court of Appeals for the Fourth Circuit. I have the order in my hand."

Judge Loomis rested his head on one hand and sighed. He pointed a finger at Gerald. "Counsel, I want one word from you. Is this true? Yes or no."

Gerald swallowed. "Yes."

"All right. Now, is there any reason why we shouldn't throw out this case as the commonwealth requests?"

Gerald said nothing. "Are you admitted to practice anywhere?" Judge Pilcher asked sadly. "We could do it *pro hac vice* for this case."

"Not if he's been disbarred," said Loomis.

Townsend shook his head. "I have to agree. If you're not admitted to the bar of this court, there's no argument. You can submit the case on the briefs, but I have to say they don't impress me."

Pilcher looked at their table. "Mr. Harper has three minutes' argument time left," he said. "Is there anyone there who is a lawyer in good standing?"

Gerald nudged Mark to his feet. "Mark Clayton for Wayne Harper," he said tentatively. "I haven't been admitted to practice before the Fourth Circuit, Your Honor."

"Well, you've only got three minutes. Let's make it quick. Do you solemnly swear as an officer of the court to conduct yourself uprightly and according to law and to support and defend the Constitution of the United States?" Judge Pilcher's eyes turned to Reiner. "This isn't a formality."

"I do," said Mark.

"Welcome to the bar of the Fourth Circuit, Mr. Clayton. You may proceed."

"The evidence presented to Judge Lyttle," Mark said carefully, "demonstrated an actual conflict of interest. The state has conceded that habeas relief was warranted on that basis. On this appeal . . ." He stopped. What exactly has happened on this appeal? Judge Pilcher nodded encouragingly. "They have tried to defend the conviction with new evidence submitted for the first time on appeal," Mark said. "But that evidence is tainted by the involvement of Roman Fleischer. If anything, that casts further doubt on the legitimacy of Mr. Harper's conviction. The district court's judgment should be affirmed."

Judge Townsend nodded. "Thank you, Mr. Clayton. The case is submitted. I believe we'll rule on this one from the bench." The judges withdrew to the robing room.

"Nice work," said Gerald. "I'm sorry about putting you on the spot like that. I didn't think they'd figure it out so fast." Mark nodded, trying to collect his whirling thoughts. Beth Harper and Anson had worked together to offer up Wayne instead of his brother, assuming the death penalty was impossible, expecting the Hampton institution. When the scheme miscarried, they'd gone too far to back out. That was the only explanation that matched the facts. If Wayne was innocent, then the DNA test must have been altered. Roman Fleischer, he remembered from the summer associate memos, would explain that. But Jeremy Rothbardt? Disbarment? What was all that about?

Kite approached their table. "You must be crazy, coming back like this. You think you can get away with that kind of stunt?"

Gerald regarded him calmly. "What are you going to do about it? I'd say you've got problems of your own."

"We'll see about that," Kite said. "Mr. Rothbardt."

The marshal's gavel announced the panel's return. The judges took their seats. "*Wayne Harper* versus *Commonwealth of Virginia*," Judge Townsend said. "The decision of the district court is affirmed. The commonwealth will release Wayne Harper or bring further proceedings within twenty days. So ordered." Kite threw his papers down on the table, then started to gather them. Judge Townsend brought him up short. "The Court is disturbed by the conduct of your office, Mr. Kite. You will be hearing from us."

"We should be getting out of here," said Gerald. "Let's go."

For two blocks Gerald set a brisk pace. Under a hotel awning he stopped. "Congratulations," he said. "You just won your first appeal. How does it feel?"

Mark blinked against the setting sun. "What just happened?" he asked.

"I'm not entirely sure," said Gerald. "I guess Fleischer did the first test. The HLA DQa looked promising. He must have been disappointed by the RFLP-VNTR. It didn't come back a match, but maybe it was close enough that he figured he could improve it a little. And who knows what he thought? Maybe he believed the sample had gotten contaminated. You read the stories about these guys, they all think they're doing the right thing. So he tells them he's got the perfect match, and they believe him. Of course they do; they have a confession. The prosecutors aren't going to be skeptical about guilt. You take a side in this game and it affects the way you see things.

"But then things get more complicated. Fleischer gets caught in some other case, and now his work's no good. The prosecutors have to throw out all his results and start over. Which they did; they weren't trying to game the system. Maybe they didn't get past the preliminary DQa typing before Anson Henry said he'd be pleading guilty. Maybe Henry suggested they stop there, told his contacts in the office he'd enter a plea if that was a match. I wouldn't be surprised; the last thing he'd want would be something that would clear Wayne." He paused. "The family wanted a conviction, I could see that from the start. And it's all over by the time the Virginia Supreme Court says you have to give Fleischer's defendants new trials. The Virginia people . . . well, it was wrong for them to try to hide Fleischer's involvement, but I suspect they really believed they had the right guy. They took what they thought were appropriate remedial measures, and now suddenly the court's saying that's not good enough. If they admit that Fleischer worked on the case, the conviction automatically gets set aside, and they're looking at a trial where the defense can argue it's a frame-up. Probably by that point they'd thrown out their crime-scene sample anyway. They thought they'd be able to defend the conviction with the evidence they had. But then you uncovered the conflict of interest, and Lyttle asked about the other test. They must have known it would come if they retried him. We'd get all the records, we'd see Fleischer's name. So they tried to get it by you on appeal.

"The state's not the bad guy here. Even as a defense lawyer, I have to admit it. Virginia wasn't trying to convict an innocent man. He had his family doing that for him. Wayne was lucky, if you think about it. Funny kind of luck. He was lucky that there was someone else trying to frame him."

"No," said Mark. "I mean, who are you? How did you figure this out?"

"It was Katja, really," Gerald said, shaking his head. "She's the one who got the original version of the report. I just knew Roman Fleischer. In another life."

"What do you mean?"

"Well, I wasn't entirely honest when I said I was a journalist before coming to Morgan Siler. Gerald Roth was, or he would have been if he'd existed. But Jeremy Rothbardt was a criminal lawyer. I was one of the good guys. Really. Lots of pro bono. The other cases paid for it."

"So what happened?"

Gerald smiled ruefully. "When I say I was a criminal lawyer, I don't just mean a lawyer who defends criminals." He stopped. "The short version is I got too close to one of my clients."

"What?"

"It was drug money," Gerald said. "I knew it. But as a defense attorney, you've got to face the fact that a lot of your clients are going to be guilty."

"Even the guilty deserve representation," Mark said.

Gerald shook his head. "God, I hate it when people say that. Like that's the only justification defense lawyers have. If you're doing pro bono, you can pick and choose your cases; you can look for innocent people, or at least people who didn't get a fair trial. If you're against the death penalty, you can take any capital case and think you're in the right. But the defense lawyer who does it for a living, most of his clients are guilty, and he knows it, and all he can say is, 'The guilty deserve representation. I'm just doing my job.' As if everyone knows deep down it's wrong. 'I was only following orders,' that's what it sounds like. But you know what? That's not it at all."

"It's not?"

"It's not," said Gerald. "As a matter of fact, guilty people aren't entitled to representation, not constitutionally. You don't have a right to a lawyer for your appeal, because the state doesn't have to let you appeal at all. You don't have a right to a lawyer for a habeas petition; same reason. Why do you have a right to a lawyer for your trial?" His voice rose. "It's because you aren't guilty until they prove it. No one is. That's the meaning of 'presumed innocent.'

"Maybe that sounds like a rationalization to you. Maybe it is. Because you get cases where you know the guy did it. He's factually guilty, whether they can prove it or not. But if someone asks me how I can defend that guy, I've got a simple answer. And it's not about how guilty people deserve lawyers. I say, 'I'm not defending that guy. I'm defending his rights.' I'm defending the Constitution, just like the oath says. The Fifth Amendment, the Fourth Amendment. Crime warps the law. We set up rules to protect the innocent; they protect the guilty too, and we come to see them as annoyances and technicalities. But they aren't technicalities; they're rights. And they aren't just his rights; they're your rights too. If the government can do it to my client, they can do it to you. Guilty people are the front line of defense for the innocent. If the government comes for you, you'd better hope that we stood up and fought for the scumbag they grabbed the day before.

"Now, are they going to do it to you? Are they going to grab you up and hold you without a lawyer? Probably not. You're white; you don't have a suspicious-sounding name. They probably won't make a mistake. You're a loyal American. They probably won't grab you for their own reasons. And you're a nice kid. You probably don't have enemies who'd tell the government lies about you. But the point of the Constitution is that you don't have to rely on 'probably' and 'won't.' The Constitution means that the government *can't* do those things to you. But the only way to make sure they can't do it to you is to make sure they can't do it to any-one. Equal justice under law."

"So what happened with your client?"

Gerald looked embarrassed. "Well, that's a slightly different story. The government was trying to freeze his assets. They're allowed to do that. But I thought it was unfair. He wouldn't have been able to pay his lawyers. Meaning me. And in addition to thinking the Constitution needs defenders, I thought I needed to get paid. So I helped him move some. Hide it. Not well enough, it turned out. I know it was wrong. There's a line somewhere. Actually, there are a lot of lines. But I crossed one that I shouldn't have. And that was that. I got off with probation, but my practice didn't make it. The bar associations are pretty strict about lawyers not committing crimes."

"So what did you do?"

"Well, what was I going to do? Jerry Rothbardt the criminal lawyer was dead. I almost was too. I thought about it, just finishing what they'd started. But then I thought, I'm more than that. So I started over as Gerald Roth. Got a job as a Morgan Siler paralegal, got a law degree from night school, and started working my way back. It was easier than you'd think. Everyone was impressed with what sound instincts I had, what good practical judgment. And I followed the death penalty cases, as a hobby. Then this one came along."

"But you must have known they'd figure it out once you stood up in court," Mark said. "You must have known you were giving everything up. You did that for Wayne Harper?"

"If you'd had a cell phone, I could have just called you instead," Gerald said. Mark's jaw dropped, and Gerald laughed. "No, they wouldn't let you keep it on in the courtroom. I had to come down here anyway. And I could have just slipped you a note. But I was thinking about it that way, about sacrificing myself for Wayne. And then I thought, Maybe I'm not here to free Wayne Harper. Maybe he's here to free me. The life you save may be your own and all that. Plus, I had a couple of scores to settle with Caleb Kite. And I didn't really like being Gerald Roth, anyway. The beard was a hassle, and corporate law, Christ, what a bore."

"And now?" Mark asked. "What happens now?"

Gerald shrugged. "I don't know. They could go after the brother, but what do they have? They destroyed the DNA sample. Wayne, they could always retry him. They've still got the confession. But they've also got a record showing they tried to cover up prosecutorial misconduct, which will make it awfully hard to get a conviction."

"What about you?"

"Well, that's a different question. Wayne Harper may see next Christmas, but I think Gerald Roth has had it. How many lives do you suppose one man gets?"

"I guess it depends on who his lawyer is," Mark said.

Gerald smiled. "Maybe we'll meet again," he said. "If we do, wait for me to introduce myself." He thrust his hands in his pockets and walked away.

"'**Y**ou will be hearing from us'—that's what he said. And you should have seen Kite's face." Mark smiled broadly. Katja's expression stopped him. "I wish Harold could have been there," he said. "I know this doesn't make up for—"

"It's not that," Katja said. "It's Hubble."

"What?"

"I figured out why I couldn't remember those documents," she said. "They weren't in Texas. Anthony Streeter put them in our files."

"I don't get it."

"The five-million-dollar capital contribution," Katja said. "I checked out the filings in the Texas commercial registry. It took a bit of figuring out, but it was there if you knew what you were looking for."

"And?"

"And Parkwell didn't do it weeks before the accident. They did it about ten days ago and tried to backdate it."

"Why would they do that?" Mark asked.

"Good question," Katja said. "Why would they throw in money when otherwise the plaintiffs' lawyers would just go away? I did a little more research with the documents we brought back. It was just luck that we had them, probably because someone thought they looked irrelevant and complicated. Probably Ryan." She paused. "You know, I bet that's what they were looking for in your room in Texas. They thought Ryan knew what he had and was looking to cut a deal for himself."

"What do you mean? What did he have?"

"Some of Hubble's internal governance documents," Katja said. "Nothing relevant to the litigation. But I started looking at Hubble's corporate structure and I found this unusual class of stock."

Mark felt a moment of revelation. "It's the Parkwell securitization," he said.

Katja nodded. "When Streeter came up with the idea of securitizing Hubble to stop the plaintiffs from recovering, he must have thought it was pretty clever. Never been done before. But actually Parkwell beat us to it. They had the same idea, on a much larger scale. They saw the liability coming and they hunkered down. But the Hubble stock still held the key that could undo it. That's why everyone was available for depositions. They were throwing the case. They wanted to bankrupt Hubble. When they found out we'd securitized it, they must have gone nuts. That's when they put more money in so the plaintiffs' lawyers would stick around. They did it on purpose."

"You see some strange things, litigating," Mark said.

"You don't understand," Katja told him.

"What?"

"Think about it. Parkwell's on the ropes. If their creditors can get control of Hubble, they can unlock the securitization and reach Parkwell's assets. Parkwell needed to stop that. They needed to destroy the key. They needed to destroy Hubble."

Mark heard Wallace's voice in his head, its pleased and professorial tones. *What looked like a solvent corporation goes up in smoke. They've really got to kill the subsidiary.* Sacrificing the subsidiary to save the parent, that was hardly a choice at all. And if some people got sacrificed as well, they were just people, born to die. Only corporations live forever. "Oh, God," he said. "Oh, no."

"That's right," said Katja. "This whole thing's been about Parkwell. They did it on purpose. Not the filing, the accident. They blew up that plant just so they could get sued."

"Oh," said Mark. "Oh," he added. "What do we do?"

"There's nothing we can do," said Katja. "That's the point of securitization. You could probably get a bigger judgment against Hubble if you proved it was deliberate, but there's only five million there. You'd still just be putting it into bankruptcy, which is what they want. There's no way to get the shares from Hubble without destroying their votes."

"There's got to be something," said Mark. "And I know who to ask."

"I don't understand," said Wallace. "You're saying they caused the fire on purpose? That was my deal. I set that up." He looked at the leather-bound volumes arrayed along the wall. "Corporate practice," he said. "You never have to think about dead people."

"They should be able to recover, shouldn't they?" Mark asked.

"Recover? Oh, they'll be fine. They're in negotiations with the creditors. It'll work out." Wallace frowned. "Why are you worried about that?"

"I mean the plaintiffs," Mark said. "They should be able to recover damages."

"Oh," said Wallace. "Right. They should. But they can't. They don't have a claim against Parkwell, not since Walker got Parkwell dismissed from the suit. And even if they did, the securitization would hold up. That's the point. They could get in on the negotiations. It might scuttle the deal that's being worked out. But Parkwell would just go into bankruptcy and come back out without paying anything."

"Can't they unlock the securitization? If they knew where the key was? What if the Texas plaintiffs just asked for that stock?"

"No," said Wallace. "Hubble doesn't own the stock; Parkwell does. So you need a claim against them. But even that wouldn't work. You could seize the stock to satisfy a judgment, but that's an involuntary transfer. Any involuntary transfer cancels the voting rights. Believe me, we thought this through."

"You'd need to have control of Hubble," Katja said. "Right?"

"Right," said Wallace. "That's what lets Parkwell unlock if it wants to. But you can't get control by seizing the stock. You'd need to own it already. And I'm sure Hubble's a wholly owned subsidiary. They would have taken it private when they set up the voting shares."

Mark had a sudden vision of the wall of Felix Guzman's living room. "What if there was some stock still outstanding?" he asked.

"There might be," said Wallace. "They could leave a little bit out there as long as it wasn't enough to exercise control. And it's not. Not unless you stop Parkwell from voting its shares." He turned the issue over in his mind. So long ago, he thought. So long ago I set it in motion. Back then I probably could have figured out a way around it too. But now . . .

"You need a fiduciary duty suit," he said suddenly. "Parkwell's the majority shareholder of Hubble. It has to be loyal to the minority shareholders; it has to protect their interests. If it deliberately damaged Hubble, it violated its fiduciary duties. And you could enjoin it from voting its stock. Whoever else is out there would be in control."

"You're kidding," said Mark.

"Not at all," said Wallace, his voice firm. "They weren't supposed to trigger it like this. We didn't set it up that way. If you've got a shareholder, you can do it."

Mark looked at Katja. "Janette Guzman owned Hubble stock," he said. "Her estate could bring the fiduciary duty suit."

"Yeah," said Katja. "But we aren't her lawyers. We're Hubble's lawyers. And Parkwell's. Try to help out the plaintiffs here and you'll get disbarred. No joke."

I've seen that choice, thought Mark. Could I put my hands in my pockets and walk away? "We can figure this out," he said.

Wallace sat alone in his office, looking at the books on the wall. Mark and Katja had left with hasty steps, full of hope, eager to meet the future. They find out that things aren't at all what they seemed, and it's exciting for them. Well, of course, he thought. They haven't lived more than a tiny fraction of their lives; they don't have to worry that it's all been wasted. It's not the same when you're older. As the years go by, the danger grows. Some sudden illumination will show the past in a new light, misguided, pointless, meretricious. He lived in fear of that revelation; he looked away from flashes. I don't want miracles now, he thought. I want to know that I was right in thinking there are no such things.

And what have I just done? Twenty years of my life, and I end by tearing it down. He shook his head wonderingly, and laughed. It felt good. I'm going to go for a walk, he thought. I'm going to go for a walk, and if I happen to run into someone, I'm going to say hello.

"Discovery," said Katja. Mark started. For half an hour they had batted ideas back and forth, anonymous letters or phone calls, unexpected declarations in open court. All of them outside their role as lawyers, and all of them, she found, things she was quite willing to do. Harold was right, she thought; it's easy to be good in the face of evil. Easy to say that this is exceptional, that normal rules don't apply. What's hard is to see it as just a more extreme version of something that happens every day. To see it within the system, to see how the system resists. To see what law wants to be. "We can do it with discovery," she said. "I was putting together disclosures anyway. We're scheduled to turn a lot of information over to Macey and Schiller tomorrow. They'll figure it out. We just need to give them the right documents."

And that, she thought with satisfaction, was no more than their duty. They weren't just fighting for the client; they were officers of the court. They were lawyers. Harold had been pushing to get the discovery done quickly, and now she could guess that Parkwell had encouraged him. They were in a hurry to get to trial; they wanted to get hit with the judgment. Well, she thought, judgment's coming. Katja felt an unfamiliar happiness, a sense of completion. She felt, in some strange way, whole.

Wallace hadn't counted on running into a woman, much less an attractive one, and his confidence quailed. He went past her once, then made a quick circuit of the floor and returned. She wasn't so intimidating, once you really looked at her. She seemed familiar, in fact, though he couldn't quite place her. There were finance partners from the old days he wouldn't recognize now, but they didn't dress like her. And they didn't pace the corridors, examining the artwork on the walls. Wallace ducked behind a secretarial cubicle. *We've got some fine old prints,* he rehearsed. *There's a committee that selects them.* Pompous, inane. He stepped out into the hallway. The woman's raised fingers traced a design over the surface of a framed painting. She caught sight of him and let her hand fall, surprised.

"I'm not sure we've met," Wallace said. "Are you a client?"

Cassandra Morgan laughed.

Katja pushed her carefully sorted piles together, a day's work undone. She picked up a handful of documents. "We'll go through them again. We need the details on the stock ownership, the Parkwell securitization, the convertible voting shares. It's all in here somewhere."

Mark rubbed his eyes and consulted his watch. "This is going out tomorrow?"

"Sure," said Katja. Her cell phone rang and she consulted the display. Jason. She shook her head. *No one can make you feel the way I do*; that was what he always said. It had never seemed a good reason to take him back, but a part of her had conceded its truth. No one else had; perhaps no one would. Now, looking at the Parkwell documents, imagining the different stories they could tell, she could scarcely believe she'd ever listened to him. Those were her feelings he was talking about. Her body. Her choice. Why had this ever seemed so terrible, so beyond her control? We are who we choose to become; the past has the power we give it. That, in the end, was what Harold had shown her. The push of a few buttons blocked Jason's number. That, and one more thing. Transformation was possible. You just had to pick the right person. She looked at Mark and smiled. "You have something else you want to do tonight?"

"No, I'm not a client," Cassandra said. "That was the problem, really." Wallace the wizard, she thought. He'd sat at her table often enough, at those early dinners. His attention hadn't been on her, though, nor on his own wife. Law sharpens the mind by narrowing it. "I just came here to sign some papers. Not even on this floor. I just stopped on my way out— Oh, it's silly." Wallace looked expectant. "Well," Cassandra said, "I picked out some of these paintings. I thought it might be nice to see them once more."

"You're a decorator?"

Cassandra shook her head. "No. It's personal business. I signed . . . what was it? I signed an agreement not to contest ownership of my house."

"I see," said Wallace, confused. He considered. "I have a house," he said. Silence hung between them, and Wallace berated himself. The assertion had sounded right in his head, potent and reassuring, but now that it was out in the air, even he had to admit there was an odd ring to it. What was it that was special about the house? Why had he thought it would appeal to her? "With some nice things in it," he continued. Shapeless images moved through his head. Well, the truth was simply that he'd always thought of owning your own house as the ultimate achievement. How foolish, how naïve.

Cassandra smiled at him. "I should be going," she said. "I've got a lot of thinking to do." She had known when she met Peter Morgan where he was headed. Whatever he said now, he had always had only one future. The rest was decoration; she could see that, even if he couldn't. The firm drew him like a magnet; it called him by their shared name. Through the years she had watched it, growing on the horizon, consuming more of his life. She had gone there with him. She had known what it would mean; she had feared what it might make him. But in all her worries and thoughts of prevention she had made a fundamental mistake. She had failed to understand what he'd been from the very beginning; she had thought to preserve a man who never was.

Wallace felt his heart sink within him. Then, unexpectedly, it rose and expanded. "Listen," he said urgently. "There's a place near here. They serve tea. And other things, to eat. Would you?"

Cassandra's surprised laugh lilted in the air. "Are you asking me out? That's very courteous of you. But . . ." She hesitated, peering over a precipice, balancing like a coin on edge.

Mark watched as the story unspooled through Katja's precise hands. It was all there, as she'd said. First the securitization of Parkwell, the impregnable shield, walling off its assets from any creditors. Then the back door, the key hidden within Hubble's voting stock. Parkwell's financial misstep, the massive liabilities looming. They'll get it, he thought. Obviously the next step is the destruction of Hubble, and we don't need to tell them anything about that. Just one more thing. The owners of record of Hubble's voting stock, including Janette Guzman and her twelve and a half shares.

What happens now? Mark wondered. Once they figure it out, the plaintiffs will have the leverage to ask for almost anything. It's a whole new ball game. Mark imagined Robert Macey at the negotiating table, prospects of astronomical contingency fees capering behind his impassive face. Is that justice? Well, it's law. Law would value the lives lost; it would assign the rights and liabilities, and what more could you ask of it?

Walker had an answer, Mark supposed. You could ask for elegance, coherence, beauty. Walker had been seeking absolution after all, Mark realized. Absolution for letting his feelings get in the way of his intellect, escape from a job that confronted him with such choices. He had found it; he had ascended to his heaven of theory, Yale or Harvard, or some-place like that. There he would explain to his students the inner logic of doctrine. He would demonstrate that it all made perfect sense, that law worked itself pure. But sitting on the floor of the conference room, Mark couldn't help thinking that the beauty of the law was somehow beside the point.

Leges sine moribus vanae, he thought, the Penn motto: Laws without morals are useless. He'd seen it every day at school, carved in one of the courtyard walls, and thought it a relic of older times. Everyone knew that law and morality were distinct. But now he was seeing the aphorism in a different light. It didn't mean that you needed morals in the law. It meant you needed them in the lawyers. Wiping out Hubble had been an easy choice, and the law wouldn't have stopped it. But whoever came up with the scheme made a crucial mistake. They involved people. They brought Janette Guzman into it, and they brought us. A web of strange connec-tions, shadows of the law. Girls and fences, sea and sand, fire and death. They brought people in, and it's people who do justice.

"It would be an honor," said Wallace. "Truly."

Truly, Cassandra thought. Unbidden, a memory of Peter intruded. Peter with his stupid poems. *Ah, love, let us be true to one another!* He'd liked Matthew Arnold, and the Romantics too. At first it had puzzled her, and then she'd thought it showed something, a breadth of taste, a large-ness of spirit. But he hadn't liked any of them, she realized now. He just found them useful. Everything she had cherished about the man had been an act. A thought flashed through her mind. *There is no truth.*

"I don't know," she said.

Another followed. *And hence no falsehood either. There is only what we decide.* And how, she wondered, could I have lived with a lawyer for so long and not realized that?

She smiled at Wallace, felt herself step into the spinning air. "Why not?"

Mark sipped a tepid cup of coffee and watched dawn glow faint through the window. The conference room they were in had once been someone's corner office, with a view out over Rock Creek Park, where the rising sun sparked amid the trees. Katja raised her head and pushed back her hair. "That's it," she said. "We've got it all. We're done here."

Mark nodded and yawned. "Do you think it's worth going home?" he asked. "I've got some stuff to do today. I could just stick around." For a while, at least, he thought. There would be consequences to face. Firing was not outside the realm of possibility, nor was general conflagration. For Parkwell it was apocalypse; maybe for him too. Maybe for the firm. Probably not, but in some ways it was comforting to project the results to that scale. If everything ended, there would be no aftermath in which to deal with blame. Just a new world for others to build.

Katja was aghast. "Oh, God, no," she said. "At least you've got to get outside for a little bit. Let's take a walk."

The building's lobby was deserted, the security guard drowsing at his post. Outside, Mark found fatigue lent the young day a tender, ethereal air. The few people hurrying in for an early start passed like shadows. Ryan Grady, almost unrecognizable in a suit of sober gray, offered a nod of greeting and walked by them without a word. Mark looked upward, to the Morgan Siler floors, noting the few lit windows, the forms of lawyers that moved within like insects struggling against the glass.

Katja slipped her arm through his. "Come on," she said, and tugged him gently toward her.

A new world to build, Mark thought. Maybe more than one; maybe multitudes, for the firm, for him, for everyone who took the chance. They turned away, down the tree-lined avenue, into the faint mists of morning. Behind them a long black car pulled silently to a halt. Peter Morgan was arriving at work.

ACKNOWLEDGMENTS

This is a work of fiction. I have had the good fortune to work for some excellent law firms and admirable judges, and I hope that those experiences have helped me in lending realism to the imagined scenes and circumstances of this novel. With the exception of a few historical personages, however, no character in this novel is based on or intended to resemble any real person, living or dead. I have also attempted to keep the law accurate, though when it collided with the necessities of fiction, it gave way.

I am grateful to more people than I can list for their assistance in the writing, editing, and publication of this book. Tina Bennett's representation made everything possible; her unflagging enthusiasm and critical acuity made the editing process both more pleasant and more productive. Jonathan Galassi and Annie Wedekind at Farrar, Straus and Giroux helped me to see the book my manuscript wanted to be. Joo Hyang Kim gave me aid and comfort through the writing process. Eric Bardawil's detailed analysis of an early version guided subsequent revisions. My parents, my sister, Corinne, and Larry Hardesty showed superhuman patience in reading each iteration and helping me through the problems that arose. A host of friends provided valuable comments, among them Joan Cheng, Rochelle Chodock, Ashley Evans, Eleni Gage, Jo Guldi, Rachel Hannaford, Karen Lantz, Anne Long, Jin Hee Kim, Sidney Kwiram, Jonathan Roosevelt, Danny Shivakumar, Tai Lui and Tai Ching Tan, Rebecca Tushnet, and Lara Veblen.

In developing the environments, characters, and themes of the novel, I have also benefited from a number of sources. The account of

Archie's clerkship with Justice McReynolds relies heavily on the memoir of an actual McReynolds clerk; it was rescued from obscurity and edited by Dennis Hutchinson and David Garrow, published as *The Forgotten Memoir of John Knox* (University of Chicago Press, 2002). Caroline Weymar re-created for me the dating scene at Wellesley in the 1960s. Other references I found helpful include Lincoln Caplan, *Skadden* (FSG, 1993); Alan Dershowitz, *Chutzpah* (Little, Brown, 1991) and *The Vanishing American Jew* (Little, Brown, 1997); Judith Hope, *Pinstripes and Pearls* (Scribner, 2003); Duncan Kennedy, *Legal Education and the Reproduction of Hierarchy* (New York University Press, 1983); Anthony Kronman, *The Lost Lawyer* (Belknap Press, 1995); Sol Linowitz and Martin Mayer, *The Betrayed Profession* (Johns Hopkins University Press, 1996); George Bernard Shaw, *The Perfect Wagnerite* (Dover, 1898); and Barry Scheck and Peter Neufeld, *Actual Innocence* (Signet, 2000).